Maya Blake's hopes of b⟨...⟩ born when she picked up ⟨...⟩ thirteen. Little did she kno⟨...⟩ come true! Does she still pinch herself every now and then to make sure it's not a dream? Yes, she does! Feel free to pinch her, too, via Twitter, Facebook or Goodreads! Happy reading!

Canadian **Dani Collins** knew in high school that she wanted to write romance for a living. Twenty-five years later, after marrying her high school sweetheart, having two kids with him, working at several generic office jobs and submitting countless manuscripts, she got The Call. Her first Mills & Boon novel won the Reviewers' Choice Award for Best First in Series from *RT Book Reviews*. She now works in her own office, writing romance.

Also by Maya Blake

Snowbound with the Irresistible Sicilian
Enemy's Game of Revenge

Diamonds of the Rich and Famous collection

Accidentally Wearing the Argentinian's Ring

A Diamond in the Rough collection

Greek Pregnancy Clause

Also by Dani Collins

Marrying the Enemy
Husband for the Holidays
His Highness's Hidden Heir
Maid to Marry

Diamonds of the Rich and Famous collection

Her Billion-Dollar Bump

Discover more at millsandboon.co.uk.

WANTED: HIS HEIR

MAYA BLAKE

DANI COLLINS

MILLS & BOON

First published in Great Britain 2025
by Mills & Boon, an imprint of HarperCollins*Publishers* Ltd,
1 London Bridge Street, London, SE1 9GF

www.harpercollins.co.uk

HarperCollins*Publishers*, Macken House, 39/40 Mayor Street Upper, Dublin 1, D01 C9W8, Ireland

Wanted: His Heir © 2025 Harlequin Enterprises ULC

Crowned for His Son © 2025 Maya Blake

Hidden Heir, Italian Wife © 2025 Dani Collins

ISBN: 978-0-263-34463-9

05/25

This book contains FSC™ certified paper and other controlled sources to ensure responsible forest management.

For more information visit www.harpercollins.co.uk/green.

Printed and Bound in the UK using 100% Renewable Electricity at CPI Group (UK) Ltd, Croydon, CR0 4YY

CROWNED FOR HIS SON

MAYA BLAKE

MILLS & BOON

straight with the welcome reminder that she hadn't done anything wrong.

During her frantic internet searches once she'd woken from her coma and discovered she was pregnant, most likely with Nick Balas's baby, she'd come across pictures of this man. But even without the revelation that Crown Prince Azar was friends with Nick, whose car she'd been in that awful night, she knew what kind of man she was dealing with.

Ruthless. Conceited. Silver-spooned. With unfair good looks to match—and, in this one's case, the breathtaking title of Crown Prince to go with them. And a mile-wide attitude that screamed that the whole world owed them adoration and worship.

Men like her father, who threw their power and privilege around just for the sake of seducing unsuspecting women, whose hearts and lives they shattered irreparably before walking away.

Her mother was one such woman, Eden the product of that kind of careless treatment. The reason her mother had lived in misery her whole life, pining for a man who'd treated her deplorably while lauding his power over her. The reason Eden actively detested men like the one standing before her.

'This isn't a costume party, and it isn't Halloween, so what is it? A prank or a dare?'

His regal head turned, probing the corners and drapes in the room before arching a masculine brow at her.

'Are your friends recording us right now, ready to jump out with their phone cameras? FYI, I will sue them all for every last cent if they dare to do such a thing. Or is it just something to giggle over later on your own?'

Despite his easy stance, thick layers of tension laced his words. Enough to make her spine of steel sway a little. But the surprising side effect of what she'd been through these last three years was the discovery that she could bend a long way, but she would never break.

The reminder tipped up her chin. 'Should I not be asking you that? It's your birthday party after all. So what is it?' She echoed his question back at him. 'Play a joke on the help? See whose life you can toy with by getting them fired?'

She blurted the words into her swelling panic. Dear God, if she got fired, paying her rent this month would be near impossible. She was already on the last few hundred in her savings. This double shift was the miracle she'd prayed for.

'I would've thought that would be more the speed of privileged frat boys—not grown crown princes who should know better.'

Dear God, Eden, shut up!

Sadly, the unfairness of it all was choosing tonight of all nights to spill out. Months of keeping it together, of working her fingers to the bone, of lying awake at night praying for that essential gap in her memory to return so wouldn't feel so…so lost, had eroded the last of her civility.

She wanted to punch and pummel and scream her frustration.

'Excuse me?'

His words sizzled like ice on a hot griddle as regal fury blazed at her.

'You had your people manhandle me in here—'

'They didn't touch a single hair on your head,' he interrupted, with blade-sharp precision.

'They didn't need to. You waved your hand and they went into intimidation mode. Is that what gets you off? Standing back and watching others dance to your tune?'

'From where I'm standing there's very little dancing and a whole load of sass going on,' he grated. 'Not to mention a stupid attempt to cling to whatever lies you're spinning.'

'What the—?' Eden took a breath and uncurled fists that had bunched without her conscious knowledge. 'Look, I know you're a big deal in royalty, with legions of acolytes on social media and around the world. And I'm sorry if your royal ego is affronted. But the truth is we've never met. I'm here on a waitressing gig.'

She waved her hand at the door, every bone in her body straining to sprint for it. But she knew those muscle-bound bodyguards would be waiting—that all it would take for them to restrain her would be another flick of his hand.

'Maggie, my boss—the woman your people hired to cater your party—is out there, supervising the wait staff. She called me three hours ago and asked me to fill in for a sick colleague. If you don't believe me, ask her.'

His gaze flicked to the door. Eden almost expected Maggie to materialise out of his sheer willpower alone. A moment later he pinned her again under those ferocious quicksilver eyes she swore could see beneath her skin.

'You truly want me to believe you think you've never met me?' he breathed in rumbling disbelief.

For the first time, Eden's certainty fractured. She was reminded of those moments when shards of memory attempted to pierce the otherwise impenetrable fog shrouding those lost months three years ago.

Was he…?

Did he…?

The visceral need to know propelled her towards him, when she should've been ending this absurd confrontation and retreating.

The Good Samaritan she'd tracked down weeks after waking from her coma—a man who'd found her with a life-threatening head injury, wandering along the road near a remote truck stop in Southern California—had known very little of what had happened to her. The police, when they'd eventually turned up at the hospital, had only been able to trace her last known whereabouts to a hostel in Vegas, leaving her with no clue as to how she'd ended up in California—save for the possibility that she'd been going to see her mom—or what had happened to rob her of several weeks of her life.

The only tenuous connection—discovered desperate weeks later, after almost driving herself ill to the point of re-hospitalisation—had been the memory of snippets of conversation with Nick, in the Vegas casino where she'd worked.

Nick—another silver-spoon-fed millionaire who had frequently visited the casino where she'd previously worked—had not taken her firm refusal to go on a date with him with good grace. He'd been relentless in his pursuit. Throwing offers of riches and luxury at her feet until he'd realised that she wouldn't be moved by them. That, in fact, she was repulsed by his obscene display of power and wealth.

He'd changed tack then, and stopped tossing around trips to Paris and life-changing shopping experiences. Instead he'd bought her a hotdog that time he'd caught her on a break. Walked her to the bus stop instead of thinking he could sway her with a ride in his Lamborghini.

It had been during those two curiously well-timed meetings that she remembered him dangling the offer of a job... somewhere. A job lucrative enough that she'd been tempted. But she had no clue whether she'd taken the job, and with the authorities' very tepid reaction to her half-clues she'd drawn a frustrating blank.

And with Nick dead, and her sole attempt at contacting his family having resulted in the immediate harsh threat of a lawsuit, she'd accepted that dead end.

Her heart leaping into her throat now, she opened her mouth to ask. Only to recall her doctor's dire warning not to go probing.

Familiar frustration and the naked fear of living permanently with this hole in her memory clawed through her.

Shaking her head, she pushed both heavy sensations away. 'Are we done here? I'd like to salvage what's left of my shift, if that's all right with you?'

* * *

She was lying. Playing games. She had to be.

And yet if she'd been an actress, Azar would've fully endorsed an award for that performance.

'You may leave,' he said eventually.

He watched her head for the door, her hip-sway admittedly less prominent than it had been the last time he'd watched her walk away, but still hypnotic. Still enough to warm and rouse his shaft. To make his fingers curl into a fist with the need to touch.

Absolutely not happening.

But...

One last test.

'Eden?'

She glanced over her shoulder in the exact way she had that last time too, the defiant tilt of her chin at once challenging and enthralling. That night it had been enough for him to stalk over to her and demand one last kiss, unaware that she was leaving his bed and going straight into betraying him with his best friend.

She was watching him warily, her breath turning a touch agitated, bringing his attention to the seductive curve of her breasts. 'Your Highness?'

He ignored her tart tone and delivered his message. 'We will meet again.'

There was no disadvantage to forewarning her. Now he'd found her again she would need supernatural powers or the help of Houdini himself to slip through his grasp again.

Her silken throat moved, but stopped shy of a swallow. It was almost admirable, the way she fought not to show her alarm. But it didn't matter. Whatever game she was playing, he would get to the bottom of it.

Then pay her back a hundredfold.

'Not if I can help it,' she parried.

Then she slipped through the door, slamming it behind her.

He waited all of ten seconds before he yanked the door open. Ramon and his men hovered outside the door, along with his half-brothers.

Teo and Valenti sauntered in, eyes the same colour as his examining him keenly.

'Want to fill us in on what's going on?' asked Teo. 'I mean, she's hot, sure…but you can't just ditch us and—'

'You don't remember her?' This came from Valenti.

Teo frowned. 'Should I?'

Valenti's droll gaze said he was internally rolling his eyes. 'She's the girl. From Arizona.'

Teo's jaw dropped, but before he could speak Azar raised a hand, directing his next words to his security chief.

'Follow her. Do not let her out of your sight. I want to know where she goes, who she sees, where she lives. I want to know everything there is to know about Eden Moss by midnight. Understood?'

CHAPTER TWO

'*WE WILL MEET AGAIN.*'

The words reverberated in her head as she walked out of her neighbour's apartment, Max's warm weight nestled in her arms.

'Thank you so much for tonight, Mrs Tolson.'

The old woman waved her away, wrapping her thick shawl around her shoulders as she leaned heavily against the door. Eden felt a pang of guilt for her reliance on the old woman, whose robustness had dwindled since her hip operation. It was her insistence that she missed Max and wanted to spend time with him that had made Eden finally give in, but undoubtedly she'd been a godsend in desperate times.

'I love spending time with this cheeky darling—you know that. And it was only for a few hours.' She stroked Max's cheek, earning a drowsy smile from her sleepy son before she glanced at Eden. 'Do you know what you're going to do after next week?'

Her insides clenched at the reminder that Mrs Tolson was moving to California, to be closer to her son, and taking Eden's reliance on her much-needed occasional childcare with her.

'Something will come up, I'm sure.'

Worry and scepticism creased the older woman's face, but she nodded, caressing Max's cheek one last time before stepping back into her apartment.

'Come by for pancakes in the morning,' she said, then raised a hand when Eden opened her mouth to refuse. 'I insist. I need as much Max-time as possible before I leave.'

Feeling a clog building in her throat, Eden nodded and turned towards her apartment door, twenty feet away.

Maggie had thankfully not given her grief over her fifteen-minute disappearing act with Prince Azar. She'd been more curious than annoyed, which suggested she hadn't heard about Eden's rude comment to the Crown Prince. It also meant she had much-needed money in her bank account, which would keep a roof over her head for the time being.

And after that?

She swallowed and summoned a smile when Max stirred, rubbed his eyes and delivered a heart-melting smile. 'Mama?'

'Yes, baby boy, it's me.'

His smile widened and his arms wrapped tighter around her neck as she burrowed into his warmth.

'Mama!'

She laughed, feeling lighter as she went into her bedroom. 'Did you have fun with Mrs Tolson?'

She tuned everything else out and basked in his sweet, childish babble about Lego and giraffes. He sang half a theme tune of his favourite cartoon as she gave him a quick bath and wrestled him into his pyjamas. Holding him to her chest, she breathed in his sweet baby scent, her heart lifting and swelling with love as he fell asleep.

That same heart squeezed with anguish when she laid him down in his crib, her fingers tracing his cheek before lingering on the dip in his chin. The faintest slash of memory made her breath catch, but knowing it would go nowhere, as usual, she pushed it away and pulled a light blanket over her son.

But as she undressed and readied herself for bed the events of the evening flooded her, giving her no chance to suppress them.

'We will meet again.'

The titanium-strong conviction behind Prince Azar's promise shook through her, jostling her confidence. She was certain there was some mistake—because even with the gap in her memory she couldn't fathom any scenario in which she would ever cross paths with the heir to the throne of one of the wealthiest kingdoms in Europe, never mind make an impact enough for him to remember her. Even in Vegas.

Her brain insisted this was a mistake.

But...

No.

Seeing the news of Nick's accident in Arizona, weeks after waking up from a coma with an awful three-month gap in her memory, she'd hoped it would shed light on his possible connection with her own mysterious trauma, but the police had been closed-lipped about giving details. She suspected they'd also been threatened by Nick's family with the same lawsuit she had. Not even her shame-tinged confession that she was pregnant, and that Nick was the strongest contender as father of her child, had swayed them.

She'd returned home to Vegas pregnant, with no clue as to who the father of her baby was. Short of tracking down the hundreds of trust fund billionaires, socialites and royalty among the friends and acquaintances littering the late Nick Balas's social media pages, she'd had to quickly resolve to embrace single motherhood. She'd decided to focus on caring for the baby growing in her womb—the baby she'd already been heads over heels in love with. That way she had also avoided exposing herself to the kind of appalling slut-shaming her father had subjected her mother to before callously disavowing Eden's paternity.

Eden punched her pillow and flipped over, her thoughts peeling back those weeks when she'd attempted to contact Nick's family and quickly been reminded that men like her heartless father still existed—that they remained as vile as her own parent had been, thinking nothing of viciously informing the child they'd so carelessly created that as far as they were concerned they'd never been born. That their existence meant less than nothing to them.

She'd also been reminded that men like that could shatter lives with a single call to their lawyers. The same way her father had devastated her mother, leaving her a shell of herself. Leaving Eden with a searing promise never to risk walking in her mother's shoes. *Ever.*

Only to discover she might well have.

She'd heard the many horror stories of influential families wresting custody of a child from financially unstable mothers. Still, she'd given in to a sliver of granting them the benefit of doubt.

Only to receive a *'cease and desist'* letter from Nick's brother and father. Containing the labels she'd most dreaded.

Grasping whore... Heartless leech, preying on the memory of our dead family member.

Their vicious response had killed any desire to tell them that she might be pregnant with Nick's son. That Nick, with his dark hair and faintly tanned colouring, might be her son's father, even though Max's eyes were more a silver-grey than Nick's faint blue.

Nick. Who would have been thirty-six today...

As she rose from bed the next day at the crack of dawn, Eden wondered if it was wise to continue the ritual she'd started with Max last year, of laying flowers at Nick's graveside.

While a part of her had questioned what she was doing, a greater part had been adamant about acknowledging the man who might have fathered her child. If—*when*—her memory returned, and she discovered differently, the worst that would've happened was her having paid respects to a man she'd known briefly.

That resolution didn't stop her stomach from churning as she showered, dressed and went to wake Max.

'Is that what you want for yourself? For him?' he prodded softly.

She sucked in a shaky breath, her eyes darkening with a swirl of emotion. Her soothing hand had worked, but his clever son could clearly sense the tension in the air, and was watching him with an intensity Azar silently applauded.

Now that he'd delivered the unsettling scenario, he was prepared to relent. *Just.* 'Pack what you will both need for the day. We'll return to my hotel.'

For now.

'Then what?' she parried wisely.

He shrugged. 'I've already delayed my return home for a day. I can probably toss in another. That should be enough time for you to wrap your head around the fact that your life isn't going to remain the same. No matter how much you wish it.'

To her credit, she was packed in fifteen minutes. Although judging from the meagre things she'd glumly thrown into a backpack, she didn't intend for it to be a long-term outing.

Azar stifled his objections, reminding himself that Max was his responsibility too now, and whatever the boy needed would be more than adequately provided for.

'You don't have a car seat?' he asked.

Her delicate jaw tightened. 'I don't have a car.'

That explained why they'd walked back from the cemetery. He turned to his chief of security. 'Ramon—?'

'Already taken care of, Your Highness. I suspected we might need one and sent Alfredo out to get it. It'll be here presently.'

This was the reason he'd kept his childhood friend on as the head of his royal guard, even after his brother Valenti had started a very successful security consultancy, and he always excused Ramon's occasional grumpiness and rigid sticking to protocol.

He nodded his thanks. Then at last he approached his son, where he sat on the carpet, playing with a giraffe and a tower of Lego.

Crouching down next to him, he caught the faint baby scent mixed with talcum powder. A scent that was instantly imprinted on his senses for ever.

'May I?' he muttered to Eden.

He saw her swallow before, eyes wide, she assented with a tiny nod.

Azar reached out, touched the thick curl resting at his son's temple. Smooth. Springy. Then he moved his hand lower, over his warm, soft skin.

A shudder went through him.

Then more powerful, *alien* emotions invaded his very bones.

A need to protect. To cherish. To *claim*. In a way he'd never been cherished nor claimed. With affection and acceptance— not out of militant duty and obligation because of the title destiny had thrust upon him.

Max glanced up, stared solemnly, and then, with a smile breaking out on his cherubic face, he held up his toy. 'Gi-waffe?'

'*Sí*...yes. Giraffe. He's very handsome,' Azar murmured, lying through his teeth.

The toy was worn to the point of being tattered, but it was clear it was much loved. He tossed a trip to the toy store into his immediate itinerary as he indulged himself with another caress of his son's cheek. Obsession bloomed, and he felt his heart pounding as emotions filled every corner of his consciousness.

He was a father.

'Prince...um...?'

'Your Highness.'

His head snapped up. Ramon stood a respectful distance

away, holding the car seat. Eden stood next to him, rebellion and apprehension sparking in her eyes.

He'd been completely lost in his son's presence and he didn't feel one iota of guilt. Going one better, Azar wrapped gentle hands around Max and stood, his small, precious weight making Azar inhale shakily.

'Are you ready to go an adventure, Max?' he asked.

The wide silver-grey eyes he'd seen reflected at him since childhood—from his father, and in recent years from his brothers—blinked at him.

'Out?'

'Out,' he confirmed thickly, moving to the door.

He only realised he was holding his breath when it was released at hearing Eden's footsteps behind him.

Five minutes later, as they were pulling away, a previous thought returned, demanding an answer.

'Earlier, you mentioned being threatened by Nick's people. Did you tell them about Max? That you thought he was Nick's?'

The very idea of anyone else attempting to claim his son lanced jagged fury through him.

There was a moment's hesitation, then she shook her head. 'I thought about it, but I didn't in the end.'

Her eyes flickered, then her lashes swept down as a wave of heat coloured her cheeks. Azar was faintly amazed she could still blush.

'I wanted my memories to return,' she continued. 'To be absolutely sure.'

He suppressed the peculiar sensation whistling through him at being so forgettable to a woman—an unheard-of thing before this one, whether by design or accident.

Instead, he dwelled on her answer. Commended her for it, in fact.

Because he knew what she meant.

There were those who knew better than to pick a fight with

the powerful Domene family and a kingdom like Cartana. But a few had tried to slap false paternity on Azar, thinking they could use the widely known circumstances of his birth to their advantage. They'd soon learned the folly of that.

He was secretly thankful that Eden had waited. The last thing he needed with his father's ill health was for his grand-son's paternity to be gossip fodder.

'A wise decision. It'll prevent any unpleasant publicity.'

Unreadable emotion flicked across her face, then she turned away to fuss over their son. The urge to cup her chin and re-direct her gaze bit at him. He forestalled it, plucking out his phone and placing the first of many calls in the fifteen min-utes it took them to arrive at the discreet entrance of his five-star hotel.

Once he had the nod from Ramon, he plucked his son from the car seat and entered the private elevator that shot them up to a floor reserved solely for his use.

'About damn time you turned up.' The deep voice echoed from the royal suite's living room. 'Not sure what you're play-ing at, but pulling a no-show isn't cool. I don't care if you're the Crown Prince or not.'

Azar stifled a groan. He'd forgotten about his brothers and their brunch plans today. Hell, he'd relegated every damn thing to the *go to hell* list the moment he'd seen Eden and the toddler at the cemetery.

Now, as he carried his son into the room, he watched his brothers' shrewd gazes flit from him to Eden to Max. Then stay on Max. Lingering for long moments and seeing the exact thing he had the moment he'd seen his son up close.

They both grew slack-jawed with shock.

'Holy—'

'Watch it. Young ears and curse words don't mix, brother.'

Eden watched the slimmer of the two men shove at the hand that had covered his mouth before he'd released the curse.

Azar Domene's half-brothers—the ones the Crown Prince had spent most of last night with out on the terrace during his birthday party. The two other parts of the trio every red-blooded woman had ogled and whispered feverishly about throughout the event.

Their combined magnetism had cautioned her to stay away from them the moment she'd spotted them on arrival. And she'd *almost* succeeded.

She couldn't remember their names, but she'd come across many articles about them on the internet while looking up Nick's accident—especially the talkative one who ran a renowned haute couture label.

She recalled him being a little wild—a playboy who attracted women likes flies to a feast. Not that the identical brother didn't command the same attention, but his was a brooding, jarring sort of intensity, unlike the Crown Prince's fiery, magnetic force field that gripped and compelled and didn't let go no matter how much you tried.

'Are you just going to stand there, *Your Highness*? Or are you going to introduce us?' the Playboy muttered.

He hadn't taken his eyes off Max, and a peculiar expression drifted over his face when Azar moved closer to them.

It seemed anyone who met her son was completely enthralled by him. She understood the sentiment. Hadn't she fallen deeply in love the moment the doctor had placed him in her arms? But their infatuation didn't diminish the apprehension spiking through her.

She'd seen Azar's reaction the moment he'd touched Max.

Had known without a shadow of a doubt that he was making irreversible plans where her son was concerned.

Just as she had seen and hadn't been able to dismiss the clear resemblance between father and son...the inescapable reality that her suspicions last night had been correct.

Crown Prince Azar Domene of Cartana was the father of her child.

Which meant she'd had sex with this man at some point three years ago!

'I know. He has the same effect on most women.'

She jumped at the mocking whispered comment and snatched her gaze from where it had latched on to Prince Azar, to find the Playboy a few feet away, his hand unfurled in greeting.

'That's enough, Teo,' Azar grated.

'Really? I've barely started.' He stepped closer. 'Let me formally introduce myself. I'm Teo Domene.'

She offered her hand and suppressed a gasp when he started to raise it to his lips. A thick rumble from Prince Azar made him freeze. He smiled and winked, before shaking her hand formally and releasing her.

'Eden Moss,' she murmured.

Before he could say anything else, the brooding one nudged him out of the way. He didn't offer his hand, and his gaze was direct, but not as piercing as his brother's. 'Valenti Domene,' he returned. Then, after a moment, 'You're Eden Moss.' It wasn't a greeting—more like a calibration of past events. 'Three years ago. Arizona. The Magnis Club.'

'The Magnis Club?' she echoed dazedly. Then his words truly sank in, making her inhale sharply. 'Wait… You know me? You remember me?'

His stare intensified. 'Any reason why we wouldn't?'

He opened his mouth, but Azar interrupted. 'No, there isn't.' When both men turned to him, he said, 'We'll have to reschedule brunch. As you can see, there's been a development.'

Both brothers' focus switched to him, then to Max.

'The understatement of the century. But understandable,' Valenti rasped. 'Is he well?' he asked gruffly.

Eden barely stopped herself from rolling her eyes as Teo held up his hands.

'No. Wait… You can't just throw us out. I have so many questions,' he protested.

'They'll have to wait. But you can say a quick hello to your nephew before you leave.'

The dizzying rollercoaster that had been revving up since Prince Azar had turned up on her doorstep took another one-eighty loop.

'You don't know yet that he's yours,' she blurted, voicing the same objection as before.

Three pairs of eyes swung her way.

Then Teo barked out a disbelieving laugh. 'You'd have to have been living in a cave without internet access or to be stone-cold blind to mistake this angelic rascal as anyone but Azar's.' Approaching his brother, he smoothed a gentle finger down Max's cheek, much as Azar had done. 'How similar is he to that childhood photo of Azar at the same age, Valenti?' he murmured softly.

'Similar enough to fool my security software for a minute or two,' his brother replied. 'Show her.'

Teo dropped his hand long enough to fish out his phone. Within seconds he was striding back to her, displaying an image that made her heart jump in her chest.

Until that second, Eden had held out some half-hearted hope that the obvious wasn't true. That once her memory returned there would be some far less overwhelming explanation for what was unfolding.

Reality battered her with hurricane force, driving home the fact that she really had—at some point—shared touches, kisses, *bodies* with this man. This man who, on paper, was so like her father—everything she abhorred about wealthy and powerful men and the way they wielded that power.

The way they only needed to snap their fingers to alter lives.

Like hers. Like her son's.

And yet heat scorched her at their continued scrutiny and

the thoughts cartwheeling through her head. Thoughts of what that moment—*those moments*—had been like.

Had she enjoyed it?

Had he blown her mind and she his?

Her nipples started to tighten, and she swiftly averted her gaze to her son. Her beautiful, caring, harmless son.

Who was now second in line to a European throne.

Stumbling to the nearest chair, she sank into it uninvited—protocol be damned. A moment later a glass of water was pushed into her hand, and she looked up into the eyes of Valenti Domene. His fierce examination had her murmuring quick thanks and refocusing her attention on the plush carpeting.

She didn't care if she looked weak. She needed to get through the next few minutes, collect herself and plan her next move.

Because what Azar had suggested—that she and Max would never be going back home—was preposterous.

Wasn't it?

'Hasta luego, hermanos,' Azar repeated pointedly.

Valenti was the first to move, pausing to slide Max a half smiling look before clasping his brother's shoulder briefly. Then Teo repeated the gesture.

Seconds later, they were gone. And Azar was moving towards her.

Max reached for her, and Azar reluctantly handed him over. She'd hoped having him in her arms would focus her attention, but the compulsion she couldn't seem to fight dragged her gaze to Azar's again.

'You'll have to make a list of what he needs and I'll make sure—' He stopped when a knock came at the door, his nostrils flaring with displeasure. 'Yes?'

A man slightly older than Azar entered, his steps slowing when he saw them. 'Your Highness, I've made the alterations to your schedule, as requested. Do you need anything else?'

The Crown Prince hesitated for a second before he beckoned him in. 'Eden, this is Gaspar—my private secretary. He'll ensure the transition runs smoothly.'

Unlike the Prince's brothers', Gaspar's face remained carefully neutral as he nodded to her. He was probably used to the eclectic demands of royalty.

'I need you to draft a press statement to be released by the palace after I speak to my father and the royal council.'

'Right away, Your Highness.' The man's gaze darted briefly to her, then to Max, before returning to his prince. 'And the subject matter?'

Azar's lips flattened for a moment. 'I have recently discovered that I've fathered a son. He was born...?' He raised his eyebrow at her.

Rebellion, and the stomach-hollowing reality that she was losing control of the situation, urged her to withhold the information. But she knew his clever minions would unearth it within the hour. In clipped tones she supplied it, then listened as he gave succinct instructions about the wording of his statement.

It was neither flowery nor stark. But it didn't hide the naked truth despite withholding specific details. It merely stated that at some point three years ago he'd fathered a son, whose existence he hadn't discovered before today. It left little doubt that Azar Domene intended to claim his son and proudly insert him into the dramatic fabric of his life, groom him to take the Cartana throne one day.

The raw facts shook her to the foundation of her soul, made the blood roar in her ears until it blocked everything else out.

'You have objections?'

She looked up and realised that Gaspar had left. That she could freely express her deep reservations. 'Of course I do. This is madness. You're moving too fast.'

'Let me guess: you're still hellbent on insisting you have unbreakable ties to that apartment? Or to your mother, perhaps?'

Her insides chilled. 'What do you know about her?'

He shrugged. 'I would prefer you tell me. I don't wish to harm your recovery by supplying information that might unduly distress you.'

A tiny, bewildering knot unwound inside her. This small display of consideration, so unlike any she'd known before, was certainly not something her father would've granted her mother under similar circumstances. But it meant nothing. It could very well be a lure to achieve his ends. She couldn't risk lowering her guard around this man whose determination to wrest her son from her was anything but quiet and understated.

'The last I heard from her two years ago, she was in a commune near Joshua Tree.'

She saw a layer of tension ease off him. 'That ties in with what you told me about her being in California,' he said.

Her eyes widened. 'I told you that three years ago?'

He stared at her for moment, then nodded. 'Now we've established she isn't a mainstay in your life, what other hurdles do we need to overcome?' he asked archly.

Irritation replaced bewilderment. 'Please don't belittle my concerns.'

'Tell me you truly want to stay in this city, in that apartment, with my son, working menial jobs while an old woman who can barely stand up straight looks after him, and I'll endeavour to take your concerns seriously.'

The accurate assessment of everything she'd yearned to better in her circumstances brought a guilty flush. But she wasn't ready to give in. Not by a long shot.

'Just because my circumstances aren't as ideal or as rosy as yours, it doesn't mean I'm going to you let you ride roughshod over the direction of my life.'

'*Mi linda*, I hate to remind you again, but you slept with a crown prince three years ago and bore his son. The only direction your life is going to take now, if you wish to put him first, is to secure his birthright. And making that happen involves him transitioning entirely to his fatherland and taking his rightful place as first in line to the throne.'

'First? Don't you mean second?'

The flash of bleakness in his eyes was searing. 'No. I don't.'

The gravity of that response, words uttered with no further elaboration, washed over her, and then settled deep to weigh her down.

'What's the hurry? If he's first in line surely he can have a normal li—?'

'No,' he interjected forcefully. 'He was born extraordinary. The quicker you wrap your mind around that, the better. Besides...' His voice dropped, and further dark shadows rushed over his face. 'There's little time to lose.'

'What's that supposed to mean?'

For a moment his sensual lips remained pursed. Then, dragging his fingers through his hair in an aberrant show of agitation, he said, 'It means that my father's health is failing. He's abdicating in a matter of months. It means that our son will soon become first in line to the throne. I've already missed more than two years of his life. No more, Eden. You and I will take him home and we will do the right thing. So he can, with minimal turmoil, take his rightful place in due course as the Cartanian Crown Prince.'

And because she knew that influential, powerful men like him created their own versions of right and wrong, she insisted on clarification.

'What exactly does "the right thing" mean?'

'The only way my son can rightfully inherit the throne when the time comes is for us to be married.'

CHAPTER FOUR

EDEN WAS GLAD she was sitting down when his hallucination-inducing words tunnelled into her brain. Her fingers dug into the plush velvet padding and she wondered whether she would pass out from the shock.

She concluded that would be impossible.

Because he couldn't mean them.

'I— What?'

Her babbled response fell in dizzying whispers. She blinked up at him, and part of her brain computed the ruthless determination on his face. The growing realisation that he was serious.

'I— You're crazy!'

Another flattening of his lips distracted her briefly, until he responded. 'I assure you I am of perfectly sound mind.'

'But… But I'm a w-waitress. With potholes in my memory. I can't be your—your—' She stopped. 'Look, I think this has gone far enough!' she snapped, her conviction that this was all some sort of elaborate game gaining momentum.

Her father had done enough of that, taunting both her and her mother from his lofty position. She would absolutely *not* take it from this man.

The lethal blaze growing in his eyes quickly abated when Max, deciding he needed to include others in his joy, pulled himself upright and started towards her, holding out a colourful storybook.

But a few steps from her he glanced up at Azar—his father—and changed direction.

Azar scooped him up, with a glint of pleased satisfaction in his eyes. She watched father and son, attempting not to feel slighted by Max's innocent betrayal.

After a moment granting his son his attention, Azar shifted his gaze to her. 'You think this is some sort of game?' he asked, his voice deadly soft.

She shrugged. 'You were pretty upset with me last night about something besides my not knowing who you were. Are you going to deny that?'

Shadows drifted across his face and his jaw clenched once. 'This is neither the time nor the place—'

'I think it's exactly the time and place. Or do you often go around tossing out proposals to women you don't like?'

And not just any proposal. One that guaranteed she would be *queen*. Which was just—absurd.

For a long stretch he studied her, almost dispassionately. 'You're the first to receive a proposal of marriage from me. But you'll also recall that I have said this is entirely for the sake of my son's destiny as heir to the throne.'

She noticed starkly that he didn't address the subject of not liking her, and chose not to examine why it left a dark hollow in her belly.

'*Our* son. He's not just yours—no matter how much you wish it so.'

A flare of colour stained his cheekbones at her speaking look at the way he clutched Max to his chest.

'I'm not going to pretend I don't feel possessive over the son I didn't know existed until three hours ago,' he bit out, redirecting his gaze to glide with open possession over Max.

That hollow in her stomach widened, intensifying that feeling of being left out in the cold that had been a far too familiar sensation since childhood. Because her father's treatment of them hadn't forged a bond between her and her mother. It had done the opposite, stripping her mother of every last ounce of self-esteem and sending her looking for love and affection in all the wrong places. The end result of which was that Eden had been abandoned to find her own way in life.

As much as she wanted to deny it, she knew wounds like those festered. Scarred. Left hearts and emotions intensely wary.

Striving to suppress the echoes of anguish, she opened her mouth, but he beat her to a response.

'As for your profession…it's nothing we can't spin to suit the circumstances. It's not common, but it's not rare either.'

'A prince plucking a downtrodden single mother from destitution into untold luxury and status?'

She'd meant it to sound caustic. Cynical in the extreme. But it emerged a touch breathless, wrapped in undeniable echoes of that dream of an unrealistic happily-ever-after that made her cringe.

'Exactly so,' he concurred, ignoring her abrasive tone. 'Provided you play your cards right.'

'What's that supposed to mean?' She almost snorted as she said the words she seemed unable to stop parroting. 'If you think I'm going to jump through hoops for—'

'It means there's a mountain of protocol and a strict code of behaviour you'll need to adhere to as my wife and princess. You'll need to be guided through it.'

The title was too nerve-shredding to contemplate just then, so she brushed it aside in favour of his other statement. '"Code of behaviour"? It's almost as if—' It was her turn to narrow her eyes as her insides shrivelled. 'You don't think very highly of me, do you?' she murmured, then inhaled sharply. 'Something happened three years ago, didn't it? Something you're judging me for?'

The tightening of his face told her she'd hit the bullseye.

'Tell me what I did,' she demanded.

'Even if I was inclined to rehash your past, your doctor

was at pains to advise otherwise. I may be many things, but I'm not a monster who'd blithely risk your health for my own purposes,' he bit out.

That confused her. Surely he wasn't looking out for her? That would make him almost…considerate…

'Mama!'

Max choosing that moment to demand her attention was both frustrating and mollifying. Azar handed him over, reluctantly, then crouched before her. She grew far too aware of the arms he rested on either side of her thighs. Hands that had touched her, caressed her when they made a child together…

'What does he need?' he enquired when Max continued to fret.

Switching into 'mom mode' took effort. 'He's tired,' she said. 'His morning has been overwhelming. A snack and some warm milk usually do the trick.'

Azar nodded, and she watched—with that punch of surprise she'd experienced a minute ago—as he rose and went to the phone. Minutes later, a butler wheeled in a sterling silver trolley with tiny bowls of everything a toddler might want to snack on, and a jug filled with warm milk on its own silver platter.

Under any other circumstances Eden would have joked at the sheer over-the-top-ness of it all. But she knew she was getting a tiny glimpse of what the future held for her son. Possibly for her.

A life surrounded by people who thought nothing of using their wealth and influence to buckle people to their will—like her father.

A life far removed from the simplistic one she'd secretly dreamed of.

Could she do it?

Even for Max's sake?

Near silence reigned as Eden placed Max in the sleek-looking highchair that had appeared. It was only broken by his enthusiasm for his snacks.

But then, 'What happened in the past doesn't change a single thing about what needs to happen for our son's sake now,' Azar murmured as they both watched Max eat. 'He's the most important thing. *Sí?*'

Turning her head, she met his implacable gaze, and in a split second a serrated white-hot memory pierced her brain, causing a gasp.

'What is it?' he enquired sharply.

She shook her head, her hand going to her midriff as her heart pounded. 'It's— Every now and then I get a...a twinge. A memory attempting to break free, the doctor says.'

'Is it triggered by something specific?'

Sí. That word, spoken in lyrical Spanish with that almost seductive cadence.

Her face flamed as his eyes probed, awaiting her answer. 'Sometimes,' she prevaricated.

He stared for another handful of seconds, then exhaled. 'I have meetings and calls to make. The butler will show you the guest suite when you're ready. But, Eden...'

'Yes?'

'Be prepared to give me an answer when I return.'

'Or what?'

A slow, heart-thumping smile curved his lips. 'Don't ask questions you won't like the answers to, *cara*. Suffice it to say, I always get what I want. And trust me when I tell you that claiming the son I didn't know I had, and ensuring I don't miss a second of making up the time I've lost with him, is number one on my list of desires.'

Long after he'd brushed a kiss on Max's head and left the room she was grappling with his grave words. Registering that while her father had done the opposite—ruthlessly cutting her off, then ensuring she would never be a threat to him by doing everything in his power to ensure she never thrived—

Azar was using his power to *claim* his son. To name him his *heir* within hours of meeting him.

But surely she was simply dealing with the other side of the same coin.

Wasn't she?

Telling his father of his first grandchild's existence was easier than Azar had anticipated, with the wry reminder that similar circumstances were the reason Azar's own twin half-brothers existed easing the knots in his gut as he relayed the news.

'I would prefer my sons don't make a habit of following too closely in my footsteps, though,' King Alfonso said, with a grunt that dissolved alarmingly into a hacking cough.

Azar's fist tightened around his phone, his insides churning as he waited for his father to catch his breath.

'Not that I would give any of you up for the world,' King Alfonso added. 'You and your brothers are the manifestations of a dream I believed would never come true.'

Then why didn't you fight to prevent the nightmares of our childhood?

Azar grappled with the resurgence of bitterness as his father fell into the story he loved retelling, of how the palace doctors had pronounced him sterile after a bad case of mumps in his late teens. How he'd struggled through accepting that he would never father children and then, straight after finishing university, had gone on a months-long hedonism streak through Europe with a swathe of women. Only to discover after returning home that he'd got not one, but two women pregnant.

Azar's right to the throne had only come about because he'd been the one born first—a fact he knew had always been and remained the subject that caused severe friction between his mother and his twin brothers' mother.

Hell, it had been the reason why their respective mothers had spitefully connived to keep them apart until well into their early teens…a situation King Alfonso had been either laughably ineffectual at battling or blindly naïve about until too much harm was done.

Now here he was, following directly in his father's footsteps. Alfonso had married the woman who'd birthed his first born in a hastily arranged wedding that had surprisingly withstood the test of time, despite her senseless rivalry with the mother of Azar's twin brothers. And despite the questionable machinations from his mother that had warped Azar's childhood and left him certain that marriage was anathema to him.

Yes, he'd known from the moment he'd been able to make such deductions for himself that there would come a time when he'd have to marry, to further the Domene line. But despite the recent rumblings through the royal council, telling him that it was time, he'd managed to put it off. Had given himself the mental deadline of age forty before selecting one of the many 'suitable' women lined up to be his queen.

Between that, his father's failing health and the earth-shaking news of his son's existence, he was surprised he wasn't knocking back several whiskies to numb the shock.

Blinking, he refocused as his father asked, 'What's his name?'

He pulled in a long, sustaining breath, his chest doing that curious squeezing thing when he thought of his son. The boy he would move heaven and earth to protect from the acrimony and indifference he'd suffered.

'She named him Max.'

His father hummed in approval. '*Excelente*. A good, strong name. Your great-grandfather was named Maximiliano, if you recall?'

He did, and when he'd first heard it he'd wondered if Eden had chosen the name deliberately, attempting to gain an advantage with that stroke of familial evocation. Her condition put that into doubt, though.

If it was true…

While the greater part of him believed her amnesia diagnosis, he couldn't help but remember how effectively she'd pulled the wool over his eyes with her false innocent act three years ago. For weeks he'd bought that act, believing her to be a good woman caught in a bad situation, until the truth had slapped him in the face.

She'd cleverly played Nick and him against each other. Expressing interest in him before inexplicably switching to his friend, then back again. It had been the first time Azar had experienced raging jealousy, and he'd detested the turbulent emotion as much as he'd detested its instigator.

She should have been a run-of-the-mill hook-up—taken, pleasured and forgotten in the usual sequence of his liaisons.

Instead, he'd discovered that he'd bedded a virgin.

Then discovered that she'd selected him only because she'd seen him as the highest bidder.

While he'd felt a primal, borderline uncivilised satisfaction in claiming that prize, he'd been livid when she'd given herself to his best friend. When both she and Nick had taunted him with his expendability that last time before she'd slid into his car.

'You've had your fun but give it up. She's with me now.'

'Yes, Azar. I'm with Nick now.'

Words that reminded him that even after all this time he wasn't over the searing anathema of coming second best. *Mommy issues*, Teo had called it. He'd rolled his eyes yesterday. Mocked his brother. But the truth resided just *there*, in a sharp starburst of indelible pain, beneath the layers of muscle close to his heart. Was it any wonder that thus far the thought of reliving any of that by saddling himself with a wife was abhorrent?

And, yes, he'd hated his own friend for that too—a situation that had only compounded his guilt when Nick had perished before they could make amends.

Those weeks in Arizona they'd both discovered their weak

spot. A stunning woman called Eden. And as the final betrayal she'd chosen his best friend, slid into his sports car after witnessing the lowest point of Azar's life—fighting over a common woman—intending to sail into the sunset with Nick.

Only for his best friend to wrap his car around a tree and for Eden to fall off the face of the earth.

She'd done that to him. And it remained a spike stuck in his gut.

'Azar?'

He started, realised he'd lost himself down another bitter memory lane and forgotten his father. *'Sí, Papá?'*

'I asked when you were returning home with my grandson. That is your intention, yes?'

It was couched in a question, but it was an order. And, while his father might have grown frail far too quickly over the past year, King Alfonso still commanded with an iron fist. It was a shame that iron fist had never succeeded in stamping out the acrimonious battlefield that had been Azar's childhood...

'Yes. I... We'll be home in a day or two. Three at most.'

No matter what feeble protests the cheaply dressed siren next door threw up.

He was still in combat mode when he left his office two hours later. Gaspar had advised him that his son was taking his afternoon nap. Which made it the perfect time to finalise his discussion with Eden.

He found her on the terrace, with a glass of what looked like mineral water in one hand and the other hand gliding through the rich, dark butterscotch abundance of her hair. She'd discarded her coat, revealing skinny leggings that moulded her shapely legs and rounded behind. The snug hem of her beige top was bordering on threadbare, emphasising her trim waist. While she'd possessed curves in all the right places the last time he saw her, he realised again that her hips had thickened slightly.

Mouth-wateringly.

He paused in the French doorway to compose himself, un-welcome heat rising as memory struck again—this time of sinking his fingers into that heavy silk mass, gripping it tight in a sensual direction that had made her scream and turn him inside out with a scorching pleasure it had taken an infuriat-ingly long time for him to forget.

Long after he'd left Arizona he'd considered whether that response too had been manufactured.

His jaw clenched now as he dismissed the memory and stepped onto the terrace.

'Eden.'

She whirled around, her eyes going wide. Her curvy bust jiggled with her motion and Azar stifled a curse when his temperature rose several more notches. This was merely re-sidual effects of that unwanted trip down memory lane. Noth-ing more.

'Um… Max is taking a nap.'

'I'm aware. Have you had lunch?' He recalled she hadn't eaten the pancakes this morning.

She shrugged. 'I don't have much of an appetite.'

Whether or not that was a dig at him, he chose not to con-template. 'Nevertheless, I'd prefer you eat something.'

'Because you think whatever you're about to throw at me requires I have sustenance?'

He allowed himself a grim smile. 'I don't just think, *cara*. I know.'

Her nostrils quivered. 'I don't know if that's a joke or a veiled threat, *Your Highness*. But I'm not amused.'

Azar stiffened slightly, wondering if she remembered she'd used that same prim little voice to say his title three years ago. At first it had been to pretend she wasn't interested in his ad-vances. Then it had been because he'd demanded it while she was on her knees, driving him to heaven and back.

Now it was meant as a dig, and it would've been amusing

had there not been so much awful stagnant water beneath that particular bridge.

He sensed Gaspar hovering behind him and turned to give the nod for their lunch to be brought out. Striding to the set table, he pulled out her chair and waited beside it.

Her gaze took in the set places, then rose to his. 'Did you hear what I just said?'

'I'm not deaf, Eden. Come…sit.'

He knew his even tone confused her. It had been carefully cultivated, purely for his mother, by the time he was seven years old and had come to realise that answering her shrill machinations with tantrums only made her act out more. That treating the Queen with sometimes impersonal kid gloves, like his father did, was the only way to defuse her volatile moods.

That lesson had served him well in his sexual liaisons in adulthood, effectively dismantling any foolish aspirations.

In the aftermath of Arizona, Azar had realised—to his bafflement and too late—that *he* was the one who'd lost control of his emotions. And that he had played expertly into Eden's hands. She'd used his unfettered passions to manipulate him, much as his mother had before he'd gained the upper hand.

But Eden Moss would learn that very little threw him off course these days. That his passions were very much tethered. Granted, the day's events had made this a unique day, as had those weeks they'd spent together in the desert…

No. He wasn't about to wonder why most of the distinctive events of his adult life involved this woman.

'I don't have an answer for you,' she pre-empted, defiance edging her husky voice.

One corner of his mouth twitched. 'You will. Today or tomorrow. Either way, things are now set in motion that cannot and will not be undone.'

'Such as…?'

She moved from the railing, approaching with a graceful glide that drew his eyes to her swaying hips. His fingers tapped the back of the chair, and after another charged second she sniffed and took the seat.

Azar took his own seat before responding. 'Such as my father, the King, having been informed that he is a grandfather and insisting on meeting Max at the earliest opportunity. Which means presenting my son in Cartana by Friday at the latest. Such as the private doctors at the palace waiting to provide the DNA and other tests—'

'I didn't agree to that,' she protested.

Her fingers tightened around her knife and for a moment he wondered whether she would use it, much as his mother had attempted to attack him when he was twelve and he hadn't answered one of her manic questions quickly enough.

The memory dampened his already downturned mood.

'Unfortunately, that forms part of the protocol I mentioned...' He hesitated a moment before deciding to divulge the rest of the news. After all, she'd discover the reality before the weekend. 'With my father being unwell, anyone admitted to his presence needs to be medically approved. And before all of that happens we need to make a stop in Milan or Paris.'

'Why?'

His gaze drifted over her, lingering on the faintly frayed neckline of her top. On the creaminess of the skin those cheap clothes caressed.

Focus.

'The Royal Family of Cartana requires adherence to certain immutable high standards. Where we stop depends on which of Teo's boutiques is ready to accommodate a complete wardrobe fitting at such short notice.'

'Teo?' she echoed. 'He has a fashion house, right?'

Azar tightened his gut against the needles of disgruntlement triggered by the awe in her voice. It was far too reminiscent of the jealousy he'd felt three years ago. But he couldn't curb the grating sensation when he responded. 'The House of

Domene fashion brand, yes. Does that sway you into agreement?' he bit out, before he could stop the betraying query.

Her face immediately tightened. 'You think a bunch of designer clothes and accessories are all it takes to swing a life-changing decision in your favour?' she hissed, with more venom than he'd anticipated.

He shrugged, demolishing that tiny hollow inside, made by her disappointment in him. 'Is it? Either way, your life is going to change. If this smooths the way, then what does it hurt?'

Her eyes flashed with more venom before she pursed her lips. 'You realise all you're doing is confirming that you don't like me very much? And I know you don't think it matters, but it matters to me.'

'Noted.'

Her lashes descended, then she flicked a glance at him. Azar noted her cheeks were lightly flushed, her chest rising and falling in a higher rhythm.

Her tongue slicked across her plump lower lip. 'Can I ask you something?'

'You may ask, but I don't guarantee an answer.'

'I get the feeling you're hiding behind Dr Ramsey's advice, but—' Her flush deepened and the stirring in his own groin intensified. 'Did we—? Was it a one-night stand—between us?'

'You're asking if I took you more than once?'

Her expression remained veiled. 'Y-yes.'

He shifted in his seat, the combination of her innocence and his need to know what she was thinking stirring further restlessness through him.

'Without going into memory-endangering details, the answer is yes.'

So many days. So many positions. So many capricious emotions he'd thought left behind in his teenage years. If he hadn't witnessed the perils of drugs and alcoholism at a young age, and vowed not to indulge in the former and severely limit his intake of the later, he might have thought he was under the influence of both during that heady time in the Arizona desert.

But every intoxicating, emotionally turbulent moment had come from this woman alone.

A combination of relief and unease flitted across her face, triggering his keener interest.

Basta!

Reaching for the nearest cloche, he lifted it to reveal the lobster bisque his memory had reminded him that she loved. Sneaking a glance from the corner of his eye, he watched her eyes widen slightly before she licked her lips in blatant hunger. He spooned two ladles full into bowls and exhaled in satisfaction when she picked up her spoon to sample the exquisite meal.

In silence, they ate, then moved to the next course.

Calm. Unruffled resolution.

That was the way forward with this woman some cosmic entity had deemed fit to bear his child and therefore wear his crown.

Tempestuous emotions from the recent and distant past would not be given a place in their union.

He simply wouldn't allow it.

Every argument she'd thrown up had disintegrated beneath the weight of the one hurdle she couldn't overcome.

What was best for her son.

It had driven her into pacing in the guest room while Max slept in a new, exquisite cot, complete with dramatic muslin netting, until the need for fresh air and clarity had drawn her to the terrace. There she'd been bombarded with the sights and sounds of Las Vegas, the most decadent city in the world.

The last place she'd dreamed of raising a family.

Which begged the question: why was she hesitating to take the silver platter offered?

She knew why…

Crown Prince Azar Domene. Even his title was melodramatic. Like an overwhelming piece of theatre just waiting to sweep the unsuspecting off their feet.

Beside remaining a force of nature, and she deemed it imperative to keep him from gaining an inch because it would be the surest way to get flattened by him, she also sensed that he despised her. Something had happened in those weeks in Arizona. Something that kept this formidable wall of resentment between them.

For an instant she regretted calling Dr Ramsey. Maybe without that express deterrent against delving deep into her memories Azar would've been more forthcoming. Although his own expression suggested it wasn't a time he relished revisiting.

The idea that she'd behaved in any way like her mother caused waves of horror to wash through her. Landing a rich, ageing Hollywood studio executive had been a trigger for her mother's dreams of fame and fortune, only for her to be scarred for life when she was left high, dry and pregnant.

Being told by her father never to contact him again had left a teenage Eden with an impression of men that had unfortunately been affirmed by the men she'd met in her mother's desperation for companionship.

That one disastrous episode had led her mother to search for an easy way out of the tribulations of her life. Her resulting career as a barely-scraping-by lounge singer had triggered a series of disastrous relationships that had earned her deplorable labels and slurs even her seven-year-old daughter had understood and been ashamed of.

Could she look beyond this Crown Prince's tarnished view of her—whatever it was—to do what was best for her son?

She held that question at arm's length now, and asked the question activated by something he'd said. 'You said your father isn't well. What's wrong with him?'

Shadows drifted across his face. He didn't answer for several seconds, and when he did she suspected he'd weighed the value of telling her and somehow worked her son more than her curiosity into the equation. She suspected 'in the interest of Max' would heavily feature in how Prince Azar dealt with her henceforth.

Eden told herself she didn't care, but the cold pang throbbing in her middle reminding her that yet again she was alone in this, wouldn't be so easily dismissed.

'He was diagnosed with heart disease several months ago. A serious case that needs careful monitoring. Unfortunately, he also recently contracted pneumonia, which doesn't help his weakened immune system. Everyone who visits must be carefully vetted by his doctors. So you see why this precaution is necessary?'

'Yes,' she said—and then realised she was half accepting that she would be travelling to Cartana with Max and his father. While her stomach churned at the very thought, she asked herself if she had a choice that didn't include a full-blown fight with the heir apparent to a powerful kingdom?

And, as he'd pointed out, what was she fighting for? The right to keep worrying and working herself into the ground just to keep a roof over her son's head? When his destiny was already set in concrete?

Eden put her cutlery down, started to reach for her mineral water, and stopped because her hand was shaking too much.

Tucking both into her lap, she forced her gaze to meet his. 'We'll come with you to Paris. And then to Cartana. But just for a visit.'

The tiniest gentling of his features went much further than she wanted to admit in soothing her. Which, again, was absurd. Because he was the enemy. Wasn't he?

'A half-step is admirable. And I get that this has been a shock. But you're only delaying the inevitable. Max is my heir and he will inherit the throne one day. Having me chase you around the globe to assert my rights as his father will not stand. So let's make the transition scandal-free, shall we?'

'You're accustomed to a life of duty and protocol. What makes you think I'll fit in?'

Her father was Hollywood royalty, and even he, living in a land of make-believe, hedonism and wall-to-wall scandals, had been repulsed by the idea of an illegitimate child.

A hard light ignited in his eyes and Eden suspected he wasn't thinking about her in that moment, but reliving a memory.

'Ultimately, how much or how little you do and what you devote your time to is entirely up to you. But be warned that the Domene Palace is a living, breathing entity that operates its own hierarchy and ecosystem. Loyalty will be rewarded. Non-compliance will be...unfortunate.'

'That sounds like a melodramatic threat.'

A cynical smile curved his lips. 'There are those who like to promote melodrama within the palace. I suggest you don't emulate them.'

She opened his mouth to ask what he meant, but steady footsteps stopped her. She glanced behind her to see Azar's private secretary, Gaspar, standing a respectful distance away.

'The young Prince is awake, Your Highness,' he said.

Eden's breath caught. It was the first time she'd heard her son referred to by his inevitable title.

Again, Azar's regard morphed, turning almost pityingly gentle before it hardened again. 'Stay with him for a moment, Gaspar. We will be in shortly.'

He remained silent after Gaspar retreated. And she knew she'd run out of time.

Max. She was doing this for Max. Ensuring she would always be there to protect him from the abandonment she'd suffered.

But...marriage. Being the mother of the heir to the throne. Palace life. Being the wife of a crown prince.

Eventual queen.

Her mouth dried as the titles fell like anvils on her shoulders, threatening to sink her. There should be lightning and fireworks in the sky to mark the screeching turn her life was taking. And yet there was only heavy silence. And her…stuck with only one answer to give.

'Yes. If you're…'

Sure, she wanted to say. But resolute affirmation blazed in his eyes, making her question redundant.

So she cleared her clogged throat and gave an affirmation of her own. 'Yes.'

She'd suspected Azar was only waiting for her response to set things in motion, but she'd imagined it would be at freight train speed. Not the unstoppable rocket force it turned out to be.

Gaspar's return to Max's room, where she and the Crown Prince—who seemed determined to insert himself into every corner of his son's life—had been watching him gleefully tear into the batch of expensive toys that had just arrived, had been to ask for her apartment keys. It had stopped her in her tracks.

Azar had coolly informed her that there was a team waiting to pack up her entire life and ship it to Cartana.

He'd told her that Ramon was already in the process of arranging Max's expedited diplomatic travel papers via the Cartanian Embassy, and it was barely mid-afternoon!

Before she could fully compute that, another knock heralded the arrival of a chicly dressed woman and a younger man, wheeling in a sleek garment rail.

'I thought a change of attire for tonight and tomorrow might be in order,' Azar said.

It was an evenly paced statement with an explicit directive underlying it. One not worth fighting, considering she'd already agreed to the wardrobe stopover in Paris.

But her gaze shifted to her son.

'Go. We'll be fine,' Azar said firmly.

Max looked up, a smile breaking out as he held up a red toy train which had already become a firm favourite.

As much as her heart squeezed at leaving him, Eden knew that thus far one thing was true. Azar Domene was obsessed with the son he hadn't known about until this morning. And if there was a fierce fire burning in her heart to ensure Max was not emotionally harmed, then a fiercer one burned in Azar—for unknown reasons of his own.

Reasons she intended to keep a keen eye on.

She went with the woman and the young man.

And, after struggling not to ogle the luxurious brands so casually offered, and settling on a pair of silk palazzo pants and an asymmetric batwing top firmly recommended for travel, with shoes to match, she gave in and allowed the male assistant to perform the quick make-up session he heavily hinted she needed.

A full hour later than she'd expected to be, she walked into the living room, stingingly aware of the brush of silk warming her skin, the smoky eyeshadow emphasising her eyes, even the arch of her feet in the new four-inch heels.

It was a predicament made even more pronounced when both Azar Domene and his private secretary froze after one look at her.

For tense seconds they stared. Then, slanting a narrow-eyed look at Gaspar, the Crown Prince said something sharply in Spanish that startled the other man, turning the tops of his ears red, before he executed a shallow bow and made himself scarce.

'Is something wrong?' she asked, hating the hesitancy in her voice.

Sardonic amusement tilted Azar's lips before his gaze moved over her, slightly more heated than she remembered.

'Not at all. Although having fair warning might prove to be a useful thing.'

She blinked. 'Fair warning of what?'

'Your effect on unsuspecting victims.'

His hard-edged tone drew a shiver from her.

'What—? I don't know what you're talking about.'

The magnificent Crown Prince stared at her for a long stretch, and then, casting a glance in his son's direction, to make sure he was still happily playing, he prowled towards her.

'The innocent waif act may work with men like my private secretary, but you should know that as long as you keep it harmless your life will be as smooth as you wish it. Stray beyond that and there will be consequences. Understood?'

He knew he'd given far too much away when her eyes rounded—even more alluring now, after whatever magic the damn stylists had created. She blinked again, and he stifled a breath as her long lashes batted against the top of her cheeks.

Dios mio, when had he ever noted the sexiness of a woman's eyelashes?

It's a good thing you're marrying her, no?

Was it, though? When his primary reason for doing so was to keep her in position when it came to his son's wellbeing and nothing else? Hadn't he warned himself against raking over disagreeable emotions? Yet here he was, already snapping at Gaspar for staring at her too long, and feeling his manhood thicken at the sight of her face and the seductive sway of her hips.

'Are you warning me against...*cheating* on you?'

The word fell from her glossy lips with such contempt he would've thought he was dealing with someone else entirely had he not known first-hand what this siren was capable of.

But, while his friend Nick had been many things—rabidly competitive, shockingly obstinate and borderline obsessed with one-upmanship—he'd never outright lied to Azar.

In his darkest nights, Nick's accusations rang through his nightmares.

'I saw her first. Just like you to slide in and take what's mine, isn't it? You should be thankful that she returned to my bed last night. She spent all night apologising. For the sake of our friendship, I suggest you stay away from her, though. She's mine now.'

Except things hadn't remained as cut and dried as that.

Crown Prince Azar of Cartana, a man renowned for his integrity and his tough but fair dealings with heads of state and unruly family members, had succumbed to temptation again.

And again.

Because this woman had played this same act and seduced him. And, yes, he knew the hypocrisy of blaming the woman. Knew and accepted that a large swathe of blame lay with him.

He'd succumbed to lust and desire. Rowed with his best friend over a woman. Watched that same woman choose his friend over him.

Hours later, Nick had been dead.

Sorrow and fury congealed into a hard ball in his gut, effectively slaying his blazing arousal.

Frustration cannoned through him at the reminder that she didn't even remember any of it.

'I'm advising that only your most exemplary behaviour will ensure a smooth transition for our son. We owe it to him to play a straight bat.'

Her lips parted, but he was done with this conversation.

Turning, he strode to Max and picked him up, revelling in the faint baby smell he'd grown so ragingly addicted to in just half a day.

This was safe.

This was less mind-bending.

And if there was the tiniest bit of cowardice in the act... who would dare accuse the King-in-waiting of such a thing?

CHAPTER FIVE

A FULL DAY later and Eden was still fuming at Azar's not so veiled denigration of her character. Whether by design or coincidence—and she was inclined to believe the former—since then they'd been inundated with staff, and the occasional guest who wanted one thing or another from the Crown Prince. A crown prince who insisted that Eden and his son were present for each meeting, the last of which had included his half-brothers.

And between one breath and the next, Eden had found herself being coaxed into having Teo Domene's creative designer as her wedding trousseau maker.

Very soon after that she'd firmly excused herself to bath Max and put him to bed—then spent a restless night swinging between the fear that she was doing the absolute wrong thing and the knowledge that there was no way back now she'd agreed.

Morning had arrived with another flurry of activity—including a surprise visit from Mrs Tolson, apparently organised by Azar, which had triggered another jolt of surprise she'd quickly pushed aside. Because of course he'd work to keep her onside until he had her firmly where he wanted her.

Still, she was glad for the chance to say goodbye, and for her neighbour to have some time with Max one last time.

Then the regal circus resumed, with stretch SUVs transporting the sizeable retinue she'd had no idea were even present at the hotel to the airport, where they boarded a jetliner the same size as Air Force One.

Eden was still reeling at the rollercoaster effect when the jet soared into the Nevada skies and winged its way towards Europe. After a half-hour exploring with Max, who was delving into his first experience on a plane with gusto and wearing himself out very quickly, she'd just settled him with a box of colourful puzzles when his father folded himself into the club seat opposite.

It was the first time they'd been alone in hours.

She cleared her throat. 'I wanted to say thanks for bringing Mrs Tolson so we could say goodbye.'

'It was nothing.'

'No. It wasn't nothing. I appreciate it.'

A spark of surprise lit his eyes—as if, like her surprise over his consideration, her courtesy amazed him. It was gone an instant later, his gaze switching to Max.

'He's such a clever little boy.'

But before the burst of pride could bloom within her he was spearing her with those incisive eyes.

'Has he ever asked about his father? About me?' he amended, as if she was in any danger of forgetting who he was.

She shook her head. 'Not in any real sense. He's too young, I think. He probably would've if he'd been in daycare...'

His nostrils flared and a fierce light of satisfaction and determination ignited the silver-grey depths of his eyes. 'It seems I came along just in time, then.'

The sting of his words sharpened her retort. 'If you're trying to laud yourself as some sort of saviour, Your Highness, you won't find me falling over myself with gratitude. You might not think so, but we were doing okay before you came along. Not everyone is born with a dozen sets of silver spoons in their mouths.'

He leaned forward, resting his elbows on the polished table

and surrounding her with the magnetism of his presence and the sublime scent that made her want to bury her nose in his throat and inhale lungsful.

'Word to the wise: feel free to use that cutting tone with me all you like when we're in private. But you will have to moderate it when we're in public.'

The delivery was even-toned to the point of icy, with zero signs of disgruntlement. In fact, he looked faintly amused.

'So I'm to walk three steps behind and ask how high when you tell me to jump or suffer the consequences?'

He reached across lazily and helped Max place another puzzle piece into its right slot. 'Not at all. And not if I express a liking for my future queen's tart tongue.'

She couldn't stop the heat from suffusing her, despite the relatively benign statement. 'I'm not changing who I am just to get on your or anyone else's good side.'

She'd watched her mother do that far too many times, with the same heart-wrenching results.

A hint of something resembling respect flitted across his face. 'Bending a little might be wise. Otherwise, get ready for a period of…friction.'

Again his words evoked steamy scenes that made her squirm in her seat. That made her far too aware of her erratic heartbeat. The tightening of her skin. The dampening between her thighs.

His silver eyes glinted again and she was sure he knew how erotically his words affected her. Straining to distance herself from the sensations, she snapped, 'We're getting away from the original subject, I think.'

The subject of his son refocused him, as she'd known it would.

He gave a brisk nod. 'We are.' Another taut pause, then, 'I wish to tell him who I am. Sooner rather than later.'

Eden looked out of the window at the puffs of cloud several

thousand feet beneath her. Up until yesterday morning she'd believed her son's father had died in a car accident.

A part of her couldn't deny she was glad Max's father was alive and well and eager to claim him. And, yes, while the level of his claim was staggering, as long as she had breath in her body she would shield her son from any hurt and harm.

She met Azar's piercing gaze and nodded. 'Then you should tell him.'

He surged from his seat immediately, came around to her side and crouched down next to Max, where he was strapped into his seat. Max paused in his play, the distinctive eyes she'd tried to downplay so similar to his father's, wide and inquisitive.

Emotion flashed over Azar's face as his son offered him a puzzle piece. Instead of taking it, Azar wrapped his much larger hand over Max's, bringing his pudgy fist to his mouth and dropping several gentle kisses on it before he brought it to rest on his chest.

As if knowing the gravity of the moment, Max didn't fuss at having his playtime interrupted. He remained silent as Azar said in deep, low tones, 'I am your father, Maximiliano. Your *papá*.'

Her clever son caught the emphasis of the word, or perhaps it sounded familiar enough that he blinked once, then repeated, 'Papá?'

Watching an emotional shudder move through this powerful prince Eden had no recollection of creating her beautiful boy with dragged a lump to her throat. Not wanting to draw attention to herself, she remained frozen as Azar's head moved in a nod.

His Adam's apple bobbed once before he replied, '*Sí. Papá.*'

Even while registering that there were several issues between them to be resolved she held this moment close, happy for her son. And it was made all the more precious because it was a million miles removed from the savage outcome of her attempted reconnection with her own father.

Paris was everything she'd dreamed it would be.

And viewed from this lofty perch, beside a crown prince who commanded an entire realm, it was even more breathtaking.

Because of course they were flying by helicopter from Charles de Gaulle Airport to the top of their five-star hotel.

And of course they were ushered straight into the royal suite, where another clutch of staff stood ready to fulfil their smallest desire.

But the person who had snagged Eden's attention immediately was a drop-dead stunning woman, who stood almost six feet tall, wearing a brown leather pencil skirt and a ruffled chiffon layered top with a boat neck that displayed a bone structure most women would kill for. Satin-smooth dark caramel skin draped over high cheekbones served as the perfect platform to showcase her almond-shaped honey-brown eyes.

Eyes that flitted over Azar and, after a courteous greeting, returned to Eden, then to Max. Like most people who met her son, her face warmed in a smile, before returning to Eden.

Eden discovered the reason for her scrutiny a moment later, when she turned on killer legs, one sculpted arm outstretched.

'Lovely to meet you, Miss Moss. I'm Sabeen El-Maleh, Teo Domene's creative director at the House of Domene. I'm to fit you with a new wardrobe before your trip to Cartana.'

Her voice was a deep, sexy husk that Eden was sure must draw the opposite sex like bees to honey.

Eden hated the faint pang in her midriff, the compulsion to see if Azar was in any way affected by this breathtaking beauty, but his attention was entirely on Max as he scooped up his son and held him against his chest.

'We'll leave you ladies to it,' he said.

With that he walked away, just as another staff member

arrived with a tray of refreshments, effectively making any protests Eden had thought to make redundant. A little overwhelmed, and a touch irritated, she was learning that the royal machine was oiled by heavy doses of extreme politeness hiding determined steering.

But she accepted that Sabeen had taken time out of her likely busy schedule to attend her at short notice.

Taking the seat offered, she glanced at Sabeen. 'Pardon me, but do creative directors usually undertake such tasks? I thought you'd have minions or stylists for that?'

A peculiar expression passed over Sabeen's face, quickly veiled as she shrugged. 'I was already in Paris for the week and Teo... Mr Domene asked me as a personal favour.'

Eden noted the slip and changed cadence in Sabeen's tone but ignored it. It wasn't her place to comment, and she had more important things to worry about.

But she couldn't help but add, 'If that means he owes you a favour, you should totally collect. I'm learning quickly that the Domene men are a domineering force who require occasional checking before they flatten you.'

Sabeen looked up from a large satin case she'd been examining, surprise lightening her eyes before she gave a low, forced laugh. 'Great advice, thanks.' She paused, her gaze darting to the double doors Azar had exited through. 'And if you don't mind my saying so, be sure to keep that one on his toes. Men like him get away with far too much, in my opinion.'

Their eyes met and held in silent reinforcement of welcome solidarity. Eden could and would stand her ground.

Then, with brisk instructions, a veritable feast of the most gorgeous designs Eden had ever seen outside a magazine were presented to her.

Quickly growing overwhelmed as her mind conjured up just where she would need to wear such exquisite clothes, she resigned herself to nodding at most of the selections and discarding the too risqué ones she knew she'd never be able to pull off wearing.

They'd moved on to accessories and make-up when approaching footsteps interrupted them. The tingling at her nape and between her shoulder blades signalled who their visitor was before she turned.

Azar's gaze dragged over her before locking on her face. 'Everything all right?'

'Should it not be?'

His eyes narrowed and she realised she'd been snippy again. But she couldn't bring herself to care. Instead, she watched him stride across and settle himself into the seat opposite from her.

His scent assailed her, and for the life of her she couldn't quite catch the breath that had come so easily moments ago.

'Max—?'

'Is fine,' he said. 'He has three of my staff making fools of themselves to keep him entertained and is thoroughly enjoying the attention.'

'Oh...and you're staying here?'

'Any reason I shouldn't?'

'Well...don't you have things to do? Meetings?' She plucked the word feebly out of the air.

He shrugged. 'I did. Until my meeting got cancelled.'

She snorted before she could help herself.

One eyebrow rose, his eyes glinting. 'Something amusing?'

'I seriously doubt that anyone would cancel on a crown prince.'

Eden heard a muted gasp from one of Sabeen's assistants, but was too embroiled by the look in Azar's eyes to heed it.

It held the smallest trace of amusement, plus that sliver of respect that loosened a knot of tension. If he liked her standing up to him—and he seemed to—maybe this exercise wouldn't be so dreadful after all. Because healthy banter was surely a good foundation for serious communication?

Among other things?

'When a minister's pregnant wife goes into early labour, requiring his presence at her side for the birth of their first child, then, yes, he is allowed to cancel on a crown prince with impunity.'

'Oh...'

'Since we've got the wardrobe and accessories mostly settled, shall we discuss how specifically you wish to be styled?' Sabeen asked, her expert eye roving Eden's form. 'Perhaps you have a signature look in mind? I can suggest a few things. We can go as simple or as elaborate as you want. Perhaps a shorter hairstyle—'

'No.' The growled word made them both turn to the full force of Azar's glare. 'She will not be cutting her hair. It stays the way it is.'

The kick in her midriff should have been born of outrage. Instead, it unfurled into a blaze so powerful its heat seared her insides. Her nipples tightened and her thighs clenched as forbidden delight lit through her.

God...what the hell was wrong with her? Hadn't she only just warned Sabeen about the domineering attitude of the Domene brothers? Yet here she was, falling for the same masculine display.

She barely heard Sabeen excuse herself, gather her assistants before quickly leaving the room. The soft snick of the door drove the exquisite tension in the room higher.

'Shouldn't that be my choice?' she demanded.

God, why did she sound so breathless? And why did her heart rate triple when he surged powerfully to his feet and prowled towards her?

He shrugged. 'Ultimately, I cannot stop you, of course. But why dispose of such a striking asset when you don't need to?'

'You think my hair is "striking"?'

Heavens, could she sound any needier?

With a deft move he reached behind her and plucked the

clasp holding her hair back from her face. Set loose, the long wings framed her face and Azar's gaze ran feverishly over it.

Maybe she was imagining the depths of his penetrative gaze, but Eden couldn't recall ever experiencing such intensity. Her lips parted as she tried to drag air into her lungs.

'If memory serves...' he rasped, and then his hands disappeared into the tresses, his fingers lightly running through them before gripping a handful. 'It still feels like the most exquisite silk. Even from across a room it is extremely eye-catching,' he finished, almost to himself.

At her unguarded gasp his fingers tightened, setting her scalp tingling delightfully. He leaned closer, his lips scant inches away. She couldn't help running her gaze over the sensual curves of his mouth. It was unfair that he knew what their kiss tasted like, while she was left to wonder. The need to know made her sway closer, her heart pounding with sweet desperation.

'It would be positively sinful to shear even a millimetre off this...' he breathed.

Oh, God, how was it possible that a discussion of her hair could get her this hot?

'Tell me you'll leave it alone.'

The demand was edged with that customary imperiousness she suspected was bred into his DNA.

'If you feel that strongly about it, then yes,' she whispered.

Then she watched his eyes darken, his gaze dropping to her mouth.

A sound left her—a cross between a protest and a whimper that would have made her cringe if she hadn't felt so very needy.

Kiss me, she wanted to demand. *Please*.

Noticing that her hands had somehow crept up to his chest, and feeling his steady heartbeat, indicating he wasn't as affected as she, common sense slowly rose, then prevailed—although it stung a little when she saw the composure reflected in his eyes.

She was still scrambling to understand her confused emotions when he released her, strolled several steps away, then pivoted to face her, his hands slotted suavely into his pockets.

Eden ignored how that sexy stance threatened her common sense.

'We're dining out tonight,' he told her.

She forced her brain to keep track. 'Are we?'

He gave a brisk nod. 'Now that you've agreed to marry me, we need to set the stage appropriately for what comes next.'

Her heart lurched. 'Which is…?'

'Ensuring the right publicity so the effect of our announcement has the right impact. We must be seen in public a few times before we spring our news on the world.'

She frowned. 'So we're to put a gloss on things? Pretend this is some sort of love-match rush to the altar? Isn't that disingenuous?'

A muscle rippled in his jaw. 'You'll discover soon enough that, while sceptics abound, most citizens still prefer their leaders not be embroiled in messy relationships or emotional strife. Like it or not, we're duty-bound to be aspirational, which means we have a role to fulfil.'

'Does that scepticism apply to you as well?'

His expression grew grave, coldly contemplative. 'For our son's sake we'll endeavour to be cordial and civil to one another at the very least. You'll agree that's essential and non-negotiable, yes?'

'Put like that, it would be churlish of me to refuse, wouldn't it?'

'Meaning what? That I'm stopping you from demanding more?'

Her mouth twisted. 'Won't "demanding more" make me a gold-digger, striving to reach above her lowly station in life, or earn me some other deplorable label levelled at women like me?'

It was an insult her father had thrown at sixteen-year-old Eden that day at his gaudy Hollywood mansion.

A faint flare of colour lit high on his cheekbones, telling her she'd hit the bullseye with that observation. Which sank her spirits.

'Have the women you've dealt with in the past really been that venal?' she asked.

A sardonic smile twitched his lips. 'You believe that's only limited to your gender?'

She hid a flinch. 'I don't know whether to feel sorry for you or feel angry that you're lumping me in with everyone else.'

His eyes flared in surprise. Perhaps because she appeared to be pitying the man soon to ascend to an honest-to-goodness throne of a European empire—the kind of prince historians would write reams about—as if he was just a common man who deserved her kindness.

'Save your sympathies, Eden. I learned to expertly navigate the dangerous pools of avarice and duplicity before I was out of adolescence.'

She lifted her chin, despite feeling her chest continuing to squeeze at the realisation that most of the things she'd heard about the vagaries of being royal might be true. That the grass truly wasn't greener on the other side.

'In that case, I guess my most important question is who's going to take care of our son while we put on this...show?'

He had an efficient answer to that, of course.

It turned out that while they'd been flying to Paris from the West Coast of the USA, Azar had been flying nannies from the palace at Cartana.

Her mind continued to boggle at just how involved he'd become in the role of fatherhood even as her gut churned at this continued usurping of her control.

CHAPTER SIX

TWO THINGS STOPPED her protesting.

The first was the young nanny, Nadia, who was delight-fully cheerful and whom Max adored immediately.

The second was that she could hardly protest at leaving him for a couple of hours when she'd so often left him with Mrs Tolson for hours to go to work.

Still, she delivered extra kisses to his chubby cheek, her heart twinging as she watched him toddle off to bed, his hand clutched in Nadia's.

'He'll be fine—or else someone will need to have serious answers for us,' Azar threatened, with that chillingly even tone that made her double-take, because she could never tell whether he was truly ruffled or not.

His resolute gaze stated that he was deadly serious.

Which, again, shouldn't have elevated her temperature or eased that tightness. But there she was, her steps much lighter, as she walked beside him to the private lift.

Bodyguards flanked them as they exited the hotel and moved towards the stretch limo awaiting them. The first she knew of the paparazzi's presence was when a flash erupted on her left. Then another from her right bounced off the gold crystal-covered bustier and velvet skirt she wore.

Sabeen had returned to finish her wardrobe consultation, and Eden was glad for the confidence boost the exquisite

House of Domene outfit, matching heels and clutch purse gave her.

Her hair had been pinned back off her face and left to fall in newly washed and styled waves down her back. She'd baulked at the priceless jewellery offered, her nerves way too frayed to add taking care of what she suspected was a nose-bleedingly expensive collection to her worries.

To his credit, if Azar had feelings about her lack of jewellery he'd chosen to remain silent on the matter, and his heated gaze raking over her told her that at least he didn't find her too lacking.

'Ignore them,' Azar rasped, his hand in the small of her back guiding her to the open back door of the limo, heating her up in ways she didn't want to dwell on.

Her senses were still erratic when they arrived at their location ten minutes later, and Eden stared up at the matte black and silver edifice of Le Cramoisie, wondering why her senses tingled so fiercely.

Stepping out of the car, once Ramon had given the driver the nod, she walked with Azar into the restaurant—and drew to a stop.

Low ambient lights illuminated a solitary impressively laid table, its two chairs set at perpendicular angles to each other. All the other tables and chairs had been lined up on the sides like silent soldiers, and not a single other soul graced the Michelin-starred establishment.

'We're the only ones here?'

'I booked the place for the evening, so we won't be disturbed,' Azar replied.

She'd seen it in movies, read about it in glossy, unrealistic magazines. But despite having served some of the world's wealthiest men at the Vegas casinos, and rejected the advances of several, Eden had never imagined such a thing would happen to her. And, yes, while it was OTT in the extreme, she couldn't stop the waves of excitement that rolled through her.

'If that's okay with you, of course?' he tagged on.

She curbed the fizz of fireworks exploding in her belly with the timely reminder that there was always a price to pay. It quickly soured her excitement.

'And if I said it wasn't?'

'Then we would have wasted one of the most renowned Michelin starred chef's entire evening and possibly got ourselves blacklisted.'

There was an arrogant note in his voice that said he didn't give one single damn even if that had been the case.

She looked around, noting the touches of Asia in the decor. 'This is a Japanese restaurant, right?' The name didn't give it away, but somehow she knew…felt another tingling of… *something*.

'Yes. It is,' he confirmed.

Sensing his keen gaze on her face, she glanced at him. 'Something's up. Are you going to tell me what?'

Only the barest lift of his chest gave him away. 'Is it?'

She sighed. 'I'm getting that it's a strategically advantageous tactic to answer a question with a question, but it's getting old very quickly. Either answer the question or don't.'

That light she'd noticed when she'd stood up to him before glinted again, and foolishly ignited her own fire.

'I'll bear that in mind,' he said. 'Ah, here's our host now.'

Hiding a spurt of frustration, she smiled as the Michelin-starred chef reached their table and bowed from the waist.

'Your Highness, Miss Moss, good evening. I'm Ike Kono-suke. I'll be personally preparing your meal this evening. Do you have any preferences or allergies?'

Eden started to answer, then closed her mouth, uncertainty making her hesitate. Was it possible to develop allergies later in life?

'She doesn't have any allergies,' Azar replied, slanting her a gaze simmering with intimate knowledge that had heat scything through his cool answer.

'Very good. Then, if I may, shall I suggest a *plateau de bouchées* encompassing the whole menu?' the diminutive man offered with a smile.

Azar nodded. 'Everything but the *foie gras*. Eden strongly dislikes that.'

Her breath caught, and her eyes snagged on his as the chef departed and a *sommelier* took his place.

She nodded absently at the offer of champagne, then immediately leaned forward once they were alone. 'The only way you could know all that is if you'd hacked into my medical records or...'

'Or?' he prompted redolently.

Heat consumed her whole. 'If I told you that when we...'

'When I had Konosuke flown over to Arizona three years ago and we ate his sushi naked in bed in...inventive ways? Yes. I'm well versed in your preferences.'

If she'd thought she was burning before, she'd had no idea. Every inch of her body was ablaze with the flame of his words.

Fighting not to squirm in her seat, she pushed at the memory he'd so surprisingly offered. 'That's why I remember the name of this place?'

'You declared his food your absolute favourite. All except the *foie gras*, of course. An objection to the process with which it's made, I remember.'

'Why are you telling me this when you didn't want to divulge anything before?'

He paused for a second. 'I read up further on your condition. Your doctor is right, but he may be erring on the side of overcaution. Supplying benign information isn't detrimental if it nudges your recovery in the right direction.'

She wasn't sure whether to be surprised and thankful that he'd researched her condition, or sceptical as to his ultimate motive.

The hit of champagne bubbles when she took a sip fizzed

alongside the excitement of moments ago, and for good or ill Eden chose the former. 'Thank you.'

He stiffened, his eyes searching her face. 'That's the second time you've sounded surprised as you've thanked me.'

She froze, clearing her throat when a few bubbles threatened to go down the wrong way. She considered a vague reply, then went with the truth. 'It's because I've learned that nothing comes for free—especially from influential men.' She dropped her gaze for a moment, wrestling back her composure. 'My wariness is inbuilt for good reason.'

He studied her for a long stretch, his gaze completely unfathomable. Then, 'If there are skeletons to be found, it's best to air them now rather than later.'

Because of his royal status and all the infernal protocols? Eden kicked herself for forgetting that for a second.

'You seem to know a lot about me already—what makes you think I have more to divulge?'

His face hardened a touch. 'You've been reticent about discussing your past. But you don't have the luxury of that now, *querida*. Courtesy of my brother, you now know you were in Arizona—'

'Which still tells me nothing. I tried looking up the Magnis Club. It's super-secretive... I'm assuming a billionaires-only resort or something?'

'Yes,' he confirmed dismissively, making a mockery of the two hours she'd wasted scouring the internet last night. 'Do you know why you chose not to return to Vegas when you left Arizona?'

'How do you know I didn't?'

'How do you think?' His voice was cool silk wrapped in electricity.

He'd looked for her? Why?

Pursing her lips, she toyed with the stem of her glass as she contemplated where to start with the sorry saga of her life. 'As far as I can remember, I had plans to work my way towards California.'

'Hopes of a career in Hollywood?' he asked, not masking his cynicism.

A tiny snort escaped before she could stop it. 'Nothing so fanciful or unrealistic.' And if she'd had such hopes her father would've doubled his efforts to squash her. 'I was on my way to a commune in Joshua Tree to bail out my mother. She'd found herself in another predicament.'

'Did this happened often?'

'A few times here and there.'

Shame dredged through her and she fixed her gaze on the glass, then jumped slightly when his finger brushed her chin, firmly nudging it up.

When she met his gaze, he rasped, 'Go on. Why were you chasing after your mother?'

'She'd been left stranded after yet another man— After her relationship ended. The guy she was seeing had left her with a few bills and she needed help.'

A few *dozen* bills—including a bail bond she'd naively and shockingly signed her name to and become responsible for after the man had absconded.

Azar's hand dropped and she immediately missed the warmth of his touch. 'Were you in the habit of bailing her out of "predicaments"?'

An echo of the judgy voices she'd heard so many times in the past, from friends and strangers alike, throbbed through his voice. 'Does it matter?' she asked.

His censorious gaze said that it did, but he didn't vocalise it—for which she was somewhat thankful.

'She was facing jail if she didn't come up with a way to settle her bills. So she called me. I... I couldn't pretend she didn't need my help.' Unwilling to delve into her fraught relationship with her mother, she changed the subject. 'Tell me about the Magnis Club. Was I working there?'

His jaw clenched. '*Si*. You were a hostess.'

Shards of memory pierced her. 'I'm assuming it was the job Nick mentioned?'

He stiffened, his eyes boring into her. 'I wouldn't know, but it's safe to assume so since you need a member who vouches for you even if you're staff.'

Her own shoulders stiffened with the tension engulfing them. 'You're giving off unpleasant vibes again. I was Nick's croupier when he visited the casino. Nothing else. And if you're wondering whether I promised him anything in return, I don't remember—but I know myself enough to be certain I'm not that kind of woman.'

They both stopped as the chef headed towards them, two servers bearing trays one step behind him. The elaborate presentation cooled the temperature between them, and for the next ten minutes they enjoyed the beautifully prepared bite-sized helpings of blue lobster croquettes with caviar, truf-fle-vinaigrette-coated scallops and grilled shrimp rolled in buttered lettuce.

Every morsel elicited from Eden an inner groan. And by the third bite a tiny bit of her tension had eased—especially because Azar, for whatever reason, had chosen to let the matter drop.

When the black stone slab of their *omasake* was delivered, he expertly caught up a rolled sliver of sea bass in his chopsticks, dipped it in a sauce and held it out to her. 'Try this.'

Her mouth watered, but something in his voice made her ask, 'Why?'

'Because you adored it before,' he said simply. 'Let's see if you still do.'

Utterly self-conscious, she leaned close, parted her lips and let him feed her.

The last platter contained half a dozen exquisitely hand-rolled bites of sushi. Racking her brain, she couldn't recall sampling those at any other point in her life. She'd grown up poor, in a dilapidated suburb of Las Vegas, eating a depressingly bland and monotonous regimen of cereal for breakfast, toast for lunch and ramen for dinner. On the odd occasion when whatever man her mother was dating had felt generous, they'd been treated to fast-food takeout.

Until she'd realised the toll of accepting even such small gifts on her mother's self-esteem and begun to refuse them.

Recalling the rows with her mother over dating men who were even more deplorable copies of her father—chameleons who started out seemingly decent, only to be revealed as cruel misogynists—shredded her heart. The worst of those fights had brought the seemingly inevitable 'You ruined my life', snarled by her drunken mother. But there had been a harsh kernel of truth ringing in it, sending Eden fleeing to Hollywood in a wild bid to salvage an unsalvageable family.

It had turned out to be the worst decision of her life.

A dart of pain stabbed at her temple, and her hand was shaking as she reached for her glass.

Azar's gaze zeroed in on it and frowned. 'What's wrong?'

'Nothing.' The pain had dissipated as fast as it had arrived. 'I'm fine.'

He watched her for a few more seconds, then served her another roll of sea bass. 'Did you ever make it to Joshua Tree?' he asked.

The piercing pain flashed again. 'No. By the time I woke from the coma and left the hospital my mom had moved on.'

After spending a three-week stint in jail for not honouring the bail bond—something else that had somehow been labelled Eden's fault.

His gaze probed but she kept her eyes on her plate, the ceaseless guilt that underpinned her relationship with her mother dredging through her.

'Does she know about Max?'

She took a breath. 'Yes. I told her when I was six months pregnant.'

'Eden?' The pulse of her name from his lips jerked her gaze up. 'Is inviting your mother and father to our wedding going to be a problem for you?'

Her eyes widened at the unexpected question. Through the relentless cascade of events she hadn't thought about what part her parents would be expected to play.

'My father has never been part of my life. As for my mother, I...'

'Not inviting her will prompt more questions, but the situation can be managed if that is what you want.'

'I'll think about it.'

It was purely a placeholder answer, both to buy herself time to brace herself for contact with her parent and because a tiny bloom of warmth at his consideration was baffling her emotions.

'Speaking of mothers, am I to meet yours?'

His eyes shadowed, a familiar chilled expression passing over his features.

So they both had Mommy issues...

Thinking about it, that odd toast she'd heard from Teo during Azar's party made sense now.

'Eventually,' he bit out.

She let it go, because her headache had gone from intermittent pangs to a dull throb. 'Is this enough for your publicity stunt?' she asked.

A current of tension returned to the able. He sprawled back in his chair and contemplated his wine glass before he answered. 'Not quite. Breakfast tomorrow, with a walk along the Seine, and then a few more events this weekend, once we're in Cartana, and then we'll make the announcement next week.'

The thought of being bombarded further with his overwhelming presence made her insides swoop and dance, even as her head pounded. Easing a hand up, she surreptitiously rubbed at her temple.

'What's wrong?' he repeated tersely.

She thought of downplaying it—then gave up. 'I have a headache.'

He tossed his napkin on the table. 'We'll leave now.'

'No, it's fine. I just need to…to not think about the past too hard if I want to keep it at bay.'

He inhaled sharply. 'And you let me quiz you about your mother?'

'I'm fine—'

'Stop saying that.' He came behind her chair and helped him up.

The chef rushed out, but a look from Azar had Ramon intercepting the frazzled man.

A minute later they were back in the limo. The return journey was conducted in silence, Azar mostly watching her like a hawk.

It was a relief to return to the mundanity of checking on Max, lingering over her sleeping son. And she was relieved further when Azar, after bringing her two tablets for her headache, offered to walk her to her suite.

She refused, because these alarming acts of care and consideration were at odds with the picture of the man she'd drawn up in her head. The one who was a carbon copy of her father. And until she worked out his true character she would be best served by keeping the distance between them.

She'd taken enough blows in her life already.

Except distance was out of the question when they had to put on a show the next morning.

Walking along the Seine, Azar's hand slipped into hers, their palms rubbing, and she couldn't stop the shiver that went through her.

He glanced sharply at her, his eyes turning a little molten as his steps slowed. 'We have this going for us, at least,' he murmured.

'What?'

'I touch you and you react so…responsively. This kind of chemistry can't be faked.'

She reminded herself that it was all an act. 'But it doesn't matter in the grand scheme of things, does it?'

His eyes turned flinty. 'Meaning?'

'You said so yourself—we're doing this for Max. How we react physically to one another will never become a problem we need to deal with.'

'You think not?'

'Unless you're about to admit uncontrollable feelings for me, then no.' Her voice was thankfully firm enough to make her next breath easier.

'Uncontrollable? Hardly. But noteworthy, perhaps.'

'Shall we keep walking or stand around playing word games?'

He remained exactly where he was, exercising his regal right to do things exactly the way he wanted. In her peripheral vision Eden saw their bodyguards expertly steering tourists around them—which had the predicted effect of garnering more interest. Which His Royal Highness played to maximum effect by lifting their linked hands between them, his eyes never leaving hers, and bringing her knuckles to his lips.

He took his time to brush his warm, sensual lips over each one, then laid her hand on his chest as he stepped even closer. His other slid over her nape, his thumb tilting her chin up until their eyes were locked. Then, just like yesterday afternoon, he leaned close, his gaze dropping to her mouth. As if on cue, her lips parted, and her breathing became hopelessly shallow despite knowing he was toying with her. That this was all for show.

'*Sí, querida.* Just like that,' he rasped huskily. 'Forget word games. One more minute of this and you'll be well on your way to winning accolades for this performance.'

CHAPTER SEVEN

THEY LANDED AT the airport in the Cartanian capital, San Mirabet, and just like in Paris were whisked away by a sleek helicopter with the Royal House of Domene crest etched boldly into the paintwork.

Unlike in Paris, though, their arrival was orchestrated in streamlined secrecy, the red carpet leading to the covered walkway devoid of any people bar the pilot, the flight attendants and Azar's guards.

Azar noticed her puzzled look as he buckled Max into his seat. 'Until the announcement is made, there's no point in inviting a circus to disturb us,' he told her. 'It'll happen soon enough.'

'When?'

He shrugged. 'That depends on my father. Once we've visited him this afternoon we can take it from there.'

She thought he was hedging now, on the very thing he'd been pushing for—until three hours later when, showered and styled by her new personal staff, helmed by a no-nonsense woman named Silvia, she clutched her son's hand outside a soaring set of doors, gilded in what she suspected was solid gold filigree. They'd been escorted here by Silvia and Gaspar, who stood behind them like the efficient sentinels they were trained to be.

Curbing the wild emotions rampaging through her wasn't easy. The sheer magnificence of the Domene Palacio Real, poised on top of a hill at the northernmost point of San Mirabet, gave it a forceful presence in and of itself. Stepping over its splendid threshold, feeling the weight of its history, and an opulence literally built from the ashes of its vanquished enemies, had started a cascade of sensations she was still grappling with as solid, steady footsteps approached.

She surreptitiously passed her sweaty free hand over the ruched silk midi dress she'd chosen for its warm, comforting dark caramel colour as the doors were swept open.

Azar had showered and changed since she last saw him. His dark hair gleamed in the mid-afternoon sunlight and the white shirt and dark suit highlighted his deep, vibrant vitality.

He held her gaze, then nodded a dismissal at the staff behind her.

Max peered up at Azar, then his face broke into a smile. 'Papá.'

Azar's eyes darkened, and a trace of the bleakness disappeared.

Still wondering at what had caused it, she watched him scoop up his son, then rasp, 'Come.'

She followed him through an elaborate private living room, down a corridor with doors on either side, then through another set of double doors, which were swept open as they reached it.

Eden's steps faltered momentarily.

When Azar had told her his father was unwell with a heart condition, she'd assumed it was serious, but manageable.

The man propped up against a mountain of pillows in pristine bedding was a far cry from the man she'd searched on the internet, when she'd realised their meeting was inevitable. The once-vibrant, commanding King of Cartana had notably lost weight, his figure shrunken in the antique four-poster bed with elaborate hand carvings that spoke of a bygone era.

Azar lightly grasped her arm and led her to the two armchairs placed close to the bed.

'Papá, meet your grandson, Max. And Eden, his mother.'

King Alfonso's direct gaze landed on her son, examining him thoroughly, before he exhaled deeply. He reached out his hand to Max and her sweet son immediately offered his.

The King swallowed as he took another deep breath. 'Maximiliano.'

His voicing of her son's name seemed almost like an affirmation. A blessing. An acceptance Eden had never felt for herself from either of her parents—especially her father. She hadn't even been aware of that problematic knot in her belly until it eased, helping her breathe that little bit easier.

'Is he calling you Papá already?'

King Alfonso smiled at his son, who shrugged.

'He's mine. There's no point dancing around the truth of it.'

The old man's gaze rested on Azar for a moment, then shifted to her, the signature silver-grey eyes he'd passed down to his sons pinning her in place. She accepted then that he was far from diminished. That while his body might be failing him, his centuries-old warrior spirit was very much present.

'And you, young lady? How are you to feature in the great and elaborate landscape that is my family?' he asked, his rich accent inflecting the words.

She executed the shallow curtsey Silvia had taught her. 'It's an honour to meet you, Your Majesty.' Swallowing around a dry mouth, she hesitated momentarily, then responded. 'My priority will always be Max, no matter what. As long as he's happy and healthy, everyone who cares for him will have my utmost co-operation.'

His stare remained direct. 'And if they don't care for him?' he prodded.

Azar's gaze lanced her where she stood, his own interest in her response almost feverish.

'Then I'm afraid I won't be very easy to live with. And I won't be averse to taking whatever steps are necessary to change that.'

Truth and purpose shook through her voice, but the notion

that she was standing up to a king didn't escape her. Trepidatious shivers raced under her skin, but she ignored them as best she could, knowing that this wasn't the time to show weakness.

King and Crown Prince exchanged indecipherable looks, the corners of their mouths twitching in almost identical motion.

And when the oldest man in the room looked at her again, a layer of that formidable willpower had been replaced by something approaching approval.

He watched them, his eyes still pinned on Eden as Azar waited until she sat down, then sat himself, leaving one hand propped against Max's back, where he was perched on the bed next to his grandfather.

'You're not afraid to express yourself. An admirable quality that will prove useful in the position you find yourself in, I think.'

The warmth around that loosened knot inside her expanded, pushing hard at her need to remain fortified against any misleading inclinations. The scars from her father's rejection remained a real, horrifying reminder.

Hell, she was in this room only because she'd had Azar's child. She didn't doubt that Azar Domene might have sought her out as he'd promised the night of his party, to seek whatever passed as payback for her slights against him three years ago. But beyond that? To go as far as to put a ring on her finger? That was all for Max's sake. And while that was a good thing for her baby, she needed to leave her emotions out of it.

'…abdication and your coronation…must bring it forward even earlier.'

Shock reefed through her and her head jerked up. 'I'm sorry…what? Even earlier?' she blurted. She was cringingly aware she was breaking several protocols by not using the right form of address, but she couldn't bring herself to backtrack.

King Alfonso's gaze returned to her, then narrowed at his son. 'Your intended doesn't know?'

Again, Azar shrugged. 'It's only been two days, Papá, but yes, she knows. I didn't think it prudent to bombard her with too much though.'

Her hands clenched in her lap. 'Stop talking about me like I'm not here. You said the coronation was a matter of months away, and now it's earlier? Explain what's going on.'

Azar waited a beat. Then exhaled. 'My father has decided to abdicate earlier than planned. I'm to take the throne in two months instead of three. One month after our wedding. And you, by ordination, will become my queen.'

And that was just the first of many left-field episodes that peppered the most dizzying weeks of her life.

Contrary to her expectations, she didn't meet her future mother-in-law for another whole week. Azar's mother cited one excuse after another until two Sundays after they'd arrived. And when the moment eventually arrived it was a frosty reception that couldn't have made it more patently obvious that Queen Fabiana Domene believed her son was marrying far below his class.

To her credit, her dismissiveness didn't stray into cruelty when it came to her grandson, which meant Eden didn't need to unleash her mama bear claws. And Max was oblivious to the disparaging remarks during the Queen's icy quizzing of just how Eden had happened to cross paths with her son, and the vapours of disdain that positively oozed from her pursed lips.

It was for the sake of her son that Eden withstood that seemingly interminable meeting. The moment it was over—the second she returned to her suite and saw Azar standing at the window in her living room, the epitome of regal composure, power and unruffled magnificence—everything she'd been holding inside for the last two hours frothed over like boiling milk.

'How did the meeting with my mother—?'

'Badly,' she interrupted. 'She doesn't like me, and thinks you're marrying far beneath you, but I don't give a damn about that. She's entitled to her opinion.'

His eyes narrowed, a film of tension weaving over him. 'And yet something is bothering you?'

'Yes! This is all going too fast.' She dragged her fingers through hair that had been painstakingly styled and layered for her audience with the Queen, relieved that it was the only appointment on her schedule today. 'We need to postpone. Everything.'

Azar's eyes narrowed, then his tension thickened. 'No. Absolutely not.'

'Absolutely, yes. I'm—I'm not ready.'

He'd gone so still she wondered if he'd stopped breathing. And when he shoved his hands forcefully into his pockets she was almost certain she saw them trembling.

'Look, the announcements haven't gone out yet. And I've seen how the palace machinery works. It can come up with a good enough reason for moving the wedding.'

'And my father? You want him to put off his abdication for your convenience?' he bit out.

A twinge across her temple jostled her breathing, and the sensation that she'd felt this tic before sparked the usual frustration over her lost memories.

'No, of course not. But maybe we can switch things around. Coronation first, then wedding…later.'

'It's the first time I've seen you in any way fazed,' he rasped, and there was a faint, peculiar note in his voice. It sounded almost *alarmed*.

'Trust me—it's not the first time I've wanted to throw up. I've only held it together because it wouldn't be a pretty sight.'

'The thought of marrying me makes you feel ill?' he growled, molten eyes lasering into her.

'Yes!' A nanosecond after she blurted that she realised what it had sounded like. 'No… I don't mean it like that. It's just…'

She stopped, words failing her as she shook her head.

Her insides clenched as something deadened his eyes. 'Well, you've hidden your abhorrence well. The staff are all impressed with your poise.'

'The staff, huh?'

'You want a more personal opinion?'

No, she didn't. She absolutely didn't.

'It wouldn't hurt to hear what the man I'm to marry thinks.'

He sauntered closer, and it was only because she was watching him so closely that she saw that he wasn't as cool and confident as she'd thought. His probing eyes were a little too fevered. He was putting extra effort into the confident stride that commanded the entirety of her attention.

'You have handled every interaction and interview as if you were born to the role. Almost as if you've been practising for years instead of weeks.'

A twinge tugged hard at her chest, and the notion that this had taken a sour turn was sobering.

'Are you insinuating something? If you are, I'd like you to spit it out, please. I'm not in the mood for guessing games.'

Something gleamed at the back of his eyes and the quiet storm brewing within his aura crackled like the distant rumble of thunder.

'Only that it seems you're surprised at what you've been capable of. I'm saying perhaps you needn't be.'

'Because you think this is what I've secretly wanted all along?' she demanded. 'An elevation to some higher status in life?'

'I'm saying hold your nose if you need to. The rewards for this slight bump in the road will be worth your while.'

Her eyes narrowed, and a peculiar feeling expanded in her chest when she realised that, in his own enigmatic way, he was *talking her round*. That he was perhaps even quietly *desperate* for her to go through with this marriage. Which was...mystifying. And strangely warming after being locked for so long within the desolation of cold rejection. But…what if this was an illusion?

'Why are you so hellbent on this happening quickly? I've already accepted that Max is yours. And I'm sure whatever DNA test you did has confirmed it?'

'*Sí*, it did.'

'Then *what*?' At his tense silence, she pushed harder. 'You want something else? Tell me what this is really about!'

His eyes darkened, dropped to her mouth, and a new sensation started in her chest. Spread throughout her body. That chemistry he'd touched on—the one that had become buried beneath the hectic schedule of readying not just the palace but the entire kingdom for a royal wedding—was suddenly awakening into stinging life, bringing with it an unexpected surge of feminine power as she read his desire loud and clear.

The laughter that spilled from her was just as unexpected as it pulsed with that power and with her own surfeit of need.

'*That's* why you're pushing for this to happen? You're sexually frustrated? Or is it just that I happen to be the unwanted woman fuelling that sensation?'

His nostrils flared and his eyes glinted in that way she was coming to recognise as Azar Domene priming himself for a skirmish. Why that sizzled her blood was a circumstance she wasn't going to wrangle just at this moment. She fought to remain still as a head-to-toe tingle took hold of her. As he closed the gap between them, bringing the forcefield of his magnetism and that terrifying intoxicating scent of man and sandalwood with him.

Molten eyes raked her face. 'You think I don't want you?' he breathed, disbelief tingeing his deep voice.

'You're a king-in-waiting and I'm the woman you're stuck with because I gave birth to your son. It isn't a stretch to imagine you're just making do with what's in front of you.'

She realised she'd been backing away while he advanced, and gasped when her back touched the wall.

'A sound deduction,' he said. 'But you're forgetting one thing.'

The boost of confidence made her tilt her chin in challenge, to meet his blazing gaze full on. 'What?'

'The first time we met I was just a crown prince and you were a hostess. None of this…baggage was between us. And yet you felt strongly enough about me to give me your virginity.'

Her mouth dropped open on a hot gasp. 'You were my first?'

Of course he was.

Didn't he only need to enter a room for her temperature to soar to insane levels?

His lips parted and she witnessed legions of emotions cross his face in a split second. Then that iron control was back in place.

'Yes. Freely given,' he elaborated hoarsely, 'enthusiastically accepted. Thoroughly celebrated.'

Evocative images surged to life in her head.

'Tell me about it…please,' she whispered, ignoring the shrieking voice demanding to know what she was doing.

Again, his gaze raked her face. Then his eyes narrowed. 'When was the last time you had one of those headaches?' he bit out.

'Not for a while. Please,' she pleaded.

He planted his hands on either side of her head, caging her in. His body bore down closer too, and the steel pipe of his erection pressed against her belly as he breathed in deep.

'Every nerve in my body tells me this is a bad idea…'

She waited, breathless with anticipation.

After a long moment, he exhaled. 'You were headed to the table next to mine in the cigar lounge. You stopped in your tracks the first time you saw me,' he rasped in her ear. 'Your incredible eyes went wide and these luscious lips parted…'

He passed his thumb in a whisper-light brush over her lower lip. 'A beautiful creature caught in headlights.'

'And let me guess...you laughed?'

His digit continued to slide back and forth, weakening her with his sensual magic. 'On the contrary. Your effect on me was equally acute, and troubling, and puzzling in the extreme.'

'Why?'

He hesitated for a full second. 'Because until that moment I'd never experienced anything like it.'

Her breath shuddered out. Common sense screamed at her that it was impossible. That this man, soon to exit his position as the most eligible bachelor in the world, surely would have experienced a raft of sexual experiences. But his unwavering stare insisted he meant it. Or maybe because she craved that crumb of possessive knowledge, she believed him.

'Is that why you...hate me?'

He stiffened and his jaw clenched, but he didn't move away. He only examined her face thoroughly, as if he yearned for some insight that she remained clueless about and he sought desperately.

After a moment, he exhaled. 'I don't hate you.'

'Are you sure? Because my every instinct screams otherwise.'

He pinned her beneath his gaze for an eternity before he rasped, 'Do you need me to prove it?'

She licked her lips, a sizzling craving piling into the mix of sensation flaying her. 'Maybe...' she hedged.

Because...heavens, she was much too weak where His Royal Hotness was concerned.

And because to him it might be a refresher, but to her it would be a first kiss. From a real man. The man she'd given her virginity to.

His fingers speared into the hair she'd ruffled, further dishevelling it as he used the pressure to tilt her head up. Then, taking the true answer she was too stubborn to provide, he slanted his mouth over hers.

Warm—no—*hot*. Supple. Electrifying. Possessive.

In an instant she was transported. Dizzy with need. Desperate for *more*. A helpless moan ripped from her soul as she surged towards the exhilarating sensation of being kissed by Crown Prince Azar Domene. And, oh, how he mastered the art.

A brief sweep of his tongue, tantalising and tempting hers to play, was deceptively coaxing, and the moment she parted her lips, ventured a taste of her own, he swooped, seizing control as effectively as his magic alone had kept her pinned against the wall.

The fingers in her hair merely supported her, so she didn't crumple into an erotic mass at his feet. Then, as if he knew how weak she'd grown, his other hand grasped her hips, holding her as he ground his hips into hers, moulding their bodies together as his mouth and tongue and teeth drove her towards a fevered edge that left her utterly breathless.

Dear God, she thought hazily. If he could do this with just a kiss, what could he do with—with...?

Thoughts dissolved as he increased the tempo, his hand sliding from hip to waist and then to her breast, cupping one mound and toying with her nipple. The cry smashed between their lips made him groan. Made him mutter thick words before he delved back for a longer taste.

'You see what you do to me?' he rasped against her mouth after they came up for breath.

The sound she emitted was nowhere near coherent. She was about to seize his nape, beg for another taste, when a firm rap on the door knocked some sense into her.

Her hand dropped to her side, just as his dropped from her breast. But he didn't move, leaving her flushing anew at the thick evidence of his need pressed against her stomach.

'It's just...ch-chemistry,' she stuttered forcefully.

He didn't even raise that imperious brow to mock her. They both knew otherwise. The potency of their attraction to one another defied reason and he wasn't going to waste his time debating the issue.

Instead he peered deep into her eyes, and that not-so-quiet storm wrapped around her, lashing her with urgent electricity. 'The wedding will proceed as planned. You will marry me and let me place a crown upon your head. Yes?'

Eden frowned. Wondered why he kept pushing rewards and crowns at her as if it was the culmination of a goal for him. But his proximity was addling her brain. And, really, her fundamental reason for doing this hadn't changed. Max. Wouldn't it be better to get it over and done with so she could spend precious time with her son?

'Yes. Okay.'

Again, she only saw it because she was staring as intensely at him as he was at her. The flash of relief before he stepped back, issued a command for the visitor to enter.

She wasn't even upset by Gaspar's interruption with more reams of protocol that needed to be studied and mastered before the big day.

She threw herself into it, because otherwise she would have spent far too much time dissecting that look. Stressing over just how much of herself she'd given to Azar Domene once upon a time in Arizona.

They didn't speak about feelings again—his or hers. She'd walked that tightrope and avoided plunging into an emotional landmine. And in the weeks that followed she was thankful for that distance, she told herself.

Even thankful for her decision when she saw how Max thrived beneath the attention of his father, his grandfather and the endless relatives who arrived in a steady torrent to satisfy their various curiosities about the future King and his newly discovered heir.

CHAPTER EIGHT

THE BIG DAY galloped towards her with as much drama and dread as an invading army.

Coronation and wedding rehearsals took place at the stunning San Mirabet basilica attached to the royal palace with such relentless frequency and attention to detail that Eden suspected she could recite the process in her sleep.

She knew she was reaching breaking point when her engagement made headline news around the world, with renowned journalists jostling for the right to conduct her first ever public interview, and the palace insisted she needed to comply.

'I'm not ready to sit down with anyone who wants to pry into a past I don't remember. It's not fair on me, or you and your family,' she stated firmly at dinner one night, after yet another full day of firm pushing from well-meaning palace staff. The very idea of it churned her stomach, despite one of the journalists being a woman Eden greatly admired for her integrity and plain speaking.

'Then don't do it,' said Azar.

She blinked in wary surprise. He'd been doing this a lot lately. *Accommodating* her. *Disarming* her. Any second now, the other shoe would drop. It always did. Didn't it?

'Just like that? But I thought I had to *conform*?'

Her wry stress on the word earned her a sardonic smile, then Azar shrugged.

'You'll soon learn that dealing with the palace council is a constant tug of war. It might feel like the odds are against you, but remember you hold the ultimate power. Sometimes that involves making one big sacrifice, or a series of smaller ones they don't see coming until you've won.'

She pondered that for several minutes. Then, plucking her phone from her pocket, she dialled her private secretary's number.

'Tell the council I won't be giving public interviews until after the wedding. And then it'll be an exclusive to Rachel Mallory. Yes, it's her or no one else. Thank you.'

She hung up to find Azar watching her with a fierce gleam in his eyes. 'What?'

'Taking control suits you. *Brava, cara.*'

Something pelvis-heating glimmered in his eyes. Something she furiously fought as thick silence settled on them. Luckily, a valet stepped forward to pour her a much-needed glass of red wine, and the moment was broken.

Still, she took that fighting spirit into the remainder of the proceedings, firmly refusing extraneous requests that pulled her time away from Max.

Unfortunately, it won her a few disapproving murmurs— the loudest of which came from Azar's mother. And Eden hid a grimace when, a week before the coronation, they were interrupted at dinner.

'Your Highness...?'

Azar made a low, disapproving sound in his throat, but set down the spoon he was using to feed Max his mac and cheese and glared at the hovering Gaspar. 'What is it?'

'Your mother wishes a meeting. Since you had a free half an hour in your schedule after dinner, I thought I'd arrange it?'

Eden stiffened, and immediately brought Azar's attention to her. 'I'm guessing she wants to tell you you're making a big mistake.'

'Most definitely,' he concurred sardonically, making something shrivel inside her—until he added, 'Which makes it a good thing that who I marry isn't up to her, *si*?'

The jolt of relief came from nowhere and floored her, weakening her further. 'So…you still want to go ahead?' she murmured, aware that her stomach was clenching in anticipation of his answer.

God, surely she hadn't been terrified there for a minute that he'd change his mind?

'That depends,' he said. His fingers trailed down her temple and cheek to her jaw, then lower to the pulse racing at her throat. 'Does the thought of marriage to me still make you ill?' he asked tightly.

That quiet rumbling storm had returned, along with the eerie sense that his causal query held visceral importance.

It never did, she wanted to blurt.

But she managed to cling to her cool.

Remember why you're doing this, a voice counselled. *Max. Always Max.*

'No.'

'*Bueno.* Then we are in accord.'

His movements were deliberately precise when he passed his hand over the back of hers, pausing on the breathtakingly gorgeous diamond ring he'd presented her with the morning they'd announced their engagement to the world, two weeks ago.

The belle round micropavé diamond mounted on a pale gold setting wasn't as flashy as the royal diamonds she'd seen during her tour of the royal palace's throne and crown rooms, thank goodness. And learning it had belonged to his grandmother, seeing the sombre, nostalgic look in his eyes, had prompted her to give in to a rare bout of inquisitiveness. She'd asked Silvia, who had divulged that he'd been close to his grandmother and had been distraught when she'd died suddenly eight years ago.

Eden hadn't asked why the jewellery hadn't been passed

on to Azar's mother. The tiny bubble of joyous warmth at the fact that Azar could have kept the treasured heirloom but instead had bestowed it upon her—despite the circumstances of their coming together—was something she locked away in a secret vault for herself.

'See you later,' he said now.

And so the royal circus continued.

Sabeen returned, her retinue doubled and her smile even more stunning as they met for the first of many dress fittings.

It was only when the statuesque beauty engulfed her in a warm hug, then pulled back to peer earnestly into her face, that Eden realised how much she'd missed a friendly face and ear. Mrs Tolson had been that for her.

'I hear it's been crazier than a mad hatters' convention over here,' said Sabeen. 'Even Teo is stressed, and he's three thousand miles away.'

Her mention of her boss held a distinct edge, making Eden start.

'Is everything okay between with you?' she asked.

Sabeen's lips pursed. 'You mean besides having the *Playboy Prince* as my boss? Having women drop their metaphorical and actual knickers whenever he walks into the room, and him not seeing anything wrong with that?'

At Eden's open-mouthed surprise, she grimaced. 'Sorry, that sounds unprofessional. It's fine. I'm fine. How are you?'

Such a simple question. And yet Eden fought back prickles of tears and shrugged. 'I'm pushing through.'

Sabeen clicked her tongue, then ran her hands up and down Eden's arms. 'I'd say you're more than holding your own, darling. Little birds tell me half the palace is impressed with your feistiness, while the other half are unsure what to make of you.'

Her eyes widened. 'They are?'

Sabeen smiled. 'You're keeping them on their toes, that's for sure. Including the soon-to-be-King.'

Eden shook her head. 'I don't know about that.'

'Oh, trust me. It's not every day a future king calls his brother to demand that his bride's gowns are as perfect as they can be.'

Eden's eyes goggled. 'He did?'

'Yup. Between Teo's mother demanding changes to her gown on an hourly basis, and Azar demanding updates every morning, it's a trip to see the unflappable Teo Domene...flapping about!' she finished, with a sharp relish that said she was enjoying the Playboy Prince's aggravation.

It made Eden wonder just what the deal was with those two.

'Azar even suggested the colours,' Sabeen went on. 'Your favourite is purple, I believe?'

At Eden's stunned nod, Sabeen beckoned one of her assistants and the woman pushed forward a clothing rail holding a gown covered by miles of protective netting.

'Since you'll be wearing the purple Order of Cartana sash with the diamond and amethyst tiara set, I thought your gown would be perfect with hints of purple too,' Sabeen said, then produced an exquisite champagne-coloured gown with a princess cut neckline brimming with shimmering purple-hued crystals.

For unknown reasons, staring at it lodged another lump in Eden's throat.

Azar had commissioned this exquisite gown?

'Now, I may not be a hopeless romantic, but I think it's clear your intended cares a great deal for you,' Sabeen murmured, her eyes on the gown.

'Does he?' The question came out breathlessly, even as she shook her head, holding back the swell of dangerous emotion. 'Of course, I would confirm or deny that if I could remember any of it,' she added, before she thought better of it.

Even Sabeen's bewildered frown was gorgeous, and had she not been thoroughly enamoured by her warmth and friendliness, Eden might have hated her a little.

'You can't remember…?' she echoed.

Aware of their audience, Eden pursed her lips.

'Excuse us for a few minutes, please,' Sabeen said firmly to her team, then turned back to her the moment they were alone. Concern filmed her beautiful honey-brown eyes.

'I don't know if you know the details of how Azar and I met, but… I don't,' Eden told her. 'I've lost my memory of the time I spent in Arizona…'

Sabeen's concern deepened. 'You poor thing. You remember nothing at all?'

She shook her head. 'And my doctor has strictly forbidden Azar from telling me anything that might distress me. So I'm sorry if I don't jump at the idea that my future husband has feelings for me. I don't have any evidence of it.'

Again, she stopped her words far too late. But, to her surprise, Sabeen nodded briskly without an ounce of judgement.

'Then play your cards as close to your chest as you wish and reveal them only when you're ready. It won't hurt one of the Domene men to take a turn twisting in the wind.'

The flush that followed Sabeen's grave advice said she hadn't meant to be so open with her emotions either. For a few frozen seconds they shared a deep, bewildered feeling of kinship.

Then Eden sniffed. 'Can we talk about something else, please?'

'Of course,' Sabeen replied smoothly. 'Lace is back, and I've got a to-die-for gown for your wedding day…'

'Dios mio, if you pull on your cuff one more time you'll ruin it! I made that suit, so I know for a fact there's no magic wish tucked away anywhere, and definitely not up your sleeve. So stop pulling at it.'

Azar frowned at the ridiculous statement. Then looked down and saw he was doing exactly what Teo was grinningly ribbing him about.

He should've heeded his far too many valets and assistants, who had hinted that it was too early for him to get ready. This bout of...of *nerves* wasn't familiar to him, nor was it anywhere near enjoyable.

Nor were the recurring bolts of alarm he'd suffered since Eden had blurted that she wanted to postpone the wedding three weeks ago. He'd dispensed with that nonsense—because surely every woman desired a crown on her head?—but admittedly in those few minutes, and far too frequently since, the searing disquiet that she'd change her mind, choose an alternative to marrying him, had taunted him more often than he liked. As had the steady drips of the possibility that his suspicions about her behaviour in Arizona might be unfounded, rooted in one of Nick's games. Perhaps even cleverly orchestrated by his supposed friend?

If that was the case—if he'd acted on false evidence—could she...would she reject him? He shook his head. She wouldn't. Even if just for Max's sake.

He held on to that belief, grounding himself in the moment, ignoring the hollow in his belly at the thought that *he* merited blame, too.

The moment was here.

His wedding day.

No matter how much he'd prepared for it, he still reeled at the fact that he had a son and was about to acquire a wife. A wife who didn't remember anything of their time together. Call him devious, but he'd tested her in minor ways over the weeks, and eventually concluded that no woman could fake such a thing for so long. That knowledge had added a twist to already churning sensations far removed from the titanium control he preferred.

Hell...if anyone dared label it, they might say he was suffering from the *jitters*.

Because what if she remembered and decided she'd been wrong to give such ready consent to be his queen? Besides his mother, she held the singular position of being the only woman to do so. And, *sí*, that remained a thorn far too close to his chest for comfort.

His jaw tightened. If she decided she'd made a mistake—

'I don't envy you, but it's not exactly the gallows, *hermano*. Lighten up, hmm?'

His jerked at Valenti's prompting. Of the three of them, he was the quietest and the most severe—which was something, considering Azar knew he terrified most people with his intensity on a daily basis.

'Or, if there's a particular problem on your mind, I'm all ears.'

The offer came with piercing scrutiny that would have raised his hackles if he hadn't known what his brother had been through.

What Valenti had suffered—taking a literal bullet for another, then dealing with the harrowing fallout of that split-second decision—would've felled most men. But the Domene blood running through his veins had lived up to its fearsome reputation. Still, sometimes he worried...

'No, I'm good, *gracias*.'

'He's good, yet he's ruining his damn suit! If I didn't know better, I'd think you're freaking the hell out. Worried your bride won't turn up?'

Teo started to laugh, then thought better of it when neither brother joined in.

The truth was, Azar was marrying a woman with a spine of steel beneath the beauty and gentleness she portrayed. That meant that even though she'd given her word, there was no guarantee. And...he couldn't exactly force her. Gone were the days when a Domene man could declare a woman his, give her little choice in the matter, and have her bear his name and his children.

And, yes...the tiniest sliver of him wished for those days. But since he couldn't get them back, and didn't really agree with those Middle Ages practices, he tugged on his cuff one last time—earning himself another glare from Teo—then strode for the door.

So what if he was getting there fifteen minutes early? It would keep the guards and the royal timekeepers on their toes. Not to mention earn him some points with the media as an eager groom.

Win-win.

'Wait. Is he—? He's leaving?' Teo exclaimed. 'Dammit, it's not time yet! I don't care if he's almost a king—that is *not* cool.'

Valenti joined him. Together, they ignored the complaining Teo as they headed out to the fleet of silver Bentleys.

It was a good thing he'd been groomed from birth to nod and wave when necessary, because all he could concentrate on was whether or not Eden would turn up.

Why the question had suddenly taken up so much room in his mind.

And what he'd do if she didn't.

Chantilly lace, with a train embroidered with white alyssum, the national flower of Cartana. Those flowers also formed part of her gorgeous bouquet, bordered by purple lilies. It was hands down the most exquisite gown Eden had ever seen. The gown several Cartanian institutions had already promised her the earth for if she would donate it to their collection, even without having seen it yet.

While Sabeen had grown misty-eyed when Eden had donned the gown, Eden's own tears had come from a deeper well of swirling emotions.

Bells pealed from the basilica with the precision of a Swiss watch the second Eden stepped out of the exquisite four-horse-drawn royal carriage, and the soaring of meticulously trained white-tailed eagles overhead in salute drew a roar and thunderous cheers from the gathered throng who were throwing themselves wholeheartedly into the day that had been declared a holiday kingdom-wide.

Since her father would never figure in her wedding plans, or in her future, and the King was too feeble to walk her down the aisle, Azar's uncle—a rather stern-faced bishop—had been chosen for the task.

Eden was partly glad she didn't need to make conversation with him, and partly sad for the absence of any support for a jittery bride—especially one thrown into such extreme circumstances as she. Especially after her mother had eventually admitted, after much prodding, that she'd been newly released from rehab and, on her counsellor's advice, wouldn't attend. News the palace had scrambled to hide, and Eden had shed silent tears over.

Enough of that—woman up!

Long, deep breaths as they reached the imposing doors of the basilica calmed her a little. Enough to steep herself in the moment, pushing away thoughts of what her future with Azar would be like.

She'd made this decision with her head, so even if her heart seemed inexplicably to be ramming itself against the fortifications she'd thrown up to protect it, so be it.

The staggering number of dignitaries, heads of nations and celebrities had been one thing when they'd been mere names on a list—seeing them in person lent even more gravity to the occasion.

Queen Fabiana sat ramrod-straight in her barely contained disapproval, her nose in the air, while a slightly improved King Alfonso and Max sat next to each other, their heads together in whispered conversation that made the old man smile. The press release about his existence—coupled with that uncanny picture of Azar as Max's age—had been a stroke of genius that had had the kingdom instantly falling in love with her son.

But, as always, her gaze was compelled to the imposing figure poised at the altar, flanked by his half-brothers. The multi-hued sunlight streaming through the basilica windows fell dramatically upon him, casting his dark bronze hair, his profile and his whole body in a celestial glow she would have thought was photoshopped if she hadn't been staring at the real-life, jaw-dropping thing.

Against the protocol drummed into them during their wedding rehearsals, he had turned to watch her progress with an interest that bordered on rabid. Those eyes connected with hers through the filmy veil, and the weak-kneed, shivery sensation that jolted through her body almost made her stumble. In that moment she was grateful for the bishop's arm, but even that grew insubstantial when she finally arrived and Azar held out his hand.

Imperious. Possessive.

No hope for escape.

She stepped up to him and... Was it a trick of the light, or did he exhale in what looked like relief?

But the almost arrogant possessiveness in his gaze when it slid over her told her it had all been in her mind.

Again discarding protocol, he seized her hand, lifted it to his lips and rasped, *'Eres diosa de la belleza.'*

Half a dozen of the two dozen knots inside her eased. And while she didn't entirely understand his words, she caught *goddess* and *beauty* and greedily let their confidence boost wash over her, grateful for one right, if superficial, thing.

And perhaps it was that possessive streak that kept his hand clasped around hers, or perhaps he sensed she might do the unthinkable and bolt from the centuries-old basilica, the hundreds of guests assembled be damned. Or perhaps it was something as simple as him doing her a strategic kindness.

She chose that option to keep her grounded, present enough to register that she was indeed marrying Azar Domene, tying herself to him for life.

The vows were said.

Priceless rings exchanged.

The official wedding pictures were taken.

And while it all felt as interminable as every royal task seemed, seeing her son dressed in a dashing formal suit, smiling and looking as cute as a button, soothed her with a swell of love so strong it made her blink away tears.

Or maybe it was the overwhelming sense that she was now tied for ever to the Royal House of Domene. That her name henceforth would be Princess Eden Domene of Cartana. Soon-to-be... *Queen*.

She gulped at the thought, and felt Azar's razor-sharp gaze on her.

'Are you in need of bolstering again, *tesoro*? I'm happy to help.'

Remembering just how he'd bolstered her in her last bout of shaken confidence, she quickly shook her head. 'No, thanks. I'm fine.'

The faintest trace of amusement twitched his mouth. 'That's disappointing.'

'There are a dozen photographers in here. Whisking me into a corner for a dirty little fumble will cause a scandal.'

His lips twisted. 'Not really. Not when they've all sworn in blood to remain loyal to me and are trained to overlook salacious things like a king and his queen engaging in...dirty little fumbles.'

Surprise punched though her. 'Are you serious?'

His amusement intensified, and she vaguely caught a flash-bulb as one of the cameras captured the Crown Prince's moment of humour.

'About the blood? Not quite—our bloodthirsty days are behind us. But you get my general meaning.'

She did. Like his father before him, he commanded the utmost respect and loyalty. For some reason, that show of humour, eased the tension inside her. Enough to tease out a smile of her own.

His eyes darkened as his gaze raked her face. And right

there another moment of intense connection snapped between them. It was broken once more by the flash of a camera that made her want to grit her teeth and snap at the photographers to leave them be.

'Easy, *mi reina*. Our wedding day isn't the right time to unsheathe your pretty little claws. There will be time for that later.'

Her breath caught, and the urge to demand to know when pounded through her. She curbed it, and sat through another fifteen minutes of picture-taking, all the while painfully aware of being under intense scrutiny—especially from her new mother-in-law.

Queen Fabiana was the only person not fully embracing the momentous event of her son's wedding. Even now she sat primly in a wing-backed chair, surrounded by her retinue who wore equally disapproving looks mostly aimed at Eden.

It was a relief when the royal event co-ordinator announced that it was time to move on to the reception—a much smaller event hosting a few hundred specially selected guests.

For the next hour she danced in her new husband's arms, then with both brothers-in-law—one all sly smiles and ribbing her about the traps of matrimony she'd willingly walked into, the other his polar opposite, with piercing eyes probing far beneath the surface.

'What exactly are you looking for?' she asked Valenti Domene. 'Maybe if you told me I could save us both the silent third degree?'

'Treat my brother well, and you and I needn't have a problem.'

She gasped. 'Are you threatening me?'

He shrugged. 'When it comes to my family and those I care about there's nothing I won't do. Remember that, Your Highness.'

Before she'd summoned a response Azar was there, smoothly reclaiming her, his gaze ten times more potent than his brother's.

'What was that all about?' he enquired silkily, even as his deep voice pulsed with slivers of danger.

'Looks like your mother's not the only one who doesn't like me.'

His eyes grew sharp. Deadly. But it was directed at his departing brother. 'What did Valenti say to you?'

Striving to retain her dwindling composure, she asked a question that seared in its delivery. 'Do you care?'

His frown rumbled louder than a thunderbolt. 'I care. Tell me.'

She shook her head, fixing a smile on her face as a couple of dignitaries waltzed past, the woman's gaze sparking clear envy. 'It doesn't matter. I'm used to being tarred with a certain brush because of my mother,' she muttered, then grimaced inwardly.

When was she going to learn to keep past turmoil from dogging her present?

'I don't wish you to be hurt. Or for the sins of your mother to be visited on you. By anyone. Including my brother.'

That final sentence was a gruff admission. One that made her gaze fly over his chiselled chin and that infernally hot dimple within it to his meet his eyes.

His slight hesitation hurt, despite her knowing that he was entirely justified to take his brother's side.

'It's okay,' she muttered airily, fighting to keep her smile in place. 'He's your family. I understand.'

The fierce gleam in his eyes deepened. 'You are my family too—or have you already forgotten our vows?' he rasped.

The hurt deepened. But the sudden flash of remorse in his eyes stopped her blurting out something she might regret.

'*Perdoname*. That wasn't deserved,' he said. 'You have risen to everything admirably.' He hesitated for a beat, then added, 'And I don't wish to start this with discord.'

Eden swallowed, blinking rapidly when emotions surged. Maybe she should've given in to the urge to bawl her eyes out this morning in the bathroom, when the enormity of the day, of knowing she'd be going through it alone, without a loving family, had weighed her down. Maybe then she wouldn't be feeling quite so…overwhelmed now.

Digging deep, she shook it away. 'Then let's not.'

She attempted a more genuine smile, and to her surprise felt her heart lurch wildly when he reciprocated. And when Sabeen swayed towards them, holding an enraptured Max and trailed by a surprisingly sombre Teo, Eden didn't bother debating if the smile had been for her or for their son.

'I think this little guy wants his *mamá* and *papá*,' Sabeen said, her smile beatific as she smiled down at Max.

Azar claimed their son with one arm, while keeping the other around her, and Eden told herself she wasn't going to wish for a few more of those smiles, just so she could test herself and see if her heart continued to leap in that maddeningly thrilled way again.

Instead, she joined Azar as he threw away the protocol book, wrapped her and his son in his embrace, and swayed across the floor. Applause rang out in the ballroom when Max kissed her cheek, and Azar followed suit with a kiss on the other.

She was brought back down to earth when, after being whisked away by a fleet of royal SUVs to the mountain retreat where generations of Cartana royal couples had spent their wedding nights, Azar showed her to the suite adjoining his, asked if she needed help taking off her gown, and after she said no merely inclined his head.

And walked away.

'Good morning, Your Highness.'

She shot an exasperated glare at Gaspar, his insistence on bowing and using the still disconcerting title souring her mood further.

Three days they'd been at the mountain retreat. Thankfully

Max, after she'd had to spend her first ever night away from him, had now arrived with Nadia. But even he only occupied only half of her time. She was nowhere near used to having great swathes of her life organised with military precision.

And apparently part of the operation was Azar meddling where he wasn't wanted.

'Where is he?'

She forced an even tone. It wasn't Gaspar's fault if she was bristling with unspent energy after discovering what Azar had done.

'Having his breakfast on the west terrace with the young Prince. He said you weren't to be disturbed if you wanted to sleep in.'

Her lips pursed. She wasn't going to worry about what the staff thought of her and Azar inhabiting separate suites. They were probably used to such arrangements. Still, she couldn't avoid that barb in her heart as she tossed her freshly styled hair and hunted him down.

Only to slow metres from the French doors, her attention rigidly captured by the sight father and son made, resplendent in the morning light.

They were completely absorbed in each other, carrying on a conversation that had them both wreathed in smiles, even though she was fairly sure Max was mostly babbling. The barb turned into an acute yearning, digging in deeper where it really shouldn't. Uncovering her secret desire for love and a family that she'd buried for so long.

Azar's head snapped up, his eyes zeroing in on her.

'*Buenos dias*. Something on your mind, *cara*?' he murmured, although the probing gaze searched her face for more. Just as it had done since they arrived here.

It was almost as if he was waiting for…*something*.

Eden pushed that mystery away and stepped out onto the terrace.

'You've moved my mother to *a mansion*?'

She'd seen the jaw-dropping floor plans. The list of staff that included a butler, maid, gardener and chef.

Her mother's call out of the blue half an hour ago had triggered in Eden that age-old yearning that maybe *this time* her contact would be selfless. That her parent would be seeking her out for something other than a handout.

She had been...to an extent. Her mother had called beside herself with shock and excitement at her new son-in-law's generosity. But while Eden had been pleased for her, the alarm bells shrieking in her head couldn't be ignored.

His eyes flicked to the phone she was waving at him, then reconnected with hers. He was the picture of regal casualness, a completely magnificent creature even the sun worshipped, its golden rays perfectly framing his aristocratic bone structure.

'She's the mother of my future queen and the grandmother of a prince. She's just finished rehab. You expect me to leave her in a halfway house one street away from a place un-ironically known as Crack Cocaine Alley?'

Effrontery dripped from him, as if he was aghast that she dared question him.

'I— Of course not— But I don't know what you want in return.' She knew it had been a poor choice of words when his face clenched hard. 'Look, I didn't mean—'

His raised hand told her to stop speaking, and she bristled as he said, 'Yes. You did.'

'I'm sorry, okay? It's just that nothing in this world comes for free. And I'm not telling you anything you don't already know.'

Slowly, he rose to his feet. 'Very well, then. What are you offering in return for my generosity?'

Her eyes goggled. 'What?'

He laughed. Low, deep, and so sexy she wanted to slap her own face to restore her fast-fleeing sanity. And wouldn't that be hilarious in the extreme?

'You're such a sexy little contradiction...aren't you, *tesoro*? You insist nothing in life comes for free, and therefore expect to pay a toll, and yet when I suggest you do so you look shocked. Even before I've made—for all you know—the most benign of requests.'

Sexy. The word ricocheted in her head, setting off little fireworks throughout her body until she was once more— *dammit*—a mass of seething need.

'You're suggesting I'm wrong?' she asked.

'I'm suggesting you don't jump the gun so enthusiastically.'

'Fine. What do you want, then?' she asked, unable to contain the breathless hitch in her voice.

He pinned her with his gaze as he slowly walked towards her. 'Three things. You ride with me every morning. When I have to tour the country by train before autumn sets in you and Max will come too. And for the next year when duty requires that I travel you'll both come with me.'

Her eyes widened. 'That's it?'

One corner of his mouth lifted in amusement. 'What did you think? That I would demand payment in flesh?'

A flush engulfed her face, and her body reacted predictably to the rising heat in his eyes. 'It isn't out of the realm of possibility...'

'Because I'm a red-blooded male and you're a beautiful woman?'

She couldn't stop the punch of pleasure and heat at his compliment, but she pressed her lips together to stop herself from blurting out the *yes* that rushed to the tip of her tongue.

He was continuing anyway. 'That may be true—and, yes, I'm aware our chemistry still blazes hard and true—but I've never bartered for sex, *querida*, and I'm not about to start. Especially with my wife. When you come to my bed it'll be of your own free will.'

'*When?* You're that sure of yourself?'

'When you can't get through a conversation with me without staring at my mouth and my body…wondering or trying to recollect what came between us and squirming with consuming need which you stoically attempt to throttle? Yes, *mi linda*. I do believe it's just a matter of time before you succumb.'

Her laugh emerged husky, and not at all as carefree as she'd hoped for. 'I'm almost tempted to bet everything I own on that never happening.'

His nostrils flared in a blatantly masculine scenting that made her pulse race faster.

'A wise choice not to—since I'm certain you will lose.'

'If this is some reverse psychology thing—'

'It's a stating facts thing. And in the short term, when it happens it entirely up to you. But take this with you when you flounce away, as I'm sure you're about to. It's only a matter of time before you're naked on all fours, with all that exquisite hair coiled in rope around my wrist to hold you still as I drive into you.'

She'd half expected him to argue with her when she came out here. Instead she was drowning in a storm of licentiousness when he leaned down and brushed a shockingly platonic kiss on her cheek.

'Now, are you joining us for breakfast?'

'I… I don't think I have an appetite.'

'Have a good day, then, *cara*. I look forward to our first ride together in the morning. And the many rides to come after that.'

CHAPTER NINE

SHE REALLY SHOULDN'T have been so thrilled at the turn of events.

For starters, she suspected her mother's next call, a mere twenty-four hours later—'*just to see how you are*'—had been part of the grand scheme that came with Azar's gift.

She was touched, but also aware that until her mother gave her attention free of conditions, and until they cleared the air of past acrimony, she shouldn't open herself up to it. And yet she ended the call with a lighter heart, feeling happier with their relationship than she'd been in a long time. Even hopeful that, in time, their interactions might be less transactional and more bond-forming. As much for herself as for Max.

But if she was so susceptible, what else would she fall for? Especially when it came to the man who commanded the very ground she walked on and who, it seemed, could pull miracles out of the air.

A little scared to contemplate that fully, she shoved it way down on her to-do list and prepared for her first ride with Azar, fighting the blush at the remembered *double entendre*.

A pair of white jodhpurs and a matching top, polished boots and an elegant little cap had been laid out for her by Silvia when Eden stepped out of her shower the next morning. At this point she'd already stopped being awed by the efficiency with which their lives were run.

Dressed twenty minutes later, she was transported by a

sleek little electric buggy to an area of the mountain retreat where a row of stables and an open paddock housed stunning thoroughbreds.

And there, making her despair at just how incredible he looked, was Azar, dressed to ride. His white jodhpurs clung to muscled thighs, the black belt and polished boots bringing every line of his powerful body into heart-stopping relief.

He turned away from her to watch a stable hand walk out with two mounts—one a massive, shiny black beast with a swathe of white down its forehead, and the other a cream mare with an uneven splash of black and brown spots that made her all the more eye-catching. Despite the stallion's size, the mare tossed her head repeatedly at him, in a brazen show of insolence that drew a huff from the other beast.

Eden was grinning at her antics when Azar took the reins of his stallion and turned. The snap of awareness thickened in the air, and her breath shortened in that way that screamed her pleasure at being the sole focus of his attention.

'Are you ready?' he rasped, after a charged scrutiny.

She was much too aware of the sensual roll of her hips, of the tightening of her skin, the clenching of her sex as she made her way over to him.

'I'm not sure. As far as I can recall I've never ridden a horse before.'

Something flickered across his face, gone before she could decipher it.

'We'll take it easy on your first outing. Come, let me show you the basics.'

His instructions were succinct, and easy enough to follow. Not so much the scrambling of her brain as his hands slid around her waist to steady her as she placed her feet in one stirrup. By the time she was seated in her saddle Eden was hopelessly breathless, and thankful when, after another sizzling look her way, he turned to his own horse.

Since he'd laid out his conditions yesterday she'd wondered

why he wanted her along for horse-riding—especially if she was an amateur. It ceased to matter the moment he mounted his saddle.

He looked *magnificent*.

Man and stallion were made for one another, the two so infinitely exquisite it was almost unbearable to look upon them.

'Something wrong?' he asked, obviously catching her gawping.

Shaking her head, she shivered all over again when one strong hand covered both of us.

'She can be spirited when she wants her way, but she's also my gentlest, most intuitive mare. I'll take control if necessary. All you have to do is hold on.'

Firm, reassuring words she suspected held a deeper meaning.

Where she craved warmth, acceptance and safety, Azar craved control.

The knowledge didn't so much render her breathless as she was already holding her own breath, searching his dark grey eyes. For what? A sign that the reasons her emotions remained caught in a maelstrom were no longer there? That the man who'd so coolly retreated after putting a ring on her finger to secure his son had somehow morphed into one who was open to the seismic feelings moving through her?

Even before her spirits fell, before the shutters came down over his eyes, she was kicking herself for her foolish yearnings. For harbouring hopes she had no right to. Yes, Azar had been considerate, even kind, but it had all been to facilitate his own goals. To control and ease the path for claiming his son.

In between trying hard to contain those emotions and absorbing the stunning vista unfolding before them, she didn't realise how contemplative Azar had grown until he pulled both horses to a stop.

'You've ridden a horse before,' he told her. 'In Arizona. That may have been your first time.'

The tightness to his voice snagged her attention. Her spine tingled with warning. 'You… We weren't together?'

His jaw clenched for a few seconds before he shrugged. 'You were with Nick.'

'I see,' she said, then shook her head. 'Tell me why it makes you angry to talk about Arizona. I need more. I don't understand…'

For a long stretch he remained silent, his gaze on the far distance, tension tightening his shoulders.

The tiniest dart of pain at her temple made her flinch. Piercing eyes found her an instant later. Assessed her thoroughly, as if judging whether or not to divulge whatever he was withholding.

Eden fought the exasperation building within her. 'Just *tell* me! I want to know everything. But if you feel so strongly about how it'll affect me, at least tell me something about you and Nick. You claim you were friends, and yet I feel something else was going on.'

His hands tightened around the reins until his knuckles whitened. When his horse picked up on the charged atmosphere and whinnied he leaned forward, trailing a soothing hand down its strong neck until the stallion quietened.

It seemed almost unnatural for the formidable almost-King to be buying himself time, and yet it felt as if that was exactly what he was doing. That little glimpse of humanity attacked the vulnerable spot inside her.

'Nick and I *were* friends,' he eventually said starkly. 'As much as two people could be while navigating their families' hidden agendas and protocols. But he liked to play games.'

She took a moment to dissect that. 'True friendship can cut through that, surely?'

A spasm of regret chased across his taut features. 'I thought he'd outgrown it. But conditioning has a way of lingering, long after you believe it's gone. And Nick couldn't quite shake his.'

Again she drilled through his cagey words, her heart thumping as she wondered if he meant her, too. She remained silent.

'He was taught to work at every relationship and come out on top. To win every power struggle.' A hard-edged smile twitched his lips. 'I made it clear he would never win a power play with me. That's how our relationship at boarding school started. Putting our cards on the table cut through a lot of the nonsense.'

'But despite all that he never quite stopped competing with you? And I just so happened to be caught in one of your games?' she guessed, hoping it wasn't true, but suspecting it was.

His gaze tracked the horizon, his jaw taut. 'He insisted that since he saw you first, you belonged to him—despite ample evidence to the contrary.'

Heat surged into her face, but she refused to be bathed in shame. Refused to believe her mother's neediness and desperation for affection had rubbed off on her just when she'd needed it not to. But considering this man—*this maddeningly irresistible man*—was the one she'd been battling against, could she be faulted for succumbing?

Yes. Still…

'I didn't throw myself at you,' she rallied, clinging to the belief.

His imperious head turned, sardonic eyes lasering her where she sat in the saddle. 'There was no need for you to go quite that far.'

'Because you're so well versed in zealous adoration you can spot it at a thousand paces?'

He shook his head, almost pityingly. Then his face closed. 'We've been over this already, *carina*. It's because I was twice as affected. Twice as enthralled. And I'm not ashamed to confess it was the first time it'd ever happened. So, *si*, I was intrigued. Enough to decline stepping aside for my best friend.'

There went her stupid heart again, when he was only referring to chemical attraction.

Somehow she found the strength to raise her hand, bat that away. To remember that her mother had been a source of intrigue for her father once upon a time. Until he'd had his fill and cast her aside. A trend that had repeated itself with stomach-hollowing frequency.

'So if I didn't throw myself at you, and you had issues with Nick, why do I feel as I'm the vill—?'

'You're not Nick's type,' he cut in stonily. 'I'm at a loss as to why he brought you to Arizona.'

'Because a supposed two-bit gold-digger looking for a payout has no place in a billionaires' playground?' she asked bitterly. 'Or should I leave the slut-shaming to Nick's father?'

Azar's eyes blazed, his body going rigid. 'He did that?'

Her insides congealed at the memory. 'When I contacted him…thinking Nick was Max's father.' Her mouth twisted. 'He reminded me that men like my father truly are a dime a dozen.'

His face tightened. 'Your father—?'

'I don't want to talk about him,' she interrupted.

His gaze rested heavily on her for another stretch. 'Then don't,' he said. 'And, since I have first-hand evidence that you were the farthest thing from a slut, that should answer your question.'

She was still tussling with that when he sighed.

'We've strayed too far into unadvisable territory. Once your memory returns we'll pick this up from a position of greater understanding. *Sì?*'

Push, pull? Support or manipulation?

Eden's heart wanted desperately to believe this was Azar opening up and supporting her. But while those shadows and walls remained, and her memory was a locked box, how could she trust anything he said?

'Yes?' he pressed, when she didn't respond.

She breathed in deep, her own gaze now locked on the vista so she wouldn't have to keep pathetically searching his.

Was she not better off hedging her bets until such a time when she knew his true feelings? She'd seen the consequences of rushing in where fools didn't dare, like her mother did, with only pain and hurt to show for laying her heart on the line.

So, even though her chest squeezed uncomfortably tight at that decision, she dragged her gaze to his, pleased when her composure didn't crack, and nodded. 'Of course.'

And surely she misread that tiny flicker of disquiet in his eyes? His slow exhalation that seemed wrapped in the faintest dismay? Because from that moment on, as he expertly conducted a tour of the verdant mountain, it was almost as if they had been in her imagination.

They slid ever deeper into their roles of Crown Prince and consort, their well-oiled machine presenting a united front, sending even the irascible palace council into muted rhapsodies. Headlines around the world hailed theirs a fairy tale union for the ages, and Max was soon garnering his own adoring following on social media.

And as one month galloped into another Eden learned to live with the thorn in her heart, ignoring the fact that it grew larger every time Azar watched her for one second too long with those shadows still in his eyes.

She even convinced herself she had her every emotion contained.

Until one month after the wedding and several days after Azar's official coronation, with her as his queen.

The last of the dignitaries and the extensive Domene family had left, the barricades taken down from the roads where thousands had celebrated Cartana's most triumphant royal event to date.

Spotting Gaspar rushing towards them on their return from dinner with Azar's worryingly more frail father, Eden exhaled, eager for relief from the constraints of being *on* the whole time. Because even now her assistant trailed after her, reminding her that she was yet to confirm a date for the exclusive interview she'd agreed to with Rachel Mallory.

'Let's pick this up tomorrow,' she said firmly.

Then her heart lurched when she saw the uncustomary pinched concern breaking through Gaspar's composure. When Eden's gaze dropped to the fingers drumming against his thigh, alarms bells shrieked within her.

'What is it? What's wrong?' she demanded.

Azar, who'd been on his phone, quickly ended the call, striding to her side as alarm clogged her throat.

'Gaspar?' The demand was clipped. Imperious.

'Your Majesties, it's about the young Prince—'

'What about him?' she screeched, only then taking in the tension amongst the staff hurrying back and forth through the immense palace.

Gaspar looked as close to distraught as she'd seen him. 'His nanny is on her way, but it seems he's gone missing.'

'What?' Sheets of ice wrapped around her soul as she shook her head, unable to fully compute what was happening. 'When? How?'

Strong fingers wrapped around her wrist, lending her a warmth she wasn't sure she had a right to accept. Not if her child was in danger and she'd been sipping fine wine at dinner.

Eden recognised abstractedly that she was hyperventilating, her heart going ten thousand miles a minute. But she couldn't stop it. Fear had taken hold of every atom of her being.

'Eden.'

The word came sharp and piercing. Commanding her attention. Her eyes met Azar's, imploring him to send his strength into her.

'He will be fine.'

'Y-you don't know th-that. Oh, God! What if...? What if...?'

She tried to whirl away from him, to compose herself enough so she could think. He stopped her, tugged her hard into his body, wrapping her tight in his strong, warm arms. He held her long enough for a layer of fear to dissipate. Then he captured her chin and tilted her face to his. His eyes blazed with authority and implacable determination.

'He hasn't been harmed. I will never allow that to happen. Do you hear me?'

Her head moved independently of her fracturing thoughts.

Gaspar cleared his throat. 'Every guard and staff member in the palace is out looking for him—'

'Then w-we should go out there too—looking! We can't just stand here doing nothing!'

She wanted to scream when Azar shook his head. 'We will. Right after we talk to Nadia. We'll find him, *tesoro*. And he'll be fine. Do you hear me?' he repeated.

Her nod was shaky at first, but the pulses of sheer resolute faith vibrating off him slowly seeped into her. She nodded more firmly, and when he lowered his head and pressed his lips to hers, in a hard, reassuring kiss, she felt another layer of panic recede.

'Your Majesties…'

Nadia's hesitant voice pulled them apart, but Azar didn't release her completely. He kept an arm around her waist as they faced the nanny.

'Have you found him?' Eden blurted.

Even before the young girl shook her head Eden saw the truth in her stricken face.

Calm down. You're no use to Max in full panic mode.

She sucked in a steady breath, shaking her hands free of tension before she clamped them tight again.

'When did you notice he was gone?' Azar asked.

'I put him down an hour ago, and went to check on him fifteen minutes ago. H-he wasn't there. I've looked everywhere I can think of.'

A broken moan wrested itself free from Eden's throat. But, as much as she wanted to burrow into Azar's chest and sob her terror, she forced herself to think.

'Tell me what you were doing in the two hours before you put him to bed.'

At Azar's questioning look, she met his gaze.

'If he's excited about something, it's the first thing he does or talks about when he wakes up.'

The nanny swallowed and nodded. She was trained to maintain her composure, but Eden could see it fraying beneath Azar's piercing regard.

Freeing herself from his hold, she grasped Nadia's arm. 'It's okay. Just stay calm and tell me.'

Nadia's gaze latched onto hers, her forehead faintly creasing. 'He didn't want to go to bed, so I made a list of all the fun things we would be doing tomorrow.' Her eyes darted to Azar. 'He was looking forward to swimming with you before breakfast.'

Azar's nostrils pinched, and the skin around his mouth whitened briefly, but he didn't speak.

Nadia's eyes darted back to Eden. 'I also promised him we would visit the mini maze tomorrow and play hide and seek with his toys.'

A jolt went through her. 'Hide and seek is his favourite game. If he woke up thinking about it...'

Another sob threatened. The thought of her baby wandering the grounds at this time of the night...risking getting hurt. Or worse...

'Let's check his room again,' Azar barked, already striding away.

She chased after him, catching up as he entered Max's suite and crossed into the vast play room attached to the bedroom, searching for anywhere a toddler might hide.

For a cursed moment Eden wished they didn't live in a

palace—a place with hundreds of places for her son to play, blissfully unaware that his parents were tearing their hair out.

'Max?' she called. Her voice wobbled horribly.

Silence.

Three minutes later they'd searched every inch of his rooms, calling out with no success.

Eden's panic surged again when her gaze snagged on the window, latched but slightly ajar. They were on the second floor... Was the space wide enough for a child to slip through? God...he wouldn't...

'No.'

Azar said the word through clenched teeth, but he still strode to the window, tugged on it. When it didn't give immediately, he pushed it open and looked out. She saw his shoulders sag as he exhaled.

'No,' he murmured again, softer this time. With an unmissable tremor.

Relief and gratitude flooding her, she whirled about. 'He wouldn't have made it to the maze all by himself. Not without the guards seeing him.'

Please, God, let him not have attempted it.

'Never,' Azar agreed. 'Our suite?' he suggested tightly.

Every inch of their bedroom and their living and dressing rooms had been searched ten minutes later.

Eden felt fresh darts of pain lancing through her temple.

'Your Majesty?'

She turned at Nadia's hesitant voice. 'Yes?'

'Maybe the aquarium?'

'But the aquarium's on the other side of the palace. Surely he wouldn't have made it there on his—?'

'Your Majesty.'

Eden turned, her teeth gritted at the relentless formal title. Ramon, Azar's head of security, stood behind them, a tablet in his hand.

'Yes?' Azar bit out.

'We may know where he is—'

'Then spit it out, Ramon. Where's my son?' Azar grated, his composure fraying just that little bit more.

The King who craved control was seeing it decimated before his very eyes.

Eden wrapped her fingers around his, pressing into him the same strength he'd infused her with. She watched his Adam's apple bob as he stared his security chief down.

Ramon held out the tablet. And there on the screen was their son, hurrying as far as his little legs could carry him, dragging his tattered giraffe behind him towards...

'The cinema room?' Azar barked.

Nadia grimaced. '*Dios!* I promised him a movie and a lollipop tomorrow if he ate his vegetables—'

'Show me...please,' Eden interjected.

Azar grabbed Eden's hand tighter, and she almost had to run to keep up with him as they tore down far too many corridors to a door at the far end of their wing. She flew past him the moment he opened the door to the cinema, her feet muffled by the thick carpeting in the windowless, sound-proofed room.

There, on a plush velvet lounger set before the giant silent screen, was her son, curled up with his giraffe tucked under his chin, one fist clutching a large strawberry lollipop. A whole plastic tub of confectionery had been spilled on the floor in his search for his favourite.

'*Dios mio...*' Azar muttered, shaken.

Relief electrified Eden, freezing her for a moment before, muffling yet another sob, she stumbled towards Max. She wanted to snatch him up, examine every inch of him to make sure he was okay. But he was sleeping so peacefully all she could do was lower her face to his cheek, run her fingers gently through his springy hair and just...*breathe him in.*

Beside her, Azar did the same, their faces almost touching as they kissed their son.

After an age, she managed to pull back when her tears

threatened to spill onto him. Sitting back on her heels, she swiped at her face, but a handkerchief arrived in front of her. She looked up. Azar was staring at her with a fierce look in his eyes. She accepted the handkerchief, then watched him lithely rise to his feet, his shoulders lowering in another deep exhalation as the security team arrived in the room.

Ramon looked visibly relieved to see the young Crown Prince safe and sound. His gaze shifted to his boss as Azar turned to him.

'First thing tomorrow—'

'We'll set up further security measures, Your Majesty,' Ramon pledged, uncharacteristically interrupting his sovereign in his desperation to reassure him that this wouldn't ever happen again.

Eden felt his gaze on her, including her in that pledge, but she was too absorbed in reassuring herself that her son was fine and unharmed to respond.

Another sob bubbled up, and Azar gruffly instructed everyone to leave. The moment the door shut behind them he gently scooped Max into his arms. He stirred briefly, then settled against his father's chest. Azar's other arm came around Eden and he murmured soft, soothing words against her ear in Cartanian as she sobbed quietly.

With relief for his safety.

With gratitude that, for the first time, she hadn't endured a horrible experience alone.

And with sadness. Because too soon she would need to return to emotional solitude, suppress this yearning for love and a home even more.

'It's okay, *tesoro*. He's fine.' Azar's lips found the corner of her mouth in a swift, firm kiss before he gripped her nape to angle her face towards his. 'Let's put him in his proper bed, shall we?'

Nodding brokenly, she held on tight to him as they returned to Max's room.

Only to feel her spirits plummeting all over again when, in the living area of their suite, she saw who was waiting for them.

With every bone in her body she wished she could override politeness and keep walking. Her overwrought emotions still lingered on the surface, and this encounter was the last thing she needed.

'I'm told you're having trouble keeping track of your offspring,' Azar's mother drawled.

Despite addressing them both, her critical gaze remained firmly on Eden.

She looked extremely well put-together, considering it was almost midnight. Compared to her, Eden felt like a grape left too long in the sun—not fresh, almost entirely wrinkled. Grimacing inwardly, she was relieved when Azar, still cradling Max, turned to her.

'Go on—I'm right behind you,' he murmured, but he didn't wait for Eden to leave before he answered his mother. 'That "offspring" is your grandson. And if you're here to express anything but support I suggest you leave.'

Queen Fabiana stiffened, her son's tone leaving her in no doubt that he wasn't in the mood for her antics. 'I just came to see that he was okay, Azar. No need to be snippy.'

He took one more step towards her with a nod. 'Thanks for your concern, but we're all fine. *Buenos noches*, Mamá.'

Her face clenched at the blatant dismissal, and she shot Eden a venomous look, but once again Eden couldn't bring herself to care.

The pain at her temples was intensifying.

She rubbed at them as they entered Max's room. 'I get why your mother doesn't like *me*, but why does she...?'

'Actively despise me?'

At her gasp, he smiled stiffly. 'Long story short: she's never forgiven my father for fathering other offspring. She wanted him to reject Teo and Valenti. Papá refused. I was caught in the crossfire of their battle until I was old enough to remove myself from it. She's never forgiven me for forming a bond with my half-brothers and not taking her side in hating the whole world for what she deems her suffering.'

Eden frowned. 'But…she was Queen. She had everything your half-brothers and their mother didn't.'

His nostrils flared. 'You have front row seats to the reality that wealth and a royal title don't equal happiness.'

What he didn't add, and what Eden suddenly realised, was the fact that his mother was the reason he craved control. Why he was so often aloof to the point of detachment. Perhaps even why he wanted to forge a different path for himself when it came to being a father to Max.

Suddenly her throat was clogging again, her heart clenching in understanding and in foolish, dangerous sympathy. Yearning…

Because if Azar was as broken as her… If her foolish heart forged a connection…

Swallowing, she held out her hands.

Azar placed Max in her embrace where, after a moment, he whimpered as he protested at her fierce cuddle.

He started to blink and wake. 'Mama?'

'Shh…it's okay, baby. Go back to sleep.'

Letting go felt like the hardest thing, and she was grateful that strong arms wrapped around her once more after she placed him in his cot and they watched him settle back to sleep without a care in the world.

'I'm not sure whether to ground him until he's fifty or handcuff myself to him to ensure he never does that again,' Azar admitted gruffly.

A broken sob-laugh slipped out. 'Welcome to my world,' she murmured, and then her breath caught when he tilted her face to his.

'A world I'm finding I'm agreeable to inhabiting,' he returned gruffly.

CHAPTER TEN

SOMETHING SHIFTED BETWEEN them in that moment. Profound and heavy enough to still their breaths. To make Azar's eyes darken, this time minus the shadows. And whether he was the one who drew her closer or if it was she who held on tighter, she chose not to dwell on it. They didn't kiss, but they came close. And, bewilderingly, it felt even more intimate, standing there watching over their son, not rejecting the connection forging between them, even though she had no idea where it might lead.

She watched as the tightness around his mouth and eyes eased and he exhaled heavily. As if some secret, mighty resolution had been reached. And when he dropped a soft kiss on her forehead Eden found herself sighing too. Abandoning those fierce defenders guarding the walls of her heart.

Just for tonight, she would take a break from tumult.

'My father will have heard about this,' said Azar. 'He'll need reassuring. I'll return as soon as I can.'

She nodded, wrapping her arms around herself to retain his warmth as he stepped away. For the longest time, he simply stared at her. Then, turning briskly on his heels, he strode away.

She stayed, reassuring a distraught Nadia, when she hesitantly approached, that she bore no grudge.

Then, after assuring herself her baby was okay, she reluctantly left him to sleep.

Sleep for herself was out of the question, but she stripped upon reaching her suite, showered and dressed in a nightgown and robe, then planted herself in front of the TV in the living room connecting her and Azar's suites. For the first time she was thankful for the strict palace protocols that almost guaranteed that news of tonight's events wouldn't get out.

She'd just about managed to get her heart to settle when Azar walked in. He was freshly showered too, and even before her avid gaze had taken in the damp strands of silky hair clinging to his forehead and temples, to wander lower over his hard pecs and washboard stomach, her heart was galloping again.

It really was deplorably unfair how magnificent this man was.

'Nightcap?' he drawled, sauntering over the extensive liquor cabinet perched next to a Venetian wallpapered wall.

She started to shake her head. But darts of pain, one swiftly following the other, lanced her temples, made her freeze.

Azar froze too, his brow furrowing. 'What's wrong?' he rasped.

'My head hurts. I'm coming down with a migraine.'

Concern clenched his brow and her heart thudded as he changed direction, striding over to where she sat.

'Shall I get the doctor?'

And invite more curiosity? 'No, I'll be fine. It's probably the adrenaline… I'll sleep it off.'

His scrutiny didn't let up. 'Does that usually work?'

She shrugged. 'I don't know. I've never misplaced my son before,' she said, then flinched at her half-facetious, half-panicked tone. It would take her a while to get over the emotional turbulence of the last hour.

'Ven aqui.' The command was low and utterly unshakable.

Eden stood and tumbled forward, a compulsion she couldn't fight directing her. The moment she was within touching distance, he dragged her into his arms. She fell the last half-step, a sob of relief breaking free before she could stifle it.

Her cheek landed on his chest and she inhaled, deep and shaky. His arms banded her, just like before, and damn if it wasn't quickly turning into her favourite place to be.

'I don't know what I'd have done if anything had—'

'Hush, *tesoro*. He's safe and sound and tucked up in bed. See?'

Sliding a hand into his pocket, he drew out his phone, hit the monitor app that showed Max fast asleep in his bed.

'That's all you need to think about right now. We've been given an eye-opening test. We will put forward better safe-guards, yes?'

She nodded, more than ready to release that rock of fear lodged in her gut. Burrowing deeper into his chest, she ex-haled on a moan again as one arm banded her waist and his fingers dug into the tight knots gripping her shoulders. He massaged her in firm, soothing circles, loosening her tension until she all but melted against him.

With one final breath she wrapped her arms around his waist, not protesting when the arm around her waist lowered to circle her hips and lift her up in a show of easy, sexy strength that changed the dynamic from comfort to...something else.

Something that made her lift her head, angle her gaze to meet the ferocity of his.

A different sensation took hold of her. One that had been brewing with unstoppable force since the moment he'd dropped his champagne glass in Vegas and chased after her.

Possibly even before then. Because, as he'd stated before, chemistry like theirs couldn't be faked.

'You don't want a nightcap. Or the doctor. Tell your hus-band what he can do for you,' he offered, with such overpow-ering yet simple magnanimity that her defences crumbled all at once, making her foundations entirely unsalvageable even if she'd wanted to cling to her last ounce of sanity.

'What if it's something I... I shouldn't crave? Something impossible?'

Molten grey eyes, hypnotising and offering safe harbour, locked onto her soul. 'I've been known to achieve the impossible. Say it, *mi reina*,' he commanded roughly. 'Tell me what you want.'

And, sweet heaven, she was tired of fighting it. Especially tonight, when her emotions had been put through the wringer.

'I don't want to be alone,' came her raw admission.

Tonight or any other night.

'Take me to bed, Azar,' she whispered fervently, her fingers digging into his shoulders, holding on for fear he'd refuse. Reject her. For fear the lust she saw in his eyes was only in her imagination. 'Make me forget for a while?'

The flare of need and triumph that blazed a moment later told her she wasn't imagining it. And, while she knew this might ultimately be a risky path she was taking, she couldn't help the blaze that flowed through her.

The heightening need speared her fingers into his luxurious hair, gripped it tight as he drew up her nightgown, to aid her in wrapping her legs around him. The better to feel the power of his arousal, a heated rod that immediately pressed, demanding, against her core.

She ground her hips against it, causing him to curse before a thick chorus of need left their lips. It tightened their connection, their mouths meeting in feverish hunger. Thick, untamed desire born of deprived need and residual fear drove their frantic hands faster, their movements increasingly desperate, until he pinned her against one wall, his breathing truncated as he feasted on her for an age, then lifted his head.

'Again, Eden. Tell me you want this. That you want *me*.'

The demand was tinged with his usual arrogance, his imperious expectation of adoration and acknowledgment of his prowess. But, having lost chunks of valued memory, Eden had learned to search beneath the surface of words and expressions.

And she heard it. That sliver of vulnerability, of uncertainty, that spoke of a deeper need. That said that this extraordinary man, who was literally a king among men, didn't believe his dominance was absolute. That when it came to her perhaps he lacked something—minute but *essential*.

And maybe it was extreme foolishness to open her heart to that, leaving her vulnerable, but here she was doing it. Discarding any smidgeon of power she might have mined from that knowledge and instead cupping his chiselled jaw in her palm, revelling in the muscle that jumped against her skin.

And with far too much emotion moving through her, she responded. 'I want you. I feel as if…as if I've wanted you for ever. Even when maybe it wasn't wise or sane or safe. I want you, Azar. Only you.'

Flames of pure lust and indecipherable emotion leapt in his eyes. She wanted to drown in the former, explore the latter more deeply. But he was spinning, striding with purpose towards the emperor-sized bed that befitted his status. He tossed her none-too-gently upon it, his hands attacking his clothes as he watched her bounce on the surface.

And once he was gloriously naked, and had ensured she was too, he prowled over her…a sleek, beautiful jungle beast.

'You're mine, *tesoro*. Say it.'

This time she had the wherewithal to shake her head. Because she knew, like his conquering kin of old, that he saw an inch and demanded a mile. She'd left more than a crack of her heart wide open for him. She suspected he would find a way in if she didn't shore up her defences soon and effectively. But she wasn't about to hand herself over on a golden platter.

So she slid her hand up his sculpted shoulder, thrilling in the sleek perfection of him, and buried her fingers in the hair at his nape. 'You first. Tell me you're mine and I'll reciprocate.'

Those shutters didn't come down immediately. But their silhouettes shimmered into sight. That ingrained propensity to guard his emotions, to keep his control, flared high before he rasped, 'I'm not going anywhere.'

Not the same, her senses screamed.

But he was lowering his head, slanting his mouth over hers in searing possession that soon turned into fiery worship over every inch of her body.

'I'm not going anywhere either,' she returned, and then took the smallest triumph in seeing how that dissatisfied and unsettled him, hearing the lowest growl erupt from his throat.

The result was fire in his eyes, demanding mouth and hands, and a wicked edge to his possession as he quickly sheathed himself and parted her thighs. Eyes pinning hers, he kissed his way down one smooth inner thigh, then the other, his nostrils flaring as desire gripped him tighter still.

Then, with his fingers and his mouth, he tormented her long enough to drag pleas from her very soul before, levering himself once more over her, he slammed inside her, as if imprinting himself on her very soul.

Grabbing her hands, he shoved them above her head, imprisoned them against the headboard with one hand while the other captured her hip, held her steady as, with a fierce determination to conquer blazing in his eyes, he drove her right to the edge of the world, then held her there with exquisite precision. Until she was begging...then screaming.

Then she was soaring, crying out, 'Oh, God, Azar. I can't... I can't... I'm coming!'

His triumph this time was absolute, as was the restoration of his control as he plunged his tongue deep into her mouth, tasting her pleasure and her surrender.

'For me. Only me. *Si?*'

'Yes! Only you!'

Words dissolved into action. Even as she was soaring he was flipping her over onto her knees, recapturing her hips.

Then, with pure animalistic mastery, the King of Cartana reasserted his dominance. With fiery caresses, worshipful kisses and always, always, the relentless drive of his shaft, he finally gave a hoarse shout of his own, gifting her another sublime climax as he seized his.

Then, in silence, he stepped off the bed, caught up her sweat-slicked body against his own and marched them to his shower.

Eden could barely keep her eyes open as he gently bathed her from head to toe.

Or perhaps she didn't really want to look into his eyes, see those shutters back in place.

Because from the corner of her eye she caught the tight clench of his jaw, the rigid way he held himself despite the slight tremble in his hands.

Yes, they'd been caught in the wildest tempest—but it was over. And now he was shoring up his defences.

It would be in her best interest to do the same. So she went one better and shut her eyes, scooping up her scattered emotions as he wrapped her in a sumptuous towel, after washing himself, then, striding back into his bedroom suite, placed her beneath the covers.

She didn't even care that they were both naked. It would be absurd to call for modesty now, after what they'd done to each other. And it was too much effort to resist when he tugged her close, wrapped his warm, hard body around hers and instructed her gruffly to, 'Sleep now, *mi linda*.' He dropped a kiss on her neck, and added, 'Rest that rebellious little spirit that I shouldn't find quite so engaging and yet...'

Maybe it was her imagination that he'd left some words unsaid, or maybe she'd drifted off before he finished speaking.

Either way, her subconscious had other ideas.

She dreamt of sun-drenched joy, of playing with Max, and a hovering and protective Azar tossing swathes of broody, desirous looks her way, promising her the fantasy family she'd secretly yearned for.

But they quickly turned into a repetitive nightmare loop of frantic, shattered loss…a dark hellscape where she screamed her throat raw for her loved ones for what seemed like eons—until a firm hand was shaking her awake.

'Wake up, *cara*,' a deep voice commanded. Hands pushed back her hair from her face. 'You're having a bad dream.'

And when she opened her eyes to the dark concern in Azar's eyes it was to feel a piercing spike of relief, quickly replaced by the most harrowing lance of pain she'd experienced yet.

Her migraine hadn't gone away.

Hell, it was ten times worse!

She was gasping through fresh waves of pain when the kaleidoscope of memories she'd feared lost for ever zipped into life, like forked lightning in a storm.

Only once the pain cleared, the memories remained.

Of Arizona.

Of Nick.

Of her and Azar.

Of that horrendous fight when he'd seen her coming out of Nick's room after delivering a bottle of champagne to him and confiding in him that she was attracted to Azar.

Then had come the double blow of Nick warning her that Azar might not feel the same, followed by the cruel, humiliating words Azar had thrown at her soon after, confirming Nick's words.

Her pain had been soul-shattering and her despair uncontrollable. She had known everything she'd thought special and sacred about giving herself to him had been a lie. That he was rejecting her as cruelly as her father had done. That she was getting a taste of everything her mother had suffered.

Throat-searing sobbing had been followed by a profound vow to herself not to fall into her mother's trap of risking her emotions on a man. A man who would never feel one iota of what she felt for him.

She had been devastated that the man she'd given herself to thought of her as nothing but a convenient bed-warmer—a toy he could play with and discard—and she'd readily accepted when Nick had offered to take her for a drive, to get her away from Azar.

Only to suffer a different sort of terror. Nick, driving his Lamborghini way too fast, while raging—ironically—about Azar's unfair privilege.

She remembered her screams as he'd taken a corner too fast. As tyres slid and glass shattered.

Then nothing.

Sorrow stung deep now, and the anguish of loss and grief for Nick was raw with reawakened memories.

Every look Azar had levelled on her since their accidental reunion finally made sense. All along she'd suspected she was the last woman on earth he'd ever want.

Now she knew.

He exhaled slowly. Heavily. Incisive eyes drilled laser-sharp into hers. The hand caressing her shoulder dropped to the bed and a different tension replaced the harrowing nightmare.

'You remember.'

It wasn't a question.

She'd survived one category five cyclone only to be plunged into another.

She pushed him away, hating her subconscious for not protecting her from this when it had protected her from those harrowing hours that last day in Arizona. Chest heaving, she threw her feet over the side of the bed and sat up, snatching up the towel she'd dropped earlier.

'Eden?' Imperious demand throbbed in his voice.

The battering continued, firing tremors through her body. 'Yes. I remember.'

She didn't need to look over her shoulder to know he'd stiffened further. That his deep censure was back.

'I'll get the doctor.'

'No, I don't need—'

'I'm afraid this time it's non-negotiable. You've suffered enough trauma for one night. I won't risk your health.'

She wanted to laugh. Then cry. Then scream at him to stop pretending he cared for her when the glaring truth of how much he didn't was a live wire writhing between them.

She clenched her teeth as he snatched up the phone and summoned his private doctor.

'Are you sure you want to go down that route? I'm handing you the perfect excuse on a plate. A queen of unsound mind and low morals is surely worth the scandal just to get her out of the way and have full access to your son?'

His sharp intake of breath made her shut her eyes. She couldn't bear to look at him. His voice ringing clear as a bell in her head was a searing reminder of one of the many insults he'd thrown at her that night, when he'd seen her exiting Nick's room.

'Women like you are only good for one thing. And even that cheap thing becomes entirely worthless when it's spread about.'

'Thanks for the offer, but if you're trying to get rid of me scandal won't be the thing that sways me. My father has told you the story of how my brothers and I came to be born more than a few times. I won't be letting you go any time soon, *cara.* If anything, the challenge of drilling down into your choices intrigues me.'

She surged to her feet and spun to face him, fury momentarily overcoming the weakness and pain still gripping her body. 'Challenge? *My* choices? How dare you? You called me deplorable names. And you...you—'

His sharp curse came as if from a deep dark tunnel. She realised she was swaying, losing her balance, just before he snatched her into his arms. Molten censure-filled eyes drilled into hers.

'Enough of this! You have just got your memory back. We will fight, if you insist, but not until you're in a better position to throw your verbal punches.'

'You're unbelievable—you know that?' she breathed as he swung her up into his arms and returned her to his bed.

The memory of what they'd done there so gloriously unspooled like the most vibrant spectacle through her mind. She struggled to bite back a moan when he pulled covers that smelled like *them* around her.

'I want to return to my own bed.'

That regal nostrils flared, betraying the fact that he wasn't as unaffected as he projected. She didn't care. Didn't want to let it anywhere near her wounded heart.

'Again, not until we do what's necessary,' he clipped out, one eyebrow raised in exasperating challenge.

'Fine. Let's get on with it, then.'

He stepped back, exposing every sculpted bronze inch of himself in unashamed nudity. The fact that it took three seconds too long to drag her gaze from him sent waves of heat to her face, and she exhaled in thanks when she was saved by the literal bell at the door.

Despite having been woken in the middle on the night, the doctor was impeccably dressed, and unflappable as he gently but firmly went through the file Dr Ramsey had transferred to him before standing up.

'I'd like to perform a more thorough examination in the morning, Your Majesty. But for now everything seems fine besides the headaches. Those are to be expected.'

His gaze darted to Azar, who stood narrow-eyed, his hands on his hips, thankfully having thrown on a pair of lounge bottoms.

'As long as you don't overstress yourself you in the short term.'

'Are you saying I can't make love to my wife, Doctor?' Azar demanded brazenly.

'Azar!'

She couldn't, of course, blurt out that she had no intention of letting him anywhere near her now she'd recalled his true feelings for her. Until she decided how best to protect herself and Max, she still had to maintain this ruse of being a happy family.

'Well?' Azar pressed, completely ignoring her sidelong glare telling him to shut up.

The middle-aged doctor, no doubt used to the eccentricities of royals, barely reacted. 'I wouldn't want to impose a pause on the physical if you don't wish it, Your Majesties, but I strongly recommend you…moderate yourselves.'

She slapped her palms over her burning face, caught between fury at Azar and hysteria at this absurd conversation. 'Oh, my God…'

Could this night get any worse?

She started to shake her head, thought better of it, and dropped her hands. 'Thank you for the advice, Doctor. And I'm sorry to have bothered you at this time of night.'

'Not at all. It's my privilege to be of service to you, Your Majesty. And I'm glad that you're on the road to full recovery.'

Azar's brows clamped at the doctor's twitch of a smile. He remained grimly watchful as he handed her pills to ease her headache and then, with a shallow bow, wished them goodnight and left.

'You!'

That infernal sexy eyebrow arched. *'Sì?'*

'You have a nerve…assuming I'll let you anywhere near me!'

His face tightened. 'Let's not close the door quite yet on what works best for us, *cara*.'

Gritting her teeth, she flung off the covers, thankful when

she felt sturdier on standing. Her head was still pounding, but she knew it would grow worse if she stayed there.

'What works for *you*, you mean. I'm only good for one thing. Isn't that what you said in Arizona?'

His lips firmed, and the skin bracketing his mouth paled a little while the tops of his ears reddened. On anyone else it might have looked like self-flagellation, or even unease. But he was masterful at controlling his feelings, and it was gone a moment later.

'Get back into bed,' he said, with unexpected gentleness.

But she suspected that too might be a tactic.

'No. The only bed I'm getting into is my own.'

She rubbed at her temple, averting her gaze when his chest swelled with a deep inhalation. Knowing he was about to press the point, she tightened the belt of her robe and headed determinedly for the door.

'Goodnight, *Your Majesty.*'

His harsh exhale just before she slammed the door behind her was her only response.

'Eat something.'

Azar's belly clenched hard as Eden's gaze flicked in his direction, started to rise, then stopped halfway up his chest before returning to Max.

While he couldn't fault her for showering their son with her attention this morning, he found he very much minded that she was freezing *him* out. That the eyes he'd stared so deeply into in the throes of the most profound lovemaking of his life were being denied him in the light of day.

Hell, he even felt the tiniest most uncharitable sensation of wishing her memory hadn't returned just yet. Because he'd selfishly wanted time to grapple with his own bewildering emotions. With the persistent possibility that he'd relied too heavily on past crutches in his interaction with Eden three years ago, and been too quick to heap blame on her.

The possibility that Nick was not blameless...

He killed the self-deprecating laugh that growled up his throat. That hinted at the impossible notion that he might be floundering on a subject he didn't want to delve into and—holy of holies—that he might be feeling the tiniest bit sorry for himself.

Hell, no.

It had never happened before, and he was damned if he would allow such useless emotions to vanquish him.

'I'm not hungry,' she murmured, with barely an inflexion.

It was the same tone she'd used since they'd dressed and gone to fetch their son for breakfast. Her mood was only transformed when she addressed Max. Then pure joy and gratitude shone from her eyes.

And, *diablo*, he was not about to admit to feeling jealous of his own flesh and blood. That would be the lowest of low.

So he shifted in his seat, reached for fresh fruit, sliced it before placing it on her plate.

'Try. You need your strength, and we have much to celebrate.'

That drew her attention, as he had known it would.

'Do we?' she echoed hollowly.

'*Sí.* Your memories have returned. Surely that's a good thing?'

Her gaze dropped, veiling her expression once more. Was it wishful thinking, or did he catch the shadow of regret in her eyes?

'Well, if nothing else, I guess we both know where we stand now.'

His belly clenched tighter. 'What's that supposed to mean?'

She didn't answer straight away, choosing instead to shower more attention on Max, who was devouring his favourite breakfast of pancakes painstakingly made in the shape of his favourite creatures by the palace chef.

After wiping a syrup-covered cheek, she slid Azar another no-contact glance. 'A mere waitress could never hold her own in your world, never mind be Queen. Or something to that effect.'

'You wish to turn every word I said to you three years ago in Arizona into a whip to flay me with? Before you do, remember that I was going with the evidence before me.'

'What evidence? I did absolutely nothing to give you the impression that I had loose morals. Hell, you saw the "evidence" when I slept with you. And if we're playing *Remember when*... Remember when you all but beat your chest in primal smugness when you discovered I was *a virgin*?'

She whispered those two words, her cheeks flushing as she glanced furtively to where the staff waited just beyond hearing range.

Azar stared, wondering how he could have blocked so many obvious details from his mind.

With a heavier dose of the unease that had been eating away at him since last night, he forced himself to remember those flashes of innocence when they'd touched.

But, Nick's possible scheming aside, *she had still chosen him over Azar.*

Yes, she might have been settling for second-best, but he couldn't overlook the fact that the choice had been made.

And he, having spent his childhood coming second to his mother's rabid ambition to elevate herself in life *at all costs*, had felt something crack in him when she'd made that choice.

It had been unforgivable then.

It was...*should be*...unforgivable now.

Unless she'd struck out in blind self-defence? Had her *'I'm with Nick now'* been designed to hurt with words and not an actual truth?

But even as those niggles of doubt swelled bigger inside him he was fighting not to reach across the table, to experience the silky smoothness of her warm, firm skin all over again.

Arizona hadn't been enough.

Last night had been nowhere near enough.

He was beginning to entertain the jarring possibility that what he was facing was a challenge without end.

He pushed every single disconcerting thought aside and nudged the fruit one inch closer. 'The doctor is waiting for us. And he will most definitely not consider it progress if you turn with an empty stomach.'

Her frown deepened. 'I can see him on my own.'

'You can, but you won't. Even if you can't stand the sight of me right now, we have appearances to uphold—remember?'

'And that includes invading my privacy?' she bit out.

The signs of her fire were better than her chilled distance, even if she was using that fire to push him away.

'What privacy, *tesoro*? You already had Dr Ramsey share your history with me. There's nothing more to hide, is there?'

Her eyes flashed with the pure fire he'd hoped to provoke. And, *sí*, maybe he was playing dirty, but he was *that* unsettled.

When he had her attention, he nudged the plate another daring inch closer.

Unfiltered exasperation was stamped in every inch of her body, but he watched her devour the fruit. And when he slid her a plate of buttery croissant, ham and eggs, he enjoyed watching her consume that too with way more satisfaction than he should have felt.

But he didn't even fight it. Theirs was a conundrum hidden in a maze. It would take time to unravel.

And if he sensed time already slipping through his fingers…? That she might make another choice, leaving him in the cold once more…?

The constriction in his chest froze his breath. *No.* He would not permit that to happen.

What if the choice isn't yours?

'I'm done. Let's go and get this over with.'

She stood, blissfully unaware of the tectonic chaos unfolding within him.

Max was tidied up, and she caught him in her arms and strode for the door, her intention not to leave him clear in every sinew of her beautiful body. It was a plan he wasn't about to argue with. The thought of those hours last night still sent faint ripples of icy horror and dread through him, along with the knowledge that any harm befalling his son would've destroyed him.

But in the clear light of day he also realised that the ordeal had done something else. It had cut through his deep need to claim and establish a relationship with his son and turned it into a deeper yearning for *more*. And not just with Max.

He wanted more with Eden, too.

For a full minute he remained frozen as the knowledge embedded in him. Burrowing into all his alarmingly vulnerable places. Rushing through his chest like a tropical thunderstorm until he was drenched with pure, unadulterated need.

Rising, he followed his wife and son at a steady pace.

He would *not* be left behind. He was the King, after all.

But as he joined them, planting himself by Eden's side as the doctor did his tests and pronounced her healthy and on the way to full recovery, he wasn't so confident of the battle ahead to win his wife.

But, *he was the King*. And he had the blood of past warriors flowing in his veins. He only needed to find a way to achieve this *more* without fully exposing himself to any vulnerabilities.

Right…?

CHAPTER ELEVEN

AZAR WAS CHANGING the rules on her.

Somehow he'd decided, the morning after she'd regained her memories, that what had happened in Arizona—the denigration of her character, the belief that she'd been playing him against Nick, deliberately inciting his jealousy, and that she'd even gone as far as to choose Nick over him—was merely a bump in the road they could overcome.

At first she'd been nonplussed, to the point of speechlessness. Then angry—because how dared he? But now, in the third week since regaining her memories, Eden had become intensely curious as to why and how he believed they could carry on as if he *hadn't* levelled the vilest of accusations at her. As to how long he intended to try and sweep her off her feet every time she so much as cleared her throat to address the giant elephant in the room.

So far, he'd taken her to every cheesy tourist spot in San Maribet and Cartana, eagerly couching it as 'the honeymoon phase' for the palace. He'd also shown her out-of-the-way haunts he'd visited as a boy with his father, like the private cave two mountains over from the mountain retreat where they'd spent their wedding night.

Today, the spectacular six-course meal he'd arranged there, across the lake on an expertly crafted royal raft, lit only with phosphorescence, was so magical Eden wasn't sure she'd taken a full breath throughout. And now, after dinner he offered revelations when she asked why only his father had featured in these outings. Revelations she would have thought unbidden if not for the strained look on his face that told her this too had a purpose. One she couldn't immediately grasp.

'If you haven't noticed already, my mother doesn't care about appearances,' he said. 'Her only abiding desire is to further her own interests.'

She flinched at the caustic words. She opened her mouth, to say what she didn't know. But he shook his head, pre-empting her.

'Don't bother with platitudes. I have recognised and accepted that ours will never be the normal mother and son relationship. And in all these years nothing has prompted me to believe otherwise. She is what she is.'

She frowned, not entirely sure why his words sent jagged unease through her. Perhaps it was because while her situation with her own mother bore some similarities to his, she hadn't given up on forming some semblance of a relationship with her, whereas it sounded as if Azar had.

Was that so he could control never being hurt again? Did that control extend to every area of his life. *To her?*

'So, in essence, where Max is concerned, you're following in your father's footsteps?'

His mouth twitched—not with cynicism at her observation, but with something close to fondness. 'He said the same thing when I broke the news about Max.' Then all traces of humour were whittled away. 'And I cannot fault him. If he did one thing right, it was ensuring my brothers and I forged a relationship—despite all the opposition. I don't intend to allow anything to stand in the way of what I mean to achieve.'

Something urgent pushed her to test that control. 'With Max, and probably with me, but not with your mother?' When his jaw tightened, she continued. 'You speak as if that's set in stone. As if you can't change things even if you truly want to.'

He sent her a speaking look that made heat flare into her face and her heart lurch. 'It's not the same,' she defended hotly.

Expecting an imperious counter argument, she was surprised, then vastly troubled, when he finally nodded. 'It's not. Because while I accepted the way things were with her even before I turned ten years old, I'm not doing the same with you.'

She shook her head. 'You can't just command things to be the way you want, you know?'

His nostrils flared, and in the glowing lights around them he resembled a fallen angel, intent on bending rules and kingdoms to his will.

After a moment, he reached out. 'Get better quickly, *tesoro*. Then we can joust on a more even battlefield.'

I want to fight now.

But she held her tongue, because this place he'd brought her to, one that was special to him and his father, was wreaking sweet magic on her. She was loath to spoil it with disagreement. And also, deep down, the promise of fighting him for what he wanted sent too large a thrill through her.

For the two nights in a row after that, when the magic wrapped tighter, she came within a whisker of succumbing to the goodnight kiss he brushed over her lips, to the intensity in his gaze when he stared down at her, willing her to take things a step further. Or perhaps a step back, so she would be in his bed?

The clawing need when that happened felt like an uphill battle she was doomed to lose.

Caught in deep thought on just how she could save this heart of hers, which seemed to be flinging itself headlong, with zero caution, into the hands of a man she still couldn't trust to treasure it, Eden forgot all about protocol as she opened the door to her father-in-law's living room to retrieve her exuberant child and take him for his afternoon nap.

King Alfonso, who'd finally got rid of his pneumonia and was remarkably stronger, insisted he was fit enough to withstand Max's frenetic pace, but Eden knew he needed a day or two between Max's visits.

'Don't think I can't see it, *mi hijo*.'

Eden stopped in her tracks. King Alfonso was talking to Azar.

She'd had no idea Azar would be there—and honestly, she'd been cowardly and avoided him for most of the last few days.

She feared she was falling in love with her husband, despite the insurmountable barriers between them. Her heart was a foolish organ, she'd decided upon waking this morning. And it needed a serious time out.

She needed to walk away. If nothing else, she could trust that Azar would ensure Max didn't tire his grandfather.

'See what?' Azar replied.

Her feet stalled, her heart thumping wildly.

'The strain between you and your wife. Put on a show for the public, but you can't fool me. I know the challenges of dealing with an unhappy wife, remember? This path you're on...leaving things to fester...it'll only lead to further strife.'

'You don't need to worry about us. We're making it work.'

His father snorted, then coughed for a few minutes before chuckling. 'You've never been one to bury your head in the sand, Azar. That you insist on doing so now makes me think you're afraid.'

'Afraid?' he scoffed. 'Because I don't subscribe to some false notion of baring myself wide open in order to satisfy someone's grand expectations?'

'Tell me what hiding your true feelings has achieved for you?'

'Papá...'

'You're a skilled negotiator in diplomacy and lately, with the help of your wife, very skilled at getting the whole world to fall in love with our beautiful kingdom. But you're terrible at seeing what's right in front of your face. Do the right thing. Drop the pretence and be straight with her,' he warned.

'Doing "the right thing" is one thing. Strangling a relationship with unwanted emotion is quite another.'

Through the dull roaring in her ears, Eden heard the former King sigh. 'I should've insisted your mother do better with you, shouldn't I? Should've put a stop that silly rivalry before you and your brothers were caused irreparable damage.'

Tense silence. Then, 'What's done is done. There's no point dwelling in the past,' Azar said.

She didn't need to be in the room to know he was pacing. He'd be hating not being able to control the whole nonsensical notion of love his father was pushing on him.

A notion he was dismissing out of hand.

'Is it done when it's affecting your future? Wake up, Azar, before it's too late.'

Something she recognised as hope shrivelled within her as Azar's bitter laugh caught her right in the chest, snagging hard at a very soft spot.

'I appreciate the advice, Papá, but for the sake of my son I can't—won't—risk upsetting the status quo.'

'Not even if it'll bring you greater happiness?' his father pressed, even though his voice had weakened with fatigue.

The long stretch of silence wrecked her to her core.

Then, 'I haven't seen any evidence that it'll be worth it. So, no. Things between my wife and I will stay the same.'

An imperious declaration that completely shattered her, and her breath caught on stifled sobs as she stumbled away towards the privacy of her suite.

'I've arranged to visit my mother. Max and I are leaving in three days.'

His espresso cup froze halfway to his mouth. 'When was this decided and why am I only hearing of it now?'

She was doing that thing again—staring at his chest instead of meeting his gaze.

The Great Unnerving—as he'd taken to calling the sensation inside him which had only intensified since his father's wholly unsolicited counselling—surged higher. At this rate he'd be completely engulfed, would drown without knowing what exactly was killing him.

Really? You don't know?

'I spoke with her last night. You know she's never met Max. And now, thanks to you, she's able to host us.'

There was no sarcasm or rancour in her voice—and, yes, he wished his magnanimity wasn't returning to bite him in the behind in the form of facilitating this separation.

'And how will your sudden absence be explained?' he rallied.

She shrugged. 'Get the palace to spin something. They've done an exemplary job for the past few months, haven't they?'

'They may well have done—you seem to have them in the palm of your hand, after all. But even if I agree to you going, I'm not sure I want to be parted from Max.'

It was a purely selfish, rash means of ensuring she returned. Because for a blind minute he couldn't cast off the notion that if he let them go he would never see them again.

Now she met his gaze—with fire and brimstone.

'You think I'm going to leave my son behind? I will fight you to the ends of the earth before that happens. I dare you to try it!'

For the second time in his life he knew the meaning of blazing jealousy. Of feeling control slipping through his fingers. The other time had been when he'd seen her with Nick. When he'd assumed—falsely, as he was now accepting—that her interest in him was anything but platonic.

The wife and Queen he'd lived with these last months, had watched interact with his people—several of whom were falling over themselves to gain her friendship—even deal with his mother, had too much integrity to be putting on an act. She wore her true emotions on her sleeve.

Now he was jealous of his own son.

He clenched his teeth as shame whistled through him. The whole situation was shaming him, emphasising just how dependent he'd become on seeing her—seeing *them*—at his table every morning and night. On knowing she was within reach, even if she'd taken to avoiding him more effectively in the last few days.

Even while he despised that uncontrollable dependency, he knew he needed it. More than he'd needed anything for a very long time.

Sí, it vastly contributed to that Great Unnerving.

'How long do you propose to be away?'

The subject of her leaving without his son was closed. He couldn't separate them any more than he could stop breathing.

Relief flashed across her beautiful eyes—and, yes, he despised that too.

'Then do something about it.'

He pushed his father's voice out of his head in time to offer the most selfless boon he could. 'Two weeks,' he said.

She frowned. 'What?'

'You have two weeks. I'll find an explanation for your absence.'

She shook her head. 'One month.'

His lungs flattened, suffocating him. 'Absolutely out of the question.'

She glared at him, rose from her chair and turned away, her arms wrapped around herself. 'Three weeks. And I'll throw in some diplomatic work. I seem to know my way around that well enough by now.'

Ice filled his veins. 'You really want to get away that badly?'

Her eyes shadowed, then she shrugged and looked away again. 'I'm not ready to write off any relationship with my mother. I'm going, Azar.'

And, as much as it ravaged him, he hung his hopes on that integrity and let her go.

* * *

Eden had been half afraid that the camera had lied about the transformation she'd seen in her mother during their video calls.

But, whether it was the Californian sun that seemed to have taken years off her or an unknown root cause, Liv Moss looked miles better than Eden had seen her in ages.

The fact that there was no self-serving man there, offering false promises and responsible for her mother's warm smile when she threw the doors of her Azar-gifted mansion open? Even better still.

And perhaps her newfound self-esteem and emotional clarity was what kept Liv from probing too deeply when Eden changed the subject every time she tried to talk about Azar.

Sadly, it didn't last very long.

Five days of exploring the quiet exclusive Santa Barbara beaches with Max and only a handful of bodyguards in tow was all she got before her mother cornered her one evening, while Max played with his toys.

She delved right in. 'You're not talking to your husband. Why?'

Eden's grimace earned her a wry glance. She scrambled for myriad excuses. But did she really want to rekindle a relationship with her mother and yet hide such an important aspect of her life?

No.

Her gaze flicked to Max, to the soft features already such a powerful reminder of his father that she wondered how she'd believed he was anyone else's but Azar's.

In the end, the facts she hadn't wanted to admit to herself came tumbling out.

'He doesn't want me. He only married me because of his son. I thought it would be enough to do it for Max's sake, but I don't know if it'll be enough in the long run.'

'Of course you know. Or you wouldn't be here,' Liv said briskly.

'What—?' she started, but her mother was shaking her head.

'And it's absolutely fine to feel that way. You shouldn't settle for less than you deserve. But, sweetheart, I think you're wrong.'

Her insides lurched. She wished to be wrong. 'Why?' she asked anyway.

'Because it's the twenty-first century, Eden. And, as much as respectability means to these people, they don't need to marry someone to validate their claims. Even if they do, courting scandal by stepping out of their marriage vows will only get them more attention. And these days any form of attention can be spun into good attention. He married you because he wanted you *and* his son. Don't make hasty decisions before you find out. I made the opposite mistake with your father. I wish I'd seen the light much sooner than I did.'

The echoes of her mother's pain triggered memories of the most distressing period of their lives and made her prod deeper. 'I'm sorry about that. But what about the other...?'

Her mother gave her a sad smile. 'The other men I tried to replace your father with?'

At Eden's hesitant nod, her mother swallowed, then blinked back a surge of tears.

'Because they made me forget my pain for a while, and some of them even made me feel loved. But it was never the real thing.' She reached across and grasped Eden's hand, the lighter shade of the green eyes she'd inherited pierced her with its earnest intensity. 'If you have a chance at the real thing, don't walk away from it, honey. You'll regret it, and if you're not lucky it'll be far too late to do anything about it.'

'And if it's not the real thing?'

Her mother sagged back in her chair, but the look in her eyes never wavered. 'If it's not, and you decide to walk away, don't settle for second and third best. Don't make my mistake. Because you'll lose more than yourself.' Her eyes flicked to Max, her eyes filling when they returned to Eden. 'You'll miss the chance to feel an equally meaningful kind of love. I missed a lot with you, sweetheart. And for that I'm sorry. I know I don't have the right to ask but…can we start over? I would very much like to stay in both your lives.'

Swallowing the lump in her throat, Eden nodded. Her hands were shaking as they gripped her mother's. If nothing else, she would repair this vital relationship with her mother, regain everything she'd lost when her father had let them both down.

'I would like that very much, Mom.'

As her mother threw her arms around her, salving a wound left far too long unattended, Eden couldn't shake the feeling that in his own way, Azar had facilitated this for her. Even while his own tumultuous relationship with his mother festered.

'I haven't seen any evidence that it'll be worth it. So, no. Things between my wife and I will stay the same.'

She swallowed another wave of hurt at Azar's devastating words. But was her mother right? Was she writing something off that was potentially salvageable? Could she stand having her heart crushed by pursuing a subject her husband had already ruled on?

As if intuiting her thoughts, Max toddled over, holding out the sleek phone Eden had given him to play with. 'Papá.'

Her heart lurched, and for a second she believed—*hoped*—Azar was calling. When she realised her child was making a demand, asking to call his father, her chest squeezed.

Azar had video called Max every evening before his bedtime. And while he remained cordial with her, she'd read the intent in his eyes. Her three weeks were counting down. And she suspected he wouldn't give her a second longer.

Why did that thought send fireworks through her when she needed to be standing her ground?

But what if that ground wasn't as cold and desolate as she had initially believed? What if there were priceless gems to be discovered if she dared to dig deeper?

'Papá,' Max insisted, his bottom lip threatening a full-on wobble if his demands weren't met.

Before she could decide, her mother reached for the phone. 'Let me do it.'

Her tears had receded, a sheen of mischief taking their place.

'Why?' Eden asked a little warily.

Liv smiled. 'Just a little experiment to see how the land lies. Max gets to talk to his father, and you get to take a long bath...think about what you truly want. Win-win.'

She made shooing motions and Eden found herself heeding them. But just before leaving the vast living room she paused, taking care to remain out of sight as her mother dialled the first number in the contacts list.

'Liv? Where's Eden?' he demanded.

It was imperious, but she heard the sharp edge she knew well now. The edge that said he wasn't as in control as he portrayed.

'She's occupied with something else. But your son wanted to talk to you so I—'

'Occupied with what?' Azar interrupted sharply.

Eden's heart jumped at the frantic disgruntlement in his voice.

'Papá!'

'Here's Max now. Enjoy your call.'

Her mother sailed on smilingly, securing Max in his high-chair, then walked away before Azar could question her further. Liv rounded the corner where Eden stood, hiding an enigmatic smile.

'Just as I thought,' Liv murmured.

'What do you mean?' she asked, her heart still galloping. 'What are you doing?'

Her mother cupped her cheek. 'Nothing. Go, honey. Have your bath.'

She went, torn between interrogating her mother and not wanting to know what she meant.

Because she didn't want to hope.

For the first time in his life Azar wished the palace machinery had failed. But they'd expertly mixed enough public engagements into the three weeks he'd grudgingly granted for Eden's trip for it to be hailed a triumph as she met with first ladies, industry experts and charitable organisations. Her popularity already on a steep upward trajectory before she'd left, had now gone stratospheric. Even more tourists were flooding into Cartana, wanting to breathe the same air as its royal couple.

And his wife didn't display a single crumb of homesickness. Hell, she seemed to be positively *enjoying* herself, speaking about Cartana with a poise, charm and expertise that had made his jaw drop and his palace council fall over themselves in rhapsodies.

It's happening despite you never making your kingdom her home. You've pushed her away...just like you were pushed away.

With every glimpse of her, and with every brief, stilted conversation before she passed the phone to Max, he felt the distance between them stretch wider. A mere ten days had felt like six lifetimes. And with each second the drum that beat into him, telling him that he should be doing *something* wouldn't relent.

'What are you going to do?' Teo asked, for the dozenth time.

His brothers had turned up to spend some precious time with their father. And, while he didn't begrudge them a single minute of that time, he wished they'd find someone else to pester while their father was resting.

He suppressed the urge to snap at them, demand to be left

alone, as he looked up from his phone—*another call unanswered by Eden*—and realised his hand was shaking.

Again.

Dios mio, she was the only woman to make him tremble so damn much. She drilled holes in his control without even trying. And, astonishingly, his heart—his soul—was making peace with the fact that he would relinquish that control if it meant having her...*keeping* her.

'Why do you care?' he lashed out.

Teo looked momentarily pained, an expression that pierced regret through Azar before the all-encompassing terror reclaimed his whole being.

'Look, it's clear to everyone that you miss your family. Even I miss Max. I've grown fond of the little rascal. And your wife isn't half bad either. You can bury your head in the sand about it if you want, but lately you've seemed...' He shrugged. 'I don't know...less sour-faced? Passably tolerable?'

'Seriously. Shut up, Teo,' Valenti growled from his position of solemn watchfulness in the corner.

Unflinching, Teo sauntered over with glasses of the premium cognac he'd poured and handed them out, watching, with one brow arched as Azar downed his in one go.

'I'm going out on a limb here, so bear with me,' he mused, ignoring Valenti's venomous look. 'If this is still about Nick and what happened in Arizona, you need to handle it quickly.'

'Teo...'

He ignored his twin. 'You chose to overlook his faults and, while he was great at hiding them, he wasn't *that* good. So what I'm saying is, are you willing to lose your family over whatever is holding you back?'

Azar had jack-knifed in his seat when Teo started talking, but now the bracing words made his insides shrivel. Because it really was that simple. And the answer was as clear as the blue skies outside his window.

He wanted her. He *needed* her.

And unless he took careful, calculated steps, he might lose everything.

So he stood, ignoring his brothers' probing stares, and walked out.

Unfortunately, a whole day later he, the clever strategist everyone claimed him to be, hadn't devised an effective strategy to win his wife. Instead, he was reduced to *texting* her. With idiotic hands that wouldn't stop shaking.

You're ignoring me.

The words made him seethe, and they terrified him.
A whole five minutes passed, then:

You're a king, with realms of adoring subjects. You'll survive.

He gritted his teeth, even as his belly swooped with fear. He looked around the room—her suite, which he'd taken to wandering into because her scent lingered in the air. And he found he needed that, too.

I won't survive without you...

He started to type the words, then quickly deleted them. Carefully. Because accidentally sending it would...would...
What?

Reveal, once and for all, the true, fathomless depths of his feelings? Reveal that his aberrant outburst in Arizona had been the unstable precursor of what he hadn't recognised was his love and obsession for her? That he would give up everything, including his cursed control, if she would forgive him and love him back?

He swallowed...blinked hard as the truth settled deep and immovable in his heart.

Come home. Please.

Delete. Delete. Delete.

Come home, por favor.

Right. Because begging in his father tongue was less emasculating? Why not simply text his true feelings too and be done with it?

He paced faster, eyes glued to the screen, then froze when the speech bubble appeared.

We agreed a time and duration for my trip. What's changed?

Everything, his senses screamed.

Then he forced himself to stop. Think.

He'd shamed and rejected her publicly once. Shouldn't he make amends the same way?

Dragging himself from her suite, he entered the living room where his brothers were enjoying a nightcap.

When Azar flicked Valenti a glance he was waiting, one eyebrow quirked.

'What do you need?'

About to shake his head, to send them both away so he could deal with this alone, he felt a jagged thought shimmer into life. Slowly it took shape and solidified.

It was a risk. But if there ever was a time when being King should count for something, surely it was now? When his very life was on the line. Because now he'd had a taste of what the rest of his life might look like, he was confident he wouldn't make it.

'I need you to find someone and bring them to me. As soon as you can.'

Valenti barely blinked before he nodded. 'Give me a name.'

* * *

Another three days passed before Eden accepted that she couldn't stay away the full three weeks with the subject of where she stood in her marriage, in her heart, hanging over her head.

Maybe she could reach him some other way.

She called her personal assistant.

'We never nailed down my interview with Rachel Mallory. Can we make it happen while I'm here?'

'Leave it with me, Your Majesty.'

Eden wasn't expecting the response she received when her private secretary returned her call five minutes later.

'Your Majesty, it looks like Miss Mallory won't be available to interview you.'

She wasn't so full of herself that she was upset by it, but she was surprised.

About to shrug it off, she stopped when her assistant added, 'But you might see her in Cartana after we return. She's been summoned by His Majesty for an interview due to air tomorrow night.'

Eden's eyes goggled, her emotions running riot. 'What? She's in Cartana? Are you sure?'

'Quite sure, Your Majesty.'

Azar was giving a public interview? For what purpose? His father's condition hadn't changed. The former Queen hadn't done anything scandalous enough to require managed publicity.

The King of Cartana giving a public interview was a big deal...

Surely he wouldn't be so cruel as to end their marriage by giving a world exclusive?

Hand shaking, she dialled Azar's number. It rang and rang. Then went to voicemail. The idea that he was paying her back for her near-silent treatment seared her heart.

Unwilling to leave a message when every fibre of her being shook she tried texting instead.

I'm not sure what's going on, but I hear you're giving an interview? Azar...if this has anything to do with us...for the sake of Max...call me.

Dear Lord, could she sound any more desperate?

Hastily deleting it, she replaced it with a less emotive message.

We need to talk. Call me.

Then she watched as the speech bubble rippled for a heart-stopping twenty seconds before disappearing.

Fury rising to mingle with the anguish of her heart cracking, she took a deep breath and dialled his number again. Listened to the ring tone with her fingers wrapped tight around the device.

Just when she thought he'd ignore that too, the call connected.

But it wasn't Azar who answered.

'Good afternoon, Your Majesty.'

'Put me through to him, Gaspar.'

A taut pause. Then, 'I'm afraid His Majesty is indisposed. Perhaps I can pass on a message?'

Her heart cracked wider. When her legs lost power, she sank to the side of the bed.

'It's eight in the morning. I know he's about to sit down to breakfast and I know he's deliberately avoiding me. Put me on speaker so he can hear me.'

'Your Majesty—'

'Do it, Gaspar. I don't care if the whole world can hear me.'

'Yes, Your Majesty.'

The fact that he complied forced another spike into her heart. But she scrounged up the last bit of her composure.

'I'm going to keep this simple, Azar. I know you don't want

me. And you can do whatever you want to me, but if you do anything to hurt my son with this interview I'll never forgive you. I'll make sure you regret it for the rest of your life. Do you hear me?'

She hated the quivering in her voice, but she'd got her message through.

And when she heard a muted rough exhalation she knew he'd heard it loud and clear.

Yet ending that call felt as if she'd stopped her own heart from beating.

CHAPTER TWELVE

'IT'S NOT TOO late to change your mind.'

Both Azar and Teo swivelled their heads to Valenti, who scowled at them for a second before staring out of the window of the media room of the palace.

'I swear I didn't switch bodies with him. I'm still Teo.' Teo turned to his twin. 'What the hell has got into you? I should be the one to tell him that, even though I'm told women love it when you make a fool of yourself over them.' Teo eyed Azar up and down. 'And you've got that tortured lover look down to an art.'

'Enough,' Azar growled, wishing he could open another shirt button.

But he'd pushed things already by conducting this interview minus a tie, sending the palace council into apoplexy. If he told them it was because he couldn't breathe properly they'd have him trussed up in an emergency room before he could explain it was an entirely emotional condition, not a physical one.

'You can both shut up. Or leave. This is the only way.'

They stopped talking. And the roar in his ears grew louder, his heart slamming against his ribs as Eden's words echoed in his ears.

'I know you don't want me...'

'I'll never forgive you...'

The raw pain in her voice had shrivelled his soul to noth-

MAYA BLAKE 181

ing. He'd spent a sleepless night wondering if this decision was the right one. He, a man known for cutting through the dross to the heart of any given situation, was floundering desperately, unnerved by how wrong he'd got the most important relationship of his life. To the point where he'd been avoiding the most important person in his life. The person who held his heart and soul in the palm of her beautiful hand. Avoiding her for fear that he'd wreck that too, before he came within a hope of salvaging what he'd destroyed.

'Your Majesty? Miss Mallory is ready for you.'

Valenti glanced over at him. Azar thanked his brother with a curt nod. Not that it had been a huge effort to get the world-renowned broadcaster to drop everything and fly to Cartana for a global exclusive with the King.

Clenching his belly, he strode to the blue-cushioned, gilt-edged chair opposite where the middle-aged woman sat.

'Your Majesty, thank you so much for granting me this interview. It's an honour to speak with you.'

He nodded briskly, but didn't reply. She got the message and moved on, touching on economics, social standing, human rights.

He cut across her ten minutes in. 'You've done your homework, I'm sure, Miss Mallory, so you'll know our GDP is healthy, our healthcare and gender equality are ranked among the top five in the world, et cetera. But I didn't bring you here to waste time talking about what you already know.'

She hesitated for a minute, wondering if she could smell a trap, before obviously deciding that whatever was coming would be worth it.

'What would you like to talk about, then, Your Majesty?'

His heart leapt one last wild time, then settled into a rapid thudding. 'I would like to talk about my wife. My queen,' he replied, and the pulse throbbing in his voice made everyone in the room—perhaps everyone tuning in—sit up and take notice.

Which was exactly what Eden deserved.

Rachel Mallory nodded. 'Of course.'

'As you and the world know, we met some three years ago in Arizona. What you don't know is that at the time I misjudged her terribly. She was trying to make a living in the most honest way she knew how, and I allowed my past and adverse influences get in the way of seeing her for who she truly is. A generous, warm, supportive and intelligent woman who puts those she loves above everything else in her life. She tried many times to let me know I was wrong in my thinking and...'

He paused, his chest caving in on itself under the overwhelming weight of his guilt. Teeth gritted, he pushed his way forward.

'I refused to believe her. I was wrong.'

'Say more,' Rachel Mallory encouraged, her focus unwavering. Almost daring him.

'All my life I've felt... I'm not quite enough.' Azar's lips twisted at the sceptical look in her eyes. 'And, yes, I see you don't quite believe that, because I'm a king. But first I'm a human being. With feelings I've long suppressed because it hurt too much to feel.'

There was movement in his peripheral vision. No doubt palace advisors, wondering where he was going with this, alarmed that he might be revealing too much. But he didn't care. Not any more. If baring his soul, relinquishing control, was what it took, then so be it.

But then he felt a unique sensation.

Felt her.

Swivelling his head, searching past the spotlights, he saw her.

Dios mio, she was here. To make true on her promise? No, he would expose every last crumb of himself before he let that happen.

Rachel Mallory followed his gaze, her eyes widening before she quickly pivoted. 'Your wife, the Queen, is here. Do you mind if she joins us, Your Majesty?'

'It is entirely her choice,' Azar replied, though his whole being was straining for Eden.

When his fingers twitched, rising towards her almost independently of his thought, his breath snagged in his chest.

To his shock and awe, she stepped into the light, her eyes pinned on his as she accepted the invitation, swaying and poised and so damned beautiful he wanted to drop to his knees in worship of her.

She was here.

Perhaps all was not lost.

She took his hand and sat in the hastily produced chair, barely acknowledging their interviewer. 'Go on,' she encouraged him, her husky voice composed.

He cleared his throat of the surfeit of emotion. He had a confession to finish. The most important of his life.

'We all seek validation in some form or other. And when that validation is withheld from us by one of the most important people in our lives, and repeatedly given less priority, it has a way of eroding self-worth. I have every material thing I could dream of at my fingertips, but the most important thing...the love I thought—knew—I deserved...was withheld by...'

He shook his head. The issues between him and his mother were private. He would not air her inadequacies now. Maybe never.

'Deep inside I knew better than to accuse one person of another's behaviour, but reality goes out of the window when feelings you've never truly experienced rip your insides out.'

'What are you saying, Azar?' Eden whispered, her fingers convulsing around his.

'I was falling in love. Deeply. Irreversibly. And I didn't know what do with those feelings. So when I believed you'd chosen someone else, I let that colour my judgement. And I lost you because of that.'

'Azar—'

He shook his head, ploughing on with a desperation he hadn't felt in a long time. If ever.

'I wasn't good enough for you then. You had every right to walk away. And I haven't been good enough for you since you agreed to be my wife.' He reached for her other hand, his insides shaking like a leaf in a thunderstorm. 'But you have my vow, here and now, that I will not rest until I'm worthy of you. And if it carries me into the afterlife, I will spend an eternity winning you back.'

Her fingers trembled as they threaded with his, and he saw her nostrils quivering as she tried to hold back her emotions. Then she went one better and cupped his undeserving cheek.

'You don't need to win back what you have never lost, Azar. You only need to open your eyes and see what is in front of you.'

His jaw dropped, and he knew he was the furthest thing from cool and calm when he sucked in a sharp breath. 'Eden. *Mi reina*. I—'

'I forgive you for all of it, Azar. Just tell me what I want to hear.'

He swallowed, then laid the last of himself bare. 'I love you, *mi corazón*. With everything I am. Inside and out. With every cell of my body. I love you, and I would be honoured if you would spend this life with me.'

For the longest second she simply stared at him, her eyes beautiful, her spirit glowing bright with the merest hint of reproach.

'Took you long enough,' she murmured.

The moment she swayed towards him he scooped her up, deposited her in his lap, then gruffly instructed her, because he was still a king after all, 'Kiss me, my queen.'

She spiked her fingers in his hair and dragged him down to meet her lips.

Gasps echoed all around them. Feet shuffled. Some people probably attempted to give them privacy.

All Azar Domene cared about was that the most precious thing in his life was where she belonged.

Her cheeks were a deep pink and her beautiful eyes bright when they parted, and she clutched at him. 'We're breaking two dozen protocols…do you know that?' she whispered, her sweet breath brushing his mouth.

He ignored the rolling cameras and carded his fingers through her hair. 'I'll break three dozen more just to keep you right here, in my arms.'

When her bottom lip quivered, he dropped his forehead to hers.

'I'm so sorry for everything I've put your through, *tesoro*. I was a coward who hid behind his pain and distrust.'

She swallowed. 'I should never have gone with Nick that day. I should've stayed and done everything in my power to show you how wrong you were. But it's behind us now. I love you, Azar.'

He groaned under his breath, then rose, hitched her up more securely.

Then he walked out.

Ten minutes later he was deep inside his wife, in their bed, with her arms and legs wrapped tightly around him as if she'd never let him go. He planned never to let her.

'Tell me again,' he pleaded.

'You first,' she taunted throatily as he pushed even deeper, as if their newly revived souls were rising to wrap around each other.

'Maybe these three years apart were exactly what I needed. Because your every breath, your touch, your scent, your love is so much more precious to me now, Eden. I will give up everything for you. I love you. I love you… *Dios*, I love you so much.'

Tears dripped from her eyes as the words poured out of him. 'And I love you, my king. With every one of those breaths. For ever.'

EPILOGUE

Eighteen months later

AZAR WALKED INTO their suite, then stopped dead at the sight
of his wife…wearing her wedding dress. It took a second for
him to clock the fat candles dotted around the room, and another nanosecond to take in the various flower arrangements
giving off pleasant fragrances, the bucket of champagne and
what looked like a platter of food from her favourite French
Japanese restaurant.

Then his gaze was back to her, answering the siren call he
never wanted to resist.

'What's this?' he rasped, crossing the room to where she
stood, her hands tucked innocently behind her and her head
wantonly tossed back, watching his every move.

As always, knowing he was her sole focus caused a thrilling and exhilarating kick to his chest, and the roar in his ears
announced loudly that he was alive. And loved by this woman
he loved back more than life itself.

Her smooth skin gleamed in the flickering candlelight and
his fingers itched to touch. To taste. To worship.

'I thought we could enact a different ending to our wedding night.'

Regret stabbed him deep, for letting fear get in the way of
what should have been the start of this profound, meaningful
life he'd found with her.

So of course he nodded enthusiastically, without a single reservation. 'What do you need from me, *mi corazón*? Shall I carry you over the threshold?'

She mused on that for a second, then shook her head. 'I can do without that, thank you. Besides, you've done a different version of that already, remember?' She laughed.

The video footage of him walking out of the palace media room with his queen in his arms had been played several billion times. It had even acquired its own meme, and was the most searched for video clip in the world. Cartana had been awarded the title of 'most romantic destination of the world', and once Azar had agreed to open up his private cave to the public it had become the most popular venue for marriage proposals. Eden had once been filmed feeding him chocolate in a hot air balloon, and immediately gained another two million followers for the official palace social media platforms.

'Do you wish to eat your favourite meal off my body, then have your way with me?' he asked hopefully.

Her head tilted, her smile widening. 'While both of those things are highly tempting, I don't want our bed to smell of sushi.'

'Tell me why you're wearing your wedding dress again, then, my love?'

'Because I just saw the doctor. In a few months I won't fit into it, so I wanted to do this now.'

The roaring in his ears made his heart shake, but the soaring in his blood told him he'd heard her right.

'*Dios*...another baby?' he rasped. His chest felt tight. Ready to explode with love for this incredible woman.

She held out her arms and he rushed into them. It was the only place he wanted to be.

'*Sí, mi rey.* You're to be the father of twins in a little over seven months.'

Azar hadn't quite got over how quickly she'd learned his

language. And how much it touched his heart...and other places in his body...when she spoke in his tongue.

He fell to knees now, this extra blessing finally flooring him. 'Twins?'

She nodded, her ecstatic smile taking his breath away.

'Are you happy?' she asked.

He swallowed. 'More than I ever imagined. More than I ever expected. You're a miracle and I'm so blessed.'

'Then get up, my love. Let's repeat our vows, and then you can show me how much you love me.'

He did so—eagerly.

And in the aftermath, so replete he didn't think he could move, he combed his fingers through her hair. 'What are you thinking, *mi amor*? I asked you that the first time, do you remember?'

'I remember.'

He smiled. 'You hedged a little, then, didn't you?'

She nodded. 'I had to. I was terrified by how you'd made me feel.'

His nostrils flared. 'Tell me now. What were you thinking?'

'I was thinking how much I wanted you to be mine. How much I wanted to belong to you. Always.'

'*Tesoro*... I was yours then. I just didn't know it and hadn't accepted it. But my heart knew. It remained empty, hungering. Desperate to find you again. And it did. So I'm yours. Today. Tomorrow. Always.'

* * * * *

HIDDEN HEIR, ITALIAN WIFE

DANI COLLINS

MILLS & BOON

To Doug,
who is willing to brainstorm ideas with me
even though I reject almost everything he suggests.
Thanks for being such a good sport. I love you.

PROLOGUE

BRIELLE HUGHES WAS cutting the crusts off her three-year-old daughter's toast when the keypad on her rent-stabilized Brooklyn apartment beeped.

"It's only me," her mother called out. "I came to ask if you saw the headlines."

"About?" Bree ignored her phone in the mornings, preferring to give Sofia her undivided attention until she dropped her at day care and was headed to work.

"Your boss getting married. Good morning, good morning." Melissa Diaz showered affectionate kisses on both of them, looking and smelling fantastic.

"I made a picture for you, Gigi." Sofia tilted an earnest smile upward.

"Another one? I'm so lucky." Melissa had moved with them to New York from Virginia Beach two years ago, to help Bree with day care. Last year, she had married the love of her life and now lived a few blocks away, but often dropped by unannounced as she headed out to start her own workday.

She was a stunning woman in her mid-fifties thanks to the skincare regimen she had developed as a beauty queen in her teens. Her startling blue-green eyes against chestnut brown hair and a honey-gold complexion meant she was often called "exotic," which annoyed her, but her unique look continued to land her modeling gigs. They were usually ads for antiaging cream and book covers about midlife wellness, but they were a nice addition to the thriving photography business she ran with her husband.

Bree took after Melissa with a similar tall, slender build and unusual eyes, but she wore her hair in a sleek bob that she touched up with a straightening iron every morning.

"It's on the fridge." Sofia was their outlier, taking after the Italian American Bree had only known for a day. Sofia had dark brown eyes and near black hair that curled into ringlets when bound in a pair of pigtails like today.

"I'll take it home when I come next time, so I don't wrinkle it while I'm out today."

"Are you talking about Sheila?" Bree asked as she slid the triangles of toast to Sofia. "She's been married for years. I was at her twentieth anniversary last August."

"Tank you, Mama," Sofia said from her booster seat.

"You're welcome, baby," Bree said absently, watching as her mother pulled out the chair across from her.

"Your real boss." Melissa clicked on her phone and quoted, "'Domenico Blackwood married Evelina Visconti in a private ceremony yesterday, sending stock prices soaring.'"

"That must be a misprint. We're not allowed to *say* the V-word at work. There's a huge feud between the families."

"That's what I thought you told me when that story came out a few weeks ago, about those two being stranded on an island in Australia."

"That's also something no one dares mention around the office," Bree said wryly.

"Well, they're married now." Melissa offered her phone.

Bree still had to dress and drop Sofia, but she quickly scanned the article, astonished to learn that yes, the owner of WBE, the hotel chain where she was an associate manager in operations, had married a woman purported to be his sworn enemy.

The press release was short, but a related article speculated what it meant for the competing hotel chains. Bree skimmed the recap of the legendary feud and glanced at the photos. The first showed the newlyweds, who were objectively gorgeous. There was a snapshot of Dom with his father, who had died before Brielle started at WBE.

A third photo showed the Visconti family: Evelina with her parents and—

"Oh, my *Gawd*." She nearly dropped her mother's phone into her scrambled eggs.

"What's wrong?" Melissa frowned with concern.

Bree was incapable of speech. She used her trembling fingers to enlarge the image, focusing on the middle brother's face.

It couldn't be.

She flicked to the caption, reading it again, looking for the name Jax or Giacomo. How many times had she searched those names, lacking a surname and having only the vaguest sense he lived in Naples and had a family cottage on Lake Como? How many times had she tried to find him—or at least *see* if she could find him—despite the fact they had agreed their affair would only last one magical afternoon?

A single day that had created a miracle.

She flicked her gaze to Sofia, who was blinking curious brown eyes at her while licking peanut butter off her finger.

Bree looked back at the caption.

Evelina Visconti with her parents, Romeo and Ginevra, and her three older brothers, Nico, Jackson, and Christopher.

Jax.

He hadn't lied to her. They'd both skipped full names so she couldn't fault his keeping quiet that he was Jackson Visconti of the Visconti Group. They were WBE's biggest competitor for more reasons than a family feud. Their hotel chain was renowned worldwide, with a head office a few blocks from where she worked for WBE.

She was aware that the Visconti properties were operated by the brothers, each with his own territory, but she'd never had reason to look them up, otherwise she might have found Sofia's father sooner.

Here he was, staring up at her with an aloof expression and the undeniable sexual charisma she hadn't been able to forget.

Or find in any other man.

"Bree," Melissa said in a mother's mixture of crossness and worry.

"I'm okay. Just surprised." She passed the phone back to Melissa, who didn't miss the way it wobbled in her grip. "Come sit with me before we leave," Bree coaxed Sofia.

Her hands were cold as she gathered her daughter into her lap and hugged her, dropping a kiss on the part in her sweet-smelling hair.

"I don't understand." Melissa looked at the screen then back to her. "This marriage won't affect your job, will it?"

Bree bit back a semi hysterical laugh. It could affect a lot more than that!

"The middle brother." Over her daughter's head, she widened her eyes with significance and nodded at Sofia.

"What!" Melissa got it right away and was equally shocked. "Will you tell him?"

Bree opened her mouth, thinking about how many times she had wished she could. From the moment she'd learned she was pregnant, she had wished she had not left his number behind in a fit of pique.

But would he want to know about their daughter? Bree's father hadn't wanted her. Not really. She would never want Sofia to experience that same cruel indifference. At least when she hadn't known Jax's full name, she hadn't had to take that risk with her.

Now she had an avenue to reach him, but the reality of bringing him into their lives when she had built her world around being a single mother loomed as such a huge shift, she could only say truthfully, "I don't know."

CHAPTER ONE

Four years ago, Lake Como

AFTER TWELVE DAYS of traveling alone, Bree decided it was actually a blessing her mother hadn't been able to come to Italy with her.

She loved Melissa to the moon and back, but for the first time in her life, she was truly self-reliant. It was an important coming of age she hadn't realized she needed until she was living it. This wasn't flying solo to Chicago as a preadolescent to visit her father, or the pseudo independence of heading off to college to live in a dorm. It wasn't playing house with her college boyfriend, Kabir.

This was a far too brief, single-woman-on-a-mission-to-find-herself journey that was reassuring her that she would, in fact, be okay without a man in her life.

Mom had promised she would be. They had survived after Daddy left, hadn't they?

Bree had been devastated by Kabir's rejection. She had wanted to crawl into bed and never come out, but her mother had urged her to, "Take a trip anyway. It will be good for you. Haven't you always wanted to go to Italy?"

The lease was running out on the apartment she had shared with Kabir, so Bree had put her few belongings into storage, closed out the streaming accounts they had shared, and hopped on the plane. After landing in the chaos of

Rome, she'd traveled south to Pompeii, then came north to sample wines in Tuscany. She'd spent three days soaking up the art and architecture of Florence, browsed boutiques in Milan, and spent this morning on a six-mile hike along the shore of Lake Como, weaving in and out of quaint villages and sweet-smelling bowers of nature.

Thanks to her mother's shrewd financial planning, Bree's student loans were manageable, but she was still desperate to get into the workforce to pay them off, otherwise she might have stayed in Europe all summer. She had planned to follow Kabir wherever he found work, but now she would be on her mother's pullout as she built her adult life from scratch.

She turned her mind from that daunting prospect and made a beeline toward an outdoor café. Despite the dwindling balance in her savings account, she was treating herself to a late lunch overlooking the vivid blue water, where the fragrance of wisteria wafted from the trellis above. A sprinkling of guests occupied nearby tables, but the midday rush was over. She was given a seat near the rail and asked for a glass of white wine, then removed her sunglasses so she could browse the menu.

When she heard the maître d' say "Giacomo," with delighted surprise, she glanced up.

Oh.

She'd seen a lot of good-looking men here in Italy, but this one took her breath with his black, curly hair styled a fraction too long. His complexion was swarthy and he wore a shadow of stubble sculpted to accentuate his lean cheeks and strong jaw. On any other man his striped linen trousers and button-down shirt with rolled sleeves paired with a thin scarf would have appeared to be trying too hard. On him, it was casually elegant. Chic and confident. Worldly.

It didn't hurt that he was built like a top-class athlete. His shirt sat against the musculature of his chest and shoulders. His trousers strained across his hips before hugging his long, lean thighs in a way that was both flattering and subtly sexual. His hair was wind tousled, his eyes covered by mirrored sunglasses that…

Was he looking at her?

A sting of self-conscious pleasure touched her cheeks. She looked back at the menu, but her ears strained to hear his voice. He and the maître d' were speaking Italian too quickly for her rudimentary grasp of the language. She couldn't help smiling faintly at their affection, though. Were they related? From the corner of her eye, she caught the way he angled his head to allow his cheeks to be kissed by the shorter man. Perhaps he wasn't interested in heterosexual women?

He's not interested in me. Who would be?

That dark thought was leftover insecurity from Kabir's callous, *You said living together would be convenient and affordable. It was. Now I'm going home.*

The memory was sharp enough to leave her chest feeling freshly impaled. Her next few breaths stung. She reminded herself that she was off men and dating. She didn't care if a stranger looked at her. She wasn't part of the insta-lust, hookup culture. She'd had one boyfriend. Their relationship had been a slow burn and lasted almost three years. She had expected she would marry him.

She'd been kidding herself, though. Wasting her time. Succumbing to Daddy issues.

Her eyes burned and the menu blurred before her eyes.

She *had* to stop pining and wallowing in maudlin self-blame, punishing herself for not being able to keep a man. The whole point of this trip was to leave Kabir and all her dreams for their future in Europe so she could go home and start with a blank page.

"The view is better at this table, Alphonso." The deep voice spoke in affable English with an American accent. A masculine hand descended on the chairback across from her. Mr. Tall, Dark, and Gorgeous waited until she'd lifted her startled gaze to ask her, "Would you like company?"

He *did* like women. Masculine interest radiated off him so unabashedly, he nearly gave her a sunburn with it.

"You're American."

She was more surprised by that than his request to join her. "How did you know that I am?" Was *she* trying too hard, wearing her new shoes from Milan and her sundress from Rome?

"My sister has a similar handbag." He nodded at the tote her mother had given her after modeling it in a photo shoot. "They're made in New York and not well-known enough to have knockoffs yet. May I buy you lunch?"

"Um…" A tingling glow filled her, one her ego drank up like a magic elixir. She was flattered that she'd gained the attention of a man whose magnetism was so tangible. She *had* been mooning over him. And berating herself for not moving on.

This was a bigger leap than she had had in mind, though. If she wanted to start dating, she ought to cut her teeth on a quiet-spoken claims adjuster from Des Moines, not a man with this much overwhelming confidence. She had the sense she could easily be pulled into his orbit and absorbed like light into a black hole.

She was willing to risk it, though. Because this was the new Bree, a woman who was self-sufficient and autonomous and secure in her worth.

"I can buy my own lunch," she said as a precaution, so

nothing would be misconstrued. "But company would be nice. My friends call me Bree." She stood to offer her hand across the table.

"Mine call me Jax. Or Giacomo." He nodded to Alphonso while his hand engulfed hers. He was at least six feet tall with a warm, strong grip and a self-assurance that made her feel special simply because she'd been noticed by him. He pointed at her glass. "The same, Alphonso, *per favore*."

"Of course. I'll tell Chef you're here. He'll be pleased."

"Are you a celebrity?" Bree asked in an undertone as they sat.

"Not at all. Alphonso used to work for me."

"At home? Or do you live here in Italy?"

"Naples, but my grandparents had a cottage here." He waved toward the far side of the lake. "It was their first home when they married. My sister bought it from the estate after Nonna passed. The house is doing its best to slide into the water, but she won't tear it down and rebuild. She wants it saved. She is not here, however." He made that pronouncement with good-natured, put-upon disgust.

"She's in New York?" Bree guessed.

"Yes. She enlists me every week or so to come deal with plumbers or painters."

"Oh, dear." She was both amused and sympathetic. "Is she your only sibling?"

"We have an older brother and another between us. You?"

"Three stepsiblings from my dad's second marriage, but I was basically raised an only child by my single mom." She shrugged, trying not to feel alienated after all this time. "That part of my life is a bit of a hot mess, so I don't talk about it much."

"Let's talk about something else, then. What brings you to Italy?"

"Another hot mess," she said wryly.

Alphonso arrived with Jax's wine and an amuse-bouche. He relayed the chef's suggested menu of three courses. Jax nodded agreement before Bree had finished the mental math on her budget.

When in Rome, she reasoned, and glanced out at the lake.

A soft breeze came off the water and the sound of outboard motors buzzed in the distance. The sun dappled through the greenery above them and music played beneath the lilt of nearby conversation.

It was movie set romantic so naturally she ruined it.

"I'm coming off a breakup," she confided when they were alone again. "I was living with my boyfriend while we were getting our degrees. I thought he would invite me to go to India with him when we finished, so I could finally meet his family. He said they didn't know about me."

Jax's dark brows shot up.

"He said his parents were looking for a wife for him." She swallowed the ache in her throat, but it remained like a scuff behind her sternum. "My takeaway was that he would rather spend his life with a stranger than me." She tried for a light, self-deprecating tone, but she was still deeply hurt.

"You're nursing a broken heart." His mouth twisted with rueful dismay.

Which gave her the thorniest pang of yearning and embarrassment.

"I shouldn't have told you. That's so cliché, isn't it? This is my first date since before I met him. Can you tell?" She shook her head at herself.

His phone buzzed and he took it from his pocket to glance at the screen.

And there he went, she thought, expecting him to use the message to make his escape.

He removed his sunglasses as he read, revealing irises that were dark as black coffee. His mouth tightened.

"You don't have to stay," she said to forestall his rejection. "I realize you thought this might turn into something else."

"I came here for a meal, not to prowl." He turned his phone face down on the table and set his sunglasses beside it, sounding vaguely insulted. "If a vacation fling is *your* goal, though?" His tone turned intimate and self-deprecating. "I would be happy to oblige."

Her heart did a somersault and she couldn't help her smile of amusement.

"How long has it been?" he asked.

"Six—No, seven weeks. But I've started to realize he left months ago."

"No sex?" he guessed.

"That had fallen off, yes," she admitted, cheeks stinging at how rebuffed she'd felt by his lack of interest.

"Literally?" he drawled.

"Might as well have. I never saw it."

They both chuckled.

"I blamed exam stress, but—" She sighed. "You know what? I'll stop talking about him. I've been brooding this entire trip. This is my last day before I catch a train tonight and start my journey home. I'm determined to enjoy it."

"Let me make you this promise, then." He leaned forward. "I don't prey on women who are in a vulnerable place. However, I will buy you lunch and compliment you without mercy, so you know exactly how attractive you are. Later, if you decide to exact quiet revenge by enjoying the best sex of your life, I would be very pleased to deliver that. If not, at least you'll have the satisfaction of having turned *me* down."

Bree nearly swallowed her tongue.

Their server arrived to switch out their course.

Jax leaned back and said, "Tell me what you've seen while you've been here."

He wasn't kidding. He applied himself to making her feel beautiful and interesting and desirable. It worked.

Bree blossomed under his attention, leaning in and talking animatedly with her hands. When she accidentally brushed her ankle against his shin beneath the table, awareness sparked in her belly and never abated. At one point, he caught her wrist so he could study her bracelet, which was a pretty silver bangle she'd bought in Florence with a matching one for her mother. He caressed her wrist before releasing her, leaving her bloodstream fizzing like champagne.

He asked about her degree, which was in business administration. She told him about her father's suggestion she work in health care, which had been one of the few times he'd taken a moment to show an interest in her life.

"He's a heart surgeon so I know how demanding the health care sector is. I'd prefer something with lower stakes that might have opportunities for travel. I'll see what's available when I get home."

"Where's that?"

"Virginia. Is all your family in New York? Do you get home much?"

"They are, but I prefer Italy." His tone cooled enough to let her know that's all he wanted to say about it. "What does your mother do?"

"She's a model. My father was still in school when I was born. Times were tight so she took any work that was offered. I still sometimes walk into a bank and see my mother's face on a poster, advertising high-yield savings accounts."

His mouth tilted, then the heat of admiration filtered into his gaze. "If you look like her, I can imagine she's in high demand. Your eyes are like this water. Blue? Green? Changeable and enigmatic."

"A misrepresentation. I'm actually very boring." She resisted putting her sunglasses back on, feeling naked.

"I disagree."

She reminded herself he was only doing what he'd said he would do, but she was charmed all the same. He was so ridiculously attractive! Her gaze kept attaching itself to his mouth and watching his expressive hands and staring into his eyes. She wanted to touch his hair and press against his chest and tuck her face into the nook of his throat.

The sexual tension simmered as they chatted through their exquisitely prepared meal, splitting a bottle of wine, then lingering over espresso and sharing a pistachio granita.

As their last dishes were removed, Bree looked for their server. "I was serious about buying my own meal."

"Don't insult me. It's already taken care of."

"When? It takes more than lunch to seduce me, you know." It was a lie. She was already looking forward to their goodbye kiss. Already thinking about more.

"I haven't even started trying to seduce you, *bella*. You'll know when I do." His gaze met hers and sent a hot spear of pure lust into her belly, exploding with heat in her loins. "Where is your luggage?"

"At my pied-à-terre. I booked it before my girlfriend asked me to meet her in Zurich so I—" she cleared her throat "—have it until I leave this evening."

"I'll walk you."

Her knees felt too weak to support her as they left. Alphonso waved them off without presenting a bill, but she had lost interest in that. Her world had become the smooth hand that clasped hers as she led Jax down the hot shadows of the streets between the closely set buildings. Her stomach was full of butterflies, her senses piqued with anticipation.

"I've never done this," she confessed, pressing her shoulder against his so she could keep her voice down. "Brought someone home who I've just met."

"You don't have to do anything you don't want to do." His hand loosened on hers, offering to let her pull away.

"I do want to." She tightened her grip and drew him up the outer stairs to the tiny, wrought iron porch of the studio flat.

The single room was dim and cool. She'd closed the blinds against the sunshine before leaving this morning, but the spicy fragrance of the nasturtiums in the window box filled the air. There was a double bed, a small table over a red area rug, and a kitchenette with a microwave and a kettle.

"I'm nervous," she admitted as he closed the door behind them. "I've always considered myself a relationship person. It feels strange that this isn't the start of one. Which I don't expect," she hurried to add. "Frankly, I don't *want* anything serious. I want rebound sex. I just don't know how to do it."

"Allow me to show you." He drew her toward him and pressed her back to the door.

Her heart spun as she reoriented herself with her naked shoulder blades against cool wood. Her hands reflexively went to his chest as he braced his arm over her head and dipped his mouth toward hers.

Wow. His chest was warm and contoured and *solid*. Deliciously intriguing.

"This, by the way, is me seducing you," he teased, and his lips brushed hers.

An electric buzz shot through her system. Her lips parted,

but he didn't accept the invitation. He nuzzled her cheek-bone and temple, nibbled the rim of her ear, murmured something in Italian that sounded pretty and was probably filthy.

His free hand caressed her throat and drew a line along her shoulder and down her upper arm, making her nipples tighten with anticipation, but he didn't touch her breasts. He only trailed those tickling caresses along the skin of her arm while she tried to chase his lips.

She had to slide her hand up to his neck and curl it behind his skull to urge him to come down farther. To seal his hot mouth over her eager lips and *oh*. He kissed her with such slow, drugging impact, she melted against the door.

At a distance, she thought, *This is different*.

Not because there was novelty in kissing someone new, although there was that, but also because his effect on her was so profound.

He lifted his head briefly, eyes glittering with something she couldn't decipher. Heat and revelation, maybe. As though he was also surprised.

Then his lips dragged across hers again, the pleasure sharp and deep and expansive. Maybe it was the freedom of having no history or future with him. It allowed her to let go in a way she wouldn't have if she'd expected to see him again, but she let herself become more and more immersed in their kiss. Letting him feast in his unhurried, claiming way.

Today was her *only* chance to know him in an intimate way, though. She found herself greedy to consume him in one gulp. She didn't want to be coaxed or treated gently. Through lunch and all the light flirting, he'd kindled her curiosity and sensuality. Now raw sexual hunger caught and burned within her. It went beyond yearning. It was craving. Urgency.

She licked into his mouth with blatant invitation and felt him stiffen.

That made her feel powerful, but her smile of satisfaction had barely touched her lips when his hand slid up from her waist and massaged her breast through the light cotton of her dress. His kiss deepened, becoming more demanding as he dragged her into a miasma of passion. His hungry mouth trailed into her throat and her nipple stung where his thumb teased it through the fabric of her dress.

She writhed, pinned beneath the unforgiving door and the press of his weight. When she wormed her hand between them to find the stiff shape pressing against her hip, his breath hissed in.

"Are you sure you've never done this?" he asked in a graveled tone.

"I'm not a virgin, if that's what you mean."

In many ways she felt like it, though. She had never experienced anything like the way he was making her feel. The greed. The *surrender*.

He bent to scrape his teeth across the tip of her breast, then sucked at her nipple through cotton and bra. The intense sensations grew until she whimpered. He straightened. His mouth came back to hers, rough and commanding. Somehow, he had picked up the hem of her skirt. Air danced across her thighs. His touch skimmed her plain underwear, then his wide palm arrived between her thighs, claiming her in a firm squeeze that made her abdomen contract with alarmed excitement. Heat flooded into the press of his hand.

What had she unleashed?

Turning her head, she gasped, "Do you have a condom?"

"I don't need a condom for this, *bella*." He slid the placket of her underwear aside and his fingertip delicately slid into her soaked folds, making her groan with pleasure.

She felt his smile before he smothered her with another kiss.

The sounds from the street below carried in, but all she really knew was the breadth of his shoulders and the drag of his mouth and the way his touch rolled and dipped and circled, making her stomach tense and tremble with anticipation. They kissed in flagrant licks and passionate clashes. She squeezed his erection through his trousers, hoping she was delivering as much erotic delight as she was receiving, but she was losing her hold on reality.

"We should..." She could hardly form words.

"Die your little death, *dolcezza*. It's what you want, isn't it?" His lazy touch slid in a delicious, unrelenting rhythm, invading and retreating.

She couldn't fight it. As climax rose to overtake her, she clutched at his shirt and bit her lip. She pushed her face into the hollow of his shoulder while her inner muscles clamped on the finger that impaled her. Waves of joy rolled over her, making her moan with abandon while he continued to caress her.

He held her close in the aftermath while she leaned weakly into him, panting in astonished joy.

"That is how it's done, *bella*," he said against her ear. "You give me the freedom to touch you and I make you forget where you are."

"Yes, please." She let her head fall back.

He kissed her again, tasting of deprivation. Demand. It thrilled her.

They began pulling at each other's clothes, barely speaking.

CHAPTER TWO

Jax settled onto his back after discarding the condom, still damp with perspiration, head pillowed on his arm, heart rate not yet steady, mind blown by the intensity of his orgasm.

He wasn't sure why their lovemaking had been so potent, but he'd actually forgotten where he was as well. His only point of consciousness had been the way their bodies rang in unison.

Why? It hadn't been that long since his last affair. He was twenty-eight, wealthy, and good-looking. Women threw themselves at him all the time. When they were clear about wanting a brief and uncomplicated encounter, he indulged.

He didn't *need* sex. He merely liked it. A lot.

But as he heard his phone buzz yet again from the pocket of his discarded jacket, he kicked himself for lingering to indulge today. And wondered why it had felt so imperative.

"Do you need to get that?" Bree asked drowsily.

"No." It was his brother, demanding a status report. Nico was up early in New York. Very early. It was a testament to how important it was for Jax to get to Naples and deal with Blackwood. If he had left as scheduled, he would be there by now, signing the deal Nico was badgering him about.

He should leave. Now.

But Bree curled into his side with a sigh of satisfaction,

the kind his ego delighted in. Her head found his shoulder and her soft curves rested against his side.

"Good," she murmured.

He wasn't a cuddler, but he liked the way she fit against him. He liked the smell in her hair where strands caught in his stubble. He liked the taste of her on his lips. Her thigh rested on his own and her fingers traced patterns from the middle of his chest to his navel, making him loath to move.

A tryst with a tourist had been the last thing on his mind when he'd left Nonna's. He'd come to Como for exactly the reason he'd given her. After flying in last night, he had monitored some work this morning, then stopped for a bite on his way to the heliport. Alphonso had been his head of catering until a year ago. He'd also been a running partner. Alphonso had left when he'd fallen in love with a chef, and Jax had provided financing for their enterprise. He dropped in when he could, to check on his investment.

His mind had been on Domenico Blackwood. Despite the financial beating Jax's family had recently delivered, Dom was not staying down. In fact, he was driving up the price on the property Nico wanted, thus Nico wanted Jax in Naples, closing the deal.

Jax thought Blackwood was bluffing. He would overextend himself if he kept raising the bid, but Jax never shirked his responsibility to the family or the Visconti Group.

Almost never.

The second he had arrived at the *ristorante*, his inner caveman had clocked a pretty woman sitting alone. His interest probably would have leveled off at admiration if she hadn't glanced over, arresting him.

Her sea-green eyes had delivered a sexual punch that took his breath. The rest of her was equally compelling. Her lips were heart shaped, feminine, and wearing a pink gloss that set off her golden tan. Her hair was a rich chestnut brown that had been gathered into a messy ponytail behind her neck. The breeze lifted flyaway strands that he wanted to smooth with his hands.

Her sundress was printed with lemons and had narrow straps that would only need a gentle brush off her shoulders to drop the silk around her feet, revealing what his practiced eye discerned were firm, lovely breasts and a lush ass. The lower half of her tanned thigh and bare shin was visible beneath the flirty length of the dress, ending in a chic sandal.

Everything about her called to him in a way he'd never experienced, not even when he'd been engaged to be married.

The painful fallout from that broken engagement was firmly behind him, but it was the reason he stuck to flirtations and flings. He'd assumed his lack of deep connections since then had been a deliberate choice. *He* would decide when he was ready to feel something more than superficial attraction.

He hadn't expected a magnetic sort of carnality to hit him square between the eyes. Or the middle of his chest. Or take hold of his groin like a barbed hook.

American, he had judged her. It wasn't just the handbag. It was the fact she'd met his gaze so boldly. He liked Europe for the fact most people kept their nose in their own business. Americans were always heads-up, eyes locking in readiness to meet, assess, and connect.

He could have—probably should have—left when he realized she was rebounding from heartbreak. Perhaps he would have, if she hadn't been so candid about her desire to move on. If she hadn't been so enchanting and responsive to his slightest touch, blushing when he caressed her wrist.

He'd been utterly entranced by her, watching her lips, losing himself in her eyes.

Her nervousness as she'd led him back here had been another yellow flag, telling him she lacked the sophistication of someone who could separate physical connection from emotional. He'd been prepared to leave if she changed her mind, but when they kissed, she grew bolder, then shattered under his touch.

Good sense had gone by the wayside at that point. He always carried condoms, and it had taken all his control to put one on before falling onto this bed with her.

Somehow, he'd kept from unleashing the full force of his inner beast, but that hadn't lessened the intensity of the culmination. It had been prolonged and so satisfying, it damned near tore him in half.

He still felt turned inside out.

He still felt *hungry*.

It wasn't garden-variety horny, either. Yes, he was recovering and itching with renewed arousal. He had a very healthy sexual appetite, and he couldn't help respond to the feel of her soft curves and the trail of her fingertips against his abs and the brush of her lips as she turned them against his pec.

A deeper sort of insatiable desire was digging claws into him, though. Something that felt thwarted despite the fact they were sated and she was inside the crook of his arm. He was trying not to acknowledge it, but he wanted more. Not just more lovemaking, but more time. More of her.

The last time he'd allowed himself to become deeply entangled with a woman, he'd been forced to choose between his love for her and the kind of man he thought he was. The kind of man he wanted to be. That push-pull had frayed things inside him to the point of nearly snapping. He still hated himself for the way things had played out.

Leave, he ordered himself and drew a breath.

She stretched against him. "You're a man of your word, aren't you?"

"I try to be. Why?" Had she heard his inner thoughts and wondered about his personal code of ethics?

"That was the best sex of my life. As promised. Thank you." She shifted to sprawl herself across his chest, breasts sitting warmly against his rib cage. Her pretty mouth, bruised by their kisses, held a smug smile, but shadows flickered behind the screen of her lashes.

She was remembering sex with someone else, feeling disloyal for comparing.

Jealousy bit him. It was completely misguided. That other man was already out of her life. Jax would be soon as well.

There would be others, though. She was far too passionate to deny herself, and he was inordinately resentful of those future lovers she would take.

He rolled her beneath him. "Best so *far.*"

"Oh?" Her eyes flared with excitement. "I thought all those texts meant you have places to be."

"They can wait." They couldn't, but he brushed aside the veil of obligation that tried to descend on him and used the superior strength in his thighs to open hers. He settled his thickening erection where she was molten and silky, then kissed her until she was buttery soft beneath him. Until she whimpered and rocked her hips, seeking stimulation in the apex of her thighs.

He moved his lips into her throat and slid down so he could graze his stubble in the valley between her breasts.

"Come back," she pleaded, clasping at his shoulders, but he caught her hands and trapped them against the mattress

while he detoured to kiss all the most beguiling places—
her beige nipples and the scented underside of her breast.
The place where her ribs ended and the tremble of her belly
began. Her navel and the point of her hip and the musky
thicket of her bush.

When he was half off the bed, her thighs clenching his
ears and her fingers in his hair, he was exactly where he
wanted to be.

He could have stayed there forever, making her shudder and gasp and sob with need, but even though she was
utterly his in this moment, that primal need to possess her
forever wouldn't abate.

Rather than take her over the edge, he slipped on the other
condom from his wallet and loomed over her, catching at
his control even as he was draping her thighs over his arms,
grasping her hips and driving into her.

"Too hard?" he asked through clenched teeth, body sing-
ing with the need to claim.

"I like it," she gasped. "It makes me feel sexy." Her soft
hands drifted over his shoulders then down to his hips. Her
nails scored his buttocks, urging him on.

"You are." He thrust heavily. "Too sexy." Another thrust.
Deeper. "Dangerous."

Because he wanted to keep her.

He didn't say it. His capacity for speech dried up. Their
noises became animalistic as he made love to her the way
he was aching to, driving her into spasms of pleasure, then
shifting to arch her over his arm while he buried his mouth
in her neck. He rolled so she was straddled across his hips
and tumbled her onto her back again, riding her through one
orgasm after another, keeping her at the heights of arousal
with the pump of his hips and his mouth on her breast and
his hands caressing every inch of her.

She matched him every step of the way, flushed and incoherent with lust, nipping at his lips and lifting her hips to meet his, grasping at him in desperation. Mews of need filled his ears.

They wrecked the bed, but that wasn't enough for him. He wanted to wreck her for future lovers, so she only thought of him for the rest of her life. It was a primitive compulsion. Atavistic.

When her cries of anguished joy rose and his own need for release pressed like a branding iron, he was both fiercely triumphant and incensed that the end had arrived.

He dropped her onto her back and drove into her, trying to forge a link that would chain her to him for the rest of their lives. For all of eternity.

Jagged, ecstatic cries left her as she convulsed beneath him.

His final thrust into the contractions of her sheath was so intense, so pure, so abruptly exquisite, it tore a shout of exaltation from him.

Time stopped. He was held in that paroxysm of painfully sweet pulses. The fiery throbs bathed him in heat, the sensation acute and lasting for what seemed like hours. Days. A lifetime. Until he was hollow and defeated.

With a final shudder, he let his arms fold. He was so weak with gratification, he barely kept from crushing her.

It was only when his erection relaxed and slipped free that he realized the condom had split.

"The condom broke."

"Hmm?" Bree was made of lead. From toenails to eyelids, all of her was too heavy to function. Her brain was a bed of moss, her entire being dulled into supreme indolence. "Issokay." Even her lips were too sated to move. "I'm onna pill."

"Are you sure?" The mattress shifted.

"Yes." She made herself drag her eyes open to find his wide chest dominating her vision. The fine hairs lay in a treelike pattern that stretched toward his light brown nipples.

He was propped on his elbow, looking alert and powerful. His shoulders were satin, his mouth a stern line. His penis was naked so he must have removed the remains of the condom.

When she lifted her gaze to his, he penetrated hers with a steady stare, not nearly as destroyed by their lovemaking as she was. Angry?

"They're in the bathroom next to my toothbrush," she said of the pills, growing indignant. "See for yourself. Or do you mean…" She reached for the sheet, beginning to feel chilled.

The sheet was bunched below their knees. He was lying on the edge of it and didn't move, forcing her to lie here naked before him.

"I had a physical after Kabir left." Her friend had suggested she check that he hadn't been cheating, leaving her with more than disappointment. He hadn't. "I don't have any health concerns. Do you?"

"No. I get checked every year and always wear condoms."

"So it's okay." She quit tugging on the sheet and sat up to hug the one pillow that was still on the bed. "I can get a morning-after pill from the pharmacy on the way to the train station if you're worried." She had time, she noted with a glance at the clock.

Blues hit her as she realized she was not only at the end of her vacation, but very much at the end of her time with him. And, like the end of a vacation, stepping back into reality hit like a slap in the face.

"That would be wise." He rose to gather his clothes.

He paused when his phone buzzed. He drew it from his jacket pocket and sighed, standing naked as he read it, an erotic silhouette of the masculine form against the striped light of the closed blinds.

If her phone had been within reach, she would have snapped him like that and called it "blind passion." Amused with herself, she opened her mouth to tell him, hoping to return to some of the lighthearted humor they had enjoyed all day, but he swore under his breath.

"I have to go." Tense energy had taken hold of him. When he flashed her a look, it was almost as though he blamed her in some way.

"Is everything okay?"

"An ongoing problem with a competitor. Nothing life threatening, but I should have been in Naples by now." He pulled on his clothes. "I'll leave my assistant's card in case you need to get hold of me." He flashed another of those piercing looks at her.

His assistant? That told her where she was in his circle of intimates, didn't it?

She picked up the sheet and pulled it up to wrap across her breasts, under her arms, wondering what she had done to make him rush away—

No. No more blaming herself for men who left. Her heart might be twisting with a desire to maintain the connection they had *seemed* to share, but she'd been a one-afternoon stand for him. He hadn't tried to disguise it as anything more than that. In fact, he'd given her countless opportunities to reject him, and when she hadn't, he'd delivered exactly what he'd promised: electrifying sex that had made her forget Kabir existed.

She refused to pine and torture herself with wondering

if he would have invited her to Naples if she'd been staying in Europe longer. *She* was the one who was unavailable.

"I guess this is the part where I say thanks, this was nice?" She aimed for a flippant tone and must have nailed it because he shot her a look of arrogantly lifted brows that rejected her tepid adjective.

Spectacular was more fitting. So was *unforgettable*. She would be damned if she would stroke his ego, though.

After a charged moment, he showed her a card, then scribbled something on it. "That's my direct line. Reach out if you need to." He left it on the table with a muted snap.

So she could be left on read? No thanks.

She waited for him to ask for her number. To say he wanted to see her again.

"I enjoyed this. *Grazie.*"

He didn't sound grateful. He sounded mad.

She was still on the bed wearing only the sheet. She suddenly felt cheap and couldn't bear it. She only wanted him to leave.

"You're welcome," she said with one of her mother's stage smiles, the kind that covered anything from a wardrobe malfunction to a lost crown. "I have a train to catch so...." She wiggled her fingers. *"Arrivederci."*

His cheek ticked. *"Ciao, bella."*

The door closed behind him and she clenched her hot eyes shut, thinking, *There goes another one.*

No. She might not be the one to physically leave, but she was damned well leaving him behind.

After a quick shower and finishing her packing, she walked out with her suitcase and locked the door, leaving his card on the table without even looking at it.

CHAPTER THREE

Present day...

WHEN HER SUPERVISOR, Sheila, told Bree, "We have a meeting upstairs," Bree's knees began to shake.

It was silly. She often accompanied her boss into meetings on the C-level, usually with Sheila's boss, the COO. Sometimes it was for something as mundane as a marketing presentation.

Today, however, it was just the two of them in the elevator.

"No one else?" Bree asked.

"Dom floated something by me. I'll let him do the honors."

Dom. That was Mr. Blackwood to Bree. Was it a promotion? Her pulse lurched with the excitement of opportunity and the apprehension of the unknown.

She had never actually been in his office. It was a massive space at the top of the Manhattan skyrise with access to a rooftop garden and a view of the East River. The office itself was four times the size of her apartment, not counting whatever rooms the various doors led to. She suspected there was a professional kitchen behind one of them and likely a full bath behind another.

The main room was dominated by his contemporary desk

sculpted from steel. There was a meeting space on one side and a comfortable seating area on the other.

That's where they were invited to join Dom and his new wife, Evelina Visconti. Blackwood now. Still Jax's sister.

Brielle's head lifted off her body. Her legs turned to sand. She shook Eve's hand while barely suppressing her semi-hysterical laugh.

"Congratulations on your recent marriage. I'm sorry my hands are so cold." She feared her palm had been clammy. This was surreal.

"Dom keeps it like the North Pole in here." Eve sent him an exasperated look. "I'll keep this quick so you can get back to the tropics. Please sit. Coffee?"

Brielle accepted purely to warm her hands. She tried to keep an agog look off her face, but her heart was in her throat. Eve's resemblance to Jax was obvious, but she also saw her daughter in her. Since reading the wedding announcement, Bree had been searching Jax online, waffling back and forth on whether to tell him he had a child. He didn't seem to have any serious romantic relationships, which had been her first concern. She was still tallying all the other pros and cons, though, making it hard to concentrate as Eve spoke.

"With our marriage, the two organizations are looking at an eventual alignment of the hotel chains. This is very early days, but I've been tasked with overseeing that process. Dom and Sheila have identified you as one of WBE's key personnel who could be a valuable addition to my team. If you're interested, I'd like to forward the offer, but let me outline the key points. It's a minimum two-year commitment. WBE would grant you a leave so you wouldn't lose your position here. In fact…" Eve glanced at Dom.

"You came to my attention because Sheila identified you

in her succession plan," Dom said. "I hate losing good people because they're stagnating, waiting for opportunities. Experience on Evie's team would give you foundational knowledge of both organizations, something that would inform your role when you take over from Sheila in a few years."

There was a long silence.

Bree belatedly realized she was supposed to speak.

Professionally, this was a dream come true, but her brain was exploding. She would be working with her daughter's *aunt*.

"I—" Thanks to her mother drilling her for years on maintaining poise under pressure, she was able to recover and say something mildly intelligible. "It's certainly an offer I want to consider. You'll have to forgive my shock. I thought I was coming here to talk about the logistics problem with the linen supplier. Which has been dealt with, by the way."

They all chuckled, but it did little to ease Brielle's nerves.

"I want my core team in place by the end of the month," Eve said. "I'll forward the details today. Don't be afraid to consult with an employment agency to evaluate it."

Bree hadn't thought of herself as being at that level, but was flattered when Dom sent a look of mock annoyance toward Eve and griped, "I also don't like losing people because my wife brings them to the attention of headhunters."

Eve grinned and said to Bree, "Call me with any questions. Any at all."

Can I have your brother's number?

Did she want it? She had deliberately refused to take it four years ago. She had regretted that impulsive decision when she had realized she was pregnant, but she'd also chosen to have Sofia knowing she'd be a single parent.

They rose and shook hands again. Bree tried to catch her breath in the elevator.

"I hate the idea of you leaving my team, but I can't think of any good reason for you to turn this down," Sheila said.

Bree smiled weakly. "Neither can I."

Jackson disliked New York at the best of times. November was not the best of times. It was gloomy and drizzly and cold.

Yet, for some incomprehensible reason, his sister had chosen to host her wedding reception here this month. For some equally incomprehensible reason, she had married Domenico Blackwood in a secret ceremony six weeks ago.

Jax was still furious about that. The Blackwoods had given the Viscontis headaches and heartaches for three generations. He was furious with Nico for selling their sister into an arranged marriage to the devil. He was furious with Eve for going along with it.

He was furious with himself. He felt guilty that she'd resorted to such a thing when the roots of this disaster could be traced back to his own negligence four years ago. If he'd gone to Naples as scheduled, Blackwood never would have got the upper hand against them.

As a turn of the knife, Eve had berated all three of her brothers the last time Jax had been here, accusing them of clinging to bachelorhood instead of making a "strategic alliance" the way she had.

She had apologized to Jax later, but her remark hadn't been as cheap a shot as she feared. His broken engagement was seven years old. Eight? She had a point, and it was stuck in him like a poison-tipped arrow. He could have and should have married by now.

All of the Visconti children were expected to follow in

their parents' footsteps with advantageous unions. Like his brothers, Jax had been putting off finding a wife, but his foot-dragging was no longer about Paloma and that unpleasant history. It was about his obsession with a woman he had slept with once.

He couldn't say what agitated him more, knowing that if Blackwood hadn't demanded his attention in Naples he might have stayed longer with Bree, or knowing that if she hadn't consumed him that day, he might not have lost that property to Blackwood. That incident wasn't the whole reason things had deteriorated to the point his sister had been forced to marry Blackwood, but it was definitely a factor.

Jackson owed it to his family—to his sister—to step up with a marriage that bettered their collective position financially and socially, *especially* because of the anguish he'd caused all of them when his first engagement imploded.

At the time, he had been trying to do the right thing, reporting an assault. His fiancée had sided with the perpetrator—her brother. Jax understood that kind of loyalty, but her rejection of him, and the attacks that had followed, had left a mark on his psyche.

Jackson had not only let down his family with his broken engagement, but had caused them real anguish as Paloma's family turned their back on his, siding with Blackwoods against them, fueling those fires of animosity.

It had become so ugly, Jax's father had had to send Jax to Italy to get some peace for the rest of the clan. Jax still carried a heavy weight of thorny responsibility over it.

His guilt and sense of rejection were no reason to dodge his duty, though. It wasn't as though he was averse to marriage. Growing up one of four children, Jax had always presumed he would marry and have a family of his own. That's why he had proposed to Paloma while he was still at university. He'd been in love and hadn't seen any reason to put off starting the life he planned to live.

Love was a very troublesome emotion, though. It clouded judgment and tested loyalty and became delicate and brittle when pressed into the space between right and wrong.

He had been guarding his heart ever since, which was another reason he had pushed marriage and children firmly onto the back burner. His sexual infatuation with a tourist hadn't helped, otherwise he might have considered one of the women his mother had been throwing at him for the past several years. Everything about settling down had felt like settling.

It was time, though. Time to step up and contribute to the family instead of causing scandal and heartache.

He told his mother to arrange him a date for Eve's party.

Typically, Jax flew in the day before an event he couldn't avoid. He landed with enough time to sleep off the worst of the jet lag, ate dinner with his parents, accomplished his purpose, and got the hell out of Dodge.

This trip, however, other appointments had been shoehorned into the schedule.

"Come early for your suit fitting," his mother insisted. She feared Jax's younger brother, Christo, would turn up in flip-flops if she didn't dress him herself.

"While we're together, we'll hold strategy meetings with Dom," Nico said.

After a lifetime of rivalry with WBE, they were moving from competition to alignment between their hotel chains. Eve had been appointed to lead that endeavor, which was an excellent use of her skill set, so Jax was willing to be supportive.

Then there was their father. Romeo wasn't making any demands on Jackson's time, but ever since his surgery, he had sounded...tired. There was every chance he would bounce back over time, but Jax had to face the fact his parents were aging.

It added fuel to his decision to marry, to offer his parents peace of mind.

He arrived four full days before Eve's party. He stayed in his childhood bedroom—one of them, at least. The Manhattan apartment was the family home situated closest to the corporate offices and the primary school they'd all attended before leaving for boarding schools in Europe.

After dinner, he watched football with his father, then patiently allowed his mother to brush invisible lint from the lapel of his jacket the following morning.

"Christo will be here tonight. Remind Nico to come for dinner." She plucked to ensure his sage-green pocket square was exactly one quarter of an inch from the edge of his pocket. Her gaze swept down his black shirt and cream-colored trousers, all the way to his black loafers, ensuring there were no imperfections.

A Visconti was nothing if not well-dressed. Jackson happened to agree with her on that.

"I invited Eve and Dom. They have plans with his sister. Will you take these proofs to her? They're for the place settings and the reception program. I need to tell the printers today if she wants to go ahead." She picked up an envelope from the table in the foyer.

"We have this new thing called texting, Mom. You take a photo and send it."

"We also have couriers, which is how these came to me yesterday. Be mine today since you'll see her anyway." She offered the envelope. "This process has been so rushed. I hope when you boys marry, you'll give me more notice."

He took the envelope without speaking.

Her smooth expression grew contrite. "I didn't mean anything by that."

"I know."

She wasn't deliberately reminding him of his broken engagement. At the time, she and Romeo had thought he was too young to marry anyway, insisting he wait at least a year. None of them had expected a breakup that would turn so ugly.

"You'll like Tabitha," she said, mentioning his date for the party. "She's very bright, educated in Paris, spent time in Tuscany and loves Italy. I've known her mother for years. Her parents were already coming, so this works out well. I've seated you with them so you can get to know them as well."

He ignored the twist of resistance in him and the sensation of a rope dragging him somewhere he didn't want to go.

"I'll see you tonight." He kissed her cheek and left.

Twenty minutes later, he entered the Visconti Group building and would have been waved through, but he paused to ask Security, "Do you know if my sister is here yet?"

"She's on twenty-eight, sir."

"Thanks." He was glad for the excuse to check in with Eve away from the rest of the family. Away from her husband.

He would die for any of his siblings, but Eve had always been the one he was closest to. While she'd been at school in Switzerland, she had often stayed with him in Naples, rather than flying home for long weekends. She had never made him talk about what had happened with Paloma, but had always been available if he wanted to.

That's why her Peter Pan comment had landed so hard on him. He couldn't have known how badly things would turn out with Paloma, but that was no excuse for making her carry the load where marriage and the family legacy were concerned. If he'd taken action sooner, she wouldn't be married to Blackwood.

He should have crushed Blackwood when he had the chance, instead of getting his rocks off. God, he hated himself for that negligence.

Nothing like it would happen again. He might have given in to his libido to the detriment of his responsibilities once, but he was past puerile self-indulgence now.

Case in point, the receptionist on this floor offered him a starry-eyed look and sweetly offered to escort him to the boardroom where Eve was conducting a meeting.

"I can see the door," he said drily.

He ignored the stares as he walked through the bullpen of cubicles and peered over the stripe of frost on the boardroom's glass walls. Eve was at the far end, circling something on a smart whiteboard. A half dozen people were at the table, faces turned toward her as they listened attentively.

He knocked and entered.

"Jax!" Eve beamed with surprised pleasure. "My brother, Jackson, everyone. He runs Visconti's Euro division."

"Excuse the interruption." He sent a polite nod to the half dozen faces that swiveled to face him. "Our mother—"

Bree. The sight of her punched the breath clean out of him.

She was far more beautiful than he had allowed himself to remember. She wore a navy blazer over a turquoise-colored top that brought out her startling eyes and made her golden complexion glow. Her russet brown hair fell in a silky curtain to her jaw, framing fine-boned features while giving her a chic, businesslike air.

Was she thinner? Or were her cheeks hollow because she was slack-jawed with shock?

He was taken aback himself. By the sight of her and by the weight of desire that landed in his gut like a comet hitting the ground.

For four years, he'd been wanting this woman, only this woman. Here she was. At last.

But what was she doing *here*? He frowned, moving past shock to puzzlement. Did she know Eve was his sister?

Her gaze dropped to the tablet in front of her. A fierce blush rose in her cheeks.

"Let me introduce you to everyone." Eve's voice was a half note higher than normal. She rattled off names that he made no effort to remember, unable to look at anyone but Bree.

"And Brielle Hughes, also from WBE," Eve finished.

Brielle. Not Brianna, as he'd assumed all this time. He vaguely recollected her name from an announcement about Eve's team. He hadn't put together that Brielle could be Bree. It hadn't occurred to him that the elusive unicorn he'd thought resided in Virginia could be here in New York working for his *sister*.

At the sound of her name, Bree lifted her lashes, but her smile was…a mask.

He'd seen that expression on her face once before, when she had said, *This was nice. Arrivederci.*

She met his gaze very briefly, only long enough for him to read apprehension behind that false smile. Was she afraid he would say something to embarrass her? Or was that inability to meet his gaze something else? Guilt?

His senses prickled, trying to parse out the cryptic signals floating on the air between them. Suspicion filled him, but he wasn't sure why.

"You should join us for lunch," Eve was saying.

CHAPTER ONE

'To WILD OATS and Mommy issues. The first brought us into the world, the second has kept us on our toes and made us the men we are.'

Prince Azar Domene of Cartana groaned loudly, his crystal flute filled with Dom Perignon lowering a fraction as he shook his head. He could count on Teo making such outrageous toasts every year.

'*Dios*. You could just wish the old man a simple happy birthday so we can get on with the drinking, you know,' griped Valenti, the older of his twin half-brothers by five and a half minutes. The scar slashing just above his temple twitched as he shook his head.

Teo grinned and punched him in shoulder. 'I didn't fly four thousand miles to make mediocre speeches.'

'And watch it with the old. I'm only three months older than you,' Azar warned.

Teo grinned. 'Speaking of wild oats—'

'Don't,' Azar warned, fully anticipating what was coming.

He didn't need a reminder of those wild six months three years ago. They were branded into his brain indelibly. If there was even a sliver of comfort to be taken from the circumstances surrounding losing his best friend, it was that his half-brothers had been there to offer support.

Teo shrugged. 'Not talking about it doesn't mean it's going to go away.'

To his credit, Teo now spoke in a more sombre tone, respecting the gravity of this part of their history. Of the paths of chaos their mothers had wrought with their bitter rivalry, leading to those 'Mommy issues' his brother mocked so glibly.

'But there's a time and a place, brother,' Valenti muttered, sliding his twin a hard, speaking look. 'Azar's birthday may not be the right time. Hell, you own and run a multi-billion-dollar fashion house. How do you not know the art of subtlety and nuance?'

'You know the part of the ostrich I like?' Teo asked as Valenti rolled his eyes. Then he sobered. 'Their feathers. You can make a sexy statement with those. The burying their head in the sand part? Not so much.'

'You're so busy pushing everyone into doing "the right thing",' Valenti said, with mocking air quotes. 'What about you?'

Azar watched Teo's face tighten with a punch of curiosity and pity. Those wild months in the Arizona desert, in Paradise Valley, had taken their toll in one way or the other. Valenti had delved deeper into his usual frozen solitude while Teo, the polar opposite of his twin, had given debauched revelry a run for its money.

Although they'd never spoken of it, Azar was very aware that his brothers had arrived in Arizona straight from a visit to their father, weighed down with more baggage than usual.

'There's nothing to report,' Teo answered, surprising them all. 'Sometimes you just have to cut your losses.'

Azar watched Valenti's eyes widen and knew he was about to probe deeper, verify whether he spoke of their father or mother. Or if it had something to with the new creative director he'd hired. He was going to intercept by speaking words he wished he didn't have to. But they were necessary, if only to quiet the demons for a hot second.

'Another toast. And, yes, I can make a toast on my own birthday.' He tightened his gut and raised his glass, his chest burning with anger, regret and shame-coated bitterness. 'To absent friends.'

Teo's face shuttered. A muscle ticked in Valenti's jaw. For a handful of seconds they said nothing, all three dwelling on memories. Azar knew both Teo and Valenti felt guilty for being caught up in their own drama and not realising the chaos unravelling in Arizona until it was too late.

Teo raised his glass. A beat later, Valenti followed suit. 'To absent friends.'

Azar nodded in gratitude.

Courtesy of his father's wild-oat-sowing history—siring three sons born within months of each other by two different women—he'd learned a hard lesson in not glossing over things. Secrets led to festering wounds and shattered trust. Hell, he wouldn't be toasting his absent friend if he'd taken his own advice three years ago. Nick's death had been senseless and deeply shocking, a product of suppressed sentiments and acute misunderstanding that would've been salvaged if everything had been laid out in the open.

He couldn't lay the entire blame on Nick or himself. No, a good chunk of that laid with another. The woman who'd created carnage, disappeared from the scene of the accident that had taken Nick's life, and then seemingly off the face of the earth. It grated deeply that neither the police nor his own expert security team had been able to locate her after all this time. Depriving him of essential closure and, yes, a little retribution.

But that was an ongoing task he wasn't going to dwell on today, on his thirty-fifth birthday. Not when he had other news to impart. Since it wasn't happy tidings, he'd waited until the party was almost over. His half-brothers would need a minute to process.

'I have news,' he said, when another round of champagne had been poured.

'You're planning another months-long bender? Count me in,' Teo said.

He managed a smile, until the weight of destiny wiped it away. 'Papá is going to call you two this coming week. But I think you should hear it from me first. His health problems are worsening. His doctors say they've done all they can.'

Valenti surged to his feet, his champagne forgotten on the table. 'What? When did this happen?' His usual gravel-rough voice was even coarser.

'And why did you wait till now to tell us? You stood there and made me toss out nonsense when you knew this all along?' Teo growled, his face dark with disappointment and anger.

'The news wouldn't have been any different two hours ago. And he didn't want me to tell you just yet—'

'Because his bastard sons aren't important enough to know?' Teo grated, his nostrils flaring.

Since he knew what it felt like to be an afterthought, to be the unfortunate cog caught between warring spokes, Azar looked his brother in eye and answered firmly. 'What he thinks doesn't matter. I told him I wouldn't keep it from either of you because you deserved to know.'

He let them digest that for a moment, then breathed in relief when they both nodded. Traces of anger lingered on Teo's face but he folded his arms, his voice hard and serious when he demanded, 'Has he sought a second opinion?'

Azar's mouth twisted. 'What do you think?'

Valenti grunted. 'I'm sure he's seen ten different specialists by now.'

'Try a clean dozen,' Azar said. 'Where do you think we got our trust issues from?'

Teo's mouth twitched, then he exhaled long and hard. 'I'm calling him before morning. You know that, right?'

There was the faintest whiff of disquiet within the curt response, also familiar to Azar.

That need for a connection that repeatedly eluded all of them.

He nodded, then twisted his glass between his fingers.

'There's more?' Valenti surmised, his eyes narrowing.

There was a reason Valenti excelled as one of the most sought-after security specialists. He watched. He listened. And he missed nothing.

Except that one essential time.

A time Azar knew had scarred his brother for life, driven him deeper into his silent turmoil.

Azar nodded again, fighting the different emotions attacking him. '*Sí*. He's stepping down from ruling. I'm to become King in three months.'

Their expressions morphed from sombre to shocked surprise. They didn't offer immediate congratulations, as members of the soon-to-be-his council had, with their eagerness to switch allegiance and commence with the boot-licking and jostling for power almost nauseating to watch.

Teo spoke first. 'Are you okay with that?'

Azar debated the tough, exposing question for a minute. It was what he'd been groomed for all his life. All he knew. And despite the odd self-indulgent occasion of wishing for another life, it was all he was destined to be. That unwavering duty had been driven into him from birth.

'I have to be. For the sake of his health. For the sake of the kingdom.'

Valenti nodded, then a moment later he was offering a one-armed hug. 'Congrats, *hermano*. I don't envy you for a second myself, but you've got that kingly crap down to a fine art, so I think you'll be fine.'

Teo laughed and offered his own hug. Then, 'I'm guessing lengthy benders are a thing of the past? I'll take a six-day one, if your kingly duties can swing it.'

'Any more talk of benders and my first duty as King will be to force you both to use your proper regal titles.'

His brothers reared back, mirrored looks of horror on their faces. 'Hell, no!'

Azar suspected that their rejection of their titles had something to do with the ugly vitriol with which their mother had fought for them to be titled. His mother had fought for the exact opposite, wanting *'King Alfonso's bastards'*—as she'd so scathingly labelled his half-brothers—not to be given their due titles.

There was a certain stain to using blackmail, subterfuge and downright emotional torture to gain the upper hand in the power and prestige dynamics that left a bitter taste in your mouth. Their mothers had fully engaged in both, often with their father absenting himself and leaving his sons at the mercy of the vitriol. That he had been embroiled in all of it through no desire or fault of his own made Azar understand his brothers' inclination to distance themselves from the darker side of the throne of Cartana.

'It's bad enough that our mother insists on calling us by them in public,' Teo griped.

'And that you've been labelled the "Playboy Prince of The House of Domene"?' Valenti added, one mocking brow raised at his twin. 'A clunky mouthful, if you ask me, but if that what you need to ensure you're not doing badly on the ladies' front, then I don't begrudge you...'

Azar started to smile as his brothers mercilessly ribbed each other. Then movement from the corner of his eye snatched his attention and he stared, the blood roaring in his ears.

It wasn't.

It couldn't be.

She'd been missing for almost three years. Rumoured to have either walked away from the wreckage or even presumed dead, even though her body had never been found with Nick's.

It wasn't her.

Was it?

He was moving before he fully clocked himself. The shattering of glass signalled that he hadn't set his champagne glass down properly.

'Hey! What the hell…? Azar? Is everything—?'

'Excuse me,' he grated roughly.

But *why* was she moonlighting as a waitress? Had she fallen this far from grace? Not that being a career hostess and a leech, dedicated to extracting as much money as possible out of billionaires, was in any way a pinnacle of grace.

'Um…it's just…you caught me by surprise.'

Azar sucked in a slow, sustaining breath. 'You just admitted you know who I am.'

She nodded impatiently. 'Yes. You're Crown Prince Azar of Cartana. I've seen you…and your brothers…in the news—'

She stopped, bit her lip, and now they weren't pinched at all. They were the deep pink he last recalled them being as they wrapped around his—

'I'm sorry, I'm not sure what the correct form of address is.'

'It is *Your Highness*,' Ramon, his head of security and a stickler for protocol, supplied icily.

The tray in her hand wobbled. Her breath stalled as she struggled to keep it upright. Another flick of his wrist and one bodyguard stepped forward and relieved her of it.

'Wait—what are you doing? I'm working.'

'Not any more. Come with me.' While he was used to audiences, large and small, Azar wasn't in the mood to air this particular item of dirty laundry in public.

He turned, nodded at his security chief, and headed for the corridor leading to his private suite.

'What—? Why—? I haven't done anything wrong.'

After a low-voiced warning from Ramon, her footsteps trotted behind him.

The moment she entered his suite her escape was effectively blocked by Ramon and his crew, and the door shut behind them all. He spun around.

'Now. You have ten seconds to confess the reason behind this poor excuse for a disguise before I have you arrested.'

Eden stared at the man standing before her. The hands braced on his hips intensified his already formidable aura, rendering him more intimidating, and yet indecently *hot* enough to slam her heart against her ribcage.

She would've thought she was immune to such displays of power, wealth and privilege from drop-dead gorgeous people by now. This was Vegas, after all.

But no.

His Royal Highness the Crown Prince of Cartana was easily head and shoulders above the normal crème de la crème.

She'd been lucky to land this gig when one of the other girls had come down with a chest infection. She'd grabbed it with both hands, even though it had meant scrambling to find childcare for Max. The promise of double pay and a chance to repay her long-suffering elderly neighbour for stepping in with help was too good to pass up.

Except she stood to earn nothing at all if she got herself fired for whatever transgression His Royal Grumpiness deemed she'd committed.

She flinched as the door nicked shut behind her. Her ten seconds had passed. His security guards had left, leaving her alone with the most formidable man she'd ever met.

'I don't know what you're talking about,' she ventured briskly.

Prince Azar's square jaw, a source of infinite fascination in and of itself, with the chin cleft that was a disgraceful personal weakness for her, grew even more eye-catching as it clenched.

He didn't need to pinch the bridge of his nose in a display of fraying patience. She got that loud and clear as his hands dropped, and he sauntered closer.

Eden would have backed away if her spine hadn't snapped

The sunlight spilling through the curtains caught his dark curls, then his eyes and cheeks. Eden wasn't sure why her heart dipped into her belly, then nosedived to her toes. Millions of men had clefts in their chin. This was merely a coincidence, she insisted, as she bundled Max into warm clothes.

At the park near her apartment they made a game of picking flowers, Max faithfully reciting the colours and excitedly clutching the bouquet as they walked the quarter-mile to the cemetery.

The churning in her belly intensified as she stood before Nick's tombstone, suppressing her frustration and panic at the thought that she might never recover those three months she'd lost.

She urged Max forward. 'Come on, baby. Put the flowers here.'

She smiled shakily at his faint protest at relinquishing his colourful bouquet. But glancing up at her, and perhaps sensing her mood, he stepped forward and dropped them onto the grey marble.

Crouching down to his level, she brushed a kiss on his cheek. 'Good boy.'

She was basking in his smile when the tingling danced over the back of her neck. She glanced up. Several cars dotted the streets dissecting the cemetery, and two dark-tinted SUVs were parked a short distance away, but nothing stood out to her.

Shaking her head at herself, she silently wished Nick a happy birthday and caught her son's plump hand in hers. She wasn't going to dwell on her jumpy emotions. They were due at Mrs Tolson's for pancakes in forty-five minutes, and the older woman—a former school principal—disliked tardiness, although she was a little more flexible when it came to Max.

Smiling fondly at the thought, Eden slowed her steps to match his tiny, tottering ones as they headed home.

They arrived home with five minutes to spare and stopped at her apartment to wash Max's hands.

'Are you looking forward to pancakes, baby?'

'Pancakes!'

Laughing, she opened her front door.

Then squeaked at the tall, dark and deadly handsome figure filling her doorway. 'Y-you—what are you doing here?'

Prince Azar stared down the aquiline blade of his nose at her, his stormy grey eyes faintly mocking. 'I warned you that we would meet again, Eden. Did you think I was—?'

He froze as Max's chubby hand grasped the door and pulled it wide, his curiosity unfettered as he looked up and *up* into the face of the stranger on his doorstep.

A stranger who stared back, his eyes flaring, then probing deep. *Deeper.* His body seemed to turn to stone and a sharp inhalation lanced from his throat a long moment later.

The human brain, as Eden had unwillingly learned over the past three years, was a peculiar, fascinating and often cruel organ. Because it chose that moment to remind her of the sharp and ominous déjà vu she'd felt looking into her son's eyes two hours ago. To remind her of that alarming sensation when she'd touched Max chin's last night and lingered on the shallower version of the very cleft she was staring at now.

'I don't care what you want. I need you to leave.'

It was a plea couched as a warning.

The fact that it took several seconds for him to hear or grasp her words spoke volumes. When he did, the eyes that met hers were at once pitying and condemning. As if strongly recommending that she mourn her old life as she knew it because he was about to steamroller and subjugate it *irrevocably.*

'Who is this?'

The query was ludicrously mild, considering what his eyes and body promised. Considering his immovable position in her doorway. Considering how each bodyguard subtly positioned himself, taking cues she couldn't entirely comprehend from their prince.

Her hand moved from Max's to his shoulder, gathering him essentially closer, ready to protect, to *die* for her offspring.

'He's my son. Now leave,' she repeated.

Her voice shook, but held. As visceral as the resolution in his eyes. And she made sure he witnessed the fighting resolve in hers.

'We both know that's not going to happen.'

A sound whistled up her throat. Dismay. Fury. Panic.

Reminding herself to remain calm for Max's sake—a demeanour she absently realised this man was also adopting, although she suspected he was infuriatingly unflappable in most circumstances—she raised her chin. 'I can have the authorities here in minutes.'

'Under what charge? Visiting an old friend?' His gaze dropped to Max. 'Or something else?'

Her breath strangled in her lungs. 'We're not friends. A-and I don't know what you mean by "something else".'

His jaw clenched. 'Let me save you the trouble. You'll get nowhere by calling the police. Not least because I've committed no crime. And I have diplomatic immunity. Make no mistake: I'm not leaving until we've cleared up a few things.' Again, his eyes dropped to Max, his chest expanding on a breath. 'Perhaps several things.'

Accepting his words at face value was the quickest way to get rid of him, she suspected. The quickest way to remove his rabid interest from her son.

'At least let me take him next door.'

Silver-grey eyes darted back to her, narrowed into lethal slits. 'Who or what is next door?' he asked, in a voice draped with silk and danger.

'My neighbour. She—we're having breakfast with her. She's expecting us.' She looked down as Max, tired of the standoff, attempted to step out.

Prince Azar stiffened, his hands slowly emerging from his coat pockets as if ready to physically restrain her son.

Eden pulled him back, then yanked him into her arms when he protested.

'It's okay, baby.'

'Pancakes! Pancakes!'

Hoisting him up had brought him to eye level with Prince Azar, a foolish but ultimately inevitable move. Because his scrutiny of her son's face was immediate, and so thorough it shook the ground beneath their feet.

'Dios mio,' he breathed, on the third, fourth...*dozenth* pass.

'Please. I don't want— Don't frighten him.'

'Mama...?'

She kissed Max's cheek, smoothing a hand down his back as he wriggled harder.

'Which door is your neighbour's?'

'Five B.'

A subtle flick of his fingers and three of the six guards were repositioned in front of Mrs Tolson's door. Prince Azar stepped back, his eyes riveted to her.

'Half an hour while he eats. And we talk.'

Even though she suspected it was futile, she let her speaking glare echo what she felt about his edict.

The moment she stepped out he fell into step beside her. His presence bore down on her like a ton of bricks, but a quick glance showed his attention was riveted on Max. Who in turn stared at him with wide silver eyes.

Silver eyes... Oh, God.

She swallowed her trepidation as she arrived in front of Mrs Tolson's door. Before she could knock, one of the bodyguards stepped in front of her and rapped sharply on the door.

'Coming,' the voice echoed faintly from within.

As footsteps drew nearer, the bodyguard positioned himself firmly in front of the door, ensuring he was the first thing poor Mrs Tolson saw when she opened the door.

'Great timing. I was just— Who are you?' Thankfully there was no alarm, just the sharp query of a former educator used to dealing with people twice her size.

'Can you move, please?' Eden said, as firmly as possible without frightening her son.

'Not yet,' Prince Azar forestalled.

Then he gave one of his subtle commands.

Before his guards could act, Eden stepped closer to the door.

'Don't you dare!' Everyone froze. Prince Azar's eyes snapped with unholy fire. She didn't care. 'Whatever you're ordering them to do, the answer is no.'

'Miss Moss, security protocol dictates—'

'I don't care.' She cut across the guard who'd chastised her last night. 'You will not invade my neighbour's privacy.'

'Eden? What's going on?'

Sidestepping the bodyguard—to his bristling displeasure— she managed a strained smile. 'Do you mind having breakfast with just Max for now, Mrs Tolson? I'll join you shortly.'

No matter what the Crown Prince dictated, she intended the encounter to be short. And uneventful.

Please, God.

She set a wriggling Max down and everyone, including the bodyguards, watched him toddle off into the apartment and head straight for the box of giant Lego Mrs Tolson kept solely for him.

'Yes, of course,' her neighbour echoed, but her worried eyes flittered over the men gathered behind her, inevitably lingering on the most formidable one of all. 'Doesn't answer my question, though.'

The Crown Prince stepped forward then, and it irritated Eden no end that his guards took a respectful step back, giving him room to slot himself next to her.

She took a breath and her stomach tightened.

Sweet heaven, he smelled delicious. Mouth-watering in

a way no one hellbent on harassing a single mother and her child had a right to smell.

He held out his hand to Mrs Tolson and Eden watched her elderly neighbour's cheek flush as she caught her first proper glimpse of Crown Prince Azar.

'I'm Prince Azar Domene. Eden and I would be grateful if you could be with... Max for a while.'

Had his voice caught, saying her son's name?

Eden's insides zapped with wild currents as she watched his gaze fly to Max and *linger.*

'Oh. Well, yes, of course. But—'

'*Gracias,*' he slid in smoothly. Then, with another charged stare, he stepped back. 'Two of my guards will keep you company, if that's not too inconvenient?'

Courteous words that didn't give a single ounce of room for negotiation. Mrs Tolson's head was already bobbing as he turned to Eden, clasping her arm and steering her back towards her apartment.

'Invite me in,' he said at the door.

Tension knotted in her chest. 'Do I have a choice?'

He shrugged. 'There's always a choice. No matter how much you might want to convince yourself otherwise.'

She felt the barb lodge itself beneath her breastbone, despite having no clue what she'd done to deserve it. She entered her tiny one-bed apartment, telling herself she didn't care what the shabby but neat space looked like to a man born into royalty, with unfathomable riches, power and influence.

But a tiny part of her couldn't dismiss that knowledge of falling short. The reminder that, as a child, she'd dreamed of the white picket fence and the loving two-point-four children and family life. And even growing up with the often debauched excesses of Vegas, with very rare glimpses of wholesome, loving families, that kernel of hope had somehow not only survived, it had also grown with the arrival of Max.

One touch...one kiss on top of her newborn's head and that

kernel had sprouted into a towering vow to do everything in her power to create a loving home for her son. Even if that home was just for two.

Those dreams would never come true for herself. But she would take pride in knowing it hadn't been for lack of trying. A vindictive father who'd never accepted her but ensured she could never claim anything meaningful from him for herself had seen to that. And maybe she wasn't entirely over the heartache that the man who'd so cruelly told her he wished she'd had never been born had gone out of his way to use his money and influence to keep tabs on her, killing job opportunities before she could secure them, but as long as she had breath in her body she would *not* be cowed.

Pushing the bleak thoughts away, she flinched when the door clicked ominously shut behind him.

'Speak.'

'Excuse me?'

His nostrils flared, giving him an air of impossible regal authority. 'I'm hanging on by a thread here, Eden.'

The faintly lyrical enunciation of her name started a shiver through her system. One she desperately clamped down upon before it took complete hold of her. This wasn't a time to be finding anything about this man attractive. Not when her senses were shrieking of a danger far more potent than the kind she was used to from powerful men like him.

'And that's my fault how?' she snapped—then held up her hand, reminding herself that she needed to get through this as quickly as possible and get back to Max. 'Look, I don't know what you want me to say. You seem to think you know me, but I assure you I have no recollection of our ever meeting.'

And yet more and more she suspected he had something to do with her missing memory. And that terrified her more than anything.

'Are you for real?' he asked.

'You asked me that last night. My answer hasn't changed.'

His jaw clenched so hard she feared it would crack. 'I ought to commend you, Miss Moss. In my whole life, only one person has been able to pull the wool over my eyes so effectively. Not once, as I thought, but twice. Would you like to take a guess who that person is?'

Dread turned her bones to lead. 'Me...?'

'You.' His smile was almost self-chastening. 'Which would stun most people. Because usually I'm an excellent judge of character.'

'What can I say? Can't win them all.'

The last vestiges of his smile disappeared, and that ferocious gaze pinned her in place once more.

'What were you doing at Nick's graveside an hour ago?'

She gasped. 'You were there? Watching me?' At his sustained, pointed silence she blurted, 'Why?'

'Answer my question.'

'Because I... I knew him?'

His eyes narrowed. 'Is that a question?'

No way was she going to tell this man about the most harrowing few months of her life—especially when she still didn't remember most of it.

'What do you care?'

The flash of bleakness that shadowed his chiselled features was immediately chased away by fury.

'Mr... Prince... Your Highness,' she said, 'I'm going to say this once, and then I'd like you leave. Because if you don't, I will call the police. And, contrary to how powerful you think you are, the authorities here don't take kindly to intruders who outstay their welcome.'

That faint trace of amusement lifted the corners of his lips again, but it evaporated in a nanosecond. 'This should be interesting.'

She ignored his arid cynicism in favour of gathering her composure to revisit a period of her life that had the ability to make her soul quake. Because it remained shrouded in thick, dense fog, with her every effort to uncover it frustratingly unsuccessful.

'I remember Nick Balas from his visits to the casino where I worked here in Vegas three years ago. I was a waitress there, and he—he was nice to me.' A sharp shard of memory attempted to intrude, but it soon danced away. 'At least I think so...'

She paused when the Prince's eyes narrowed.

'I caution you against speaking ill of the dead, Miss Moss...'

'If you're going to threaten me about Nick, too, save your breath. I've had all the warnings I can stomach—'

'What do you mean by that? Who has threatened you?'

The bark of laughter charred her throat. 'It's more like who didn't.' She shook her head. 'We're veering from the subject...and I want to get back to my son.' She paused when he stiffened again, his eyes flashing with a fierce light before he gave a brisk nod. Sucking in deep breath, she continued. 'I remember talking to Nick a few times...and then I woke up in hospital three months later...pregnant, and with no recollection of who I was. I was told I'd been found on the road in the middle of nowhere, but I don't remember.'

His eyes widened fractionally. Then deep laughter rumbled from his throat.

Despite the laughter being at her expense, Eden couldn't stop herself from gaping in wonder at the breathtaking transformation of the man. He looked carefree, as if he had everything he wished for at his fingertips, in that way he was portrayed in glossy magazines that made even the most cynical woman stop, stare and sigh. That made women *hope* despite suspecting those hopes would never be fulfilled because he was so far out of their league as to be in a different galaxy.

She stared. Every cell in her body tightening and straining at that soul-slashing rumble of sound. Then it was transmitted straight between her legs. Dampening her core. Plumping her flesh. Triggering a stark, breath-stealing *yearning*.

Even after that brief, stunning transformation was wiped away, and his implacable displeasure was re-established, the sensation remained.

'Amnesia?' The word was drenched with abject scepticism. 'That's how you want to play this?'

For a moment she was bewildered by that response. Then the fact of being ridiculed over something so vital to her sparked fresh anger. 'How dare you?'

He stepped up to her, his face etched with superior regal effrontery. 'How *dare* I? You think I should tolerate you vilifying my friend and simply accept it?'

She blinked, shock unravelling through her before a degree of understanding layered over it. 'Is that what this is all about?' When his face clenched again, she rushed on. 'You think I'm playing games? I can prove I'm not.'

Keen eyes dissected her, then he nodded. 'Fine. I'll bite.'

She shook her head. 'Not until you give me some answers. Why are you here? Why did you follow me?'

'No, Miss Moss. That's not how this is going to go. Let's see this proof you have first.'

Eden hesitated, wondering if she'd been too rash. She didn't know this man, after all, and baring her medical secrets to him shouldn't have been her first choice. But the warning shrieking at the back of her head, telling her to be rid of him asap, wouldn't let her prevaricate.

Pulling her phone from her pocket, she dialled the number she'd used far too many times in the last three years.

It was answered after three rings. 'Dr Lloyd Ramsey speaking.'

'Hi, Dr Ramsey, it's Eden.'

'Eden? You're not due for a check-up for another month. Is everything all right? Have you had any memory issues?'

Prince Azar stiffened, his eyes narrowing at her pointed glare.

'Um...no. Everything's fine. But... I'm here with...with someone who is a little sceptical about my condition. I'd like you to explain it to him, please.'

A slight hesitation ensued. 'Unfortunately this isn't the first time one of my patients has faced this, but I'm reluctant to do this over the phone without—'

'I'm happy for you to record my consent, Dr Ramsey. I just need to you to tell Prince—him—about my condition.'

The doctor sighed. 'If you're sure. Am I on speaker?'

'Yes. Go ahead.'

In brisk words he explained her diagnosis of retrograde amnesia, how there was no telling when or if her memories would return, and the importance of her not unduly stressing over it—which was easier said than done.

Prince Azar Domene listened to the prognosis with a thunderous frown which didn't disappear once she'd thanked her doctor and ended the call.

In silence he paced the small space, and she felt the atmosphere charging until she was seconds from exploding.

'You visited Nick's graveside with your son,' he bit out, and the sharp edge to his voice jangled her nerves anew.

'You already know that, since you had me followed.'

A tic rippled in his jaw, and there was a curious hesitation in his face before he bit out, 'Is he Max's father?'

Heat crept up her face. As much as she wanted to be worldly about it, or consign it to her amnesia, she couldn't help but feel a sting of chagrin and shame for her situation. Because this time three years ago she wouldn't have believed herself capable of sleeping with a man she'd just met—especially a spoilt trust fund playboy who believed the world was his for the taking.

'I... I think so, yes.'

His nostrils pinched in a sharp inhalation. 'You mean you don't know?'

Exasperated, she waved her phone at him. 'I can call Dr Ramsey back, if you'd like him to go over it again?'

'He's only given me your diagnosis. He doesn't know everything you claim you can't remember. You obviously knew Nick. Do you remember sleeping with him?'

The edge in his voice was deadlier, his eyes boring into hers with a ferocity that made her every nerve quiver with apprehension.

'My private life is none of your business, Your Highness,' she bit out, cursing the new wave of heat that rushed up her face. 'But for the sake getting rid of you for good, I can tell you one of my last memories of Nick is of discussing a job with him. I don't know whether or not I actually did this job. That's the last thing I remember of my life here in Vegas before I woke up in hospital three months pregnant...' She paused, the overwhelming memory washing over her. 'I was told someone found me hurt and wandering near a truck stop in California.'

'California?' he echoed sharply, and disbelief, shock and scepticism were in his gaze.

'Does that mean anything to you?' she asked, equally sharply.

His nostrils flared, but he shook his head. 'Go on.'

She bristled at the command, but she'd opened this door. She needed to finish quickly so he'd leave her alone.

'I had no identification with me, so no one knew who I was until I woke up from my coma. Now, have I satisfied whatever morbid curiosity makes you think we're connected?'

He stared at her for a charged minute, then he prowled close. Closer. Until she could see the flecks of molten silver in his light grey eyes. Until she feared she would be sucked into the mesmerising vortex of his aura.

'No, Eden. We're nowhere near done. Do you want to know why?'

She didn't. She *really* didn't. Because she was suddenly terrified of his answer. Terrified of the real reason he was here. The reason he'd reacted so viscerally to her last night.

'Not particularly. And for the last time, you need to leave.'

CHAPTER THREE

AMNESIA.

Such a simple cluster of letters for a profound, life-changing turn of events. As an immutable safeguard, considering he was heir to a powerful throne, a DNA test to establish true paternity was unquestionably necessary. The doctor's credentials and connection to Eden would also need to be verified.

But Azar *knew.*

He'd known the second he looked into the boy's eyes.

Hell, he'd known it from fifty yards away as he'd sat frozen in the back of his SUV at the cemetery, watching Eden and the toddler placing flowers on his friend's grave.

He had a son.

Abstractedly, he praised his strict palace childhood tutors for his ability to keep standing, breathing, *reasoning* when waves of shock threatened to drown him. When an avalanche of *possibilities* unravelled, pure and urgent, wrapping around his soul with the promise of doing things differently, of being the parent he'd always yearned for as a child—a desire he'd believed he'd rid himself of years ago.

Every instinct screamed at him to stalk next door, drop to his knees and just...*stare* at the beautiful child he'd help create.

And the boy was beautiful. If nothing else, Eden Moss had given him a healthy son...

'Is my son well? Healthy?' he asked, with a compulsion he couldn't deny.

Her breathing stalled completely. 'What are you talking about? He…he's not yours—'

'He is.' He knew it to his very core. 'He has the Domene eyes. He is mine.'

She lost a shade of colour, but even in her shock Eden Moss remained stunning. Eye-catching in a way he couldn't believe still had such a raw effect on him, considering everything she'd done.

But that was an issue to be tackled later.

He turned on his heel and headed for the door.

'Where are you—? Are you're leaving?'

He clenched his teeth at the naked hope in her voice. Had it been anyone else, he would have felt a sliver of sympathy.

Every Domene since the fiery birth of Cartana half a millennia ago had sealed the formidable reputation of the European kingdom.

Those who'd imagined they might subsume or conquer the relatively small land mass sharing its borders with Spain, France and Italy had quickly learned that size mattered not one iota.

Enemies had been dispatched with brutal efficiency until its dominance had been widely and thoroughly accepted and respected.

These days the Domene men attempted to slap a veneer of civility and sophistication over their outward dealings on the world stage. But behind closed doors…in a matter such as discovering the next heir to the throne of Cartana was living in a squalid one-bed apartment in the back alleys of the world's most decadent city, being raised by a woman who'd shown him the true meaning of duplicity…

Mercy was non-existent in the potent gaze he levelled at her.

'No, Eden Moss. I'm not leaving. I'm going next door to see my son. To speak to him. To touch him for the first time.'

The words launched a seismic wave through him, changing his very essence from the inside out.

'You can come with me, or you can stay here and pack your things. Either way, when I leave here in the next hour he's coming with me.'

Her lips had parted with his first words. By the time he was finished her delectable mouth was gaping, the weight of his resolution widening her eyes.

And perhaps he wasn't completely heartless, because that sliver of sympathy *did* flash through him. But he killed it in the next instant, when she blinked, then stepped determinedly towards him.

'No. Wait!'

He didn't. A simple equation had supplied his son's age, reminding him of every small and big milestone he'd lost.

More than two years.

He'd never got to see his son take his first step. Hear his first word.

Dulce cielo.

Urgency propelled him down the corridor, and one bodyguard swiftly opened the elderly woman's door. He entered the apartment and saw him—Max—tucked into a highchair, carefully setting down a cup that contained what looked like milk.

A plastic plate containing the remains of cut-up pancakes and fruit sat on a coloured mat decorated with prancing fish. His chin, mouth and cheeks were liberally sticky with some sort of syrup, but it was the cheeky grin of enjoyment on his face that wedged Azar's breath in his solar plexus.

His son looked up. Azar saw the hint of a cleft in his chin, deepening the certainty in his soul that he was looking at his son and heir.

The urgency of that mandate pounded harder—to do better than had been done to him. To ensure his flesh and blood lacked for nothing emotionally. And, yes, he wasn't entirely certain how he would achieve that, seeing as he'd often been referred to as 'the Cold Crown Prince', and hadn't entirely rejected that moniker, especially when it served his purpose. But didn't he thrive on the direst challenge?

He'd suffered a cold and distant mother who, despite being Queen, had been determined to wage a war of attrition on the woman she'd seen as her rival, and a father seemingly unwilling or unable to mediate in that war, resulting in his sons, especially Azar, being perennially caught in the crossfire. And hadn't there been times past when he'd wondered whether the fallout of those battle wounds had ever healed? Enough to overcome his bitterness long enough to forge a half-decent marriage when the time came?

Only to conclude that it wouldn't matter in the end. That all he needed was to ensure any prospective spouse and queen understood there would be strict intolerance of melodrama or vitriol.

If that directive had to be adjusted now, in respect of how he believed he'd tackle fatherhood, at the unexpected appearance of his flesh and blood, then by God he would rise to the challenge.

He dragged himself from the past to see Max's grin had begun to slip—until he looked past Azar and it re-emerged.

Azar didn't need to look behind him to know Eden had followed hot on his heels. She zipped past him, sending him a wary look before she positioned herself defensively next to her—*their*—son.

'Mama! Pancakes!' the boy exclaimed.

She brushed her hand over his curls and leaned in to kiss his cheek. 'They look yum-yum! Are they good?'

'Yum-yum,' he concurred.

Azar made a note to supply him with as many pancakes as he could handle. The boy picked up a plastic fork, speared one square and started to offer it to his mother—then froze at Azar's stare.

'Maybe you should sit down? Let's take the...tension down

a notch?' her shrewd neighbour said, her gaze darting between them.

As much as he wanted to scoop up the boy and hightail it to his private plane, he took a beat and paced away exactly three steps. He couldn't stomach a greater distance.

He might be able to call upon his diplomatic immunity status for many harmless things, but he was certain the authorities would frown upon him prising his son from his mother's arms. Not to mention the scandal and stress it would cause his homeland and his ailing father.

The father from whom Azar couldn't quite maintain his customary cold detachment, despite the unsettling dysfunctionality that had marred his formative years.

So he curbed the urgency rampaging through his blood, pulled out a chair that didn't look as if it would support his weight and sat.

'Coffee?' the neighbour asked.

About to shake his head, he met her steady stare and changed his mind. It was obvious she cared about Max. This might go smoother if he chose sugar instead of vinegar. *'Sí, gracias.'*

Her eyes widened at his response, then her cheeks flushed lightly as she rose to fetch a cup.

Eden glared and he curbed the smile, welcoming the tiny distraction. Until his son's gaze found his again and he was thrown into a vortex of unfamiliar emotion.

He wasn't sure how long he stared. At some point his coffee was placed before him. He sipped it, smoothly hiding his grimace at the poor taste.

But everything and everyone else might have ceased to exist, for all he cared. Well, everyone bar Max's mother. Her mother hen act was hard to ignore. Not to mention the allure that had captivated him three years ago, which remained potent enough to drag his gaze repeatedly to her.

That was how he knew she was stretching out the moment. Delaying the inevitable.

He put an end to that by draining his cup five minutes later and staring pointedly at her.

A faint flush rose in her cheeks as she grabbed a napkin, cleaned the boy up, then started to gather the dirty plates. At his nod, one of his bodyguards stepped forward and relieved her of them, took them to the tiny kitchen.

Azar rose. 'Thank you for the breakfast, Mrs Tolson. We'll take our leave now.'

'No thanks needed. Max is adorable. Eden's doing a great job raising him.'

The clear warning and pointed endorsement triggered a dash of admiration and respect for the old woman.

Not so much Ramon, who visibly bristled. 'You need to address His Highness correctly when speaking to—'

Azar held up his hand. 'We'll let it slide this once, Ramon.' This woman had looked after and fed his son, after all.

His gaze slid to Max, who now clung to his mother, one hand fisted in her hair. 'Shall we?'

Another flare of rebellion lit her eyes and, *maldita sea*, it shouldn't feel this hot to be locked in silent battle with her. A battle she conceded after ten seconds, her feet gliding gracefully across the floor towards him.

As he turned to head out, he was too busy suppressing his suddenly inappropriately roused libido to heed the whispered conversation between the women. But he breathed easier when Eden reassured the older woman with a murmured, 'It's all right. I'll be fine.'

She might not be entirely fine—not if he discovered even a crumb of misinformation in her narrative. But that was an issue for later.

At her door, he met her intensified glare. Skin tingling, he was startled to admit he hadn't felt this enlivened since— In a long while. The dark gloom surrounding his father's illness had dimmed his already sombre temperament. That was why he hadn't had a liaison in several months.

Only his brothers' insistence on keeping their birthday tradition had placed him on the royal jet to Vegas a few days ago.

To think if he hadn't come he would never have discovered this life-changing event that had come and gone without so much as a butterfly's wing fluttering against his skin, never mind the sonic boom it deserved.

The enormity of it firmed his resolve.

'You have half an hour left.'

'You can't just toss about edicts and uproot Max from the only home he's ever known. I won't allow it!'

His eyes shifted to his son and a different tingling overcame him. He wanted to touch him. Hold him. But what she'd said needed addressing first.

'You claim you don't remember—'

'It's not a claim—it's the truth,' she hissed, then smoothed a hand down the boy's back when he whimpered.

He swallowed a growl of frustration. 'Very well. You've had a little time to absorb the fact that he's the future heir to the Cartana throne. But, as much as I'm sure you would prefer swathes of time to come around to the idea, unfortunately it doesn't work that way. As we speak there will be several media entities wondering what I'm doing here. It's only a matter of time before the paparazzi arrive and camp outside this apartment building, hounding your neighbours and digging through your trash.'

It was a slight exaggeration, since he'd been meticulous about evading the media, if only for a short time, because those bloodhounds could sniff out news buried on an asteroid circling the Milky Way. But he intended to use every tool in his arsenal to move things along quickly.

Far be it from him to turn histrionic, but *destiny* itself pounded at him. And he wouldn't be denied.

"Your group?" He reluctantly dragged his attention from Bree to his sister.

"Gosh, no. They get enough of me in here. Dom is coming to get me. Invite Nico. You're going upstairs to meet with him, aren't you?"

"Yes. I only came in to give you this, from Mom." He offered the envelope, but his mind was turning over the fact that Bree hadn't seemed as surprised to see him as he was to see her. In fact, now he really thought of it, that initial look on her face had been *alarm*.

"Thanks." Eve took the envelope. "I'll walk you to the elevator."

"Not necessary." He glanced again at Bree, wanting to talk to her, but she was avoiding his gaze. Her profile was stoic, her posture so still he had the sense she was forcibly trying not to reveal her agitation.

"Jax?" Eve opened the door, waiting until he'd walked out and the boardroom door had closed behind them before she hissed, "Keep it in your pants!"

"Excuse me?"

"Oh, please. She's very pretty, but you know the rules."

"She doesn't work for me." It was a reflexive response from a place that didn't want to hear no.

"This is a workplace, not a nightclub. I thought Mom was fixing you up with Tabitha? She has a daughter, you know."

"Tabitha?" That was information he should have been given.

"Bree," she corrected with exasperation.

"She's *married*?" It hit like a kick to the stomach.

Was that why she'd looked so uncomfortable? Did she think their long-ago tryst would get back to her husband? Who was this other man, anyway? Jax had no right to the jealousy that pierced him, but it struck like a viper.

"No, I don't think the father is in the picture." Eve was keeping her voice down as they navigated the bullpen. "She said something about her mom being nearby to help with day care. We're all still getting to know each other." They arrived at the elevator and she stabbed the button, then glared at him. "She's off-limits, is what I'm saying. Definitely not someone to notch your belt with."

He didn't tell her they'd already had sex, but his brain was exploding over the memory of a broken condom. Now she had a little girl? How old?

No. He was overreacting. It had been four years. Plenty of time to have a baby with someone else. And she'd been on the pill. He had left her his number. If her daughter was his, she would have called him.

Wouldn't she?

Tamping down on the wild suspicion trying to bubble up inside him, he stepped into the elevator. Now that he had Bree's full name, it was easy to call up her socials.

Her posts were stale with nothing more recent than a year ago. In the few photos of her daughter, she had kept the girl's face off camera, only showing the back of her head. He stopped scrolling on one with a woman asleep in a hammock. She was an older version of Bree. Her mother, Jax presumed. She held a baby in a sun hat face down on her shoulder. The caption read "First birthdays are tiring for everyone!"

It had been posted in early April two years ago. That meant her daughter had been born three and a half years ago, which was a very coincidental *nine months* after he'd met Bree the previous July.

The doors opened on Nico's floor, but Jax stood there until the doors closed again. The car didn't move, but it could have been plunging into the basement for all he knew.

It wasn't possible that Bree had had his baby. He had only just decided he was ready to consider marriage again. He wasn't ready to be a father.

He wasn't sure he was *fit* to be a father. Children needed love and when he loved, he caused pain.

News like this would only produce a fresh scandal and worry them. This wasn't an unplanned pregnancy, allowing time for everyone to get used to the idea. It was a *child*. One he'd neglected for *three years*. How did a man make up for that?

No. She couldn't be his. He refused to believe it.

But deep down, in the roiling pit of his gut, he knew that she was.

Bree was still hyperventilating when they broke for lunch.

The project team was small because they were still in an information-gathering phase. So far, the work was interesting and challenging. After heavy deliberation, she had taken the position because the pay was excellent and the experience an asset on her CV. It allowed her to develop relationships with top executives in both companies, something she believed would serve her in the future.

Which meant she had also met Nico as well as Eve. Nico was a slightly older, more buttoned-down version of Jax. She had tried not to stare, but she'd had the same overwhelmed reaction while speaking to her daughter's uncle as she had had to his aunt.

This whole situation was so bizarre, she kept pushing the reality of it to the back of her mind. At the same time, she had been mentally counting down to the wedding reception this Saturday. It was *the* party for the elites of New York, falling the weekend before Thanksgiving when anyone who was anyone was preparing to leave the city for family visits and Christmas vacations and warmer climates.

Bree wasn't going anywhere, but she had given herself until Friday to decide whether—and *how*—to tell Jax he was a father. She hadn't expected him to waltz into the boardroom *today*.

When Eve had exclaimed, "Jax!" Bree had had one second to swallow her soul back into her body before being struck afresh by how compelling he was.

He had eschewed a power suit for a checkered jacket over tailored trousers. His natural charisma immediately captured the attention of everyone in the room, including her.

Oddly, she had been so stressed at the idea of telling him about Sofia, she hadn't been prepared for the heat that engulfed her or the vivid memory of writhing with him in the throes of ecstasy. Where had she found the audacity to behave like that? It was mortifying to think back on in the professional setting of her workplace!

Maybe he won't even remember me, she had thought with equal parts dread and hope.

Then his polite but indifferent gaze had locked with hers and lit up. It was the same energy he'd projected four years ago, as though he was saying, *There you are*. All his masculine energy looped out to snare her, exactly like the first time.

Heartening as it was that he recognized her and still found her attractive—or considered her easy, more likely—the stakes were entirely too high. If she hadn't been a mother to *their* child, she might have been persuaded to follow him anywhere. All he had to do was crook his finger.

Instead, the pull of attraction crashed into the decision she'd been putting off. Tell him? Or keep Sofia to herself?

Through Eve, she knew a little more about the Viscontis.

They were tightly knit. Bree was envious. She'd never felt close to her stepsiblings. Her father's family weren't interested in Sofia, either. If anything, that disinterest made Bree more reluctant to tell Jax. What if he and his family were ambivalent, or worse, hostile to Sofia's existence?

Telling Jax was a huge gamble, the kind that could pay off or devastate her.

After he walked out, the morning passed in a blur. She had no idea what she said or did. She was on guard the whole time, aware he was in the building. The walls pulsed with his presence. When everyone rose to leave for lunch, all she could think was that she desperately needed air.

"Okay, Bree?" Eve hung back as everyone else filed from the boardroom.

"Totally," she lied, slapping a big, fake smile on her face.

"Good." Eve didn't look convinced. She nodded toward the elevators as they stepped out the door. "I'm having lunch with Dom and my brothers. If I'm not back by one, will you take lead on the supply chain mapping?"

"Of course." As she followed Eve's glance to where the three men waited near the elevators, she saw Jax staring this direction as though he'd been waiting for her to emerge.

A fresh wave of anxiety assaulted her, one so strong her knees nearly melted out from under her. She mumbled something about water and dived into the coffee room.

It was a galley style with a coffee machine, a refrigerator, a sink, and some chipped mugs. There wasn't anywhere to sit so it was empty.

She poured herself a glass of water, making herself sip while trying to form a rational thought. All she could think about was her complete abandonment with him. She couldn't let him undermine her willpower like that again.

"Bree."

She choked and nearly dropped the glass. Water splashed against her sleeve and she had to wipe her chin as she spun around.

A fresh rush of hot-cold attraction-dread washed through her. Her physical response was monumental and her emotions zigzagged all over the map.

I can't. I want. Look at him. Run.

He raked his attention down her office attire—a simple jacket and wool trousers with a light knit top. The touch of his gaze was as tangible as his hands had been that day, as though he remembered every place he'd touched as vividly as she did.

When he came back to meeting her unblinking stare, there was a fierce light in his eyes. A demand for answers.

"Where's Eve?" She looked past him, wondering if he could hear her heart since it was pounding hard enough to deafen her.

"Powder room. She told me you have a daughter."

Oh, God.

She wanted to close her eyes, but she was transfixed like a deer in headlights, watching his eyes narrow. Feeling the truth bearing down on her.

Say something.

Her throat was too tight. She could hardly breathe. All of her went cold. She suspected she was ashen as a ghost.

"Mine?" he asked under his breath.

She couldn't lie. Her voice was as faint as her vision. "Yes."

CHAPTER FOUR

"WHY THE *HELL* didn't you call me?"

Bree's eyes widened in alarm, making Jax realize his voice had come out like a gunshot. The floor was mostly empty since it was lunch hour, but the silence across the bullpen turned expectant.

A gut-chilling sense of deception and betrayal hit like nausea. He had left his number. He had tried to do the right thing.

She had cut him out anyway. Pushed him out of his daughter's life. *Why?*

He had spent the past two hours telling himself he was jumping to asinine conclusions, but now he barely kept control of himself. All he could do was step back and point to the boardroom where he'd first seen her.

Bree swallowed and ducked her head, leading the way.

"Jax." Nico's voice resounded with warning from the elevators.

He ignored him and closed the door, pressing his hand on it to ensure no one would interrupt them.

"How?" he demanded.

"The condom broke," she reminded, body language tense with distress.

"You said you were on the pill. You said you would take the other kind."

"I did! But I bought a take-away meal on the way to the train station and started throwing up as soon as I was aboard. My friend actually had to take me to the hospital in Zurich because I was so dehydrated. We barely made it to London in time for our flight. By the time I got to Virginia, I was a wreck. I crawled into bed to sleep off the jet lag and didn't even think about the pills until I came up for air. By then it had been almost a week. I thought I'd wait for my period then restart them but..." She swallowed.

"I left you my number," he reminded her grimly.

"I—" Her mouth firmed and her chin came up in rebelliousness. "I didn't take it. I left it in the room."

"On purpose?" She had to be kidding. *"Why?"*

"You didn't ask for *my* number. Why should I take yours?"

"For this. *This* was the reason I gave you my number," he said through his teeth.

"I didn't think it would happen, did I? I wasn't sick when I walked out without it."

"Have you been sick this whole time? You've had *four years* to contact me."

"How?" she snapped. "I didn't know your full name until a couple of weeks ago."

"You could have called Alphonso at the restaurant in Como."

"And said *what*? Hey, you know that guy who picks up women when they're dining alone? I was one of them. Can I have his number? How often does he field *that* call?" She clamped her lips together and looked past him, expression closing up.

There was a rap on the door. Eve stared crossly at him through the glass.

"What are you doing?" Her voice was muted, but Nico and Dom stood behind her, glaring with suspicion.

"Go to lunch without me," Jax barked.

"I will not." Eve pushed on the door. "Let me in."

He yanked it open. "This is a personal matter."

"Bree?" Eve prompted. "Would you like to come with me?"

"What do you think I'm going to do to her?" he demanded. "We're *talking*."

"I'm fine," Bree assured Eve, but her sallow complexion and the way she had her arms coiled tightly around her torso told a different story. "We actually met once. I should have mentioned it, but I wasn't sure he would remember. I'm fine. Honestly."

Eve swung him a look of disgust. "You hooked up and ghosted her? Nice."

"This is none of your business, Eve. Get out." He jerked his head at the bunch of them.

"This is literally my business," Eve insisted. "Bree works for me so let me have a moment to speak with her—"

"*No*. Come with me," Jax said to Bree.

She touched the strap of the tote bag slung over her shoulder, then nodded jerkily.

"You're obviously upset," Eve said as Bree brushed past her. "You don't have to go anywhere with him."

"It's okay." She didn't look at the men as she kept walking.

"What the hell are you doing?" Nico challenged as Jax came out of the boardroom.

As if there was a comprehensible answer to that question. Until he was able to wrap his own brain around this news, there was no way he was sharing it with anyone else.

Jax ignored his brother and followed Bree, aware of the blistering glares behind him.

At least they didn't try to follow them into the elevator. When the doors closed, he pivoted to face her.

"*How* long did you say you knew who I was?"

"I saw your photo in Eve and Dom's wedding announcement." She spoke to the middle button on his shirt.

"So you've had *weeks* to reach out." The cynic in him was adding up these details into something nefarious. A plot that meant she was targeting him. Deliberately trying to damage him in some way. Maybe she was just taking advantage of timing. Maybe her daughter wasn't his after all.

"From the moment I realized I was pregnant, I believed I would raise Sofia alone," Bree said defensively. "When I finally knew who you were, I needed time to consider what it meant to involve you."

He wanted to leap on her dilemma as evidence her daughter wasn't his, but his attention was snared by a greater detail.

"Sofia? That's her name?" The musicality of it was a heart punch, bending his white-hot anger into prisms of emotional colors: curiosity and protectiveness, worry for her well-being, and yearning for the time he'd missed. "I want to see her."

Bree clicked her phone and held it out.

Jax had meant he wanted to see her in real life, to judge for himself, but the image on the lock screen was another hammer-blow against any doubt. The round face with black ringlets and dark eyes and tiny white teeth looked too much like Eve as a toddler for him to dismiss her as anything other than a Visconti.

Still he fought it. He didn't trust easily. Not anymore. He had learned the hard way that humans were complicated, self-serving creatures. He moved among them with an alertness to the fact they could turn on you without notice.

Bree might not have acted maliciously in keeping Sofia from him, but she hadn't been as forthcoming as she could have been. He shouldn't take her word for it. The sensible thing was to wait for a paternity test, but his gut had told him Sofia was his.

Even if she wasn't, he wanted her to be.

That thought staggered him. What did he know of being a father? Parents were supposed to protect their young, weren't they? He was a scandal magnet. He would only let down his daughter the way he'd let down everyone else.

He absolutely should not want Bree's child to be his.

But he did.

For no reason other than he wanted Bree.

The elevator opened. They walked across the lobby, out the rotating door into the bluster of harsh wind and spitting rain.

"Where are we going?" Bree asked in a small voice.

He looked at her blankly, still trying to put his thoughts in order. They needed somewhere private to talk.

"The Visconti Signature is three blocks that way," he decided.

They didn't bother with a taxi. Bree hurried alongside Jax, not complaining about the pace his long legs set, even though she wore low pumps. The biting wind was trying to shear her clothes from her body. She wanted off the street as quickly as possible.

She wasn't given time to admire the inlaid marble and chandelier and grand staircase of the Signature's lobby. The front desk manager recognized Jax and hurried to give him whatever he wanted—which was the Presidential suite, apparently.

One private elevator trip later, they entered a palatial apartment. She'd seen photos of comparable rooms in WBE hotels, but had never had a reason to go into one. It was more residence than hotel room with two bedrooms, a full kitchen, a fireplace, a dining nook, and a terrace overlooking Central Park.

Jax walked straight to the bar, poured a drink and knocked it back. He hissed as he refilled his glass. "Do you want one?"

"Yes." She was in her own state of shock. "Look, I'm sorry you had to find out like this. I knew you were coming to town and I've been trying to figure out when and how and whether to tell you. It never occurred to me you'd guess."

As she accepted the drink, her fingers brushed his. Her insides were still trembling, especially when his expression was so ominous, but that tiny contact sent a spark into the kindling of awareness she was trying to ignore.

They locked eyes and she saw his pupils swell, as though what had happened within her was reciprocated in him.

She nervously backed off and set aside her purse, then shifted to sit on the sofa, putting the coffee table between them. She sipped and the scotch replaced the heat of desire with an acidic burn that felt just as dangerous. She sipped again, then said the one thing she had rehearsed for this moment.

"I don't expect anything from you. It was my decision to have Sofia. Unless you want to be in her life in a meaningful way, there's nothing you need to do."

"Of course I want a relationship with my daughter," he said starkly. "What kind of man do you think I am?"

"I don't know, Jax. We spent one afternoon together. We're strangers."

He muttered a frustrated curse and moved to the windows that overlooked the rain-washed city. His free hand gripped the back of his neck, then he dropped it to speak over his shoulder.

"She's definitely mine? What about that other man you were with before you went to Italy? What about the rest of your trip? Was I really the only man you brought back to your room?"

She was so insulted by that, her jaw locked.

He turned. "I'm not judging."

"You are so judging," she choked. "And that's rich from a man who picks up tourists and uses cheap condoms."

His cheek ticked.

"No, Kabir is not her father," she said astringently. "We weren't having sex before he left. Remember? And since you're the only other man I've slept with besides him—"

"Ever?"

He was so taken aback, she deduced he'd had scores of lovers before her and since. That didn't surprise her, given how smoothly he operated. It was none of her business anyway so she had no right to feel scorned.

But she did.

"Strangely enough, I haven't had time for all these men you think I've been entertaining. I was pregnant and constructing a life around being a working mother. If I get an evening with a book and a bath, I consider myself lucky." She rose and gathered her purse. "I don't actually care if you believe you're her father. Get a paternity test if you want one or walk away and pretend this never happened. I just told you I don't want anything from you so there's no reason for me to lie. I was hoping we could be civil, but apparently not. I'll say goodbye."

"I don't need a paternity test," he ground out, then ran his hand over his jaw. "She looks just like Lili.

"Who?"

"Eve. Evelina. We called her Lili when she was little."

A small snort of amusement escaped her. "After I met Eve, I joked to my mother that I should get a maternity test, since Sofia looked so much like her."

"Your *mother* knows I'm her father?" He was back to sounding livid.

Bree grasped the strap on her purse. "Mom was with me when I saw your photo."

"How exactly did this go, Bree? You realized who I was, then went to work for my *sister*? Does Eve know I'm Sofia's father? Does Nico?"

"No." She dropped her purse again, agitated enough to pace. "Eve offered me this role four weeks ago. From a career standpoint, I had to take it. I have a daughter to support." She paused to let that sink in. "Frankly, it was nice to be recognized for my potential. This isn't nepotism. I earned my place on her team. And yes, it gave me access to your family. I won't apologize for wanting to get to know more about you before deciding whether to tell you."

"Such as?"

"Whether you were married. Or involved with someone." Definitely asking for Sofia's sake, not her own.

"You asked Eve if I was married?"

"Not outright." She picked at a rough edge on her nail. "When she mentioned her party this weekend, I asked if there were any other family weddings on the horizon. It was friendly conversation."

He shook his head, seeming astounded by all of this. She couldn't blame him.

"I knew you were coming to town this week and that this would be a chance to tell you, but I didn't expect to see you today." She let her hands fall to her sides. "And I didn't know whether to tell you because I didn't know how you would react."

"Shock," he provided with heavy irony, then pinched the bridge of his nose. "I don't like having things hidden from me, especially something as important as a person I created."

"What did *you* do to make her except break a condom? I did all the work."

"You didn't give me an opportunity to do anything else, did you?" he shot back. "You had options, Bree. You didn't even try."

He wasn't wrong. She could have made up any story and passed a message through Alphonso, but in her experience men—*fathers*—weren't very reliable. She hadn't relished the humiliation of begging a stranger in Italy for the number of a man who might have told her she was on her own anyway. She absolutely refused to set her daughter up for the apathy she'd suffered, so she had let Jax remain a stranger she couldn't find. She had proceeded as though it would be just her and Sofia because it was less agonizing than hoping for Jax to enter their lives and wind up disappointed.

"You're telling me the truth?" The intensity of his stare squeezed her lungs.

"I can't tell if you want it to be true or not," she said with a pang of disappointment. In her perfect world, he was over the moon to learn he had a daughter. Instead, he seemed to be holding both of them off. "A paternity test would show if I was lying."

He ran his hand down his face and a shaken breath left him. "We'll do one because others will expect it, but okay. I have a daughter." His expression flexed as he fully took this information on board. His Adam's apple bobbed.

Maybe she was judging him too harshly. Of course this was a shock.

"What, um…" She hugged herself. "What do you want to do now? Take some time to process? I can leave. We can talk again later this week."

"No," he said abruptly. "You've been around Eve enough to know that family is important to us. If Sofia is my family, then she is part of my life now. In a meaningful way." He threw her own words back at her.

"And what does that mean to you?" She lifted haughty brows.

"I don't know yet. Shared custody? Isn't that what most involved parents have?"

"You'll move back here to New York?" A small chill of threat moved through her. "Just like that?"

"No." He dismissed that with a scowl.

"How do you see that working then? I'm not dragging a three-year-old across the Atlantic every two weeks." She waved toward the windows.

His restless gaze moved around the room, but she had the sense he was looking inward. "You'll have to live in Italy."

"What? No! Our life is here. You can visit her whenever you're in town."

"How is that meaningful?" he rejected impatiently. "I'll support you," he added as though money was the only thing that worried her. "You won't have to work."

"I happen to *like* working." Financial independence was deeply important to her.

"Then work remotely. Or I'll find you something in my office. You're throwing up arguments that have no bearing."

"And you're acting like I'm that pushover you met in Italy. You can't throw money around and expect me to lie down for you."

He held her stare while her words hung in the air.

She started to blush, thinking about exactly how easy she'd been for him that day. He was remembering it, too. She could tell.

The air had already been crackling with heightened emotions. Now her awareness that they were alone in this suite hummed even louder. Her body tingled as though she was a receptor for the specific sexual energy he radiated.

"I wasn't talking about sex."

"It was a Freudian slip?" he mocked lightly. "Because we can take this into the bedroom and work out the sexual tension."

"I wouldn't trust your condoms."

"Keep throwing that at me, Bree. You said you were on the pill. I happen to know the medicine chest in a room like this is very well stocked, by the way." His mouth curled with cruel enticement.

He was taunting her, but the atmosphere had altered, shifting from animosity to something more provocative. His gaze skimmed her and temptation began to hum in her ears.

I haven't even begun to seduce you.

"This is a power move," she said shakily. "You don't even like me."

"You're the mother of my child." He held her gaze as he approached. She could practically smell the pheromones coming off him. "I could never hate you. Or harm you. I'm merely angry with you."

"And I'm supposed to want angry sex?" She couldn't remember where she'd put her purse. She had a clear line to the door, but didn't move. Because she wasn't afraid of him. She was afraid of herself. Of the yearnings that gripped her. Her feet were magnetized to the floor. The rest of her willed him to make a move. It was foolish, so foolish.

"If you don't want sex, say that. We'll stick to arguing." He cradled her jaw, warm and gentle and devastating. His thumb grazed her bottom lip.

She caught at his wrist, but it was too late. He had already cast his spell. Or broken one. Her slumbering senses leaped awake. Tingling heat suffused her, tightening her skin while loosening sinew and inhibition. Swirls of desire twisted through her belly. Against her will, a sob of need panged in her throat.

He heard it and answered with a gruff noise. He dipped his head and sealed his mouth to hers.

Her lips melted, opening to seek the taste of him and he struck, releasing the full impact of his hunger. He plundered, hot and potent and ravenous. He combed his fingers into her short hair, pulling just enough to tip her head back and give him more to work with. More to *take*.

A moan of helplessness became trapped in her throat. Maybe she should have pushed him away, but her hands slid beneath his jacket, across the crisp fabric of his shirt and splayed on the warm plane of his back. She pulled herself closer to him, trying to ease the ache in her breasts. In her *soul*.

Of all the reasons she hadn't taken another lover in four years, this was the biggest one. No one else was *him*. No one smelled like spice and tang and musk. No one wore fine textures over steel, cool control over heat. No one touched her in this same casual knead of pleasure into her flesh while he filled his hands with her. No one made her feel so wanted. Craved.

She pushed at his jacket and he shed it abruptly, then his wide hands slid down to her waist, to her hip and around to her buttocks. He picked her up.

She wrapped her legs around him, expecting he would take her to the bedroom, but he balanced her on the rounded back of the sofa and pressed the column of his erection to the notch of her thighs.

A thrill of excitement bolted into that place where he rocked. She clung her arms around his neck and his kiss became blatantly sexual. She strained, moving against him to soothe herself and incite him. It had been so *long*.

When his hand found the edge of her top and sought the skin beneath, she scraped her own jacket off and arched her bra-covered breast into the splay of his hand, gleeful when he brushed the cup aside and teased her bare nipple. She offered herself to his touch even as she drank up this glorious sense that she was back where she belonged.

Which was an illusion. This was nothing more than it had been the first time: compatible chemistry. Consenting adults scratching an erotic itch.

She bucked helplessly anyway, clinging around his neck, mouth sealed to his, seeking the pinnacle.

It was only as she began to dissolve that she remembered her first encounter with him had changed her life forever.

He set his hand on her tailbone and pressed harder, intensifying her pleasure. Plunging her into a sea of sensual waves that battered and destroyed her.

CHAPTER FIVE

THIS WAS NOT what he had planned when he brought her here.

Everything in him—especially the primed length of flesh crushed to the softest, hottest part of her—wanted to carry her to the bedroom and finish this. If she had been in a dress, he would already be buried inside her, condom or not.

But the fact she had completely distracted him from their discussion was sobering. He refused to let her knock him from his priorities again.

He slid his hand from the bra cup he'd invaded and gripped her hips as her trembling legs dropped from his waist.

She tipped her head back, eyelids heavy, mouth lush and swollen, cheeks still flushed from orgasm.

He wanted to deliver a thousand of them. But therein lay her danger to him.

"Better?" he asked.

She sucked in a breath as though he'd stabbed her, then she shoved her hands against him, pushing him back so she could stand.

That had been cruel. It had. He was instantly ashamed of himself and reached out to steady her, but she slapped his hand away.

"I knew you were just trying to prove something," she spat out. "What a horrible way to behave! Why would I let anyone so mean near my daughter?" She picked up her purse.

"I know where you work," he reminded her.

Throwing him a bitter glare, she locked herself in the powder room.

He'd handled that well, hadn't he?

From his jacket on the floor, he heard his phone buzz. He picked it up and looked at the screen, but it was only Eve asking him what was going on.

Just making things worse over here.

He set aside his phone without replying and picked up the drink Bree hadn't finished. He drained it, exhaling over the burn, willing his arousal to quit tenting his trousers and his brain to re-engage.

He shouldn't have said that, but he hadn't been this far on the defensive in years. Not since Paloma had asked him in a fit of disparaging anguish, *What kind of man does that?*

The question plagued him to this day. What kind of man turned against his friend? What kind of man failed to cover up an ugly secret if the alternative would lose him the woman he loved?

Jax had understood why his fiancée had chosen to stand by her brother. He would stand by his own family through nearly anything, but he wouldn't stay silent and allow heinous behavior to happen.

He had had to make a deliberate choice about what kind of man he was: loyal, but willing to collude and hide the harm done to an innocent? Or someone who stood up for the injured, despite the cost to his relationships and social standing?

He'd chosen the latter, for better or worse. Paloma had broken their engagement, called him every vile name in the book, then her family had done their best to level his reputation. Jax had steered clear of serious relationships ever since.

Learning he was a father was not the same level of crisis. It was an adjustment, but he refused to call it bad news. It was big news. Life-changing. He was still straining under the weight of it, but his priorities were very clear. He knew exactly what kind of man he was. He had a sense of the kind of father he wanted to be—one like his own. Strong enough to be a firm foundation. A hand that guided with care, not heaviness.

Now that his shock was wearing off, he was starting to embrace the idea of fatherhood. He wanted to embrace his *daughter*.

The powder room door opened.

He turned to see Bree wearing a stiff, hostile expression. Her lipstick was fresh, but the rest of her makeup had been washed off. She avoided his gaze and picked up her blazer from the sofa, shaking it out, then draping it across her arm.

"I shouldn't have said that," he said. "I was angry, but that's not why I kissed you. I wasn't trying to prove anything."

"Sure," she said with distinct lack of interest. "But now I'm angry." She glanced at him long enough he saw the redness in her eyes. "So I'm leaving."

He'd made her cry. What an ass. "Don't."

She ignored him and walked to the door.

"Damn it, Bree, I felt exactly as threatened as you do right now so I said something mean. I won't do it again."

"*I* threaten *you*?" She flung around to scoff. "I don't want a single thing from you! Especially orgasms you deliver like an insult." Her voice cracked and she looked away, blinking fast. "No. I lie. I do want one thing from you. Go to hell." She reached for the door.

"There hasn't been anyone else for me, either," he bit out.

She spun back to face him. "Don't you lie to me."

"Where's the incentive to lie about that?"

"I have no idea, but I don't believe you." Her expression was wounded. Persecuted.

The gulf of mistrust between them was as wide as the ocean that had separated them for the last four years.

"That happened because that's how we react to each other." He pointed at the sofa. "It would have happened even without this bombshell that has exploded both our lives. But I know she's mine now, Bree. We can't go back from that. So let's reset and talk this out."

She crossed her arms defensively, hugging the blazer that was still draped over her arm, staying where she was, mouth pouted with indecision.

Finally, she sighed and said in a tone that edged toward hopeless, "That's why I wasn't sure I should tell you."

"You were afraid we'd have sex?"

"No. Yes," she allowed with a harsh, humorless chuckle. "But I was afraid you would explode her life. When we met, I thought you were some bohemian expat running a hotel in Italy."

"Flatterer."

"Once I realized who you were..." She sighed.

A chill entered his chest.

"What?" he prompted, bracing himself for one of the ugly rumors Paloma's family had circulated about him.

"There was a lot of press around Eve and Dom's marriage. I don't want Sofia subjected to that kind of attention. I've seen what happens to celebrity babies. People chasing them for photos. At the very least, there would be gossip at the office. She's *three*. It's my job to protect her from things like that. From everything."

"*Our* job," he corrected.

"If you mean that, then tell me how you plan to shield her from those things." She didn't sound obstructive. It was an earnest question.

He couldn't protect her completely. There would be press. There would be fallout.

He rubbed his jaw.

"I hear what you're saying, but I can't pretend she doesn't exist, Bree. I'm not ashamed of her. I'm far more embarrassed that I'm coming into her life so late. We'll have to ride out the attention. Frankly, being in Italy will help."

"You don't know what you're asking." Her brow pulled into a pensive wrinkle. "I'd have to give up her spot at the good day care."

"Are you joking?"

"No." She scowled at his phone. It had continued to buzz with incoming messages the whole time they'd been talking. "Seriously, you don't need Sofia. You already have a child in your life. That thing never stops demanding your attention, does it?"

He walked over to silence it.

"It's Eve. I'll let her know you're still with me and will be tied up the rest..." He swore as he scanned the stack of bubbled messages.

"What?" she asked with dread.

He began reading aloud. "Dom asked if Bree's daughter is yours."

"What?" she gasped. *"No."*

"Where are you?" he continued reading. "Is Bree with you? She went to Italy before she started at WBE. We talked about Como. When did you meet her? Call me."

"Seriously?" Bree cried. *"Do* something."

Bree pinched herself, which had never actually worked to wake her up from a bad dream, but anything was worth a try at this point.

She was still trying to reclaim herself from behaving like

an oversexed floozy, still worried he would use it against her. Now his sister had figured out Jax was Sofia's father?

She watched him bring his phone to his ear.

"Is Nico there?" he asked. "Did he hear this theory of Dom's? Good. Keep it to yourself. I mean it, Eve. Tell Dom to keep his mouth shut, too." He glanced at Bree.

Her heart lurched. His expression was severe, not the least bit reassuring.

"Because I only found out an hour ago," he said flatly. "She needs some personal time. She'll be in touch after we talk. Can I trust you to keep this under wraps or not?"

He closed his eyes as he listened again.

"Yes, I know, Eve. Stop wedding-splaining. I have to go." He ended the call, then studied Bree with an unreadable expression.

"What did she say?" Bree had thought falling apart fully dressed was the most defenseless she could feel today. Her secret was out. A secret she'd been keeping from Eve all this time. Was she fired?

"They won't tell anyone, but if Dom can guess, others can, too."

Like Nico. Or anyone on the team who'd seen the way they had reacted to each other. The crackle in the air had been like the roar of a forest fire.

"We no longer have the luxury of time. I want to meet Sofia, then introduce her to my parents before they find out some other way."

The ground seemed to shift under her feet. This was everything she'd been fearful of—the sense of exposure and lost control. She was still angry with Jax for toying with her, but she was just as angry with herself for abandoning control. For letting him see how easily he could manipulate her with her own response. It was humiliating.

His claim that he reacted just as strongly to her was a joke. He'd dropped her like a hot potato four years ago and again ten minutes ago. She didn't know how far she could trust him or how this would play out, which was terrifying.

Her arms abruptly felt empty. She needed to hold her daughter. To ground herself in what mattered most to her.

"I'll, um, call my mother to meet us at my apartment, so we're not doing it in the cloakroom of the day care center." She spoke to Melissa while Jax texted his driver.

They were both silent in the car. Bree was cold, stomach churning, fearful she was making a mistake, but she was in it now. She had to see it through.

She would have sworn Jax had forgotten she was here, he seemed so remote, but he abruptly leaned over and pressed a button. It was a seat warmer, not that it had time to work. Her shivers were more about anxiety anyway. She gave their daughter a very good life, but it wasn't a Visconti level of good. He was bound to judge her modest apartment with its used furniture and Sofia's thrift shop wardrobe. Kids grew fast. Did he realize that?

She would also be judging him, though. Which wasn't entirely fair. He'd only been a father for a few hours. She couldn't expect him to display an instant connection, but whenever she had toyed with the idea of telling him about Sofia, she'd feared he would dismiss both her and his daughter. Maybe in some dark corner of her soul, she had always wanted him to, so he would fit her skewed vision of what fathers were like. Then she could raise Sofia alone, well seated high on her horse, able to say she had tried.

And could tell her daughter someday in the future that she wasn't at fault. *He* was. Exactly like her own father.

Which wasn't a scenario she really wanted for Sofia. She was merely braced for it. She would rather know today that

Jax would disappoint them than discover his inconstancy in the future, after they'd begun to believe in him.

Ominous as it was, this meeting had to happen.

She trembled as she let Jax into her apartment.

The building was an older one with tiny bedrooms and narrow windows, but it had been updated with a new kitchen and faux hardwood flooring right before she had moved in. Location was everything, so they made the small space work.

Her mother wasn't here yet. Bree moved through the living room, flicking on the table lamps to chase away the November gloom, picking up toys and pajamas and a stray hair band as she went. Saturday was chore day and by Monday, it always looked like this. She refused to apologize. Parenting was messy. That was reality.

Jax removed his jacket and hung it on the back of a kitchen chair, then moved to the open door of Sofia's room. He didn't say anything about the mountain of stuffies or the low, narrow bed made by a preschooler. He moved to the refrigerator to study the scribbles stuck there with animal-shaped magnets, then perused the trio of photos on the wall over the sofa.

"Mom's husband is a professional photographer. Mom took Sofia for her third birthday."

He didn't respond, only stroked his jaw thoughtfully as he studied the images.

Bree found herself taking in the way his shirt fit the breadth of his shoulders and the precise line where his black hair stopped against the back of his swarthy neck. There was unconscious elegance in the way he absently touched his chin. That hand had braced her tailbone while he had driven her over the edge. She had caressed that spot on the back of his neck, arching her throat to his ravenous lips while groaning in luxury.

Why, oh, why had she let that happen? It was so mortifying.

He turned his head, catching her staring.

She looked away, cheeks stinging.

The beep of her door lock pulled her heart into her throat. She hurried around the corner to greet her daughter.

"Mama!" Sofia rushed her.

Bree scooped her up, crossing her arms beneath her bottom to snuggle Sofia's pixie-like body close and tight.

"How come Gigi got me before run and play?"

"Because I want you to meet someone." She tried to keep her voice light, but her veins coursed with adrenaline. She couldn't seem to catch a full breath.

Melissa met her gaze briefly, expression anxious, then she looked past them. Her expression smoothed into her beauty contestant smile.

"You must be Jackson. It's lovely to meet you. I'm Bree's mother, Melissa."

Bree stepped into the kitchen area so her mother could reach past her and shake Jackson's hand.

"Nice to meet you," he said, but his gaze was already pulling back to his daughter.

Sofia studied him, arms still around Bree's neck, but head up, eyes bright with curiosity.

"Do you want me to stay?" Melissa asked.

"I'll call you in a little bit." Right after she finished shedding her clammy skin and throwing up the lunch she hadn't yet eaten.

Melissa left Sofia's backpack on the hook over the shoe rack and slipped out.

"Let's take off your things." Bree removed Sofia's boots, then slid her to the floor and took her jacket to hang it.

Sofia stayed beside her, one arm wrapped around Bree's

leg as she stared up at Jackson. Bree smoothed hair that had been mussed by Sofia's winter hat.

"This is Jackson. He's—" She looked at him. Was he ready for this?

"I'm *Papà*." Jax crouched and let one knee touch the floor, then braced his hand on his thigh. "That's how we say *Daddy* in Italy. Do you want to try it?"

Bree's heart lurched.

Sofia was still hugging her leg and looked up at her.

Bree nodded, throat tight. "If you want to."

"Papà?" Sofia looked at him shyly.

"Perfect." A slow, proud smile spread across Jax's face. Sofia smiled back.

Bree's heart writhed with emotions she couldn't name. The connection was forming before her eyes. It was beautiful in the most painful way and painful in a beautiful way.

"There's something important I need to tell you, Sofia," Jax continued in a quiet, somber tone. "I didn't know about you. I should have asked your *mama* for her phone number when we met, but I didn't. That was my mistake. If I had, you would already know me. I'm very sorry it took so long for me to come see you, but I'm here now. You'll always know how to find me from now on."

Oh. Bree swallowed back the heart rising into her throat, then it was pulled clean out of her body by her daughter.

Sofia stepped across the space. Her small arms splayed out, trying to hug Jackson's wide chest. Her little head rested on his shoulder for the length of a couple of heartbeats while she said, "That's okay. We still love each other. You can do better next time."

Shock blanked Jax's expression.

Bree covered her laugh, but she was also tearing up. It was exactly how she and Sofia made up after a spat. Usually, it was Sofia kicking up and having to apologize, but Bree always reassured her that her love never faltered. It seemed her daughter had absorbed how to be gracious in accepting remorse.

As Jax's arms twitched to wrap around her, Sofia darted back to clasp Bree's leg again. She looked up at her with an anxious look that asked, *Did I do it right?*

"That was very well done," Bree assured her with another stroke of her hair, blinking the dampness from her eyes.

"Can I have screen time?" Ah, the attention span of a preschooler.

"You can wash your hands and we'll all have a snack. Then we'll talk about screen time."

"Deal!" Sofia ran into the bathroom.

There was a scraping sound as Sofia dragged her step stool to the sink, then she began to sing "Happy Birthday."

Jackson uncoiled to stand, the movement seeming to take great effort. His expression was stunned, as though Sofia had been a linebacker who had leveled him into the ground and his ears were still ringing.

That's what Bree thought, anyway, until his gaze flashed into hers, alight with purpose. Then she realized his gradual unfolding was actually the energy of a panther leaping in slow motion.

"You're coming to Italy," he told her.

"No, Jax." She kept her voice down and shook her head, but had the sense that *she* was the one who was reacting too slowly. Invisible paws were closing around her, sharp talons extending to trap her in an inescapable cage.

"Yes," he continued as though she hadn't spoken. "And I think we should marry."

CHAPTER SIX

BREE DIDN'T SAY a word to him as Sofia emerged from the bathroom and sat to eat a cheese sandwich with apple slices.

Jax stayed out of the way, sitting with Sofia to answer her questions. She had hundreds of them ranging from whether he liked dogs or cats to whether he knew Kylie with the brown hair?

Every second that he spent with her strengthened his resolve to become an integral part of her life. He had already been thinking of a future with both of them when he'd walked in here. His libido had been screaming that no matter what happened, he needed an affair with Bree and his sense of family values had demanded he bring his daughter into his home.

Not that there was anything wrong with the life Bree was providing her, but he could see they were outgrowing this apartment. Also, Bree did seem to do all the cooking and cleaning along with working full time and parenting an active preschooler.

He could and would elevate their circumstances purely because his daughter deserved a lifestyle on a level with his own.

Then this midge of a girl had hugged him minutes after meeting him. He'd been too astonished to hug her back, but she had opened a completely new emotion in him. She had smelled like crayons and laundry soap and some ancient scent that imprinted in his brain, telling him she was his. It was akin to what he felt toward his family, but was even more deeply rooted in personal pride and protectiveness. *Mine.* Not in a possessive way, but because she belonged *with* him. She was a part of him. He wanted that proclaimed to the world. He wanted her to have his name.

As he took in how small she was, how trusting and vulnerable, he felt a sharp need to be her provider and protector, while his ingrained sense of having let down his family nipped at him, making him wonder if he could be enough.

Was that why Bree had kept her from him? Did she not trust him to look after his daughter? *Them?*

He glanced at Bree and the carnal possessiveness that had been reignited at the hotel rose anew. He could still feel her thighs around his waist. Her lips had slaked a desperate thirst while leaving him parched for more. She'd burned like a grass fire, nearly incinerating him.

Honestly, he wasn't sure if their chemistry was a point in favor or against marriage. His fixation with her wasn't quite healthy, but it had lasted four years and showed zero signs of fizzling. Marrying her would make official something that was liable to happen anyway. On the other hand, as recently as this morning, he had been committed to making a calculated alliance that would benefit his family.

Bree didn't fit that directive.

When Sofia was done eating, Bree settled her on the sofa with her tablet, asking her to wear her "ear muffins" so the grown-ups could talk.

She returned to the kitchen to eat the last bite of her own sandwich and began tidying up with jerky movements.

When the silence had gone on long enough, Jax said, "Marriage makes sense. You and I are a unit now. She's a

Visconti. She deserves to have my name and all the advantages that entails."

"Telling your parents about her today makes sense. You're only in town a few days. With Eve's party looming, your mother is only going to get busier, so fine. We can tell her today. But suggesting we get married when we barely know each other is ludicrous. I'm not giving up everything that matters to me, including my independence, to go to Italy and discover that you and I can't get along."

"What makes you think we can't get along?"

"The fact that you don't listen to a word I say!"

"I'm listening. You're worried about day care. We'll hire a nanny. These are all solvable problems."

"Seriously?" Bree rubbed her temples. "If I wasn't on the wrong side of this domineering attitude of yours, I'd admire it. I thought middle children were the peacemakers."

"Nico is the one who's domineering. Eve is spoiled. Christo is a wild card who rarely does as he's told. If I don't hold my ground to get what I want, I don't get what I want." He brought her the empty plate from the table and held her gaze. "I prefer to get what I want."

"Stop doing that." Pink rose on her cheekbones. "You said you weren't trying to prove anything."

"I'm not doing anything. It's just there."

"What is? Your compulsion to score?"

"The want."

Her breath hitched and she swallowed, then turned away to clatter the plate into the dishwasher.

"Welcome to parenthood, where you don't always get what you want." She clicked the door closed and turned to face him. "I can't overturn Sofia's life for a marriage based on nothing but geography and sex. Is that really the life you want for her? To be raised in a household where her parents married for convenience and don't even love each other?"

Her mixture of disparagement and wistfulness gave him a pang, mostly because it struck him as naive. At one time, he had thought he would marry for love, but had discovered that particular emotion was actually very cumbersome.

"Convenience is for things that aren't necessary. If all we wanted was sex, marrying would make that more convenient. You and I will marry because it's practical. Being present in Sofia's daily life is a necessity to both of us."

"Talk about wedding-splaining." She rolled her eyes. "What did Eve say to you when you talked to her, anyway? Is that why you're suddenly bringing up marriage?"

"No, I thought of it all by myself." Eve had merely reminded him about her party and what was at stake there, and the fact his mother had arranged a date for him which was why he needed to tell his parents about Sofia tonight. "But Eve's marriage is a good example of one that's practical." He didn't mention the part where he still disapproved of it.

"Eve and Dom are in love," she protested.

"They're in lust," he corrected. "If they hadn't wanted to end the feud between our families, they would have had an affair."

"What a cynical thing to say."

"Because I'm not putting a romantic spin on it? Practical marriages work because they have goals beyond sentimental declarations. My parents married for social connections and wealth building. It's a very successful union. They respect and care for each other. They have four children who are accomplished and well-adjusted. What about your parents? They're divorced, if I recall correctly? Why did they marry? Love?"

"You don't have to sound so condescending." She dried

her hands on the tea towel. "They married for me, if you must know. Mom was pregnant. Which did not turn out to be a strong enough reason to keep them together. So, no. You and I won't be getting married."

"Mama, can I have five more minutes please?"

"Five," Bree agreed, brushing past him. "Then we have to get ready to go out. Your *papà* wants you to meet your other grandma and grandpa."

Bree agreed to meet his parents because she wanted the introduction out of the way. It also got them out of her apartment, which had begun to feel very claustrophobic.

Marriage? Was he out of his tree?

She hadn't been above dreaming of a big wedding as an adolescent. By the time she was living with Kabir, she had been convinced she would marry him in full pageantry. Her father would walk her down the aisle and it would be nothing but happily ever after.

The way Kabir had dismissed her as delusional for even thinking he would marry her had left her feeling foolish for wanting marriage at all, let alone a big ceremony.

Maybe she would have come around again to wanting a life partner, but she had met Jax, then had Sofia—two very strong forces that had pushed the desire for marriage from her mind. She hadn't wanted to bring a stranger into Sofia's life unless she was truly, madly, deeply in love, and there'd been little chance of that, not when she compared every man she met to the enigmatic, dynamic Jax.

Most importantly, she knew marriage wasn't something to enter lightly, especially when you didn't have genuine love and desire to be with the other person. She'd had a front row seat to the breakdown of her parents' marriage and would never want to put Sofia through that.

They pulled up to the curb before a stately prewar apartment block. The driver opened her door and Bree stepped out, then swung her bag behind her shoulder as she turned to reach for Sofia, who was unbuckling herself from her car seat.

"Let me carry you so you don't get your party shoes wet."

"I'll carry her," Jax said, looming beside her. "Move out of the rain."

Bree stepped under the awning that extended from the entrance to the curb, watching as Sofia trustingly allowed Jax to pick her up. He balanced her bottom on his arm as though he'd been doing it since day one, and Sofia hunched into him for shelter against the spatter of falling rain.

A doorman hurried to open the door for them, greeting them with a polite, "Good evening, sir. Ma'am."

"Can I walk now?" Sofia asked.

Jax set her down, but offered his hand. She took it, also clasping Bree's fingers as Jax led them into what looked like a private elevator. A brass plate read *Visconti* over the call button.

Inside, Sofia looked up at the small chandelier, the glittering mirrors and the flocked wallpaper of blue on silver. "It's pretty."

"It is," Bree agreed with a strained smile, trying not to be intimidated by the overt wealth, but she had a suspicion that was its purpose, to convey the innate power the Visconti name possessed.

The elevator opened into a foyer where the parquet floor held an intricate pattern. A staircase rose in a graceful curve and a pretty half-round table held an arrangement of fresh flowers in a vase Bree would bet was painted by hand with twenty-four-karat gold.

A butler took their coats, revealing Sofia's corduroy overalls atop a striped pullover. Bree had changed into a wool skirt with a cowl-necked sweater. Jax had approved both outfits, but now Bree worried they were underdressed.

She smoothed Sofia's flyaway curls after removing her hat, sending yet another encouraging smile to the girl when, really, it was herself she was trying to bolster.

Jax held his hands down to Sofia and she picked up her arms, letting him lift her again. Then he set his hand in the small of Bree's back, guiding her into a lounge where a man was talking.

It was his younger brother, Christo, standing in front of the fireplace. The Visconti genes were equally strong in him, but he kept his black hair longer than Jax and wore an ivory cable-knit sweater over jeans.

Christo cut off whatever animated story he was relaying and lifted his brows in amused question, sliding his gaze to Sofia, then running a distinctly masculine glance of assessment from Bree's bangs to her boots.

"I didn't think you'd be here yet," Jax said. The hand at her back slid to her hip, securing her closer to his side.

Ginevra Visconti was on the sofa, back stiffening, eyes flaring with startlement at the sight of unexpected company.

"Hello." Ginny rose and sent Bree a very cool nod. "Perhaps you'd like to introduce us, Jackson. When you texted that we would have two more for dinner, I thought you meant Eve and Dom were coming after all."

It was a very polite *This surprise is unwelcome.*

Romeo was in an armchair and Nico rose from another one where the angle of the back had hidden him. He narrowed his eyes, but didn't seem as surprised to see Bree.

"You're here, too. Good." Jax sounded more annoyed than pleased. "I can tell you all at once."

"Tell us what?" Nico was flicking his gaze between them.

Thanks to her mother's drilling in poise under pressure, Bree kept a relaxed smile on her face, but her blood was congealing in her veins.

"Mom, Dad. I want you to meet Brielle and Sofia. Our daughter."

The silence that crashed down on the room should have left the house in rubble. This was even worse than walking into her father's Georgetown mansion and his wife's circle of DC's elite. Romeo and Ginevra Visconti were high society and Old Money. They knew immediately that Bree was not One of Them.

"Are you trying to put Dad back in the hospital?" Christo drawled.

"How are we only learning of this today?" Romeo asked gruffly.

"Yes," Nico seconded in a tone of heavy distrust. "Why today? Bree has been working for Eve for weeks."

Ginny shot Nico a look, then back to Jax for confirmation, back to Bree with accusation.

"Maybe Bree thought *I* deserved to know before she told *you*," Jax said with heavy irony, then addressed his parents in a more even tone. "We met in Como four years ago. Bree was on her way to Virginia. I was needed in Naples. We lost touch."

His parents were still staring as though utterly confounded.

"This has been proven scientifically, has it?" Nico asked.

"We stopped for a cheek swab on the way here," Jax agreed.

"And?"

"It will be confirmed tomorrow."

"But you brought them here today? Come on, Jax," Nico chided. "You're smarter than that."

"We'll go," Bree decided and held out her hands for Sofia.

"No," Jax said, but allowed Sofia to tip into Bree's arms. "Nico will leave, unless he changes his attitude very quickly."

It wasn't just him. Bree felt the waves of dismay coming off his mother. It was exactly the derision she'd grown up in.

He has to let her come here. It's part of their custody agreement. Otherwise, he'd have to pay more.

"It's my job to protect our family," Nico said without apology, holding Jax's stare. "That includes you."

"It includes Eve, but you didn't mind throwing her to the wolf, did you?"

The men weren't toe to toe, but they might as well have been. They were the same height, the same build. Animosity crackled like lightning between them.

Sofia read the room and buried her face in Bree's neck, hugging arms and legs tightly around her.

"Bree wouldn't risk Sofia's well-being on a lie that could be disproved so easily," Jax continued in a tone weighted with warning. His fingers dug into her hip, keeping her pinned against him. "They're both also now part of this family. Act like it," he commanded Nico.

No, thank you.

The very last thing Bree wanted was to be force-fed to anyone. Been there, done that, and had been thrown up like a hair ball to prove it.

"She's Lili all over again," Romeo said gruffly. "Look at her. Sofia," he called gently. "Let me see your face."

At her name, Sofia picked up her head to peek at Romeo.

"See?" the older man said with a nod of satisfaction. "The truth is right there."

"Yeah. What part of this are you having trouble believing?" Christo asked Nico out of the side of his mouth. "That

Jax had a shot with a solid gold ten and blew it? Kind of par for the course with him, don't you think?"

No one laughed, especially not Ginny.

"I really wish I'd had this information sooner, Jackson. What about the party?"

"They're coming with me," he said as though that was obvious.

His mother's expression tightened.

"I don't want to overshadow Eve on her special day," Bree said firmly. "It sounds like it would be very overwhelming for Sofia, too. So, thank you, but no."

"You're coming," Jax told her, arm like iron across her back. "I've asked Bree to marry me. I'd like her to wear Nonna's ring."

Another resounding silence fell.

"Jackson," Bree said under her breath. Her eyes were bright with hurt and anger.

He didn't blame her, but this chilly reception wasn't about her. His mother was already two hundred miles down the road of marrying him to Tabitha and connecting the Viscontis to her wealthy, influential family. Coming back from that, and the explanations she would have to make in order not to offend, were consuming her in this moment.

Bree tried using the shifting of Sofia's weight to her other hip to force him to release her. She wanted to leave, but he wouldn't let her.

"Come to me, *piccolina*. Mama's arms are tired." He drew her from Bree's hold back onto his arm, liking the feel of her featherweight and steadying hand resting behind his shoulder. "Is the ring here? Or does someone have to visit the bank?"

"I'll check," his father said.

"That's really not necessary," Bree said to Romeo's back. "I haven't agreed..."

Her faint words were overshadowed by Sofia's surprised, "Did you call me a pickle?"

"I called you *piccolina*. It means *little one*." He tilted his forehead closer to hers, incapable of resisting her cuteness.

She giggled, shoulders coming up. "I thought you said *pickle*."

"Do you want me to call you *pickle*?"

She shook her head.

"Piccolina?"

She nodded.

"Stay for dinner. I insist," Ginny said firmly, gaze softening as she watched them. "Forgive me, Brielle. I completely forgot my manners in the face of this happy news."

Jax felt the small jolt in Bree's frame as though she stifled a snort.

"Please come sit." His mother patted the cushion next to her. "Sofia? Will you come, too? I'd like to know more about you. How old are you?"

Jax ushered Bree closer. She reluctantly lowered onto the sofa, where Sofia wanted to sit in her lap. His daughter was then happy to chat with her new grandmother, telling her she was three and liked to paint and draw.

Bree sat as though she was in military school, spine straight, expression stiff and unreadable. Jax stayed on his feet, moving to accept the drink Nico offered him, but keeping his eye on Bree.

Christo set a glass of white wine on the table in front of her with his signature come-home-with-me smile.

Bree's response was a tepid, "Thank you," which amused Jax for its complete imperviousness to his brother's charm.

Christo applied himself to winning over Sofia, asking

what she wanted to drink, teasing her with offers of wine and beer. "Is that not what children drink? You'll have to teach me how to be a good uncle."

"Now I know." Nico was watching, too, sipping his own scotch.

"What?"

"What kept you in Como four years ago."

It was a sucker punch, one that Jax should have seen coming. One he deserved, perhaps. At the time, Dom's father had recently died and Romeo had just retired. They'd seemingly had Dom on the ropes, financially. Jax had been confident he had the property in Naples sewn up, but his dallying with Bree meant Dom got there first. It was the first good hit Dom had landed against them and hadn't been the last.

"Don't take it out on her," Jax warned. They'd all underestimated Dom if half a day was all he had needed to gain an advantage over them.

Besides, Jax had lost more than that property four years ago. Losing to Dom because he'd prioritized sex was an embarrassment, but it would be a long time before he got over his anger at himself for leaving Bree without taking her number. Now he knew he had missed years with Sofia that he would never get back. That wasn't entirely Bree's fault.

You didn't take my number. Why should I take yours?

Bree had thoroughly captured his interest that day. His dereliction of duty had proved it. After Paloma, he hadn't wanted any woman to take up that much space in his life or head or heart. So he'd accepted the clean exit that Bree had offered him.

In the four years since, he had tried to convince himself he'd been right to keep it no-strings that day, especially since his inability to forget her proved she had the power to knock him off his stride.

He was still wary of her effect on him, but now Sofia was part of the equation.

"Don't tell me not to bring them to the party," he said to Nico. "I have to."

"You do," Nico agreed. "*You* have to be there no matter what. If we don't all show our support for this marriage, the whole exercise is a bust."

Jax snorted, thinking of Bree claiming his sister had married Blackwood for love. No, Eve's belated wedding reception was the equivalent of a state dinner where two warring factions would put down their arms and promise to live in peace from now on. If anyone refused to attend, it would give the impression they were still holding a grudge.

"Tabitha would have been a better look. This *will* cause ripples," Nico warned.

"I know." An old sting of culpability spread under Jax's skin.

He hadn't expected his actions against Paloma's brother, Tucker, to impact his whole family. He had stood by his principles when he had reached out to the victim and offered to back her up if she wanted to press charges. He had given a police statement when asked. Jax was the one who had worn the print of Paloma's slap on his cheek for days and caused Tucker to move to Brazil to get away from the notoriety.

When their family had attacked Jax, he had accepted the retaliation, but his parents and siblings had become collateral damage. Romeo had sent Jax to their grandmother in Italy to cool things off. It wasn't meant as punishment, Jax knew that, but having his family push him away on the heels of Paloma's rejection had made him hyperconscious of never letting them down again.

Then he had. By sleeping with Bree.

The very last thing he wanted to do was instigate fresh gossip, but he was about to reveal a secret daughter, looking like a deadbeat dad who had ignored his responsibilities for four years. So much for his lofty principles. That's how Paloma's family was likely to frame it. At the time, their hatred toward him had gone so deep they had cozied up to the Blackwoods in a "my enemy is your enemy" alliance.

One Jax feared would show its ugly head at the party.

"Anything less than acting loud and proud to learn I'm a father looks like I'm trying to hide her. I have to announce it immediately and drive the narrative. I need the support of the family while I do it." He sent Nico a significant look.

His brother held up a hand. "I had to ask the questions. But I agree. You have no choice but to acknowledge your child and marry her mother. You'll take them to Italy?"

"Yes." There was no way he'd leave Bree and Sofia here to navigate whatever stones Paloma's family chose to throw at her.

"Good. I'll have a press release prepared."

Exiled again.

Jax tried to forestall the thought, but it was a cut that had scarred over while remaining ultrasensitive.

Bree's profile was more remote than ever as she tried to insist to his mother that she couldn't attend the party because she had nothing appropriate to wear.

"Please take pity on my mother, Bree," Jax said. "Eve got married without telling her. She's dying to help someone shop for a gown."

"It's true. I love an excuse to shop." Ginny patted Sofia's hand. "And I have some spoiling to catch up on with this one, don't I?"

CHAPTER SEVEN

THE RING WAS on the inventory list for the box at the bank, Romeo reported, but he returned with photos of Eve to show Sofia how much she resembled her aunt. Nostalgic tales ensued.

By the time Bree saw an opportunity to rise and leave without making a scene, they were being called in to dinner.

Of all the times for Sofia to be on her best behavior! Everyone had the gall to be nice to her, too. Nico brought her books to sit on since they didn't have a booster seat, acting like a doting uncle despite the remark he'd made to Jax.

You have no choice but to acknowledge your child and marry her mother. Then you'll take them to Italy? Good.

Get them out of our sight, he meant. It was her childhood all over again.

"What of your family, Bree?" Ginny asked her. "Are they here in New York?"

As if this test couldn't get any more grueling.

"My mother is here, yes. My father is in DC. He's a heart surgeon." It was a pathetically predictable way to earn a murmur of admiration, as though she had anything to do with his ability to save lives. As though he cared about *her* life one way or another.

When Sofia yawned as coffee was being offered, Bree leaped on the excuse of an approaching bedtime. She'd had the forethought to bring a toothbrush and pajamas so she could change her before they left, anticipating she would fall asleep on the way home.

She emerged from the powder room to see Jax accept an overnight bag from the butler, saying to Nico, "We're staying in the suite at the Signature."

"I booked the Donatellis into that," Nico said with a scowl. "Haven't you done enough? You have to evict our bankers and get them on our bad side?"

"I texted him. He said they were visiting family while they were in town and didn't need it anyway."

Bree was on her last nerve, but she waited until they were in the elevator before she said, "This has already been a big day for Sofia. She'll sleep better in her own bed."

Jax gave her a flinty look, but he directed the driver to her apartment. When they arrived, he carried the sleeping Sofia from the car. As he tucked her into her bed, Bree had the fleeting thought that he had proved himself to be a more doting, affectionate father inside of twelve hours than her own had been in her entire lifetime.

But she kept hearing Nico's voice. *You have no choice…*

She snuggled Sofia's favorite stuffie under the blanket with her, kissed her cheek, then drew the door closed as she came out.

Jax was in the middle of her living room, overcoat gone, imposing presence taking up all the space. He had changed before dinner into brown wool trousers and a knitted pullover with a shawl collar. She didn't know how he made everything he wore look like a photo shoot from a fashion magazine, but he did.

"You didn't have to bring us home. Now you'll have to backtrack to the hotel."

He snorted. "Subtle."

"What did you expect? An invitation to stay over? It's been a long day." She was emotionally and physically exhausted, but also keyed up. "I don't want to go to this party, Jax. I don't want to shop with your mother and I don't want to wear a family heirloom! Did you see how they looked at me when you brought up marriage? *No.*"

She absolutely would not subject herself to being unwanted again.

"See?" He ran his hand down his jaw as he stretched it out. "We have things to talk about. The party is unavoidable." He dropped his arm to his side. "I can't go alone, then reveal I have a daughter. The first question would be *When did you learn about her?* That would bring far more attention—negative attention—than announcing it amidst the party news. If you're worried about the cost of the gown, don't. It's covered." He waved his hand to dismiss such trifling things.

She hated that he made a good point about burying the revelation in the excitement of the party. Eventually, the world would know he was Sofia's father. Her coworkers weren't blind. She had already received a few texts asking why she hadn't come back to work this afternoon. They knew something was up. Bree dreaded having to make explanations, but if the truth was announced formally, it would save her from stumbling through it.

"Fine," she huffed, pacing into the living room. "I'll go. And I'll wear whatever your mother picks out for me." The better to win her approval and blend in. "But I'm not wearing your grandmother's ring. Why would you even suggest that?" She spun back to face him.

"Because Nonna gave it to me for my bride."

"Then you should keep it for her, shouldn't you?" she said tartly.

"Our marrying is also unavoidable," he said in that same dispassionate tone. "And best accomplished as quickly as possible. Sunday afternoon, before we leave for Italy."

The floor disintegrated beneath her feet again. She kept flailing, thinking she had hold of a branch only for it to snap and plummet her deeper into a dark chasm.

"Your mother hates me." She leaned into that statement, crossing her arms defensively. "In case you didn't notice. So does your brother."

"They don't hate you." His brows came together. "Nico is on his back foot over orchestrating Eve's marriage, but he understands how important it is for me to marry you."

You have no choice...

"As for Mom, she arranged a date for me. The daughter of a friend. Now she has to gracefully withdraw from that."

"Tabitha?" Bree immediately hated herself for sounding like a jealous wife. She had no claim on him whatsoever.

His expression didn't change, but he grew watchful, perhaps wondering how much she had overheard. "Yes. It was essentially a blind date. I've met her very briefly in the past, but I don't really know her. We're not involved."

Now she felt even worse. Like she needed mollifying. Which she kind of did.

"Date whoever you want. I don't care." She looked into the darkest corner of the room, already sulking at the prospect.

"Really? It wouldn't bother you if I married a stranger and brought her into Sofia's life?"

She snapped her attention back to him. "Don't you dare."

"So you would prefer I marry someone you approve to be her mother figure?" The corners of his mouth dug in and his brows tilted into a complacent angle. "Who would that be?"

Herself, obviously.

He knew he had her, which was enormously frustrating.

It was terrifying. She was scared of being locked into an intimate relationship that was based on nothing but practicality. His lack of genuine regard for her would chip away at her self-esteem. She had fought really hard to find her confidence and autonomy and he only had to look at her to fill her with yearning. That made him very dangerous to her peace of mind.

But the alternative, where he married someone like this unknown Tabitha, and that stranger became a pseudo parent to Sofia? Like Laura had been to Bree?

No, no, no. Absolutely not.

That's what would happen, though, if she wasn't the woman who occupied that position in his life.

"Maybe we could come to Italy for a while, to see how things go between us," she conceded with great trepidation. "We don't have to marry."

"I want Sofia to wear the Visconti name. You would benefit from it, too."

"I'm not marrying for money," she said firmly.

"Money is power and you will need both, Bree. You're right to be concerned about media attention falling on both of you. It's an unfortunate reality in my life, but becoming part of the fold will give you some protection."

"Push, push, push. I just agreed to go to Italy with you and you're still not satisfied?" She waved an exasperated hand, then hugged herself, worried now about how she would be treated by the press. She considered herself a modern woman who didn't buckle to society's most limiting expectations, but she knew darned well that Jackson Visconti's baby mama would be regarded differently than his bride.

"I'm thinking beyond this weekend," Jax said. "For the next fifteen years, you and I are partners in Sofia's upbringing. Have you thought about giving her a sibling?"

"Oh, my God. Slow your roll, cowboy." She held up a halting hand.

"I'm just asking. But these are all aspects that weigh into this decision. If you want more children, it's another point in favor of marrying." The lamplight was behind him, casting his face in sinister shadows that were impossible to read. "I would be amenable, by the way. Not immediately, but it's definitely on the table."

"You don't *want* to marry me, Jax," she reminded him. "You don't want *me*." He had proved it when he walked out in Como.

"I'm arguing very passionately that I do. There hasn't been anyone else in four damned years." He stepped close enough she felt the heat off his body. "We're already lovers. I'm saying we should make official what is going to happen anyway."

You don't know that.

That was what she wanted to say, but delirious heat burst in her, likely signaling her reaction to him in a flush of bright red under her skin.

Why? Why does he do this to me?

Goose bumps of excitement rose on her skin. Her nipples pinched into stiffness.

His gaze raked down as though he knew what was happening to her. He probably did. He read her like a book. He wasn't even touching her and she was feverish with desire, mind echoing with that word. *Lovers.*

Tell him to leave. Be smart.

Instead, she turned her head and saw the open door to her empty bedroom. She thought about how he had apologized to their daughter for not being here sooner. How he had stood up for her with Nico.

She didn't know if it was true that he'd been celibate all this time, but she knew she didn't want him to be with anyone else in the future. It wasn't only about not wanting strangers parenting Sofia. It was the pull of a link that had been forged between them four years ago, one she didn't want broken again.

One she wanted to reinforce.

"Kick me out if you need time to accept it," he said grittily. "But spending the night thinking about it won't change the fact that we're going to sleep together again. So why fight it?"

Why indeed?

Why deprive herself?

She nodded and walked into her bedroom, heart in her throat as she heard his footsteps behind her.

The moment they stepped through, he filled the small space with his expansive energy. He closed the door and locked it, then began to undress, dropping his clothes where he stood while watching her fumble to do the same.

"We're going to have to be quiet," he said in a low voice as he stalked closer and dropped her bra straps off her shoulders. "Aren't we?" He slid magical fingers behind her, releasing the catch to let the bra fall, then caressed from her collarbone to the points on her shoulders and down, grazing the sides of her breasts.

His gaze on them made them tighten and swell. Her nipples were taut pebbles that brushed the wide plane of his chest. Lower, his erection brushed her abdomen, making her stomach dip with anxious anticipation. With more nerves than that afternoon in Italy. There'd been no stakes then. Now they were so high, she could barely find the courage to take him in hand and see if she could give him as much pleasure as he gave her.

"We could have been doing this all this time," he rasped, drawing lacy patterns on her breasts with his tickling touch.

"You didn't want to." Her whisper held a thick edge. "You didn't stay. You didn't ask for my *name*." He wasn't the only one who felt slighted by these long years apart.

She saw his mouth tighten, then closed her eyes, not wanting him to realize her anger stemmed from hurt. She didn't want him to have the power to hurt her. He shouldn't. Despite the child they'd made, they were strangers. But he *had* hurt her by leaving without a qualm. He could easily do it again.

That realization had her parting her lips with hesitation, but his mouth came down on hers, hungry and demanding, but tender. Soothing? Or was that merely the relief of waiting years to be like this again?

She released his erection and he pulled her closer. Naked skin met naked skin. Her arms rose to fold around his neck, easing the ache inside her. The one that had longed to be held like this again.

He shuddered and a thankful groan resonated through her. His? Or her own?

She didn't know because she was lost. Melting. Still hurt and angry, but those emotions were burning clean in the inferno of need that licked at her. His tongue danced across hers, stoking the heat while his hands swept her shape, becoming flames of their own.

His lips trailed into her throat and his wide hand slid into her underwear, pushing them down. As they cut across the tops of her thighs, he moved his palm to cup her mound.

Lightning shot into her loins, then exploded outward to her nerve endings.

"I've been thinking about this all day. Even before you came so hard against me at the hotel. The second I saw you again, I wanted my hands all over you." His whisper warmed her ear while his clever fingers delved. "I wanted to touch you like this. I've never stopped wanting you. Tell me you want this, Bree. That you want *me*."

"I do." It was a small, broken cry sent toward the ceiling.

"Shh." She felt his smile against her cheek right before his teeth scraped the edge of her jaw. "I want to taste you, but I can't, can I?" His fingertip rolled around the swollen center of her pleasure. "You'll wake her."

She pressed her mouth to his shoulder to stifle her moan of pleasure, barely able to make sense of his words. She curled her nails against his skin, dying.

"Do I need a condom?"

"I'm on the pill," she gasped. She'd called her doctor for a prescription the day she'd seen his photo.

"Heard that before."

She opened her eyes and tipped her head back, but his mouth was quirked with irony, not accusation. He inched her backward to the bed.

Her heart thudded with anticipation as he pressed her across the mattress and stole her underwear, then prowled like a panther to loom over her. He used his thick thighs to make space for himself between her legs and held himself on an elbow, watching as he guided his tip against her moist folds, teasing both of them.

"I would happily get you pregnant again," he said with primal possessiveness in his eyes. In his voice.

It was such an animalistic thing to say, her pulse lurched.

Then he lined up and pressed. She was so aroused, he slid deep with one claiming thrust, but it still pinched. The burn of his invasion felt good, though. The fullness relieved an emptiness that had been with her since they'd last been like this.

He noticed her flinch and froze.

"Hurt?" His thumb caressed her jaw.

"It's okay," she whispered. "I just really missed this." She had. There was a dampness behind her eyes that had nothing to do with discomfort and everything to do with how much she had longed for the feel of him.

He set a comforting kiss at the corner of her mouth, then swept his lips across hers in a more carnal kiss. One that drew her back into the sea of passion.

When her knees climbed of their own accord to hug his rib cage, he tucked his hand beneath her tailbone and tilted her hips so he could bury himself an extra fraction of an inch.

They both shuddered.

And when he started to withdraw a moment later, she clung with arms and legs and the inner muscles of her sheath.

"I'm not going anywhere, *bella*." He returned in a deep thrust that made all her nerve endings sing. "I'm staying right here for the rest of our lives."

She could accept his proprietary statement—could even celebrate it—when he delivered so much pleasure. Such a feeling of homecoming and being desired.

For long minutes, nothing existed except the sublime friction of their lovemaking. It was exactly like their first time. Electric. Nearly too much to bear. His skin seared her own. She ran her hands across his shoulders and cupped the sides of his head and reveled in the slow heaviness of his strokes. The controlled power.

She gasped for breath, then sought his kiss again, groaning into his mouth. Trying not to bite his lip as she fought the grunts and groans of wild abandonment.

"Harder," she begged. "Faster."

"It has to be slow and quiet." He wove their fingers together against the mattress, prolonging their pleasure. It became tantric, melding her to him in a way that nothing else could have. She was aroused to the point of wanting to scream. Each stroke was exquisitely erotic. *Necessary.*

When she was mindless, when nothing else existed but his full ownership of her body, her body surrendered for her. The first waves began to crest over her and his hand fisted into her hair. His fingertips bit into her thigh as his hips cemented to hers.

They tumbled into the abyss.

Bree woke a few minutes before her usual alarm. Her bed was only a twin and she was right at the edge. Jax was on his stomach behind her. His knee was crooked so her back and bottom and thighs were curled into the nook of space he had left her.

I like this, was her first thought. Latent satisfaction kept her relaxed as she blinked against the morning gloom, but renewed desire began to stir her nerve endings, especially when she recalled their lovemaking. It had been torture of the most delicious kind.

And a horrible mistake. Because this was exactly what she feared most—beginning to soften toward him and form an attachment, even a physical one. She had been in this situation before. At least with Kabir she had waited to share her body until she'd been more confident in their emotional connection.

It hadn't kept them together, though. Despite the love they

had declared to each other, he had walked away, destroying her sense of self-worth.

Maybe she would fare better in a situation where her expectations were low. Maybe it would be safer to involve herself with a man who gave her terrific orgasms, but didn't steal pieces of her heart. That way, if he ever did leave her, she wouldn't be so devastated.

And maybe she was rationalizing sleeping with someone who had already slid past her defenses.

She sat up, trying not to wake him, but had to bite back a groan as her muscles protested. Everything ached in a way that filled her with gratification. She kept the edge of the sheet across her breasts, but the tips peaked with renewed arousal. Her skin pebbled from more than the morning chill. *Weakness.*

"She's not up yet, is she?" he asked, voice mostly muffled by the pillow.

"No, but I can't sleep." She didn't dare look over her shoulder at his bare, golden shoulders. His arm snaked around her waist. His wicked lips brushed her lower back.

"We don't have to."

Tempting. So tempting.

"She will be up soon, though." And her whole life had to be rewritten to include him without losing herself. "I need a shower."

She removed his arm and rose, then shrugged on the robe hanging on the back of her bedroom door before she faced him. There was no call for shyness. He'd seen and touched and tasted every inch of skin she possessed, but she was still deeply self-conscious.

"Can I trust you not to kidnap her while I'm in there?" She was only half joking.

He was on his elbow in the rumpled bedding, jaw shadowed with morning stubble, eyelids heavy. "How much more proof do you need that I want you both?"

She tied off the belt and hung on to the tails, wondering why she experienced such an atavistic thrill at his possessive language when she refused to believe he actually wanted *her*.

"My parents had passion in the early days, too." She kept her voice low. Barely above a whisper. It added a note of despondency to what she was saying, but maybe that was her inner child still aching to be heard. "That's how they wound up with me. Our situation reminds me too much of that. I don't want Sofia to go through what I went through."

"And what is that exactly?"

She twisted her mouth, unable to call it abuse or neglect. Her needs had been met, if grudgingly on her father's side. Her mother had lied to her, but only to protect her. She hadn't told the truth when Bree asked if her father loved her. Who could, when the answer was no?

"Sadness," Bree replied.

"Because they divorced? We won't."

"You don't know that." At least her mother had loved her father. She had married him believing her feelings were reciprocated. "What if you fall for someone else? What if I do?"

"You won't." It was a quiet, implacable order that made her chuckle drily.

"It happens, Jax. Then you're stuck in a marriage you accepted for a child you never wanted in the first place."

"I want her."

"So do I. But asking Sofia to carry the weight of a marriage isn't fair to her."

"I don't expect her to. It's on us to make it work."

"Mama?" The knob on the door wiggled. "Who are you talking to?"

Jax had retrieved his bag from the driver last night. He rose and stepped into track pants, calling out, "It's me, *piccolina*."

"Papà?"

"Yes."

As he tied the drawstring, Bree unlocked the door and opened it.

Sofia was in her wrinkled pajamas, a penguin stuffie hugged under her arm. She blinked at him. "Why are you here?"

"Because I'm part of your family now."

He might be annoyingly domineering, but Bree liked the way he spoke to Sofia in ways she could understand. She also liked that he didn't imply they hadn't been a family before he entered the picture. He was joining what she and Sofia already had.

Sofia frowned. "But *I* like to cuddle with Mama in the morning."

His mouth twitched before he schooled his face into patience. "You still can. We'll have a big bed in Italy where we can all cuddle together."

She looked up at Bree, brows pulled in confusion. "With the elevator?"

"Not where we went last night, no. Italy is a different place."

"I'll tell you about it while I make breakfast. What?" Jax caught Bree's askance look as he finished pulling on his T-shirt. "You think my Italian grandmother didn't teach me how to cook? Come, *piccolina*." He came to the door and offered his hand. "You can help me."

Bree's chest constricted as she accepted that she had to give her daughter the kind of father she'd always longed for. It was herself she needed to worry about.

CHAPTER EIGHT

Jax was impatient to take Bree and Sofia to Italy, but he had to get through suit fittings and lawyer meetings and obtaining a marriage license first. Then they had the party and the actual wedding and Bree still had doubts about all of this.

In an effort to dispel some of her misgivings, he took them to Eve's for dinner.

Bree was suspicious. "When your boss wants to meet you away from the office, they usually hand you a box of your stuff from your desk."

Eve didn't fire her. She graciously welcomed her to the family, and they made a plan for Bree to work remotely on a very flexible schedule while she got Sofia settled. Eve also introduced Bree to one of Dom's sisters, Astrid, and her daughter Jade, who was near Sofia's age, so Sofia would have a friend at the party.

That didn't do much to ease Bree's nerves, but Jax realized she was not only preparing to leave her home country with their daughter inside of a week, but had to attend a formal ball where she would be outed as the mother of his child. Plus, her father couldn't attend their wedding.

"Did he say when his schedule might open up?" Jax asked her.

"It could be months," Bree said with an unreadable look on her face. Defensive? He wasn't sure.

All he knew was that he wanted his ring on her finger. That's where his real impatience stemmed from. Despite the way Bree gave herself up to him in bed—which was indescribably gratifying—she wore a cloak of reserve throughout the day, one that kept him from fully trusting she would go through with the wedding.

Maybe his failed engagement was undermining his confidence in her, but he was still processing the fact she hadn't tried harder to bring him into Sofia's life. Now he had this sense of impending doom as he awaited their wedding day. He wouldn't relax until his marriage was signed, sealed, and decreed.

First, this damned party.

The reception was being held in the ballroom of the WBE Hallmark property, which was across the street from the Visconti Signature. They got ready in the hotel suite.

Melissa came along to help Bree with her hair and makeup. She was spending the evening here at the hotel, enjoying the amenities until it was time to take Sofia home for a last sleepover with Gigi before they left for Italy. Bree would spend the night here with Jax. Tomorrow, they would all convene at his parents' home, where the immediate family would witness their nuptials.

"I was thinking to surprise Bree by flying us through DC on our way to Italy," Jax told Melissa while Bree was in the shower. "Do you have her father's number?"

Melissa's expression altered slightly, almost imperceptibly, but he'd seen a similar adjustment on Bree's face often enough to recognize that Melissa was about to demur in some way.

"I don't, actually." She lifted the lid off the plate of chicken fingers she'd ordered for Sofia. "Bree has always managed her communications with him herself."

Always? "How old was she when you divorced?"

She drew a breath that suggested the mere mention of that time was a firm press on a still tender bruise.

"Eight. Once lawyers were involved, he and I stopped speaking. I can't say it was my finest hour." She gathered up Sofia's flyaway curls in an absent, tender way that made him think she wasn't fully aware she was doing it. "When Bree told me she was pregnant and intended to raise Sofia alone, I knew I bore a lot of responsibility for that decision. But so does he."

She lifted her gaze to his, letting him see the fine layer of gritty bitterness along with regret. Remorse. But also, a somber warning.

"She's seen how badly things can turn. She has a right to be afraid that she's making a wrong choice."

"But she doesn't have a *reason*. I won't give her one."

"You'd better not," Melissa said pleasantly, still twirling Sofia's hair around her fingers. "I've learned my lesson about offering second and third chances. You won't get any."

Like Bree, she was tall but slender, hardly a threat to him, but he took her very seriously. It would be a grave mistake to get on her wrong side.

She cocked her ear. "I think that's the hair dryer. I'll go help Mama with her makeup." She dropped a kiss on Sofia's crown. "Come in when you've finished eating. I'll do your hair."

Sofia nodded and Melissa walked away.

Jax wiped Sofia's fingers a few minutes later and sent her into the bedroom to join the women. Then he showered and dressed in the spare bedroom before moving to the lounge, where he stood at the bar to drink the scotch he poured himself while he reread the press release that had hit the airwaves.

He hated even the blandest mention of himself in these sorts of things. This one glossed over his obliviousness to having a daughter, merely announcing his sharing of a child with Brielle Hughes and their intention to marry in a private ceremony.

They will reside in Naples, Italy, where Jackson Visconti runs the Euro division.

All innocuous details that still felt like a spotlight burning into a deeply personal place, leaving him raw with exposure. He wanted to shield himself, but also Bree and especially Sofia. Every moment he spent with Sofia unraveled the careful structures he had assembled around his heart. He was committed to protecting her with every breath in him, but in moments like this, when they were on display next to him, he had to wonder if he was up to the task.

Would he be able to give them a safe, happy life? Or would he only draw them into the rain of judgment and fire the way he had with his parents and siblings?

"My turn!" he heard Sofia sing out from down the hall.

"Your turn," Melissa echoed with amusement. "Come sit here."

He heard a rustle of silk and turned his head to see Bree had come into the lounge.

The vision she made arrested him. He may have even stopped breathing as he took in the way her hair held the glamorous retro wave of a silent film star. Her makeup was subtle, but her thick lashes emphasized her eyes and the aqua color of her irises was so deep and wide, they threatened to drown him.

With a self-conscious bite of her ruby-red lips, she gave a slow pirouette. The skirt of royal blue satin flared. It was topped by a sequined, sleeveless bodice that shimmered. It dipped in the back and left her arms and upper chest and shoulders bare.

"Your mother picked it." She gently pressed against the skirt as she faced him again, looking down to the closed-toe stiletto that peeped from beneath the hem. "She said the whole family is wearing blue except Dom and Eve." Her gaze slid over his dark blue tuxedo which perfectly matched her gown.

"You look beautiful. Perfect."

One of us.

He had to swallow because his voice was not entirely steady.

"So do you. I mean you look very handsome." She set her hand against her stomach. "I know Eve and Dom are the stars, but I'm nervous. Did the announcement go out?"

"Yes." The wheels were in motion.

"And?"

"No reactions yet."

She nodded, frowning in consternation, then she touched her earlobe. "You said not to put on jewelry, but Mom brought me some earrings. Should I get them?"

"No, I bought some for you." Not that she needed adornment, but the blue sapphire studs, each stone haloed by white diamonds, would suit her. A matching pendant was affixed to a dark blue velvet choker that he helped her put on.

"I don't know what to say." She looked at herself in the mirror behind the bar.

"Say you'll marry me." He opened the ring box, discovering that he was uncharacteristically nervous.

She gasped as she looked at it, hands tucking beneath her chin as though she was afraid to touch it.

He'd seen the ring many times. It had been as much a part of his grandmother as her ever-present smile and her iron-gray hair. He'd seen the ring as recently as this morning, when he'd picked it up after it had been sized and freshly polished. It was genuinely beautiful. Even the goldsmith had been charmed by the delicate filigree that elevated and supported the diamond. She'd praised the skill and care taken by its maker.

But as Jax showed it to Bree, it seemed to sparkle even brighter and feel heavier in his hand. It was more substantial than a simple piece of jewelry. It wasn't merely a symbol to indicate their promise to marry, it was weighted with the years it had already endured. With the thousands and thousands of moments it had witnessed. It spoke of longevity and heritage and familial lines.

Paloma hadn't worn this ring. She'd dropped the one he'd given her into the Hudson. In this moment, he couldn't be more glad about that loss.

Bree was the woman he wanted to marry. His breath backed up in his lungs as he waited for her to agree.

"Your grandmother wore this?" she asked in hushed awe.

"She never took it off. That's why it was nearly worn through." Jax showed her how the repair of the band had been disguised with a continuation of the engraved design.

Nonna Maria had thrown over the man she was supposed to marry—a Blackwood—so she could run off with Aldo, the man she really loved.

They had all adored her, but Jax had had a special relationship with her. After his engagement fell apart, she'd said one morning, *I never thought she was right for you. You cared for her. I could see that. And you wanted to do your duty by joining the two families, but she is not the reason your heart is broken.*

He had all but forgotten that conversation until this moment. His scalp tightened, as he remembered the rest of what she'd said.

You and Eve are like me. You need love. When you find your match, you'll give her my ring because you can't imagine anyone else could wear it.

That wasn't how it was with him and Bree, he told himself. Nonna had been overlooking how following her heart had started the feud with the Blackwoods. He was making a *practical* choice. He had to.

He turned his mind from acknowledging the weeks and months and years of having his eye caught by chestnut hair, of glancing at posters in banks. He ignored the fact that he had asked his parents for this ring within twelve hours of seeing Bree again.

But his voice wasn't entirely steady as he asked again, "Will you? Marry me?"

Her gaze searched his and her lips quivered as she tried to find words.

"The, um…" She cleared her throat. "The press release said I would, didn't it?"

Every muscle in his body tensed. "You can still refuse."

"No, I… I agree we should marry." She tentatively placed her trembling fingers in his palm. "For Sofia's sake. I'm her mother and you're her father. We should try to make a life together. Just promise me that… That if you decide you don't want me anymore, you'll tell me. Don't cheat. And promise you'll never walk out on *her.*"

"Those are very easy promises to make," he said with a thrum of sincerity that had its roots deep in his soul. He threaded the ring onto her left hand and something within him came to rest.

It looked perfect on her. The size and shape and intricacy suited her graceful fingers. It looked as though it belonged there. He brought her hand to his lips and kissed her polished fingernails. Her eyes glossed and her lashes fluttered.

"I wish you could have met her," he said, meaning it.

Her mouth trembled. "Me, too."

"Mama, look! I'm a princess, too."

"Sofia, wait—! Sorry." Melissa hurried up behind her, abashed at the interruption.

Sofia stopped, adorable in a dark blue velvet dress with its tulle skirt that faded to a lighter blue at the hem. Melissa had styled her dark hair in ringlets that framed her round cheeks and big, innocent eyes. She looked like a cherub from an old-world painting.

"It's okay. We have to go. Fashionably late is for the bride and groom."

They obligingly waited for Melissa to snap a quick photo, then he escorted his fiancée and daughter across the street, chest so full of pride, his shirt buttons should have burst.

Bree's stomach was nothing but butterflies as they entered the ballroom. She kept touching the ring, wondering, *Am I really doing this?*

Jax introduced her to some of his cousins and other relatives who had already heard the news of his secret child. They were curious, but welcoming.

Then he brought them to a table where they were seated with Dom's sister, Astrid, whom Bree had met the other day. Astrid's husband, Jevaun, was very easygoing, and their children drew Sofia into the adjoining room, where nannies were on hand to amuse young children with puzzles, games, and other toys.

There was a certain tension in the air, but Astrid assured Bree it was very much about the fact that prior to Dom and Eve's marriage, a Blackwood wouldn't have been caught dead in a room with one Visconti let alone all of them. The feeling was very mutual so everyone was walking around like cats on a floor full of tacks.

Eve and Dom arrived looking positively incandescent. They thanked everyone for coming. Romeo Visconti stood to welcome Dom to the family. Dom's mother welcomed Eve. Dinner was served, wine flowed, and the guests began to relax.

Bree was aware of some stares and tried to ignore it. Word was getting around so curiosity was to be expected.

There were more speeches after dinner, then Dom drew Eve to the dance floor.

After the parents joined them, Jax stood to invite Bree. Nico and Christo were already there with Dom's unmarried sisters. Astrid and Jevaun came and the children all stood at the edge of the dance floor to watch.

Bree's mother would never, ever, have encouraged Bree to enter the beauty pageant circuit, but she always credited the years she'd spent doing it as a terrific finishing school. She had taught Bree everything she learned, including how to waltz.

Jax made dancing with him easy, of course. He smoothly guided her around the floor and switched to a livelier pace when the music changed, twirling her out and bringing her back so she laughed with surprise.

At that point, she glanced to be sure Sofia was still holding the hand of Astrid's daughter and realized an older woman at a table behind Sofia was talking behind her hand while staring derisively at Bree, then sending a disparaging look at Sofia.

Bree's enjoyment of the moment drained away. Thankfully, the music changed again and Eve invited the children onto the dance floor.

After that, it became a party. The children had no concept of feuds. Their antics ensured everyone was laughing if not dancing along with them.

Bree tried to let go of her unease, telling herself she had imagined the stranger's nasty look. Even if it was real, what did she care? People had strong feelings about all sorts of things, including children born out of wedlock. She couldn't let it get to her.

An hour later, Melissa collected Sofia. Bree and Jax stepped out to hug Sofia good night, promising to see her in the morning.

As they came back into the ballroom, Bree caught that same woman giving her a sneering look.

She didn't say anything to Jax, but the whole time they were mingling their way around the room, Bree felt the small arrows of denigration and disgust hitting her. She knew she wasn't imagining it. She'd been raised with these sorts of undercurrents of being seen only because she was *not* wanted to be seen.

Jax felt it, too. Any degree of warmth in him had drained away. His voice became terse. His hand in her back was hard, no longer warm and caressing the way it had been earlier in the evening.

The final straw was when Bree stood in the stall of the ladies' room and heard a woman's voice over the drifting noise of the party and the handful of voices at the mirrors.

"Thank *God* Paloma broke her engagement to him. That man is either stupid enough to get himself trapped by a gold digger, or he's the kind who knocks up a woman and tries to wriggle out of it. Either way, that little nobody is welcome to him. Do you think that little bastard is even his?"

Bree yanked the door open with a bang. The middle-aged woman who'd been casting ugly looks her way all night stood at the mirror. The other women in the room stilled, and one said, "Odelia," in a tone between shock and caution.

"What?" The older woman lifted her chin, unrepentant. "We're all thinking it." She dismissed Bree with a flick of her self-satisfied glance.

No, Bree thought as her heart trembled in her chest. *I am not doing this again.*

Since it was Eve and Dom's party, she didn't grab that woman by the hair and wash her mouth out for the things she'd said about Sofia, but she would not marry a man who would put her in this position of being belittled and disparaged.

When she came out of the powder room, she saw Jax hovering nearby. He hadn't been farther than arm's reach all night, she realized. He looked sharply at her as she emerged.

"Is everything all right?"

"No. I'd like to go home. *Home.* And I won't marry you," she added shakily.

She started to remove the ring, but Jax caught her hand before she could. He dragged her close, wrapping his other arm around her. It was almost as though they were waltzing again, but she was trapped in a cage—one she refused to accept.

She pushed at him and flung her head back to glare with outrage.

"Wait," he commanded, keeping his arm tight around her.

He wasn't even looking at her! He was staring over her head toward the end of the hallway.

"I'm serious, Jax. I don't want to make a scene, but I will if I have to."

"I didn't want to believe she would go after you," he bit out. "Not here. But the way she was watching you and followed you the second you left my side..." He clenched his jaw.

She'd never seen anyone so quietly, dangerously incensed. His body was a twisted metal cage wrapped around her. The set of his expression was murderous.

Her own anger bled off in the face of his. "Who is she?"

The angle of his head grew more alert. He narrowed his eyes.

Bree sensed the woman approaching. Instinctually, she leaned into Jax, chin tucked, seeking his protection while bracing for a physical attack.

From the corner of her eye, she saw the woman come even with them. She wore a smirk of dark satisfaction.

"You could have left it alone, but you didn't," Jax said with contempt.

A hate-filled light exploded in the woman's eyes. "*You* could have left it alone, but you didn't."

Bree didn't know what was happening, only knew the stakes of the evening. She knew what Eve meant to Jax and splayed her hands on his rib cage.

"Not here, Jax. It's Eve's night."

He was like a pit bull, all straining muscle on the end of a leash, ready to attack and tear apart. She didn't have the strength to contain him if he chose to.

"If you need to blame me for his actions, blame me. *Do not* come after my family," Jax warned wrathfully.

"Odelia." Dom came up to them and subtly aligned himself next to Jax. "It's time for you to say good night to my stepmother."

Odelia swung a disbelieving glare up at Dom. "You have made a mistake, Domenico. He's a snake. He'll turn on you when you least expect it."

"Leave quietly. Don't make this ugly."

Odelia stalked away.

Bree might have breathed a little easier at that point, but Jax's arms were still hard around her, crushing her ribs.

"Brielle, we haven't danced yet. Will you do me the honor?" Dom asked.

She could feel the volatile energy still bottled within Jax, percolating and ready to explode. She was also aware of people casting looks their way. As subdued as the interaction had been, people had noticed.

"You need to stay a little longer," Dom added quietly to Jax. "You know you do. Let us dance. You can ask Eve."

Very slowly, as though his muscles were rusted shut, Jax released Bree and gave a barely perceptible nod.

Stage smile.

She accompanied Dom to the dance floor, where he adeptly guided her around, but she felt stiff and uncoordinated.

"I'm sorry Odelia upset you," Dom said. "My father seized any means to attack the Viscontis. It resulted in some associations that have run their course. You won't see her at any future event where I'm present. Evie is very taken with Sofia, by the way. She's already talking about our spending Christmas in Como and asking you to join us there. She wants to get to know both of you properly."

He was trying to distract her and ease her unsettled nerves. It didn't work. Not when Jax swept by with Eve. His expression was still stiff. His sister's was stark.

"Why do we have to stay longer?" Bree asked Dom.

"To show you won," he said simply.

CHAPTER NINE

JAX HAD SUSPECTED Odelia would go after Bree to get to him. She had been watching them all night and quickly followed Bree into the powder room.

At least Sofia was safely away from here. His driver had texted him after escorting her and Melissa into Melissa's brownstone.

Jax was still furious, especially because the altercation had drawn fresh attention onto him. Not everyone would repeat his old scandal, but enough would give it air. His instinct was to take Bree out of here, rather than put up with the stares, but Dom was right. Leaving would have been a concession. Staying after the other couple had been ousted was a statement as to who was welcome here and who was not.

He waited while his brothers each danced with Bree, then Bree sat with Eve and Dom's sisters for a while before Jax moved to collect her.

"You're leaving?" Eve rose the moment he touched Bree's shoulder. "You'll have to excuse them slipping away," she told the group. "They're getting married tomorrow. Jax wants his beauty sleep." She was teasing to keep the mood light.

"Your groom sets a high bar. I don't want him outshining me at my own wedding." Jax went along with the joke, even though he saw Bree's expression stiffen at the mention of their wedding.

She didn't say anything as they crossed the street and rode the elevator to the top floor, only exhaled a shaken breath as they entered the suite.

She started to twist the ring off.

"Don't. Let me explain." He moved to the bar. "Do you want wine or...?"

"Water."

Smart.

He poured two from the filtered tap and brought the glasses to where she sat on the sofa, expression rigid, hands in her lap.

"Excavating my past is the last thing I want to do," he said bluntly. "I had hoped Odelia would behave herself and I'd never have to speak of this again, but..." He scowled at the lack of bite in the sip he took from his glass. "I was engaged to her niece."

"Paloma," she said stiffly, refusing to look at him. "I heard."

And thought he was lying about there being no one since her?

"It was long before you and I met. I was twenty-four. Her father was one of my father's investment partners. We were neighbors on Martha's Vineyard so we saw them every summer, growing up. I went to university with her brother, Tucker, and considered him one of my best friends. As soon as I got my degree, I was made head of marketing at Visconti. We both wanted children right away. Marriage made sense."

"So it was a practical marriage? Or did you love her?" Now she looked at him. Her thick lashes emphasized the vulnerability in her blue-green eyes.

Your heart isn't broken.

No, but it had been dented. Badly.

"It was young love." Maybe it had been what he thought love should be. Closeness built on shared history. Fondness and sexual intimacy. "But this is how I know that marrying because you *think* you love someone isn't enough."

She rolled her lips together, looking to a corner as though being scolded for wanting love, but she didn't understand how badly those emotions set you up for anguish.

"The morning after our engagement party, Tucker and I were nursing a hangover. I noticed scratches on his neck. He mentioned someone we both knew. Corinne. I won't repeat what he said, but the implication was that she had acted like she didn't want his attention, but came around in the end."

"That's horrible." She recoiled in revulsion.

"It was. It was equally disturbing that he expected me to let it slide without calling him out for it."

"Bro code?"

"I wouldn't let either of my *actual* brothers get away with something like that, but yes. Tucker expected me to keep it to myself. All I could think was, *What if it happened to Eve? To Paloma?* In fact, I went to her first."

"Paloma?"

"Yes. She was my fiancée. He was her brother." He rubbed his jaw, still conflicted over how he'd handled it. "I warned her I was going to the police. She was upset, obviously. Corinne was one of our friends, but Paloma was equally—maybe more—worried about Tucker. She didn't want me to get him into trouble."

You can't do that to him. What kind of man does that?

"She said that if Corinne wanted to do something—or nothing—that was up to her." Now he ran his hand into his hair at the back of his skull, trying to release the old tension that gathered there. "I took her point. I hadn't even heard Corinne's side of it, but Paloma told me to drop it or she'd break our engagement. I called Corinne anyway. I told her what I knew and said that if she wanted to make a statement to the police, I would support her."

"Did she?"

"Eventually. She was devastated, but hadn't thought anyone would believe her. Or care. They'd both been drunk. She was blaming herself, but after a week or so, she spoke to the police. She hadn't had one of those kits done, though. By then, Tucker's scratches had faded. It turned into her word against his."

"But you were able to corroborate. He *confessed*."

"And I had told Paloma what he said, but she sided with her family. She told the police I was lying and hadn't told her anything about it. She said I had sour grapes because she'd broken our engagement, which she had by then. Her entire family started smearing my reputation to drown out the gossip around what Tucker had done."

"And Corinne?"

"Tuck's father paid her to withdraw her statement. I don't blame her, considering what they put me through. It was hell. At first, I didn't care because I knew I was right." He sneered at his youthful principles. "Then they joined the Blackwood camp and started including my family in the attacks. At that point, Dad sent me to Nonna and suggested I set up the Euro division."

"He banished you?" Her expression was so empathetic, so filled with sorrow on his behalf, Jax thought he might remember it for the rest of his life—the crinkled brow, the soft, sad pout of her mouth. The blink of sheened eyes.

"It wasn't like that," he said, but his voice traveled over rough ground. It had felt exactly like that. Ostracized. Exiled.

He drew a breath, trying to ease the ache of being punished for doing the right thing. Of being separated from the people he loved most.

"Dad had the whole family to think of." He cleared his throat. "Mom was getting blocked from social events. Nico and Christo were taking it on the chin, but Eve was only seventeen. When they went after her, saying some really filthy stuff, my temper was so short, I broke a man's nose. Dad put me on a plane for my own good."

This time when she fiddled with the ring, she was only centering it on her hand. "At least your grandmother was there for you."

"She was. They all were, in their way. Dad wasn't just getting me out of the city. He had his hands full with Dom and Dom's father. Sending me to run Europe was a strategic move. I genuinely prefer Italy, and Eve was starting school in Switzerland. I saw her all the time. It was probably best that Dad split up us boys, too. We stand together against an enemy, but we're competitive enough to break each other's noses when we disagree. Best to keep large bodies of water between us."

She only looked at the ring, somber. "I thought she was making sure I knew I didn't belong there. She said I'd tricked you into marrying a nobody and that Sofia was a bastard."

He couldn't help the angry curse that burst out of him, or the way his hands curled into fists. It was a damned good thing Odelia was all the way across the city by now.

"It was me she wanted to hurt. She was using you to do it. Of course, you belong."

"Uh, no," she said on a humorless laugh. "Let's be honest about that."

"I am being honest. Aside from Odelia, did anyone else make you feel unwelcome?"

"No, but…" She gave him a pensive look. "You didn't tell me who you were when we met. Yes, I could have looked at your card, but you weren't up front about all of this." She waved at the sumptuous comfort of the Presidential suite. "Was that because you thought I might have heard something about you? That I might be a gold digger?"

"I've had my share of encounters with people attracted to my wealth and name," he admitted. "It was refreshing that you saw me as a person."

"And you knew you'd never see me again, so what did your full identity matter?" Her voice husked and her brow pulled with injury.

"It wasn't that cold-blooded, Bree. I had caused my family a lot of pain. I was still trying to make up for that. I was due in Naples that afternoon to close on a property that Nico and Dom were competing to purchase. I stayed with you. That felt very selfish." He ran his hands on his thighs, conscience still pinched. "I could tell you were a bigger distraction than I could afford, especially when Nico texted that Dom was moving in on us. I was standing there realizing I'd failed my family by sleeping with you, so I didn't ask for your number. But you could have looked at my damned card."

She dropped her gaze, unrepentant, her jaw remaining set.

"I accept that you were hurt and angry tonight. And by my behavior that day. Fine. But I'm committing my life to you tomorrow and I need you to do the same. You can't pull off that ring just because a stranger is rude to you."

"I'm afraid to trust you," she said in a low voice, twirling the ring.

"Same," he said bluntly. "But we have to try."

"How?" she asked with a pang of hopelessness in her

voice. "Where do we even start? All we have between us is sex."

"Then let's start there."

"W-what do you mean?" Bree asked with trepidation.

Jax tugged his bow tie open, then drew it from his collar and set it flat across her knees.

Her heart arrived in her throat, pounding hard. He couldn't be serious.

"No?" He was watching her very closely. "You know I'd never hurt you. Don't you?"

Not physically, no, but he had already turned her inside out over different things. His engagement for one. To a woman he had *loved*. What he'd been through was still making her ache for him, but it also heartened her. A man who had stood up for someone else wouldn't want to force her to do anything she didn't want to.

It was still terrifying to draw her hands down from where she'd instinctively tucked them into her neck and offer them.

"I don't know how..." She tried pressing her inner wrists together, but he guided her into crossing them.

As he wrapped the silk and pulled it tight, binding them, her heart pounded harder.

When it was done, she gave a testing wiggle. He felt to ensure it wasn't so tight it would leave marks. His fingers settled on the pulse in her wrist.

"You're scared?"

"Yes." Her mouth was dry.

"Really scared?" He stroked his touch up the sensitive underside of her bare arm. "Or nervous and turned on?"

How did he know? Her nipples were stinging behind the cups of her bodice. She bit her lip. "The second one."

A slow, wicked smile formed across his lips.

He stood and drew her to her feet, then cupped her face and kissed her.

It started out slow, but deepened by degrees, as though he was reassuring her. As though he was rewarding her.

She flowered under that sweetness. It had been a fraught evening, from attending the party, feeling judged there, then learning more about him and how he had felt about their time in Como.

Now a white haze was filling her brain, taking over any awareness but the drugging sensation of long, lazy kisses. Arousal was detonating through her, and she started to bring her arms up only to discover her wrists were bound.

He lifted his head, eyes gleaming with lust and amused gratification.

He hooked his finger into the silk that bound her, leading her toward the bedroom.

Butterflies filled her stomach as her mind exploded with possibilities, trying to anticipate what he would ask of her. What he might do to her.

As they neared the door to the bedroom, however, he turned her toward the wall, lifting her joined arms toward the U of a tulip-shaped wall sconce. He hooked her bound wrists into it and her stomach plummeted into uncertainty.

"What, um…"

"You're going to have to be very careful, Briella *bella*," he said as he stood behind her, trailing his seductive touch along her trembling arms and the backs of her shoulders. "Don't move too much or you might knock that off the wall. Then we would have some embarrassing explanations to make, wouldn't we?"

"You're not serious," she said on a shaken breath, trying to look over her shoulder at him.

"Do you want me to release you?" His tickling caress

was sweeping across the top of her spine. His lips nuzzled at her nape, nearly taking out her knees. "Because what I really want to do, *bellezza*, is *release* you."

"What if…" They were in the hall. "What if someone walks in?"

"Does that possibility excite you?" The zip of her gown lowered, relaxing across her chest. "Close your eyes and pretend I'm a bellboy if you want to."

"Who are you pretending *I* am?" she asked with a sharp look over her shoulder again.

He chuckled.

"There is only one woman I want, *bella*. The alluring, elusive Bree I met in Como." His hand went into her hair, dragging her head back so he could scrape his teeth against the side of her throat while his other hand delved into the front of her gown. "I want to chain her in a dungeon and keep for myself the rest of my life."

He pinched her nipple just hard enough to make her jolt, but then he soothed her, rolling and teasing and sending rivulets of arousal from breast to belly to sink hotly into her loins.

"I'm glad you're wearing such tall shoes. I can have you right here. I want that very badly. Do you feel that?" His hand rode down to the notch of her thighs. He cupped her mound, using the pressure to push her backside into the erection behind his fly.

"Be careful," she gasped. "You'll stain the dress."

"We both will." He rocked his hand, making her shudder with erotic joy, trapped in such a blatant way. "I'm going to make love to you right here. I want you to know that it's safe to give yourself to me anywhere, anytime. To let me take control. And when you do, you'll like it."

Was it, though? Because despite being literally tethered

to the wall, she felt adrift. As though pieces of her were falling away. Shields maybe.

She wanted to catch them back, but her arms were bound and her skirt was coming up. He ran his hands over her buttocks and hips and thighs, praising her in Italian while sliding her panties down her thighs. She didn't understand all of it, but she understood a cherishing touch and words like *bella* and *seducente* and *la mia donna*.

My woman.

When he guided her to step out of them and his hot touch began to explore between her thighs, she leaned into the wall, turning her face against the cool wallpaper, closing her eyes as longing filled her, waiting for his caress to find the molten center of her.

Finally, he claimed her folds and the peak of her pleasure with a long reaching touch, making her shake. Making her sob with yearning.

More erotic words warmed her ear. "You're as aroused as I am. I don't want to stop touching you, but I want to be inside all this heat, *bella*."

"Yes," she moaned. "Please."

His touch left her and she could have wept, but he was opening his trousers. The fabric brushed her skin. The satin of her skirt draped her thighs as he nudged her shoes apart and stood between them.

A distant part of her had a moment of clarity, realizing how flagrant this was. He'd barely kissed her! But the broad dome of his sex was seeking her entrance, pressing. He was filling her and she groaned in ragged abandon at how good it felt.

His breath hissed in and he gripped her hips. More Italian. Earthy noises of his hips slapping her buttocks.

She was pinned to the wall, arms tingling from being

raised so long, but she didn't care. She only wanted the friction of his thrusts. The animalistic noises from his throat that told her he was as wrapped up in this as she was.

And just when she feared he would lose control and leave her in a state of abject arousal, he slid his touch to rub and press and detonate her climax.

She screamed.

CHAPTER TEN

"I CAME IN to wake you and heard you were in the shower."
Jax rose from the table to hold her chair, gaze skimming
the silk pajamas her mother had given her yesterday. They
were a frosted mulberry color with gray lace on the cuffs.

"Mom gave them to me, since we're not taking a honeymoon." She looked down at them rather than meet the heat
in his eyes. The subliminal, *I know what you did last night*.

The bondage in the hallway should have satisfied both
of them, but after they'd undressed and she'd washed off
her makeup, she had worshipped every inch of him, using
her mouth to draw him into a tensile arrow of muscle before she rode him as though she hadn't seen him in years.

The activity had left her whole body sore in the most
delicious way.

As she started to take the chair, strong hands caught at
her and drew her to face him. He cupped the side of her
neck and nuzzled her temple, lips scuffing her cheekbone.

"Thank you for last night."

She shivered under the onslaught of his tender caress. He
inhaled as though drinking in her scent.

She had trusted him and let herself go. Now she felt un-
protected. Wary. What would he do with all this power
she'd granted him?

"I could eat you for breakfast," he said with a run of his

lips into her throat, then up to her mouth. "But after today, you're mine forever so I'll be patient."

He left a lingering kiss on her lips, then slowly released her, allowing his hands a final roam across arm and waist and hip before he lifted the cover from her plate of avocado toast.

She sank down, shaken from nothing more than a good morning fondle.

"Do you need anything from your apartment before the movers take everything to storage?" he asked as he poured her coffee.

"I told them to stand down."

"Why?"

"Because I'm keeping the apartment." She attacked her food. Nerves had kept her from eating much at dinner last night and she'd worked up an appetite with him overnight.

"Your place isn't big enough for us to use when we visit. If you don't want to stay here or with my parents, I'll buy something."

"Mom and Quinto want to use it. I didn't realize they've been wanting to semi retire and travel. They were staying for me, to help with Sofia, but now they'll buy something in Virginia Beach and work here on and off."

"You're giving yourself a place to come back to," he accused.

Her pulse tripped. She had to fight to swallow her bite.

"I'm being realistic." He was all about being practical, wasn't he? "You haven't spent a night trying to soothe a child with an earache, or seen her when she's overtired or had too much sugar. Parenting might not be for you, Jax."

"I'm insulted. Have you read the prenup? You already have options if you and I arrive at irreconcilable differences."

She had. The terms were very generous—provided she give their marriage a year and attend counseling if things grew rocky.

"We're trying to establish trust, Bree. That's difficult for me when you're giving yourself an off-ramp."

"We're getting married after four days of knowing each other. Of course I'm giving myself a safety net. But it's also less stressful. I was losing my mind with making decisions and worrying I would forget something that would wind up in a storage locker. This way, Mom can send me anything I forgot. I can start paring down the next time we're here."

He pursed his mouth with dismay, but seemed to accept it.

They ate in silence until his phone pinged. He glanced at it. Frowned. Looked at her.

"What?" she asked apprehensively.

"I reached out to your father."

She sat back, taking his words like a cold knife into the chest. "Talk about making it hard to trust. Why would you go behind my back like that?"

"That's not what I was doing." He frowned. "When you said he couldn't come to the wedding, I thought we could go through DC on the way to Italy, so I could meet him."

Against her will, and a lengthy history of endless disappointment, a tiny ray of hope lit inside her.

"What did he say?" she asked timidly.

"This is his wife. She said they're leaving on vacation today."

The lightness inside Bree dropped like a stone. She swallowed the bitterness that arrived in her throat. "I told you they weren't available."

"I presumed he had surgery. It sounds like he has the day off. Does he not want to meet me?" he asked with incomprehension.

"He treats presidents, Jax. He's not impressed by you."

"That's not what I mean. I'm about to become your husband. I'm the father of his grandchild. He doesn't care?"

And there it was: the coldest, most shameful fact of her life. The one she'd spent years trying to come to terms with.

"No," she said, pushing away food that she no longer wanted. "He doesn't."

His brows came together in a dark line.

She drew a breath that felt loaded with noxious gas.

"When I was very young, I thought it was the demands of his work that kept him from coming home. He's a brilliant surgeon. Everyone says so." She wet her dry mouth with a sip of coffee, but it tasted sour. "I understood the importance of his work, so I patiently waited for the day when it would be my turn to hold his attention, but it never came. Instead, shortly after I turned eight, he told Mom he was taking a position in DC. We weren't invited. He wanted a divorce so he could marry Laura. He had found time to have an affair, but not to come to my recital."

"What an ass."

"That's not even the worst of it. He was already a surgeon when Mom met him, but he was up to his eyeballs in tuition debt. She didn't mean to get pregnant, but she did, so they married. She sold the house her parents had left her to pay off his loans. Eight years later, he was making big money so she rightfully asked for substantial alimony. Dad retaliated by demanding shared custody. He was trying to push her to lower the support payments. She thought if she wasn't in the picture, he'd make more effort to connect with me. Spoiler alert, he didn't."

And it still hurt. It made her feel inadequate. Unwanted.

"I was old enough to understand the animosity between them, if not the nuance of it. I *felt* it when I went to see him and he worked the whole time, never making time for me. Laura had three children of her own, all younger than me. She didn't need another child underfoot."

"He divorced your mother to marry a woman with three children?"

"Yes." It wasn't parenting he didn't like. It was parenting *her* that had repelled him. "I don't know how he met her. A convention or something. Her father is in politics, which is why they moved to DC, to be closer to her family. She resented having me foisted on her, but Dad insisted I be there every second weekend because of the support payments."

"Your mother couldn't do anything?"

"Like what? *Make* him want to spend time with me? No, but she could see I was miserable. When I started high school, she renegotiated so I only had to see him twice a year if he matched her contributions to my college fund. I got a part-time job purely to boost the amount," she said with spiteful humor.

"Why did you invite him to the wedding? Why do you have any relationship with him at all?"

"Because it's nice to have access to good doctors. When Sofia had that ear infection, Dad made a call, got us seen right away. Also…" She winced, embarrassed. "I thought marrying someone as illustrious as a Visconti might catch his notice. Or Laura's. I was using you. It didn't work."

"This is why you asked me if I wanted a meaningful relationship with Sofia."

"Yes." She kept her eyes on the food she wasn't eating, not wanting him to see the gaping canyon of emptiness she had kept available for her father that he had always declined to fill. "It would have been easier for me if I'd never had any expectations of him. I didn't want Sofia to suffer the same disappointment."

"And it's easier for *you* not to have any expectations of *me*. That's why you didn't want my number four years ago."

Ouch. That landed very squarely on target. "Correct."

He snorted and looked to the side.

"It's also why I didn't expect any different when you didn't ask for mine."

His gaze flashed back to hers like a scythe. "In future, *I* can make a call if you or Sofia need a doctor. You don't need him in your life unless you want him there."

She smiled flatly, appreciating the gesture and wishing it was that easy to stop wanting the impossible.

"Are you going to eat anything more?" he asked.

"No."

"Good. Let's get married."

Melissa had given her a very good life, one that had gifted Bree with the confidence that she could move through life without a man to fulfill her.

She had longed for a partner anyway. That's how she'd wound up moving in with Kabir and attaching so strongly to him. She knew fairy-tale endings didn't exist, but she wanted the realistic happily ever after where someone gave her a place to land when she fell. Someone who shared the small nonsense of life and helped her laugh about it. She wanted great sex.

If she hadn't been stinging from Kabir's rejection four years ago, she might not have been so quick to push Jax away. Of course, if Kabir hadn't rejected her, she might have been married to him, she thought ironically.

A pang of relief followed that realization, forcing her to acknowledge that all this time that she'd been carrying and birthing and raising Jax's child, she had secretly longed for a relationship with *him*. She had longed to share Sofia with him and see the pride in his eyes that mirrored her own. She wanted to know more about him and his life and make love with him and feel his arms around her as they slept.

Here was her chance. She only had to be brave enough to marry him and believe she could have all of those things.

And risk being scorned again.

That was the part that kept giving her pause, but that was life. One way or another, she would suffer disappointments and heartaches. They were inevitable.

At least she knew where she stood with Jax. Everything he'd shared about his first engagement told her he was a very honorable man. The kind of man she could trust and rely on. Maybe even love.

So she married him.

Since it was a private, afternoon ceremony at his parents' home, Bree had chosen a knee-length, double-breasted coat dress with a pill hat that had a short, netted veil. Jax was in a black morning coat over a silver vest, a white shirt and striped trousers, looking so handsome Bree had to wonder how his first fiancée had backed out.

Melissa arrived with an overexcited Sofia, who put on *another* new party dress—Nonna was determined to spoil her as mercilessly as Gigi always had—and the moment arrived for Sofia to walk her posy of flowers across the room.

The gauntlet of her new family proved too much for her. Sofia caught a case of nerves, dropped her flowers, and ran to Jax, where he stood with the officiant.

He picked her up and she buried her face in his lapel, clinging tight, refusing to let him put her down. Everyone covered their smiles.

Once Bree joined him, Sofia agreed to stand with them and listened politely while they spoke their vows.

Jax went first, pledging in a deep, steady voice to be a

loyal and faithful partner as he cherished, respected and comforted her.

Hot tears arrived behind Bree's eyes as she accepted the simple band from him that would sit behind his grandmother's ring. It was warm from being in the pocket against his heart and had a pure quality in its solid, unadorned simplicity, matching the promise he was making to her.

When she slid a slightly wider version onto his finger, and repeated the words back to him, a tremor arrived in her chest.

She hadn't expected this moment to feel so moving or impactful. She hadn't expected to *believe*. But as she looked into his steady eyes, she understood that her inner walls had to come down to give them a real chance.

It was unsettling because it wasn't just the bulwarks of defenses she had to release. As they moved forward in their life together, she had to believe, somehow, that they would hold each other up. She didn't know how that would work. She didn't know *if* it would.

There was no going back, though. They were pronounced husband and wife.

He drew her into his arms and her own bout of extreme shyness hit. They had danced together last night where all could see them, but this embrace was different. It was a declaration, a deeply intimate one. When his mouth settled on hers, it was a revelation of the passion that had brought them together in the first place. She couldn't stop herself from twining her arm around his neck or parting her lips to let him deepen the kiss.

She felt the control he exerted even as he gave in to temptation and briefly ravished her, just enough for her heart to leap and send a blush of pleasure into her cheeks.

He kept his arms around her as he lifted his head. His

gaze flashed into hers with a light of satisfaction. For the response she couldn't disguise? Or the marriage itself?

Either way, she knew in that second that the balance of power between them was not equal. It never had been. He had the wealth and resources, the physical strength and greater erotic prowess than her. He even had the unqualified love of their daughter who had yet to discover that Papà could say no just as well as Mama could.

But it was done. They signed the paperwork and accepted congratulations and posed for photos. After a convivial early dinner, they changed to go to the airport.

Bree hugged her mother, trying not to cry. She could fly Melissa out anytime, now that she had an obscene allowance on top of the salary she would continue to receive, but it still felt as though she was stepping aboard a steamer for the colonies, never to see her mother again.

Trying to hide her tears, she gathered up her daughter and left with her new husband.

Jax had left his penthouse a week ago, oblivious to the fact he would return with a wife and daughter. Bringing them into his home should have felt disruptive, but he found himself embracing the chaos of decorators converting a bedroom for Sofia and toys underfoot and little feet kicking him in the night because Sofia wasn't fully settled in her new home and new bed.

He liked being a father, he discovered, except when he had to discipline Sofia. The first time it happened, it was as though Bree wanted to punish both of them.

"It's your phone," Bree said when they found Sofia washing it in the sink, trying to destroy the evidence of her peanut butter fingerprints upon it.

Sofia knew phones were off-limits. Jax had to put her in

a time-out on the bottom stair and restrict her screen time for two days. She cried. He felt horrible. She apologized and he tried not to crush her as he hugged her.

"Do you still love me?" she asked fearfully.

"Of course I love you. I will always love you," he promised her.

"Next time I'll ask first," she promised, snuggling into him.

He resolved to keep it out of her reach from now on. He couldn't go through this again.

Feeling close and connected to Bree didn't happen as easily. Not that they were in conflict. Things were actually going as smoothly as they could.

They hired a nanny and Sofia took to her and her new preschool very quickly. She was picking up Italian words as easily as she absorbed English, outpacing Bree, who spent an hour on an app every night, trying to keep up. Bree struck up the acquaintance of a few mothers at the preschool, which also helped her assimilate and kept her from feeling isolated in a new country.

She came to work with him three mornings a week, occupying an office two floors down from his, then spent two evenings online with Eve's group back home. They often had lunch together. At home. After a quickie. Once they even defiled the stately desk in his office.

There was the real source of his satisfaction with domestic life, he supposed. Sex on tap. Yes, they had to be mindful of Sofia, but they necked all the time. He liked thinking about what he was going to do to Bree, sometimes fantasizing all day without hardly seeing her, then playing it out when they got to bed.

He liked more than the steady diet of orgasms, though. He wouldn't have called himself lonely before they married.

His life was too busy and demanding, but he liked having someone to come home to. He liked the chitchat over meals and he liked having Bree next to him when they went out.

Small things niggled at him, though. Things like the fact she'd kept her apartment in New York and her own bank account where her salary was deposited. She stayed on the pill.

She had good reasons for all of those decisions, but in his mind, they added up to a withholding of her full commitment to their marriage.

Marriage to him was a lot, though. He had to admit it.

Even in the run-up to Christmas, there were holiday parties and the frenzy of shopping. They spent Christmas with Eve and Dom in Como, where his parents joined them for a few days, then attended a New Year's Eve party at the home of a famous movie star.

Things grew even busier in January, especially his social calendar.

Bree was already a working mother. Now she was also the wife of an executive. His role at the helm of the Euro division meant he was expected at cocktail parties and charity galas and ribbon cuttings. He loved the convenience of not having to find a date for these things, but Bree was soon at her wits' end.

"*Another* ball? Can I wear my wedding dress?" She was joking, but he said, "Absolutely not."

Her wardrobe was deeply inadequate, though. She had a stylist who had loaded her up with designer ready-to-wear, but she needed more.

He booked them for a few nights in Paris and surprised her by flying Melissa in to join them. Sofia was thrilled to spend her days with Gigi, freeing up Bree to meet with designers and shop the boutiques.

"Are you afraid they'll *Pretty Woman* me? Why are you coming with me?" she asked on their first morning.

"I thought it was obvious that I have a passion for fashion." He waved at his bespoke trousers and slim-fit suede jacket over a tight black sweater. He'd almost added a vintage fedora. "I used to come with Eve. I know a lot of the designers."

Also, Bree was not nearly courageous enough when it came to spending his money.

"It's forty thousand dollars," she hissed when he told her to wear a cashmere day dress out of the shop.

"It suits you. You need a better coat, though." He picked one that cost twice as much, enjoying spoiling her.

Once she got over her sticker shock, she deferred to his taste, reluctantly admitting, "I do like it," and "It feels really nice."

On their last day, they visited a shoe gallery on Rue Saint-Honoré. Jax opened an account for Bree, then stepped outside to take a call from Nico. Through the window, he watched her try on a pair of tall black boots with a stiletto heel.

Today, she wore a tweed skirt with a chunky, peach-colored sweater with sleeves that fell past her knuckles. It was a perfect ensemble for a pair of sexy boots like that.

As she paced in front of the mirror, head tilted in consideration, he decided he would buy them for her even if she only ever wore them for him. He could already imagine how he would arrange her to best admire them.

A man passed behind him and entered the shop. Jax didn't pay much attention until he saw Bree turn and say something to him.

The man froze, then walked across to embrace her.

"What the hell?" Jax muttered.

"What's wrong?" Nico asked.

"I'll call you back." Jax shoved the phone into his pocket and entered.

"Here he is," Bree said. "Jax, this is Kabir." She seemed flustered as she introduced the tall, fit, South Asian man.

He wore a camel-colored overcoat and such yearning in his eyes as he looked at Bree, it was a punch in the stomach for Jax.

"Kabir and I dated in university," she reminded Jax with a tight, uncomfortable smile. "I was just telling him I was here with my husband."

"I didn't know you were married," Kabir said. "The last time I talked to Jessica, she only said you had a baby. That was a couple of years ago."

"A daughter," Jax provided. "Sofia. She's three."

Chew on that.

Kabir's brows went up, and he said a faint, "Congratulations."

"And you? Married? Children?" Bree asked him politely.

"I was engaged. It didn't work out." He looked like he wanted to say more, scratched the back of his head as he looked between them, then sealed his lips. His expression as he looked at Bree was filled with despair.

"What are you doing in Paris?" Bree asked into the potent silence.

"Work. I'm with my uncle's company. I promised my sister I'd bring her a pair of shoes." He looked around. "I don't have a clue where to start."

"We won't keep you, then. Are you finished?" Jax asked Bree.

"Um, yes, I've chosen some shoes, but I don't think I'll take the boots."

"No," he agreed. "A different style, perhaps." Something that wouldn't remind him of this interaction.

Jax had already opened an account. Her shoes would be shipped to Naples. He helped Bree remove the boots and handed them off to the shopping assistant.

"We should get back to Sofia and your mother," Jax said.

"Melissa's here? Say hello to her for me," Kabir said with genuine affection.

"I will. It was nice to see you."

"You, too. And, Bree—" Kabir caught at her hand as she reached for her handbag.

Jax glared so hard at that proprietary touch, the man's fingers should have incinerated and fallen to the bench in a pile of ash.

"I just wanted to say…" Kabir cleared his throat and stuffed his hand into the pocket of his overcoat, glancing warily at Jax. "Since I have the chance. I'm sorry. I've always felt bad about…" He glanced at Jax again, loathing that he was prostrating himself in front of an audience, but his gaze swiveled back to Bree, filled with a plea for understanding. He searched her gaze. "I know how things were with your father. The way things ended between us—"

"It's fine," she cut in with a breezy smile. It was the one that grated on Jax's nerves because it was so fake. "Don't give it another thought. Have a good life, Kabir. I mean it."

They left and didn't speak until they were in the elevator at the hotel. Then Jax couldn't keep it in any longer.

"He's still in love with you."

"I know."

"What do you mean, you *know*?" Waves of animosity were coming off of Jax.

Bree was still recovering from the shock of seeing Kabir in a place that was so out of context from anywhere she would have expected to run into him. It was like getting off on the wrong floor at work and not knowing it until you walked into the wrong office.

"I always knew he loved me. I just didn't know he would lie to his family about my place in his life and leave me anyway."

The doors opened to reveal a well-dressed older couple.

Bree smiled tightly at them and moved with Jax to their suite.

"Mom?" Bree called out as they entered. She checked her phone and saw her mother had texted that she and the nanny had taken Sofia to a nearby playground.

She let Jax take her coat and glanced at the bar, wondering if it was too early for a drink. Wondering what it was about running into Kabir that felt so unsettling.

"Have you been texting him?"

"*No*. You heard our entire conversation. It's the first one we've had since he left our apartment four years ago."

"But he reached out to your friend since then," he noted, pouring himself a drink.

"Jessica," she provided. "She was my roommate first year. She was in the same biochemistry track as Kabir, so they were always trading notes on assignments. She probably contacted him about job prospects." Bree still saw Jessica sometimes when she came to New York, but she had never mentioned Kabir asking about her.

"If you hadn't had Sofia by then, do you think he would have tried to get you back?"

"I doubt it. His family life is complicated. That's why he never told them about me."

"And you forgave him for that?"

"I do now, yes." She appreciated Kabir's apology. She had never allowed herself to look back on their time with fondness, too hurt by the rift at the end, but now she could see how young they'd been. It hadn't been realistic of her to think they were ready for marriage. She was barely ready for it now.

"He would have taken you back today if I hadn't been there," Jax muttered.

"Are you jealous?" she asked with shock.

"He talked to you as if he knew you."

"He did. We lived together for two years. *Before I met you.*"

"You're mooning over him."

"I'm not *mooning*. It's nostalgia for the people we were. We had happy times, Jax. Sorry to break that to you, but that's why we were together for so long. Because we loved each other. And might I remind you that you were *engaged*? You loved someone else, too. At least the people from my past don't insult our daughter and make you feel small."

He had the grace to look away.

"Jealousy is not a compliment, you know," she continued with ire. "It tells me that you don't trust me."

"It's hard to trust you, Bree. You made him sound like he'd broken your heart. Like it was over."

"He *did*. It is."

"Well, lucky him, having that much effect on you."

"Are you serious right now? His feelings for me are not within my control, but you know what? It's nice that *someone* loves me."

He snapped a look at her.

Her heart was pounding with emotions that had climbed way out of control, but this was an undercurrent she'd been avoiding and now found herself unable to escape. She was flailing in it.

"You think I don't hear you tell Sofia every single day

that you love her?" she asked with a catch in her voice. "And wonder if I'll ever hear it?"

"Do *you* love *me*?" he asked bluntly.

She was starting to think she did. He was clawing her apart right now with a chilly attitude and a few dispassionate words.

She would be damned if she would admit it, though, not when he was being such an ass. Not when he didn't trust her and was only being possessive.

"That wasn't our deal, was it?" She fought to keep her voice steady. "This marriage is practical." In this moment, it was a certifiable nightmare.

"But you loved him. You were still in love with him when we slept together in Como," he said grittily.

"You knew that," she shot back.

"Do you still?"

"No."

He only stared at her, skeptical.

"You're being very insulting right now." She crossed her arms.

"You aren't committed to this marriage. *That's* insulting."

The door beeped and opened.

"Papà!" Sofia ran straight to Jax and he picked her up.

"I didn't think you'd be back already." Melissa set down her bag to remove her coat. "I told Nanny to take a few hours off. I was going to order lunch and watch a movie with Sofia."

"Shopping fatigue. I'm going to take a bubble bath," Bree said with a strained smile.

"Me too?" Sofia asked.

"Sure." She could do with a dose of innocent enthusiasm and unconditional love.

An hour later, when Sofia's fingers and toes were wrinkly, Jax came into the bathroom to say that lunch had arrived. He rinsed Sofia in the shower, then wrapped her in a towel to carry her out to dress her.

Bree showered her own bubbles from her skin, stepping out in time for Jax to return.

"I don't know what you want from me," she said, tucking the edge of the towel beneath her arm. "Maybe I didn't give up my apartment, but I still gave up a lot to marry you. I know it doesn't seem like it. Not when you're giving me shopping trips to Paris, but I knew who I was when I was a single mom climbing the corporate ladder. Now I'm someone's wife in a strange country with no friends. I don't have Mom around the corner to lean on. Every weekend I'm paraded through some black-tie event where I have to pretend I belong. You have me looking at villas on the Island of Capri, for Pete's sake! That's not *me*, Jax. Forgive me for clinging to a few pieces of myself that are familiar."

"We got it, by the way. The villa on Capri. That's what I came in to tell you." He leaned on the counter, arms folded, ankles crossed.

"The one with the pool?" She hugged the towel around her a little tighter. "And the gardens and the view?" It had been built in the nineteenth century, but modernized into something so charming, she hadn't believed she was standing in it. Now she would live in it.

He nodded.

"I'm glad." Her smile faltered as she took in the gravity in his expression. "Are you?"

"Very. I've ordered champagne."

She wiped at a trickle of water that was leaking down the side of her neck onto her bare shoulder.

"I was being possessive," he admitted with a grimace. "Your past with him didn't matter to me until I saw you with him today and realized how much history you had with him. History that I don't have."

"Because I didn't try to find you when I was pregnant. You still haven't forgiven me for that. I know." Would he ever?

"I'm trying," he said bluntly, making her heart lurch. "Because what's done is done. It's not productive to hang on to it. I know that."

"I'm trying, too. I'm trying really hard to believe all of this is going to work out." Her mouth trembled with uncertainty, though. "Fighting with you doesn't help."

"I know." He leaned forward and grabbed a handful of the towel.

She clutched at it, keeping it from falling, but his grip pulled her into the space he made as he opened his feet.

"Kiss and make up?" he suggested.

There was no *I'm sorry*. No *I love you*. No *I'll do better next time*.

She nodded, though, needing the approximation of remorse and acceptance and promise. She needed more than a kiss, too.

He must have as well. The moment his mouth touched hers, it was as though a match lit. A flame burst to life between them.

His kiss turned hungry and he spun her, then lifted her to sit next to the sink. He dragged the towel open so it pooled around her hips.

She opened her thighs and reached for the buckle on his belt, pulling him closer. Needing connection. Needing his need of her.

He took over, jerking open his fly, hitching his trousers down and freeing his erection.

He gripped the towel beneath her, sliding her hips right

to the edge of the counter while he guided himself to part her folds, seeking the damp heat.

They were kissing again, grasping at each other, bordering on frantic. This wasn't make-up sex. It was an extension of their fight. It wasn't anger, though. It was more an expression of the hurt they were causing each other. She wasn't quite ready so it stung as he entered her. She nipped at his bottom lip and he pulled back to give her a glittering glare through his narrowed eyes.

They pulled each other closer, grappling, provoking each other with all the secret things they knew each other liked. She dipped her head to suck hard on his nipple. He swept his hands beneath her thighs, planting his palms on her hips so she was tipped back and had to catch her balance on her hands. She was constrained, but the angle stroked places that made her eyelids flutter.

He whispered flagrantly sexual things. He told her how beautiful her breasts were and how much he liked her heat clamped around him. He watched as he made love to her with steady precision, driving her arousal relentlessly up the scale until she was one humming nerve. All her awareness was centered in the place where he claimed her. The sweet burn and the coiling tension.

"No one else will ever give you this, Bree. No one else will see you like this and feel you—" He gritted his teeth, barely hanging on. "Only me. Say it."

"Only you," she moaned obediently, arching so the top of her head was against the mirror behind her, the ceiling light in her eyes. "I only want you. Only you."

It was true. So profoundly true, it shook her to the center of her being. She couldn't imagine her life if he wasn't in it. She hadn't loved Kabir. She had loved the idea of love. She had wanted the potential for stability and a secure future and had been devastated when he denied her that.

This was love. It was the delicious agony of feeling deeply connected and utterly defenseless. Of knowing her husband's flaws and being angry with him and wanting to make love with him and share her life with him anyway. Wanting to share *herself.*

"I'm yours. Always. Never stop, never stop."

The fingers digging into her hips pulled her a fraction of an inch closer so the slam of his hips struck where she needed it most.

Climax hit, detonating a sting of pleasure through her, one followed by wave after wave of pure pleasure. He bit back his own groans, throat flexing, muscles straining as he locked himself to her and pulsed with glorious, powerful throbs inside her.

Then, with both of them still shaking, he gathered her close, cradling her so tenderly against his damp chest, she wept a little.

Because she loved him. She was so fathoms-deep in love with him, it compressed her lungs. She couldn't breathe.

His kiss was gentle when he tilted up her chin. His thumb swept the tear from the corner of her eye. Concern pleated his brow.

"We'll both do better next time." The corner of his mouth dug in with irony.

At what? Lovemaking? Fighting? Meeting old lovers? Or loving each other?

He gently withdrew and the sense of loss made her ache.

She began trying to pull herself back together, but as usual, she was in pieces. Vanquished.

While he zipped his trousers and was in complete control.

CHAPTER ELEVEN

IN MANY WAYS, Bree's life was a fantasy come true.

The next weeks were taken up with decorating their new home and making the move to Capri—Capri!—where they lived from Thursday through Sunday. On Mondays, they commuted into Naples by ferry, which Sofia loved, then worked a short week before returning to their island paradise.

Their travel schedule picked up, too, which meant overnights in London, Berlin, and Madrid. Bree enjoyed it. Sofia and the nanny usually came along and Bree often had a chance to poke around the new city with or without them before she put on something a princess would wear and accompanied her husband into a ballroom.

She was growing more confident in those spaces, too, learning how to make small talk and recognizing familiar faces.

Lazy Sundays were her favorite, though, when Jax took Sofia into the pool in the afternoon and she sat on a lounger, reading or texting her mother if Melissa was up.

They would have an early dinner and remind Sofia that they were going into the city in the morning, necessitating an early bedtime. One of them would put her to bed and they would go to bed early, too, making love with unhurried passion that was always thorough and gratifying.

That's when it was hardest for Bree to hide that she loved him. Not just during, but in the quiet aftermath when they lay tangled and sated. When his heart steadied beneath her ear and their skin dried and everything felt so right, she thought she would burst from happiness.

How would he react if she told him he possessed her heart?

She probably should tell him, but she couldn't face him offering some kind of tepid response about that not being something she should expect from him.

"Everything all right?" he asked in a quiet rumble.

"Yes. Why?" She picked up her head.

"Your sigh sounded very heavy."

"It's Monday tomorrow," she prevaricated.

He swept a hair off her eyelash, delving into her soul with a long look that she couldn't hold. She pressed a kiss to his chest and rubbed her cheek back and forth like a cat against his pec.

Then he sighed, and she thought, *He knows. He knows I'm hiding something.*

It was a terrible catch-22. She was afraid to trust him with her heart, making it impossible for him to trust her.

He unwound his arm from behind her and rolled to reach for his phone. It was on silent, but with his family in different time zones, he always checked it before going to sleep.

She had got in the habit of doing the same, to be sure nothing had cropped up with her mother. On weeknights, Eve or some of her other coworkers often sent something through that was better handled immediately, so the team could keep working rather than waiting until Bree's morning when they would be finished their own workday.

Her mother had sent photos of her and Quinto beaming inside their new condo in Virginia Beach. Bree's smile was still on her lips as she tapped on the email from Laura.

Her stepsister must be getting married. The subject line was Save The Date.

Bree opened it and completely lost her temper.

Bree spat out a word she never said, not even when they were in this bed where anything went. She threw her phone across the room, hitting the wall and chipping the plaster.

"What the hell, Bree?"

She fought her way clear of the sheet, spitting out another string of filthy language about where "they" could go and what "they" could do when they got there. She thrust herself into the pajamas she wore to bed in case Sofia came in.

He rose and pulled on the briefs he wore for the same reason, then he picked up her phone to see the screen was cracked.

"What's going on?"

"It doesn't matter," she insisted hotly, eyes bright with tears. *"I don't care."*

"You clearly do care—Where are you going?"

She stopped at the door. "To break some dishes. I don't know."

"Just tell me. Is it work?"

"My stepsister is getting married. Next year. I'm invited. Do you know why? Because Laura wants me to ask you to comp them a ballroom for the reception." She was shaking, voice quivering with fury. "She's asking me to help her keep costs down because they're liable to have upward of two hundred people. She wants me to do her that favor, then sit and watch *my* father walk *her* daughter down the aisle when they couldn't be bothered *meeting* my husband when you offered to go to them."

This man's lack of connection to his daughter absolutely baffled Jax. Did he not know what a kind, intelligent, funny person he'd sired. Why wasn't he proud of her? Why was he so bent on *hurting* her?

"Tell them to go to hell," he said. "Block them. You don't owe them anything."

She only made a noise of acute anguish and walked out.

He swore under his breath and dragged on some clothes before following, but damn this big house they'd bought. He wasn't fast enough to see where she went. She wasn't in the kitchen breaking dishes and she wasn't in Sofia's room, comforting herself with a cuddle with their daughter.

It was almost March, but still very cool at night. He didn't think she would have gone outside, but when he couldn't find her in the house, he texted the nanny that they were outside and checked the gazebo, then noticed the wrought iron door to the beach stairs was unlocked.

Their shoreline wasn't a sandy beach like where the tourists flocked. It was a rugged, rocky cove where storm waves crashed in to take bites out of the brittle land. There was a jetty out to a small dock, where he could tie up a runabout if he wanted access to his yacht from here, but they'd bought the house for the view, not to swim in the sea.

Bree was at the end of the jetty, colorless in the moonlight, arms hugged tight against the wind. The tide was up so the waves churned close enough to her feet to make him uneasy.

He walked out. "Come back to the shore. It's dangerous out here."

"I don't understand why I care," she said to the water, voice thick with anguish. "I try not to. I try *so hard* not to care anymore. But I still do."

"Bree, come on." He slipped his arm around her, heart squeezing as he saw the shiny tracks on her cheeks.

She was a column of tightly wound pain, mouth pinched and eyes staring into the horizon.

"You care because you're a better person than they are."

"He saves people's *lives*," she said on a jagged lilt of laughter. "And he doesn't care about the life he made. He cares more about strangers than me. It wasn't that he didn't want to be a parent. He's a great father to Laura's kids. He doesn't want *me*."

He opened his mouth, but what could he say? The man was a fool. A cruel one. If it were up to Jax, he would cut him out of her life completely. Now.

"You're freezing," he noted, hugging her stiff body close. "Let's get up to the house, in case Sofia wakes."

"I wish I could hate him. I want to, but I always come back to wanting some little shred of proof that he…" Her expression crumpled.

"All right."

They were doing this here then, where they were raked by the wind and soaked by the mist off the water. It was cold and damp and the way she sobbed battered him like the tossing waves, knocking him against jagged emotions that tore into him, but he held her while she broke apart. He rubbed her back and kept her upright as she sobbed.

When she was weak and leaning on him, he picked her up like she was Sofia and carried her down the jetty. Then he set her on her feet and guided her up the stairs, locked the gate, and stripped her down to put her in the hot tub.

She was quiet and withdrawn now. Docile. He put her to bed a while later and promised he'd join her shortly.

Then he took his phone to the den and called Melissa.

"Jax!" she answered with surprise. "Is everything okay?"

"We're fine. I promise. But Bree's had some news that upset her." He explained about the wedding.

"God, I hate him," Melissa spat with true vehemence. "He's such a cold bastard. The ways he hurts her and thinks it doesn't matter. He does it to hurt *me*. If I could divorce him a thousand times over, I would. If I could go back in time, I never would have told him I was pregnant. He would have had nothing to do with her. *Nothing*." She took a shaken breath, gathering her composure. "Do you want me to come?"

"I actually wondered if you would take Sofia for a week. We never got a honeymoon and I threw Bree into the deep end when we got here. She could use a break. If we stay here, she'll go to work tomorrow and pretend she's fine. She's not." She was deeply hurt and deserved some time to heal.

"Of course I'll take her! We'd love that."

They worked out a few details and he called Nico, then Eve. He didn't tell them why he wanted the time and they didn't ask.

Then he called one of their Caribbean properties to book a villa.

When he finally headed to bed, he found Sofia snuggled up against Bree. Their daughter was more settled these days, not coming in very often. He wouldn't have put it past Bree to have brought her in here herself, purely out of a desire for comfort, but he didn't mind. There was something reassuring in falling asleep with both of them in the bed where he knew they were completely safe.

He would bet his entire fortune that Bree had never been welcome to sleep with her own father.

Jax couldn't think too hard about that man or he'd keep himself awake plotting murders.

He undressed to his briefs and slid in, reaching out his hand so it rested on Bree's hip, sheltering their daughter between them.

But as he was drifting off, Melissa's voice kept echoing in his head.

If I could go back in time, I never would have told him I was pregnant.

CHAPTER TWELVE

WHEN JAX TOLD Bree over breakfast what he had arranged, she cringed inwardly with embarrassment. She was already mortified at her behavior last night, acting like Sofia, throwing her toys and having a meltdown, needing to be bathed and put to bed.

She'd never been so happy as when Sofia had crept in, though.

"Where's Papà?" she had whispered.

"He'll be here soon." Bree had pulled her little body into her own like a treasured teddy bear.

"A vacation isn't necessary," she insisted now. "It would look awful. I don't want the rest of the team thinking I can just drop out on a whim and go on vacation because I'm married to Eve's brother."

"You can, though," he drawled. "We can make it a working vacation if you want, and take a few calls, but we haven't had time for just the two of us."

That was true. They had their unstructured Sundays, but Sofia was always a part of those days. She had put in the hours at work, too, arranging her own schedule to suit the time change.

"I've never been away from her that long," was her final, weak protest.

His mouth twitched. "We'll cut things short if we miss her too much."

It turned into a long day of travel. They flew fourteen hours to Virginia Beach, where Sofia happily waved them off, excited to stay with Gigi in her new apartment. Then they climbed aboard the plane for another nine hours to the Visconti property in Saint Martin, arriving at midnight local time.

"Technically this resort is in my purview, since it's governed by France," Jax mentioned as they were shown to their two-story villa by a very anxious night manager.

"Is the Dutch side not in your purview?" she asked with false innocence.

"You know damned well WBE has their own resort there."

Bree tucked her smirk into her shoulder and allowed the young man to give them a tour of the interior with its pristine white walls and splashes of colorful cushions. The ground floor held a kitchen, two lounges, a small office, and a dining area. Several pairs of doors opened to the shaded patio and the infinity pool that sat placid and glowing at their feet.

"We could have brought Sofia," she murmured when she saw the four bedrooms upstairs. Each had a balcony, but the primary bedroom had a wraparound terrace with views of moonlight on the calm water of the western side of the island.

They had eaten on the plane, but hadn't slept much, so they went straight to bed.

Bree rose early to open the doors to the terrace and stepped out to a view of palm trees, a sugar-white beach and the surreal blue the Caribbean waters were famed for.

"I forgive you for making me come here," she said over her shoulder.

"Enough to come back to bed?"

She crawled onto him and they lazily made love.

Later, when they had eaten, they walked along the beach holding hands like honeymooners. Bree was in a white dress that caressed her legs. Jax wore cropped linen trousers and an open shirt and such an air of ease, she fell in love with him all over again.

"This is a bad precedent to set. I may start pitching more tantrums if this is what my time-out looks like."

An easy smile touched his lips, but his eyes remained hidden by his sunglasses.

"I have an ulterior motive."

"Is it more sex? Because we already need an intervention."

"We do." His slow smile was deeply satisfied. "And, believe me, I've considered what the impact will be on that when I tell you what I'm thinking. I was going to wait until I'd buttered you up more." He stopped walking.

She turned to face him, catching at her sun hat as she tilted her head up, curious.

"I want to ask when we might try for another baby."

"Oh." She blinked behind her own sunglasses. It wasn't as though she didn't think about it every day when she took her pill, but things had felt so nascent between them. She hadn't felt ready to put more stress on such a new relationship.

She hadn't been sure they would last. That was the stark truth. Why put two children through a breakup when she could keep it to one?

"I have an idea what I'm asking," he said when she didn't say anything. "Easy-peasy for me, but it's nine months of discomfort for you and a not-fun time at the end. But… This isn't a guilt trip." He gave her upper arms a light squeeze. "I really wish I'd known Sofia from the beginning. That I'd seen her come into this world and—Bree."

She pulled away, arms crossed defensively as she turned to face the water.

"That's not a condemnation. I understand why you didn't tell me about Sofia. I really do. The way your father treats you is unconscionable. You deserve better." He stole her hat and set his forearm across her collarbone, drawing her into the solidness of his strong frame.

"I shouldn't let it bother me."

"You're allowed to be angry, Bree. You're allowed to be hurt. Have you got back to them?"

"No." She was waiting until she'd activated her new phone and had put that off while they'd been traveling. "I know why she asked. I've arranged discounts in the past, when they went on vacation. WBE has a family thing as long as I do the booking."

"Did they invite you to go with them on those vacations?"

"Yes. I went a few times, but it was a lot of work with Sofia being so young. Eventually, it was easier to book it for them and bank the favor in case Sofia needed a doctor."

"Speaking as your husband, I think you should tell them to go to hell. Speaking as a Visconti executive, we offer a similar perk to employees. If you want to ask the Event Co-ordinator in DC to get in touch with them and give them a quote, I'm willing to sign off on an appropriate discount. Having said that, I will also back you up if you want to tell them you're no longer employed directly by WBE or Visconti and are therefore no longer eligible."

"If I cut the cord, it's cut. No going back." Something in her tightened with resistance, hanging on out of habit, even though she was exhausted from clinging to it. "I've always thought that as long as I kept trying, kept communication open…" She clenched her eyes shut, refusing to let the sting of her gathering tears leak out. "I feel so pathetic for continuing to hope. I don't give up on people, Jax. I know you think I don't trust you enough, that I'm not committed enough, but I commit *hard*."

"I know." The hand that held her hat came across her stomach. His arms closed tighter around her, holding her together as she drew shaken breaths.

"If I throw that relationship away, what does it say about who I am? I don't leave just because things are hard. Having a baby is hard, you know," she said over her shoulder. "They never let you sleep and worry you to death. Sofia is false advertising. She walks and talks and is out of diapers, but that first year is stressful."

"I know you're scared that I won't be there for our children. I'm only asking you to think about it."

"I think about it all the time," she admitted, letting her head tilt against his shoulder. "Can we discuss it after I've decided what to do with my father?"

"Of course." He touched his lips to her temple. "But let's forget about him for now."

They did. For the next few days, they did little but walk and swim and sightsee. They shopped aimlessly, and she made him take her to lunch at the WBE resort, which Jax had to concede was an excellent meal. They napped whenever they felt like it, enjoyed intimate dinners at sunset, and made love often.

"You're sexy as hell in that," he said of her new bikini when she joined him in the pool one afternoon.

"Are you doing that on purpose?"

"What?"

"Complimenting me. I feel like we're back in Como. You

know I'm a sure thing now, right?" She held up her left hand and wiggled her fingers to indicate the rings.

"I never say anything to you that I don't mean." He grabbed her wrist and dragged her through the water into his arms. "You are sexy as hell with or without a bathing suit, but the color suits you. It's titillating to see you in it and know your tan lines as well as I know the rest of your body."

She looked down at the neon blue bandeau and the way he was arranging her legs to wrap his waist.

"If I haven't been complimenting you enough since we married, that is my bad. I've had a lot of distractions, but I notice how beautiful you are all the time. I notice what a caring mother you are and that you bring a lot to Eve's team. Anytime you walk into a room, I know I'm the luckiest man alive to call you my wife."

She chuckled and shook her head, only half believing him. Maybe a little more than half because he did make her feel beautiful. And smart. And cherished.

She felt like the luckiest woman alive and, as their bond strengthened, she found it easier and easier to ease her grip on the old, frayed line that tethered her to the past. The one that had left blisters and calluses on her soul.

On their last day, she spent an hour composing an email that was only ten words.

I'm unable to arrange a discount or attend the wedding.

She hit Send and braced herself for a painful inner schism or a sensation of being cast adrift. Instead, she felt as though a tremendous weight was no longer dragging at her. She was a sea creature freed from a thousand pounds of tangled net. She was lighter. She had never really been part of her father's family so she wasn't losing anything by stepping away from it.

Rising from the lounger as though rising from ashes, she went inside to find Jax at the desk in the office. He was frowning at his laptop.

"What's wrong?" she asked.

"Nico's asking when I'll be back in New York." He closed it, expression pensive. "I told him we're leaving in a few hours."

"Can we still visit with Mom?" They were planning to fly overnight to Virginia Beach and stay the weekend before working out of New York next week.

"We should head straight to New York."

"That's too bad. I'll text her in a minute. But first, um, I took your advice. I sent my regrets to the wedding and said I couldn't help with costs. Then I blocked Laura's number. If she reaches out to you, you can ignore it."

"Wow." He rose and held out his arms in an offering of an embrace. "Good for you. I know that wasn't an easy decision."

"It wasn't as hard as I expected it to be." She stepped into his arms feeling as though the last of her inner walls had also fallen away, painlessly. They had nothing but a bright future ahead of them. "Can I show you something?"

"Sure." His expression altered to curiosity as he followed her up to the bedroom.

She walked into the bathroom and held up her birth control pills, then dramatically dropped them into the wastebasket.

His brows went up. "Really."

"It's a day for big decisions. Unless—"

"Oh, I'm very sure." He gathered her close and kissed her with such breathtaking thoroughness, her heart was pounding by the time he let her up for air. "Shall we get started on trying?"

"It was one and done last time, champ. I probably got pregnant by tossing them."

"Let's make sure." He drew her to the bed, then tumbled her onto the mattress.

If his goal this trip had been to build her up with flattery and seduction, it had worked. She was pure confidence as they kissed and caressed and peeled away clothing. She rained kisses on his throat and chest and shoulders and stomach and the thrilling hardness of his erection.

He groaned and ran his fingers into her hair and said, "Much as I love that, it's not going to get the job done."

He rolled her beneath him and gave her the same treatment, seeming to worship every inch of her until she glowed with more than arousal. Joy. *Love.*

She was so full of love that when they were joined, moving in perfect harmony, she couldn't keep it in.

"I love you," she whispered, stroking her hands over his powerful back, arching in surrender to him and this greater force that burned like white-hot light within her. It rose like music into a crescendo. "I love you so much, Jax. I love you."

Jax felt her words twist through him with the same euphoric bliss as orgasm. Her voice turned to a helpless cry and he lost what shreds of control he still had, straining in the stasis of ecstasy with her.

It was intensely powerful. The throbs in his sex rang through his body, jarring every tensed muscle. His heart thudded so hard he thought it would explode. He tried not to bruise her with the strength of his grip, but he had to hold on to her through the cataclysm. She was his. *His.* He was both triumphant and conquered.

As the pulses faded, his muscles began to tremble with fatigue. She was panting and soft beneath him. So lovely. So delicate and welcoming.

Her heartbeat was still stumbling, but he felt it at a deeper level inside him. As though it sat against his own.

And that's when he realized what a mistake he'd made. How vulnerable he'd made her.

He untangled their limbs and rolled off her, but his arm hooked out of habit around her, bringing her into his side while he lay on his back, still catching his breath. Stunned and slowly experiencing a seep of dread.

"Did you mean it?" he asked.

"I wouldn't lie about that." Her lashes lifted and her gaze was so defenseless, it hurt to look into her eyes.

He swallowed and shifted his gaze to the ceiling. He had wanted proof of her commitment to their marriage, but hadn't realized this was her way. Not just giving him another baby, but giving him her heart.

She loved him.

How the hell was he supposed to protect her now? He *hurt* the people he loved.

"You don't have to say it back," she said in a small voice.

"You know I care about you." God, that sounded tepid.

She thought so, too. Her expression flexed with agony before she set a firm hand on his chest and tried to lever from the bed.

He tightened his arm. "I care deeply."

They gave each other incredible pleasure in bed and he enjoyed her company outside of it. She was the mother of his child. Children, potentially. For all of those things, he already loved her in a broad way, but love—

"I don't want to hurt you."

"Then don't," she said starkly.

"But it's inevitable if someone loves you that you're going to let them down. I'm doing it now." He was disappointing her, which was precisely the emotion he hated to cause most, especially in people he cared about.

He was thinking about the message from Nico.

When are you back in NY? Tucker's here.

"What do you want me to do? Apologize?"

"No."

"Because I know this wasn't our deal. I didn't mean to. It just happened."

"Bree, I'm not mad."

"Just disappointed?" She lurched away. "I need a shower before we go."

"Bree."

Don't be hurt.

"I didn't ask you to love me back, Jax." She spoke over her shoulder as she stood. "And you know why."

CHAPTER THIRTEEN

HAVING THE CAPACITY to love someone did not make her a fool. Loving her husband did not make her a fool. Wanting to be loved back did not make her a fool.

Bree felt like one anyway.

And she was so tired of it! Maybe Jax hadn't promised to love her, but she was still disappointed that he didn't. It was even more disappointing to contemplate years of being stuck—again—in this state of yearning and wishing and feeling unworthy.

She couldn't do it. Wouldn't. This was exactly the anguish she'd been trying to spare herself when she had decided to be a single mother in the first place.

They barely spoke as they boarded the jet and slept in the stateroom most of the flight.

Actually, she tossed and turned. Jax was only beside her for a few hours, barely sleeping at all.

By the time she rose, Bree had a dull headache and gritty eyes. She accepted a coffee, then remembered she was trying to get pregnant and should avoid caffeine.

Was she, though? She had left her prescription in the bin at the villa, but maybe that had been mistake. Maybe this marriage had been a huge mistake.

Jax didn't look half as wilted as she felt. He had shaved

and put on fresh clothes. When she joined him, he lifted his grave gaze from his phone.

Her declaration of love—and his inability to say it back—sat between them like compressed air.

"I've..." She cleared her throat. "I've decided to stay with Mom while you carry on to New York."

His blink was a tiny flinch, one he covered so quickly she might have imagined it.

"For the weekend?"

"I don't know, but I need time with her."

With someone who loves me.

She lifted her chin. "I need to decide whether I want to be in a marriage where I'm more emotionally invested than you are."

Something flared in his gaze, but he didn't say anything, only studied her, unmoving except for the tick in his cheek.

A knot formed in her chest, tightening and tightening.

Fight for me, she willed him. *Prove that I'm important to you.*

"If that's what you want." He dropped his gaze to the phone he held.

His words slid into her like a cold knife. A lump formed in her throat and she looked to the window, eyes hot.

The flight attendant asked them to prepare for landing.

Her mother was on the tarmac when they landed. She climbed from the car with Sofia, who hugged them with all her might, bringing tears of happy reunion into Bree's eyes.

"I'm sorry, *piccolina*," Jax said as he held her. "I have to see Zio Nico in New York."

"You can talk to Papà on my phone, though," Bree assured her as Sofia pouted.

"I'll call tonight," Jax promised.

"Let's get out of the wind," Bree said. It was a beautiful

day, if considerably cooler than the tropics, but that wasn't the reason she felt chilled to the bone and hurried to the car. She was hurt and angry and, for once, she needed to be the one who walked away.

It wasn't any less devastating, though. It felt as though she was being torn in half.

Jax helped Sofia into the car and stayed on the tarmac as they drove away. Bree didn't have to look back to see him watching them leave. She felt the force of his stare.

"What happened?" her mother asked gently.

Bree took a shaken breath, eyes welling with hopelessness. "He didn't say it back."

"Oh, my baby girl." Melissa took her hand and squeezed it.

Jax was encased in ice as he flew the final leg to New York. Bree's refusal to accompany him had been a slap in the face, but he hadn't argued with her. Now that he knew how susceptible she was to him, he feared hurting her even more if she came with him, especially considering his reason for rushing to see Nico.

He hadn't had the foresight to distance himself from those he cared about when he first tangled with Tucker. A painful sense of deprivation had accosted him the moment she had said she wouldn't come with him, but he refused to draw them into the line of fire.

In the years immediately after Tucker's departure to Brazil, the man's family of lawyers, politicians, and media personalities had targeted the Visconti Group in that country. Romeo had sold off their properties in Sao Paulo and Rio de Janeiro since they'd become less profitable anyway.

It had been a tactical error, essentially giving Dom and his father carte blanche with that territory. Christo had moved to Hawaii to oversee the Pacific Rim, including some highly successful properties in Peru, Chile, and the Patagonia region, but Dom had taken over the larger share of South America. It became another foothold to bolster his position against the Visconti Group after his father died. Jax still felt responsible for that.

Now he had a new weight on his conscience. It had taken time for Tucker to learn about his aunt being kicked out of Dom's wedding reception and put his revenge into place, but he was here and he was out for blood.

It began as a whisper campaign that Eve was pregnant and it was the reason for her quick marriage to Dom. She and Dom shrugged that off.

"Time will tell," Eve said, but it was still infuriating that she was being targeted when she'd done nothing to Tucker or Paloma or anyone.

Worse were the planted stories of bedbugs and food poisoning that began to surface online. They were false reviews, but were picked up by influencers and reported in other media. Those rumors would be costly to quash and were liable to persist for years.

Dom didn't say anything about the strain on his family relationships, including his marriage, but this had to be difficult for him. That ate at Jax, too.

"What the hell do I do? Pistols at dawn?" Jax paced before Nico's desk.

"We do what we're already doing," Nico said flatly.

They were calling in favors with broadcasters and countering the negative publicity with friendly celebrities and promotional packages. Even so, they were seeing record numbers of cancellations including two weddings and a charity gala.

Eve walked in without knocking, closed the door behind her, and declared, "*That's* annoying."

"What now?" Jax asked through his teeth.

"He got the Department of Justice to open an antitrust investigation into the merger of our two companies."

"It's an alignment," Nico said in a beleaguered tone.

"That's what I told legal. They advised we put things on hold while they figure out if they have a case. I'm preparing a statement to the team, offering full pay for a month and a warning they might be furloughed indefinitely."

"Including Bree," Jax said with a wince.

"Do you want to tell her before the memo goes out?"

Things between them had deteriorated. Two days ago, she'd called to ask with frustration, "Why am I hearing through *Eve* that Tucker is there?"

"Because I don't want you drawn into it." He was embarrassed that he was still causing his family to suffer. Having his wife and child affected would be unbearable.

"Is it dangerous?" she asked with concern. "Are you worried he would come after me or Sofia?"

"No, I don't have any reason to believe he'd resort to violence, especially when he's being so careful to keep his fingerprints off these other actions." Legal was looking into a defamation suit, but had little evidence to tie the unfounded reviews to Tucker. It was incredibly frustrating. "But he would take any chance to treat you the way Odelia did. I'd rather spare you that."

"I don't care about snide remarks. Do you want us to come to New York?"

Desperately. But he refused.

"No. Stay where you are. I'll come get you as soon as we've dealt with him."

"'We' being you and Nico?"

"And the rest of the family, yes."

On the screen, the concern left her face as her expression stiffened. He heard his own words and realized he was making it sound as though she wasn't considered family.

"Bree—"

"Yes, you can show Papà your donkey. Here you go." She put Sofia on and he listened politely as she told him about the stuffed toy that had come with the book Gigi had given her.

Every time he had called since then, Bree had given the phone to their daughter as quickly as possible. The way his marriage was imploding was eating him up, but he needed Tucker out of the way before he tried to patch things up with Bree.

So much for that. She was going to be furious.

He moved into an adjacent office and placed the video call.

"Sofia, Papà is on the phone," Bree said as soon as she answered. "Do you want to sit down to talk to him?" It was a rule that Sofia could only hold a phone or tablet while seated.

"Wait," he said. "I need to tell you something first."

He explained and watched her expression tighten.

"So I'm fired? What about my job with WBE? Should I go into the office?"

"Nothing's been figured out yet. This is a courtesy call. Eve will send out a memo with more details."

"Thanks, I guess," she said flatly, seeming to search his expression through the screen. "That's the only reason you called?"

She was giving him room to make an overture, even though it was probably hard for her.

I won't ask you to love me back.

All he had to do was say he needed her and she would hurry to his side. He knew that. But it would be the most selfish act of his life.

At his silence she said, "Here's Sofia."

His daughter's face came on and her first question expanded the fissures in his heart.

"When are you coming? I miss you."

"Soon." That felt like a lie. He spoke to her a moment, then said, "Can you put Mama back on?"

She called for Bree, then said, "She's in the bathroom."

He ended the call, temper frayed while a deeper sense of guilt ate at him.

He went to tell Eve that he'd talked to Bree and found her alone in Nico's office, curled into the corner of the sofa, eating a breakfast burrito.

"Where's Nico?" he asked.

"Gym."

Jax could use an hour of throwing weights around himself. God, he was frustrated. He was eating his heart out, missing his wife and daughter, hating himself for being apart from them. Suffering this rift over an action that was so far in the past, it shouldn't still be having this kind of impact on any of them.

"There's more if you want one." Eve used her burrito to wave at the kitchenette.

"No. Thank you." He would promptly throw it up. He dropped onto the sofa beside her. "I told Bree."

"She's upset? Understandable, but she knows we'll find something for her, right? I just talked to Dom. He's going to talk to Tucker—"

"No."

"And remind him there are pressure points he could bring to bear. An entertainment agent doesn't want to get on the wrong side of an award-winning music producer, for instance."

"Jevaun? Astrid's husband? No, Eve. I do not want *your* husband asking a man I met once to clean up *my* mess. I'll figure this out myself."

"Why?"

"What do you mean, why? Because it's not your problem to solve. It sure as hell isn't Dom's. You shouldn't even be married to him. That's my fault, too." Then he'd gone and pressured Bree into marriage when he patently didn't deserve her.

"Oh, my God, Jax." Eve set her burrito on the plate on the coffee table, then curled her legs beneath her as she faced him. "Do you remember when I graduated and went to the Amalfi Coast with friends and you wanted to drive down to go clubbing with us?"

"I didn't *want* to. Mom asked me to keep an eye on you. Why?"

"I wasn't there. I was in Budapest. Getting up close and personal with Dom."

"What?"

"We only kissed a bit." She looked away blushing, suggesting it had been more than "a bit," not that he wanted to contemplate what more than "a bit" might mean. "We didn't know who the other was, but once we realized, we went our separate ways and tried to forget about it. Then we wound up on that island last year. Now we're married. Because we're *in love*. So get over yourself. My marriage to Dom has nothing to do with you."

"I don't even know what to say to that," he muttered. "You were twenty-one."

"Two," she insisted, then added ruefully, "Almost. But at least he didn't leave me *pregnant*. How old was Bree when you were fooling around with her in Como?"

"That was different."

"Different than what? Every other couple who can't keep their hands off each other?"

"I never should have approached her. I know that." Culpability had him lurching up from the sofa to pace with agitation. "I shouldn't have slept with her. I shouldn't have left it on her to call me. I shouldn't have forced this marriage on her."

He had pushed and pushed for her to commit and she had. She'd fallen in love with him. She'd gone off the pill.

Only to have him drag her into his old, humiliating scandal.

"That's a lot of 'shouldn'ts.' Why did you do all of those things, then?"

"Temporary insanity?" He could remember so clearly that first moment of being drawn to her in a way that was different than anything he'd felt before. She'd told him she was hurting and he'd wanted to make her feel better. It hadn't been about seducing her. Yes, the sexual attraction had been off the scale, but he'd wanted to know more about her. He'd wanted to touch her and *be* with her. Make her smile and impress on her that she was perfect exactly as she was. Any man would want her. *He* wanted her. So damned much.

But he hadn't felt deserving of her. That was the stark truth. Not while he was living in exile, still making stupid mistakes like allowing Dom to get the upper hand over his family.

"Jax, I saw the way you looked at her that day in the boardroom. Every time I see you two, do you know who you remind me of?"

"Don't." He closed his eyes as if that could close his ears, but he already knew what she was going to say. He felt it in himself. He had felt it from the beginning and hadn't wanted to acknowledge it because he knew what it meant.

"Nonno adored Nonna *so much*."

Jax winced. "And look what happened when she gave in to him." Two generations of vengeful hell with the Blackwoods, all because Nonna had followed her heart.

"You think being married to Bree is going to cause something like that? How?"

"No, but she's…" The light in his life. "*I'm* the one causing *her* pain. None of this should be happening. I shouldn't be putting any of you through this again, least of all her. Bree shouldn't be affected by my past mistakes."

"Do you really see calling out Tucker for sexual assault as a mistake?" she asked with an askance frown. "You did the right thing, Jax. We're all behind you on that. We always have been. Yes, we're mad right now. *At Tucker.* Bree probably is, too. She wouldn't side with him the way Paloma did, would she?"

"No. Never." He rubbed at the tension in his jaw. "But I can't ask her to side with me. I can't ask that of you. Look what it's costing all of you."

"You've stood with me in battles and collected your share of bruises. That's all this is, Jax. And I genuinely don't care what people think or say about me because I have Dom. And you and the rest of the family, obviously, but knowing Dom loves me makes me feel able to withstand anything. That's why I don't understand why Bree's not here with you. I would swear she loves you and would want to be supportive."

"I told her not to come." It would have gone a long way to mending things between them, but he'd hurt her instead. Again. He'd seen it. "I'm trying to protect her." But he was failing. Miserably.

"Her?" Eve asked in gentle challenge. "Or yourself?"

"You think I'm protecting myself?" He released a choke of humorless laughter. No, he was punishing himself, he realized. And hurting Bree in the process, which made him feel even worse.

"What then? Do you love her?"

He sent his sister a helpless look, unable to fight it any longer. Yes, he loved his wife. With everything in him. Being apart from her was killing him.

"Have you told her?"

He looked away, growing even more sick with himself.

"Oh, Jackson," she said with deep disappointment.

Yeah. He'd messed up. So badly.

"I need to go see her."

"Yes, you do," Eve muttered to his back as he walked out.

Two hours later, he was buzzing Melissa's condo, but wasn't getting an answer.

He tried texting Bree. Nothing.

He tried Melissa. Melissa replied.

We're visiting Q's family in Miami.

With Bree?

Three dots came and went a few times, making him swear under his breath.

Finally…

She said she'll be in touch when she's ready.

He hit the button to place a video call to his mother-in-law.

"Hello, Jackson." Melissa's smile was friendly enough, if wearing a hint of tested patience.

"Is she with you?" he asked.

"No." She seemed surprised by that.

"Where then?"

"Jackson—" She held her breath, then exhaled. "I have to let Bree take lead on this."

He was standing in full sun, trapped in the oven-like alcove at the entrance to her building, but he was suddenly covered in a cold, clammy sweat.

"I've become one of those relationships you let her manage on her own, haven't I?" Like her father? The one Bree had cut out of her life for good a week ago?

Knives turned in the pit of his gut.

Melissa smiled more gently, but he could hear her telling him the night before their wedding, *I've learned my lesson about offering second and third chances. You won't get any.*

"Would you let her know I'm here?" he asked. "And tell her I'd like to know where the hell to tell my pilot to land."

"I will, but maybe go back to New York and wait for her to call."

"Thanks," he muttered and let her go.

In the car, he tried Bree again.

To his relief, the call connected. Sofia's smiling face appeared.

"*Piccolina*, where are you?" he asked.

"At home," she said, as though that was obvious.

That was when it clicked. The last few times he'd spoken to her, he'd seen only the back of a sofa and a photo above her that he recognized as one that Melissa's husband had taken showing Melissa and Sofia posed in painter's clothing near a ladder. He'd seen it in their condo when they'd dropped Sofia in Virginia Beach on their way to Saint Martin.

But that wasn't the only copy. There was another.

"Which home, Sofia?" He strained to keep his tone even. "The one in New York?"

"Uh-huh." She nodded.

"Will you please get Mama? I need to speak with her."

She called for her and Bree's voice said something indistinct.

"She can't talk right now. Nanny is coming so Mama can go see— What's it called again?"

"A headhunter," Bree said off camera.

Sofia giggled. "Not like Easter eggs."

"No, not like Easter eggs," Bree confirmed in a stronger voice. "Tell Papà I'll call him later."

"Bree," he said through his teeth, barely restraining himself from barking it, not wanting to alarm Sofia.

"You didn't ask, Jax." Bree appeared on the screen and carried the phone into the bedroom. "I thought you might want some emotional support," she hissed. "But you have made it very clear that you don't need me. If your goal was to kill what I felt for you, then job done. I have an appointment. I'll talk to you later."

She ended the call.

The sensation in his chest was so painful, he nearly wept.

CHAPTER FOURTEEN

THAT HAD BEEN CRUEL. Bree knew it as soon as she hung up.

It was a *lie*. But she was releasing the kind of anger she hadn't allowed herself to feel or express as a child, waiting for her father to notice her. Or when she'd been an adolescent, beholden to her father for payments into her college fund. Or when she'd been an adult needing a referral to a good obstetrician.

But this was different. She had laid her heart bare to Jax. Not only when she told him she loved him, but when she told him how she hadn't been loved when she had had every reason to expect it.

And yes, she knew she couldn't force those feelings out of him. It was fine if he didn't feel them. She didn't want him to pander to her.

But the part where he left her in Virginia Beach and acted as though she didn't have a place in his life? When they were married? With a child?

What a callous way to behave! She refused to stand for it. *Refused.*

So, when her mother and Quinto had left for Miami, she brought Sofia to New York. Was it underhanded and passive-aggressive and juvenile not to tell Jax that's where they were? Absolutely.

She didn't care. She was *furious*.

And now she'd lost her job.

She knew Jax would find something for her in the Naples office, but that wasn't the point. The point was to prove she didn't need him. That she would be fine without him.

Fine was a sliding scale. She was devastated at the way things were falling apart, but she wouldn't pine. No, she would build her life back to what it had been before. Better.

Or, at the very least, learn to live with this Jackson-sized chasm inside her.

The recruiter was someone who'd helped negotiate her contract with Eve's team. It had felt silly at the time. A needless expense, really, but she was glad now that she'd had a savvy eye on her contract because she had a comfortable severance package to look forward to.

The woman happened to be in the neighborhood when Bree texted her, so Bree met her for a quick chat over a glass of wine to let her know she was open to offers and to keep her in mind for anything that might be coming up.

On the way home, Bree stopped to collect takeout from Sofia's favorite noodle house. When she entered the apartment, Jax was there, standing in the middle of the living room with an air around him like a simmering volcano threatening to blow.

Her heart leaped with her usual reaction to his fiercely sharp good looks, but for once he wasn't turned out perfectly. His shirt was wrinkled and his eyes were ringed by circles of sleeplessness. His hair was disheveled in a way that suggested agitated fingers had been combing it.

A twinge of guilt accosted her. He had been under a lot of stress with Tucker. Maybe another tantrum on her part hadn't been the right move.

But she'd been so *hurt*.

"Sofia?" she asked.

"I had the nanny take her to Eve's. Astrid and Jevaun are bringing their children over. Sofia was excited to see them again. I said we would come get her as soon as we could."

Her nerves tingled as she realized they were alone, but she steeled herself against letting him know he was affecting her.

"You made good time from Mom's." She set the bag on the counter in the kitchen and removed the boxes. "Did you take a helicopter from Teterboro?"

"I'm not here to talk about my unnecessary commute to and from Virginia, Bree."

"You sound angry."

"I left anger back in Norfolk."

"Maybe you're hungry." She began plating the food.

"No, that's not it," he said in a dangerous tone.

She brought the plates to the table anyway. "What did you expect me to do, Jax? Sit in Mom's condo like a good little girl until you remembered that I exist? I chose to take your advice and tell the people who treat me badly to go to hell."

"That's not what you're doing, Bree." He came closer and leaned his hands on the far side of the table. "You probably don't remember what you said the first time Sofia had a nuclear meltdown with me, do you? The first one where you were out of the house. It was just her and me. I called you, I was so surprised by it."

"Are you suggesting I'm behaving like a child?" She crossed her arms.

"You told me it was a good sign that she lost her temper with me. You said she never kicks up for other people, only you and your mother. You said it meant she trusted me enough to push me away, knowing I'd come back. You said I should take it as a compliment."

She swallowed the embarrassed heat climbing in her throat, unable to hold his gaze.

"I can't tell you how flattered I am right now."

"Prepare to be charmed to death by divorce papers, then."

"Prepare for me to return the compliment, *amore mio*." He splayed his hands as he leaned even closer. "Because I am ready to break every piece of furniture in this room."

"Don't call me that. Don't you dare." She took a half step back, chin up with challenge, but that only left her throat feeling exposed. It left her fluttering heart feeling naked and open to another mortal wound.

"I dare, *carissima*. I dare to pull you closer when I'm furious with you because I love you."

"No, you *don't*," she cried.

"Do you need me to throw these plates across the room to prove it? Once I start, the table and chairs will go after them. Believe me, I am very angry."

A frisson of terrified thrill crackled in the air. She had wanted a reaction. Here it was, wild and powerful as a lightning storm.

"But I don't want to scare you," he muttered. "Especially when it's not you I'm angry with."

A hacked-off laugh came out of her and she looked away. "No, I don't have that sort of power over you, do I?" Her voice cracked with the despair that fractured her sternum.

"Why the hell would I be angry with you for looking after yourself? I'm angry with Tucker. I'm angry with your father. I'm so angry with him, Bree, I truly hope I never meet him. It will not go well. Mostly I'm angry with myself. Because I knew I was hurting you when I didn't say the words back. I knew you might never forgive me for that."

"Then why didn't you?" she cried, fighting the pull in her brow and the crinkle in her chin. The threat of tears scalded from the back of her throat to the back of her heart.

"Because—" His brow flexed with anguish.

She bit her quivering lip. Waiting in agony for the awful reason, the one that would reveal the true depth of her flaws.

"Because I have never deserved you," he said in a voice thinned with agonized self-contempt. "I knew it the first time I saw you. I sat there thinking you were the most beautiful, vibrant, intriguing woman I'd ever met, and I knew I wasn't good enough for you."

"How can you say that?" she asked, genuinely baffled.

"What kind of man seduces a woman who's still in love with someone else? I didn't take your number because I would have chased you down and tied you to me then." He sounded so tortured.

"Would that have been so bad?" Her soul was still crying over the time they'd lost.

"It was too big a risk. I had already lost everything I wanted once before. My future had been mapped out and it was gone." He snapped his fingers, then flicked his hand through the air. "My family sent me away. It felt like a sentence. One I deserved." He let her see the anguish in his eyes. In his soul.

It was such a harrowing sight, her heart began to ache for him.

"I was so damned lonely, Bree. Eve was there sometimes, but she had her own friends, her own future to mold. Once Nonna was gone, I was staring at a life that was empty of meaning, but I knew I deserved to feel that raw."

"No, Jax. You didn't." She took a step, one hand dropping to the edge of the table. "Don't do that to yourself."

His mouth twisted with pained irony. "Then, there you were, so pretty I could hardly breathe. You were hurting like I was. Feeling rebuffed and wanting the pain to end. I wanted to keep you, Bree. But I didn't feel I deserved to be happy. And I was immediately punished for my time with you, which proved I shouldn't be."

"Do you hear how flawed your logic is?" Why were humans so good at being cruel to themselves?

"My grandfather proposed to Nonna three days after they met. Did you know that? She was supposed to marry Dom's grandfather, but she eloped with Nonno instead. That's what started the feud between our families. It was an all-consuming animosity that went on for three generations. I never understood how she could have caused something like that. But there I was that day, wanting you with every fiber of my being, not caring what it might cost my family in the long run so long as I got to talk to you. Touch you. Kiss you…" He shook his head. "I hated myself for being so weak. I made myself leave that day. Made myself let you go. And hated myself for that, too."

She bit her lip, trying to keep it steady, trying to take in all that he was saying. Afraid to believe it, but for once his expression was unguarded. His inner pain was on full display. He was baring his soul.

"I ached for you, Bree. I looked for you wherever I went. And when I finally found you again, you'd had my *baby*." He closed his hand into a fist and swallowed. "Maybe if I hadn't been blaming myself for my sister marrying a damned Blackwood, you and I would have got off on a better foot. Instead, I was full of fresh self-loathing. At least I could be angry with you, though. For keeping her from me. That was a crime just bad enough that maybe we were on an even playing field. Maybe you weren't too good for me after all."

"Hurtful." She winced.

"I know. Especially when I realized why you thought you were better off raising her alone. That distrust of yours was hard on me, though. No. Let me say that differently. *I* didn't trust *you*. I was convinced that you would see through me at some point and know you could do better. And when you told me…" He had to clear his throat. "When you said you loved me, I guess I thought I had to *show* you why you shouldn't."

"You did."

His breath cut in as though he'd been stabbed.

"You taught me to demand better for myself. It's fine if you don't love me, Jax. But I won't let you hurt m—"

"Of course I love you," he cut in sharply. "Do you think I'd pour my guts out to anyone else like this? How did you not get that from the part where I said my grandfather fell for my grandmother on sight and I'm just like him?"

"Okay, so you implied it, but—"

"Bree. Right this minute, Dom is telling Tucker to back off or there will be consequences. Do you have any idea how much it galls me to let a Blackwood do me a favor? But I don't want you to lose your job. And I thought saving my marriage—I thought telling you I love you—was more important than anything else in the world right now. Tucker will still be there in the morning. You might not be. You are my heart. My other half. I love you, Bree. If you leave me, you will break my heart. I mean that. You already nearly snapped it in two, telling me I'd killed your love for me."

They were only a few feet apart, but as she met his gaze, she saw his remorse. She saw the canyon that had stood between them all this time, the one they had both kept between them because it was such a leap of faith to cross it.

He was extending his hand, though, inviting her across the invisible bridge. She only needed to believe it was really there.

"*Ti amo,*" he said. "*Ti amo tanto.*"

No one had ever put themselves on the line like this for her before. It was what she wanted, but it was so monumental, it made her heart feel too big for her chest. Her vision blurred with emotive tears and her lips quivered so hard she struggled to form the words she needed to say.

"I love you, too." The quake began in her voice and extended into her chest and resounded in her soul. It made her feet feel heavy and awkward as she took a faltering step.

He pulled her close, crushing her into his arms.

For a long moment, he merely held her with her ear pressed to the thud of his heart. Then she looked up at him and he set his mouth against hers in a tender kiss that felt sacred. It tasted of apology and yearning, celebration and elation. It tasted of love. The kind of love that was pure and strong and everlasting.

When he picked her up, he stood unmoving for a long minute, holding her cradled in his arms, just looking at her.

"Yes," she said, thinking that's what he was asking.

He smiled faintly before his expression sobered. "I am very sorry for hurting you."

"So am I." She buried her lips in his throat. "I could never stop loving you even if I tried. And stop saying I deserve better. We'll both be the better that we deserve."

"We will," he promised solemnly.

Jax was never more at peace than when they lay replete like this, Bree tucked against his side, fingertips drawing secret messages against his skin.

"Do you know what we should do?" She came up on an elbow.

"Collect our daughter so she doesn't think we've orphaned her?" He had missed her, too. Sending her to Eve's, when she had wanted to stay with him, hadn't been easy.

"Definitely that, too." She flicked a look at the clock, then relaxed in a splay across his chest. "But we should have a reception like Eve and Dom's."

"A big party? I'm always happy to show you off." He swept a wisp of hair off her brow. "But I thought you didn't want anything grand like that?"

"Because I don't love being the center of attention, but you can't let him think he ran you out of the city. Take it back. Show him who won."

The spark of battle was in her eyes. For him.

"I'm touched." He was. "And I will give you anything it's in my power to give, but you don't have to do that for me."

"It's for us. All of us."

"My mother *would* be thrilled to plan another party."

Three months later, after a sumptuous meal, Jackson invited Bree to start the dancing.

As a combined force, the Blackwood-Visconti clan had neutralized Tucker, sending him back to Brazil with his tail between his legs. They had won. Everything about this night was magical and drama free.

The only gossip was a few sly, amused whispers noting both Bree and her sister-in-law were eschewing champagne…

EPILOGUE

One year later...

"I MISPLACED OUR DAUGHTER," Jax said, coming to the open door of Bree's office. "I sent her to change out of her school clothes, but she didn't come back downstairs for her snack."

"Have you found her?" Bree started to rise.

"Yes. And it's going to be a late bedtime."

"She's sleeping? I thought she was over her cold." Sofia had gone back to preschool today, seeming like her energetic self.

"It was a nice day so we walked home. I think that tired her out." He jerked his head in invitation, a smile teasing his lips.

She followed him to Aldo's room, where their son was swaddled and fast asleep in his crib.

Sofia was beside him, one bent arm pillowing her head. The other was across his tiny body. They'd asked her to forgo hugs and kisses while she had the sniffles, and she had, but with the embargo lifted, she seemed to have decided snuggles were allowed again. She loved her baby brother even more than they had hoped, to the point that she'd been angry with Bree when she hadn't let him sleep in her bed with her.

"I can bring him to you when he needs his milk," Sofia had said with great annoyance.

Bree sighed with the euphoria that rose at moments like this, when the world was so perfect, her eyes glossed with happy tears.

"Thank you for this." Jax settled his arm around her. "I really am the luckiest man on earth."

She glanced up at him. "Feel like getting luckier?"

"Always."

They hurried to their room before their children woke up.

* * * * *

If you were captivated by
Hidden Heir, Italian Wife,
then be sure to check out these other
passion-fueled stories
from Dani Collins!

Her Billion-Dollar Bump
Marrying the Enemy
Husband for the Holidays
His Highness's Hidden Heir
Maid to Marry

Available now!

MILLS & BOON ®

Coming next month

HER ACCIDENTAL SPANISH HEIR
Caitlin Crews

Something else occurs to me. Like a concrete block falling on me.

Something that should have occurred to me a long time ago.

I count back, one month, another. All the way back to that night in Cap Ferrat.

I stand up abruptly, gather my things and stride toward the front office.

My mind is whirling on the elevator down and I practically sprint out the front of the building then down a few blocks until I find a drugstore. I give thanks for the total disinterest of cashiers in New York City, purchase the test and then make myself walk all the way home to see if that calms me.

It does not.

I throw my bag on the counter in my kitchen and tear open the box, scowling at the instructions.

Then I wait through the longest few minutes of my entire life.

Then I stare down at the two blue lines that blaze there on my test.

Unmistakably.

I simply stand there. Maybe breathing, maybe not.

The truth is as unmistakable as those two blue lines.

I'm pregnant.

With *his* child.

With the *Marquess of Patrias's* baby.

Continue reading

HER ACCIDENTAL SPANISH HEIR
Caitlin Crews

Available next month
millsandboon.co.uk

COMING SOON!

We really hope you enjoyed reading this book.
If you're looking for more romance
be sure to head to the shops when
new books are available on

Thursday 19th
June

To see which titles are coming soon, please visit
millsandboon.co.uk/nextmonth

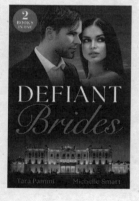

afterglow BOOKS

Afterglow Books is a trend-led, trope-filled list of books with diverse, authentic and relatable characters, a wide array of voices and representations, plus real world trials and tribulations. Featuring all the tropes you could possibly want (think small-town settings, fake relationships, grumpy vs sunshine, enemies to lovers) and all with a generous dose of spice in every story.

♪ @millsandboonuk
⊙ @millsandboonuk
afterglowbooks.co.uk
#AfterglowBooks

For all the latest book news, exclusive content and giveaways scan the QR code below to sign up to the Afterglow newsletter:

SCAN ME

LET'S TALK
Romance

For exclusive extracts, competitions and special offers, find us online:

🅕 MillsandBoon

𝕏 @MillsandBoon

📷 @MillsandBoonUK

♪ @MillsandBoonUK

Get in touch on 01413 063 232

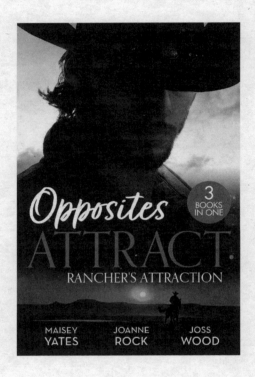

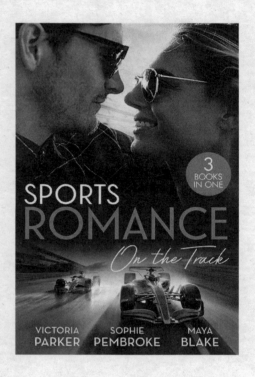